THE TEN O'CLOCK LINE

THE TEN O'CLOCK LINE

Marianne Coil

ISBN: 9798327515321

Dedicated in memory of my parents, Neal A. and Marie Ann Coil, married for 65 years.

FOREWARD

I must express gratitude to the Indiana University School of Dentistry, which retained me as a free-lance editorial consultant for graduate students submitting theses. Through collaboration with students and faculty, I gained the insight to create the character of Dr. Libby Doherty. Her kindness, generosity, and professionalism are reflections of the IU personnel I have known. Of course, I should add that nothing in this work of fiction is intended to express an official position of the university or its faculty.

Second, I am grateful to the late Wade Jennings, PhD, professor of English at Ball State University, for reading an earlier draft of this book. His invaluable critique cemented my suspicions about the changes I should make. He passed away in 2020 before I could publish this work. I am indebted to him.

Third, I would like to recognize people who offered generous support during evolutionary phases of my life: educator Gordon W. Thompson; broadcasting veteran Dick Cooper; playwright Rita Kohn; civic leader Carole Darst; and the late social-justice advocate Suellen Jackson-Boner. Every interaction with each of them created a context for reflection and personal growth. And I would be remiss if I omitted mention of the founder of the first radio station I worked for, the late Donald A. Burton.

Finally, in creating the character of police detective Gale Mooneyham, I drew inspiration from figures of law enforcement I encountered as a journalist. Several were rogues, but Gale's spirit reflects the best among them, like Officers Anderson and Cooper of the Indianapolis Metropolitan Police Department's East District. One late night about a decade ago, young vandals threw yellow paint on the cars in the lot behind my residence. Police were alerted and they notified us to come out and check the vehicles. For sure, my new car was decorated with paint, and the officers called for a fire truck to hose down the cars while the paint was wet. Then, one of the officers followed me to a dangerous neighborhood at one a.m. to a manual car wash, and he scrubbed my car. These acts of kindness would meet with Gale's expectations for good policing.

CHAPTER 1
The Present Day – Saint Patrick's Evening

The black mixed-breed dog sat at attention, staring with his mistress at the darkened bungalow. Relaxing the leash, the jeans-clad woman shifted her weight on the sidewalk, and she fiddled with the nubby turtleneck on her pullover. The sun had set, and the pair enjoyed the promise of a new moon bringing pitch-black tranquility.

The woman often stopped with her dog as they approached this house, where a ghost was trapped, albeit an innocent spirit. The dog walker thought no one sensed the presence of the elusive soul within, because neighborhood gossip never mentioned this dwelling.

A face glowed in the attic window. The face of a girl.

"Tell me what you want," the woman whispered, barely moving her lips.

The girl disappeared.

Though gifted, the dog walker tried not to interfere in the lives of people who didn't ask for help, a special kind that couldn't be announced with a sales pitch at the front door. Funny – people would answer random emails from psychics claiming to have vital information – but the same offer made in person to a stranger could provoke a call to the police.

Now listening, the dog stood. A breeze tickled the woman's brunette bangs, and she brushed them back. She zipped her windbreaker. Rounding the next corner, a Volkswagen approached.

"Let's go, Trevor," she said, resuming their slow pace. The car turned into the driveway of the special bungalow.

The resident, a business-like female, would be outside at times to mow the lawn, and the psychic believed the woman was unaware of the traffic in her own house, a portal for spirits. That lady could plod without sensing her invisible company, the dog walker judged, while predicting an overthrow of some kind.

"One of these days, Trevor," she said, as they paused, looking back at the house.

CHAPTER 2
The Present, Saint Patrick's Evening – Gale

Gale squinted, groping for sunglasses tossed on the front seat of the unmarked cruiser. He loathed Saint Patrick's Day, and making it worse, Washington Street was a straight line to the sunset searing his pupils. Driving west through an industrial neighborhood, he left a gathering at the painted-brick police lodge, which stood like a big cherry cough drop on the corner.

Seeing spots, he slowed the car and slapped on the glasses. In the rearview mirror, he spied gray curls tickling the stems of his shades. He needed a haircut. The traffic light turned red, but a patrol car shot by, tooting a clipped, abrasive warning at the intersection. The uniforms were on a run, approaching a shack missing half its siding in a near-eastside block known for drug-related prostitution and violence.

The wearing of the slime. Saint Paddy brought olfactory memories from thirty years ago, when Gale was a rookie. An intoxicated driver threw up in the back seat of Gale's squad car right after midnight as the holiday began. After a hasty clean-up and a blast of evergreen deodorizer, Gale and his partner resumed their tour at one-thirty. Taking deep breaths, they knocked on the door of a modest apartment. In pajamas, a recent bride answered, receiving notice of her husband's death in a collision. The victim's rickety pizza-delivery car, an orange Dodge Colt, was a compressed heap. A sleepy trucker hauling washing machines had run a red light and plowed into the driver's side.

Hearing the news, the brand-new widow screamed, "Oh God! Oh God!" for ten minutes in an off-key monotone, which stopped as if on a timer. Gale just wanted to go home.

3

At four in the morning, he made the discovery that sent him to a minister. Four uniforms answered a call to a residence on East New York Street. In the front yard, a housecoat-clad, middle-aged white woman was on her knees. Pointing at the house, she wailed. One officer tended to her, while the rest entered the one-story home, decorated with children's bikes chained together on the paint-scabbed front porch. Gale never forgot the banana seat bike with streamers on the handlebars. As the men walked about inspecting, the cop on the lawn shouted, "She's the grandmother. The kids are in the basement."

Gale reached the bottom of the steps first. The partially finished basement with mottled drywall had a carpet of brown shag, and a lumpy plaid sofa. On camping cots – four children, streaked with red like they'd painted themselves for a prank.

Leaning over the nearest cot, Gale felt for the child's pulse, but the boy was dead, along with two girls and another boy, a toddler. Shot at close range, they were between the ages of eighteen months and seven years. One lifeless girl clutched a blonde doll with big brushy eyelashes on half-closed lids, and a rash of blood spatters on its face.

Between dry sobs, he heard himself utter, "I . . . I . . . I . . ." He never finished the sentence, but soon he began talking low. "We're right here. We're not going to leave." When detectives arrived, he went up to the yard for air. The lawn filled with police functionaries. A plainclothes captain crouched to listen as the grandmother swayed on her knees like a buoy. Her daughter, a waitress, worked nights at a truck stop on Interstate 70, and the daughter's boyfriend, a drug addict, asked for money before she went to work. She refused, enraging him. Likely using burglary tools to sneak into the house, he shot the children, while the grandmother slept in the back bedroom. She awoke when shots resounded under the floor.

"They was like buried 'far-crackers,' " she said, with the Gothic intonation of someone recounting the slaughter of an entire village by Union soldiers. Upon hearing the intruder charge out the front door, she ran to the living-room window, which framed a ghoulish cartoon of his getaway on foot.

"And then I went 'downstars,' " she said, beginning to sob. As her mind replayed discovering the dead grandbabies, fierce pain induced a series of yells, as if she moved, again, from cot to cot, from loss to loss. The police captain bowed his head.

4

Television news teams were pulling in, and Gale saw they aimed cameras at his partner, weeping into his hands. Gale led him indoors, and they cried together, waiting for their release from duty.

A week later at home, Gale woke up at lunchtime. His wife was at work. He went to the living room and flopped on the new beige sofa they were so proud of. They'd chosen accent pillows of green and gold. In the darkened room with closed curtains, the colors reminded him of phlegm in a handkerchief. He pressed a pillow to his face. With shoulders heaving, he cried. The dried mucus from his nose stiffened the pillow fabric. He didn't care.

He called in sick for the next two nights, and on the second, he slouched, drinking beer on the back steps. Something rustled in the bushes. He tensed. Emerging from the brush, a raccoon family walked in single file to a maple tree. The coons scaled it, disappearing into the darkness above the flat roof of the detached garage. Fascinated, Gale relaxed, and then he heard a kindly whisper, "You should always have clean underwear."

He sat up straight. That was a real whisper, imparting one of his late grandmother's favorite warnings. Respectful and attentive, he thought he could go inside at last, without being rude to the invisible guest. He left his sleeping wife alone. He wasn't sure she'd believe his story. In the kitchen, he consumed a half-loaf of bread swamped with peanut butter and jelly. After the snack, he did laundry.

He considered his options. Best not to consult with the blue brethren about his supernatural experience. They'd call him crazy, and they were the type of pranksters who'd hang underwear from the ceiling before roll call. Therefore, he acquiesced to his wife, who wanted to invite their church pastor to dinner. After the meal, Gale showed him the fishing boat in the garage – nice and private – where Gale asked him about hearing the dead speak.

Since the initial parley, he met with a pastor on a regular basis. Although the personnel changed as they moved to new assignments, Gale developed a rapport with each minister. Except for the one he arrested for drunken driving. The poor cleric entered a court-ordered rehab program, and he maneuvered so that subsequent talks with Gale were polite but infrequent.

Thirty years since that horrible Saint Paddy's. Gale sighed. For the past few weeks, he'd been anxious, without cause as far as he was concerned. Maybe he was the target of a vandal, a malevolent, special-effects guy with a mental-fog machine. To calm down, Gale had taken to reading from Psalms before bed. His wife always read a prayer from a laminated card kept at bedside, and when he reached for the Bible, she said he could leave the light on.

"That's OK," Gale said. "I'll turn out the light in a minute." In the dark, he would imagine himself seated on a large rock in the sunlight. The soft rays would comfort him like warm boxer shorts just taken from the dryer.

He was glad to go home tonight. His wife, Lee Ann, a schoolteacher, had made a tuna-noodle casserole to bake when she came home. Biscuits, greens with tomato chunks, and a bowl of fresh fruit would balance the meal. He'd eat brownies while the couple drank coffee and watched The History Channel. He looked forward to snuggling against the blue crocheted throw on his recliner. Life was good, despite recent doubts, but he preferred an end to the day's Irish clamor.

When the cops at the lodge were measuring the amount of Irish in their backgrounds, they waited for Gale to take his turn.

"Kentucky hillbilly," he said. Though bored, he could enjoy getting his buddies wound up during the social hour. After a pause, he remarked, "I've got four brothers also named Gale, and the youngest died of 'tuberous begonia.' "

The others stared, until he relented, saying, "You guys don't garden much."

Remembering this exchange, he wiggled his eyebrows and tightened his grip on the steering wheel.

CHAPTER 3
Present Day, Saint Patrick's Evening – the Psychic

The woman shared her cube steak with Trevor for dinner. Happy, he sloshed and gulped water from his favorite bowl.

All day at her desk at the university, she looked forward to the meal. An administrative assistant to the Department of Social Work for twelve years, she segregated her life as a psychic from the day job. At the office, she didn't talk about her talents, nor did she reveal to her clients where she worked full time.

As she buttered a roll, tears troubled her eyes. Trevor walked over, nuzzling her right leg under the table.

"I hate it when this happens," she said. "I know it's not about you and me. I'm not afraid."

During their walk before supper, she sensed the spirit in the special bungalow was in distress. Empathizing, the psychic felt a heaviness in her chest.

"Sometimes, I just don't need this talent," she said, getting up to rinse her face at the kitchen sink. Remembering the green beans simmering with bacon on the stove, she spooned a portion and held it under her nose, inhaling the smell. She closed her eyes. She pictured bacon frying in her parents' kitchen, a ritual on Saturday mornings as she grew up, and she relaxed, releasing the pain.

CHAPTER 4
The Present Day, Saint Patrick's Evening – Libby

Libby Doherty had a home in Irvington, five miles east of downtown Indianapolis, in a block north of the Methodist church, once home to a college president. He sold his house to the Methodists in the 1920s, and they added a sanctuary. The Tudor-revival structure dominated the landscape at the corner of Audubon Road and East Washington Street, also known as US 40. The church distinguished an oval about fifty yards from the intersection. Audubon Road circled the church property and continued north. Narrow curved streets branched from the circle to houses more than a century old. A regulatory fight over tearing down so much as a garage could be bitter in the protected historic district.

Among these homes, Libby's was a three-bedroom bungalow with an attic. The previous owner reset the windows and finished the basement. The house sat atop a gentle slope, and at the bottom, pert shrubs bordered the sidewalk. The garage, accessible from a curved drive, hid behind the house at the edge of a small back yard.

Painted brown with tan contrasts, the home had the appearance of a substantial birdhouse. Electric candles shone at dusk against filmy curtains at the front windows, and the tiny beacons cast a special welcome on this chilly night. Stopping her Volkswagen outside the garage, Libby got out, entering the home's back door under a gabled wooden awning. One small lamp in the kitchen lit her way to the dining room, where she flicked the chandelier's wall switch and started for the living room.

8

Alarmed, she stopped. A cold draft sideswiped her face. This happened, often, but she couldn't find the source of the air flow. Maybe she should call a heating and air-conditioning expert. She continued into the living room.

A large painting of a mid-twentieth-century estate auction hung over the gas fireplace. The auctioneer's left arm pointed heavenward. Simple folk assessed the dining chair dangling from his right hand. In the background, a picnic spread was ignored on a table with pies and jugs of liquid. A willow tree gave shade to a woman sitting on the ground, and a baby on a blanket slept next to her. In the left foreground, a mattress rested on its edge in the back of a pickup truck.

Mauve carpeting covered the living-room floor. An area rug with faint rectangular themes in gold, burgundy, and light blue defined the locus of seating, which consisted of an Italian-leather sofa in gold, and two armchairs. They were upholstered in fabric flecked with the colors in the rug. A three-legged wooden pedestal near the west window held a cut-glass vase with fresh flowers in yellow hues. A walnut bookcase with bronzed trim stood along the wall opposite the fireplace. The shelves contained books, knickknacks, and framed photos.

A grandfather clock ticked, placed at an angle in the southwest corner. Just inside the front door, a brass holder with a floor stand supported an eighteen-inch, ivory pillar candle overlaid with wax flowers and vines. Off-white drapery with tiny mauve-and-gold chevrons framed the muslin half-curtains over the windows. The walls were painted light blue.

She checked the front closet for intruders, a habit she could never shake. Retracing her steps, she turned off the chandelier and cut across the dining room's polished wooden floor to the arch announcing the side hall. This corridor ended in the back of the house at the wall opposing the basement stairwell, and in the front, at the door to the master bedroom. Along the hall, three doors marked the bathroom and the other bedrooms. Libby went to the large front bedroom and turned on the bedside lamp.

Behind a door hidden in the closet, a steep staircase led to the attic. She peeked inside the closet, clicked on the ceiling light, and verified the attic door was shut. She turned off the light and shut the closet door. She didn't like the attic, but she didn't know why.

9

CHAPTER 5
History, February 1921 – Mary, at the Bungalow

Like most teens in Irvington, Mary Hobson attended a high school on the east side about two miles from downtown. Her mother insisted she also attend a salon twice weekly in a church basement. Given the lofty name Creedmore Hall, the salon was a cultural forum for decent girls learning etiquette, art appreciation, and morals. The group was for the young women of Protestant families who would soon live by the sentiment, "Keep Klothes Klean."

At Creedmore Hall, she met a would-be artist, Deck Whittenger, grandson of the wealthy banker Cable Deck Whittenger. Grandfather's beefy, rosy face, denture-filled smile, and ever-present wet cough deceived business opponents into thinking he was weak. Deck's handsome face was thinner, like a pale idol in the moving pictures, and he could disarm with his grin.

On Tuesdays the lecture at Creedmore Hall linked patriotism with one's duty to God. The church minister would address God's choice of America as the beacon of freedom and unlimited opportunity. One must defy the enemies of freedom because they were in defiance of God's order.

After the lecture, punch and cookies were served, and then students focused on one or two rules of etiquette. They practiced the correct way to approach a dining table to sit down. Other lessons included how to walk to a sofa and sit with legs crossed at the ankles.

The matron who led the etiquette sessions was a relic from the Edwardian era who would have rung for tea if there'd been a servant to bring it. Although she sipped from the gold-rimmed vessel of refinement, she had an unhealthy obsession with panties.

"You pretty young things with these fashionably short dresses – we don't want to see the panties when you sit down. Cross at the ankles, sit up straight, and tuck in your stomach.

"Your knickers are not for snickers." And then she would take a sip from a water glass.

Loathing Tuesday afternoons, Mary looked forward to Thursday, when the painter Deck Whittenger would give an art class. She was talented, he said, admiring her detailed, yet amusing renderings of butterflies she studied from a collection he brought.

"You give them personality," Deck said. "Do they have names?" She didn't realize he was already flirting with her.

"I can give them names, like for the big one, 'The Vanquisher.' "

"Sounds like a vigilante," he said.

"Maybe."

"Or someone who flies into your room at night," he said.

She looked at his face. His expression was innocent.

***

Mary's father was an actuary with Great Lakes Standard Security at the headquarters on Meridian Street. With an excellent salary, he could have paid a housekeeper, but conserving money, his wife gave meticulous care to their bungalow. Her fun was in volunteering for various causes.

The girl adored her unassuming father, but feared her mother, whom she loved, but could not please. When Mary won a public speaking contest at Creedmore Hall, her mother was indifferent to the stream of parents who congratulated them during refreshments.

"The stage needs a new curtain," Mrs. Hobson said, appraising the church basement.

What Mary didn't know, because her mother didn't share memories, was the story of Mrs. Hobson's childhood. Her father operated a grain elevator that caught fire, and he died trying to fight the blaze. Even though the insurance proceeds retired his debts, the widow had to sell their home and move the family into a small apartment over a dry goods store.

At first, Mary's grandmother took in sewing, but she later found work as a housekeeper for a physician who traveled daily throughout Hancock

11

County. With three children to support on a meager income, she relied on relatives who farmed to share Sunday dinners, and to donate a plot for her vegetable garden.

Raised under these circumstances, Mrs. Hobson curtailed her imagination to avoid being disappointed, and she regarded most positive events as too good to be true. In turn, she could display a kill-joy demeanor.

But the woman softened whenever she studied her daughter in a new dress, especially a blue one.

"I had one child, and then my womb dried up. I was lucky you turned out to be so pretty," she said.

But an untouchable girl was the paragon of Victorian womanhood – chaste, demure, and occupied with household affairs. Fearing a loss of prestige from challenges to this familiar role, Mrs. Hobson found comfort in the Ku Klux Klan's embrace of Victorian morality.

Condemning drinking, gambling, and prostitution, the Klan earned the confidence of white middle-class Protestants. Businesses put out the word they welcomed Klan customers, and churches abetted the secret society by calling it a pillar of the temperance movement.

The Klan had just opened its Indianapolis office, and Mary's father paid his ten-dollar dues. Still, he declined to attend gatherings.

"I don't understand why you don't go," her mother said.

"Laurinda, I respect the judgment of the fellows I eat lunch with – every day – at the hotel across the street from the office.

"They're company lawyers – really fine fellows – and they have reservations about certain Ku Klux tactics that could have repercussions for their careers."

"For example?" Mrs. Hobson said.

"Well, look – they burn the Cross on other people's private property, and that could be trespassing and vandalism.

"True – not every jurisdiction regards it as such, especially where the sheriffs are Klan members – but just in case, the lawyers don't want to risk disbarment for knowingly abetting something illegal."

"But you're not a lawyer, Barker," she said. "Why does it matter?"

"I think if something is illegal, it's illegal," he said.

"Can't you even go to a rally?" she said.

He sighed. "I just don't think I have to wear a costume to prove I'm a

12

patriot. I was too old to serve in the Great War, but I bought war bonds. And I did so with a glad heart.

"And you, my lovely, wrapped an infinite number of bandages."

His eyes twinkled. "When you were around, I kept fidgeting so your wily fingers couldn't wind me up like a dead Egyptian king."

"Oh, Barker! But really, why did you bother to join?" she said.

"It's good for business. We need to enforce Prohibition, and the Klan is all for it. And the president of our insurance company is a staunch supporter of the anti-liquor laws. The consumption of alcohol poses hazards we don't want to indemnify.

"We had underwriters in Evansville who told us how big the Klan was down there, and our president got excited.

"You know, I'll never forget the farmer who lived down the road from us when I was a boy. He got drunk out in his barn and knocked over a lantern. Burned down the barn, killed the livestock. That idiot had a wife and four children. We had to take butter and eggs to help them."

"Oh, dear!" Mrs. Hobson said. "I can't cook without butter."

"The wife stood by him, though – said he just tripped over a milking stool and dropped the lantern. I think he had a small insurance policy that paid," he said.

"And now, we have these secret drinking clubs. Those ratholes need to be cleaned out, and the Klan agrees." He sipped his coffee.

"In general, the Klan is for keeping up standards, and I don't see anyone else making the same pitch with more success," he said.

"So, I'll pay my dues, but moderation is helpful. Every cause has zealots who go too far."

Overhearing this after-dinner discussion as she carried dishes to the kitchen, Mary was let down, wanting to interject that dreadful things were happening. However, her parents taught her to stay out of conversations between adults. She'd heard at school from friends talking in subdued voices about their fathers, who went to secret meetings and didn't come home until three o'clock in the morning.

Mrs. Hobson believed in the Klan doctrine of white supremacy, and the sanctity of chaste womanhood. The woman on a pedestal was responsible for maintaining the solidarity of the Protestant white family, and she was vulnerable to black rapists and immigrants who interfered in the social order.

13

The elder tried to make Mary ashamed of her own body. Her mother said menstrual flow had a disgusting trace of sex that didn't bring forth a child. Alone in her room, Mary sneered at the illogic. She'd read medical books at the library. Every virgin in the land had these cycles, and what had she done to deserve such scorn?

But to her mother, the talking pelvis known as her daughter could have been Jezebel taking a bath for King David's viewing.

"My knickers are not for snickers," the girl muttered after a discussion about maintaining pristine undergarments.

"What was that?" her mother said.

"Nothing, Mother." Despite her reservations, after weeks of lectures about purity, Mary succumbed to the ideology and began to doubt her self-worth.

CHAPTER 6
The Present Day – Saint Patrick's Evening

Now to bed, Libby reached over to set the alarm for five-thirty, an appointment kept after laborious dreaming. Weighted by cast-iron boots, she trudged through black smoke like a fireman searching for an exit. As she emerged into daylight, her long-dead companion, Teddy, was beckoning. He held out a handful of goldfish moving their tiny mouths, and then he let the fish cascade into a fountain. With puckered lips, he gestured fins at his side and made his eyes bulge. He disappeared.

In the morning, Libby had a headache. Listening to classical guitar music, she sat at the kitchen table with a cup of coffee, a banana, a hard-boiled egg, and a grain muffin with a dollop of cream cheese. The soothing arrangement of Bach focused her thoughts on the dream. What was Teddy doing? He'd been sniffing around in her dreams since last autumn. It was odd; she didn't start dreaming about him until she moved into this house. She rubbed her temples. Whenever he appeared, she felt used up the next day. In most dreams, he approached her on the sidewalk. He'd smile and move on as if going to a business meeting. But the thing with the fish last night – that was different. She got up to put on sweats and went out the front door.

The morning was too foggy for safe jogging. Libby walked at a moderate pace. Crossing Washington Street, she headed toward the railroad tracks a half-mile hence on South Audubon Road. She passed the first historic landmark, the brick Italianate mansion once home to George W. Julian, whose brother co-founded Irvington. George won two terms in Congress in the mid-nineteenth century and sought the vice-presidency on the Free Soil ticket in 1852.

Libby approached Irving Circle. Traffic flowed around a small park and continued south. At the hub, a fountain gurgled in warm seasons. The friends of the fountain were aghast when an intoxicated northbound driver missed the curve, drove over bushes, and slammed into the fountain. Thousands of dollars in repairs later, the masonry around the pool regained its integrity, and the top third of the fountain was back where it belonged.

On the walk to the fountain from the north spoke, a bust was mounted on a pedestal. A plaque announced, "Washington Irving, for Whom the Town was Named in 1870 by Jacob Julian and Sylvester Johnson."

The visage on the bust belonged to the winning, youthful Irving, not the gouty gent photographed in later life. Though absorbed long ago into the capital city, the town honored its patron everywhere, especially at the annual Halloween festival, going strong since the 1940s. Each year, schoolchildren competed for prizes by painting the windows of merchants. For a few days in October, storefronts had crude facsimiles of stained-glass ghouls, witches, and winged creatures.

Irvington had its "haints," provoking curiosity about the historic district, where notorious Klansmen and leaders of Christian missions were once neighbors, and where churches had ghostly choirs. Artists of national repute, such as William Forsyth, lived in Irvington in the early 1900s, as well as prominent figures in the academic and publishing world. Hoping to engage with these forceful spirits, small crowds bought tickets to walk with flashlights around the winding streets, as a leader told ghost stories associated with various locations. When Libby considered buying a house in Irvington, she went on the tour and made up her mind that night. She wanted to live in this fun neighborhood.

Reaching the railroad tracks, Libby turned around, but at the stoplight at Washington, she went east, instead of crossing. Up a slight incline, she pushed to Arlington Avenue and back. At the high point on a clear day, she could see the bank buildings defining the downtown skyline. Adding a lap around the Methodist church, she was almost home. She'd gone about two miles.

Cleaned up, she pulled her hair into a ponytail. Dressed in a casual navy tunic with matching slacks and loafers, she put on a tan car coat. Outside, she looked back at the brown house, inviting her to retreat from the slowly dissipating fog to an undisturbed morning of reading poetry and drinking hot tea. Wishing she could pick up the dream about Teddy, she remembered her staff and the dental patients who depended on her. Pride and professionalism sustained her, and she drove to work.

She grew more curious about the dream. "Thanks, Teddy," she said, annoyed, pulling into a parking space. Getting out, she looked at the office building's sign. One of the tenants, listed as Shoemake & Higbee, offered no clue as to the nature of their business. Someday, she'd ask the landlord about them.

CHAPTER 7
Present Day, Summer – The Psychic

The dog walker and Trevor were out after eight in the evening, and the sun wasn't ready to set. Joggers went by, and the sound of a tree saw buzzed in the distance. Trevor strained on his leash when he smelled meat grilling at a cookout.

The dog walker was agitated, too. When they passed the special bungalow, she saw the face in the attic window, again. The sad face of a girl.

"I know you want out," the woman said in a low voice.

The girl disappeared.

"Can't you give me a sign, or something?" the woman said. Trevor whined, and they stood, waiting for a thunderclap, a temblor, an eclipse.

What they got was the sound of weeping. "I'm sorry. I'm so sorry," a female voice said, between sobs. "I'm so, so sorry."

"Oh, dear!" the dog walker said.

Trevor moaned, as if to say, "That's too bad!"

The weeping resonated like the soundtrack from an old movie made in the 1940s. She could almost see the cue blip and hear the rasp of the analog film hissing through the projector.

Searching for open windows or idling cars, the dog walker scanned the neighboring homes for a source, a logical explanation. But this wasn't like listening to the teenager next door playing drums in the garage. She knew this otherworldly performance was meant just for her.

Trevor growled. She rubbed his ears. "Did you hear it, too?" she said, shivering in the warmth of the summer evening.

18

Ambling home, the dog walker remembered the first aural message she received. She was only six years old, around 1980. Coming back from visiting relatives in Texas, her family stopped in Dallas for breakfast on the Sunday they planned to return to Indiana. They weren't going to the airport until after lunch, and her dad wanted to sightsee in the rental car.

They went to a popular chain restaurant downtown, and while her father was settling the bill, her mother took another child to the restroom. While her father turned his back, the six-year-old walked out to the curb where the car was parked.

In contrast to the bustle of the restaurant, the downtown was deserted. No traffic, no pedestrians, no rattling or creaking sounds, no wind – nothing. Maybe someone was around the corner.

The child walked, almost wafting in the stillness. She saw a big lawn with trees across the street, and a big, tall building on the other side of the lawn. "That's funny. There's an X in the window up high," she said.

Along the sidewalk near the curb, she approached a black sign with metal letters. She stopped to try to sound out the words.

Behind her, a man spoke. "They need to make a bigger sign, don't they?"

He was amused. "Don't you think it should be bigger? *I* think it should be bigger." His tone grew more mirthful. "I mean, really, don't you think it should be *bigger*?"

She was terrified, knowing she wasn't supposed to talk with strange men. She whirled, expecting to confront a bad man.

No one was there. On tiptoes, retracing steps, she looked for a space between buildings, where the man could be hiding. There was no space.

In the silence, she stared across the street, and her eyes went again to the X in the window up high.

A warm energy closed in on her left. The man spoke, again. "You know, when history is written, it's all going to come out – what they did to me." His tone was confidential and trusting. She deferred, tilting her head to the left in acknowledgment.

"Yeah, everything's gonna come out," she said, in the lazy drawl of a playmate musing about castles. She strained to hear ambient sound, but in the static calm, a penny would have hit the cement like a bomb.

Her father's voice broke the charm. Running to her, he shouted, "Darla! What are you doing? Why did you run away?" He was mad.

19

"I didn't run. I just went around the corner because I wanted to see."

"There's nothing to see. Your mother is crying," he said, grabbing her by the shoulders and giving her a little shake, not violent, but stern.

"But there is," she said, pointing to the sign. "The man said the sign should be bigger."

Her father knelt, face to face with his daughter. "What man? Did he touch you?"

"No. He was nice. And then he just went."

Her father looked up and down the street. She knew not to mention the visitor was merely a voice, because her parents wouldn't understand.

"He didn't say why the sign should be bigger," she offered.

Holding hands, they went to the sign. Her father's mouth opened, and he made a sharp pivot to gape at the X in the window up high.

"That's Dealey Plaza, and that's the book depository," he said. "I can't believe I'm really here."

Her father pulled her into a tight hug. "I'm sorry I shouted at you. Let's go back to Mommy. She'll want to drive by."

Remembering, Darla felt guilty. She hadn't visited her folks upstate in months, although weekly phone calls took place. She should see them this weekend.

"Let's jog," she said, and Trevor matched her pace.

CHAPTER 8
History, February 1921 – Deck

Deck Whittenger was a poor catch, according to the jewel-laden matrons of his social caste on the city's north side. In hushed conclaves, they spoke of lurid rumors about his days at a military academy. A classmate came home with stories. "Lights out" meant one thing to most cadets, but Deck envisioned something else.

With Grandfather's money, he bribed the sentinels and sneaked into town. He paid a local trash hauler to pick him up at his hiding place about a quarter mile from campus.

His daily activities were pacific. By the time he graduated, Deck had shown he was an artist with potential. His instructors knew that while he lacked the discipline to improve, family money would open doors that slammed in the face of far more gifted painters.

Deck's father died in the flu pandemic, and after losing his son, Grandfather spoiled Deck even more. Graduating from the military academy a few months before World War I ended, Deck went to Europe in peace time for eighteen months to study art. As his teachers predicted, he conducted a grand tour marred only by occasional attendance at lectures. He should have made progress with his use of light and shadow, but he was stuck in a Pre-Raphaelite mode. All his portraits looked the same – like a man in drag wearing different wigs. Each female subject had the same fleshy, bow-tie lips, chiseled cheeks, slightly masculine jaw, and wildly abundant hair.

But Deck arrived home as someone who studied art in the great capitals of Europe, and with the family name, he had cache with people who didn't know better. The students of Creedmore Hall would accept that he was teaching them to participate in a grand tradition.

CHAPTER 9
History, February 1921 – Mary and Bina

Mary Hobson found her best friend, Bina Schwartz, crying in the lunchroom at school. Bina was holding a magazine close to her face to conceal her distress, but Mary wasn't fooled.

"What's wrong?" she said.

"Everything – everything is ruined," Bina said, shoulders shaking.

"Maybe you should go to the dispensary," Mary said. "Are you sick?"

"That would be preferable," Bina said.

"What do you mean?"

"We're ruined. Our family is ruined," Bina said, still hiding.

"What? Did you have a fire?" Mary said.

"I wish. At least we'd have the insurance money," Bina said.

"I don't understand," Mary said.

"Papa is closing the butcher shop because the Klan is coming in. The Jew-haters already scared away our customers, and with the Klan building up, we can't stay here. We're going to my Uncle Chaim and his family in Pittsburgh," Bina said, weary of holding up the magazine.

"No! No! You can't leave. You're my best friend!" Mary said, ill.

"I don't want to leave. The business is failing, and we can't afford the mortgage on our house," Bina said in a faint voice.

"How did they scare away your customers?" Mary said, lowering her voice.

"Lots of ways. The women – They say my father sells spoiled meat. They say he 'Jews' them out of their hard-earned money," Bina said.

23

Mary was silent. Her own mother gossiped on the phone about Catholics and Jews. People were hurting – including me, Mary realized. "Please don't go," she said.

"We have to," Bina said. "I don't want to leave you. We tell each other everything."

"I wish I could go with you," Mary said.

"No, you don't," Bina said. "Uncle Chaim doesn't have room for us, but he's taking us in, anyway. Just lining up for the bathroom will be a nightmare," Bina said.

"But at least you can share the Passover with a big family," Mary said, trying to think of comforting words.

"I suppose so," Bina said, dropping the magazine and wiping her face with a handkerchief. "I guess I should splash some water on my face before I go to math class."

At home that night, Mary cried at the dinner table as she recounted her conversation with Bina. "You and your friends have destroyed *my* best friend's life," Mary said.

"Young lady, go to your room. You will not speak to me that way, and you will not create a spectacle during a meal," her mother said.

Mary threw down her napkin and slammed her chair against the table as she walked away.

"Now, Mary," her father said.

Her mother stood. She went to get a wooden ruler from the kitchen and headed for Mary's bedroom.

"Laurinda, please don't," Mr. Hobson said. His wife ignored him. Seconds later he heard his daughter plead, "Ow, Mama! Don't! Stop! Stop it! Please stop!"

"Don't ever behave that way at our table, again, or at anyone else's table," his wife said. She went back to the kitchen and put away the ruler. Standing in the archway, she asked, "Do you have room for dessert, Barker?"

"I've lost my appetite. Coffee will suffice," he said.

"Oh, my sweetheart!" she said. She hurried with the coffeepot to fill his cup.

"Tell me about your day," she said, returning to her seat.

CHAPTER 10
Present Day – Autumn

Libby finished adjusting the orthodontic braces on the last patient for the day, a boy of twelve years. As she went to her private office, she overheard the staff talking. Keisha Whitley, the billing associate, was complaining about the Chinese take-out they had for lunch.

"Why didn't you bring me a 'poke' chop?"

"Fine, *amiga*," said Marquita Baldonado, her best friend. "We're gonna start calling you 'Poke and Beans.'"

Keisha snorted. "I guess that makes you 'Refried Beans.'"

"I'm a better side dish," Marquita said.

"Don't you mean leftovers?" Keisha said.

Leaving the friends to their scurrilous banter, Libby hustled in her office. Tonight, she would treat herself to an Italian dinner after swimming laps. She put on a sweatshirt and jeans, replacing the blue scrubs crumpled in the laundry bin.

Showcased in the office window, the autumn sun wheezed over the benzene emitters of Indianapolis. Tufted clouds suspended in the coarse air wore streamers of purple and pink.

Across the street from the eastside dental office at 56th Street and Post Road, the federal building at old Fort Benjamin Harrison loomed like a severe-looking high school. The Army's finance center still operated, but the lush fort property was sold to developers. Significant acreage was taken by the state of Indiana, which created a park with a golf course close to Libby's office.

25

Toting a gym bag, Libby entered the waiting room and bid her employees good night.

"If you hurry, you can run into the rising politician in the parking lot," the dental assistant, Drew Columbus, said. She closed the window blinds.

"If he's rising, he's full of hot air," Libby said.

The subject was a deputy prosecutor running for his mentor's old job. The prosecutor resigned to take a federal position. His protégé sought to replace him, after the interim prosecutor declined to run.

The candidate occasionally visited the suite upstairs. Marquita called the bachelor, "*El Super Ratón.*"

"Which means?" Drew asked.

"Mighty Mouse," Marquita said.

"He's not a wiener," Drew said.

"But he does not prosecute a romance. I know a legal assistant who ran into him every day at the City Market. She did everything but 'danz on dee tebble-tops' to get his attention." Marquita loved to pimp her ethnic heritage, and she couldn't resist a self-deprecating shimmy.

To limit the exchange, Libby maintained her stride going out.

Indeed, he was there, clenching a tiny box of thumb drives in one hand while opening a car door with the other. Slipping from his hand, the box fell, spilling the drives, clicking like cockroaches as they hit the asphalt. Libby went over to help.

"Most lawyers carry brief cases," she said.

"Ah, but these are not briefs – something worse. Financial reports."

Hunkered down, the brown-haired man didn't look up as he collected the thumb drives.

"Then they should be labeled 'biohazards,' " she said, crouching and rising as she retrieved a stray drive. She handed it to him when he stood up.

"Thanks." He stuck out his right hand. "Jed Talbot Harkness."

Libby returned the handshake. "John Wilkes Booth."

He laughed. "What was that for?"

"Something about the three names."

"I get it," he said. "I'm so used to campaigning, I even refer to myself in the third person. Aren't you the dentist?"

"Until fifteen minutes ago." His eyes don't blink much, Libby thought.

"You have a gym bag. Are you headed for a workout?" he said.

"Yes." She decided not to give him more.

"Enjoy it. I wish I had the time. I have a fundraiser."

"But that'll generate more reports," she said, half-elated.

"True." His eyes widened, taking her in. Sensing his appraisal, Libby retreated into herself.

"Have a good workout, Dr. . . . . Booth." He waited, but she didn't add anything. "*Sic semper tyrannis*," he said, waving.

"I beg your pardon?" she said.

Victorious, he smiled, feeling his ego flutter at the edges like a curtain in the breeze. "*Sic semper tyrannis* – Thus ever to tyrants. That's what Booth shouted after he shot Lincoln."

"I see. Raise lots of money," she said, smiling, turning, and not looking back. Driving to the YMCA, she couldn't remember much about Jed, except the unblinking gaze. She gave up on candidate Harkness when she landed in the pool.

***

With piqued appetite, Libby was restless after the swim. At home she dressed in a black skirt and a teal cashmere V-neck. Piling her medium-blond mane into a back clasp, she studied herself in the bedroom mirror.

Tall, with a firm trunk, Libby had long arms toned by years of volleyball and swimming. Her outsized, blue-gray eyes wheedled for makeup, which she applied. The oval face featured thin brows, a petite nose, and lips more modest than spare. She considered her looks ordinary, but the big eyes, movie star eyes, drew people to her.

She fondled a coat but left it on the closet rack. She'd wrap herself in the invisible cloak of night air. Resuming travel, she drove six miles north to Kessler Boulevard and cut across to Broad Ripple Village, home to bars, eateries, shops, and artists' studios. Libby parked her Volkswagen on a side street three blocks from her destination.

The last time she walked through Broad Ripple after a late event, she saw two drunken teenagers urinating on the front lawn of a house. Noticing a lime-green Porsche in the driveway, one of the boys shouted, "Cool!" Startled, the other youth, producing a stream, turned sideways to gawk,

27

spraying his buddy. Jumping back, the dampened boy whined, "Oh, man!" Libby laughed, picking up her pace to escape the recriminations.

Tonight, the revelers were indoors, and she strolled, appreciating duck calls reverberating overhead from the formation flying to a nearby canal. Arriving at a window display of glass lampshades filtering mellow light, she studied the mosaic of sea green, red, and amber chips molded into novel forms, like a goldfish with a red eye. Moving along, she stopped again to admire furniture in the style of Gustav Stickley. The armchair was inviting, but too expensive for a knock-off.

Encountering passersby holding hands, she remembered the last time she held hands with a man. The memory brought sudden fatigue. Unflinching, she almost marched to Big Sal's Marble Terrace.

Big Sal greeted her at the door, or at least the putative Big Sal. Maybe his real name was Mike Jones. She declined a seat on the outdoor terrace, so he ushered her to a dimly lit room with intimate oval booths lining the walls and tables clustered in the center. Seating her at a table for two, he removed the extra place setting and left a menu.

The waiter appeared with a bottle of wine, the evening's special. She asked for a glass of iced tea with lemon, no sugar. He frowned and fetched the tea.

Glancing about, she surveyed the patrons' meals. The seafood was tempting, but surely polluted. One fellow dug into a plate of spaghetti; another worked on his veal. Libby ordered a small spinach salad with artichokes, a bowl of minestrone soup, and a sample of bruschetta. The wayward action would rest in the selection of a dessert.

Sipping the tea, she eavesdropped. Voices drifted like drunken winos lurching about. To her left, a man said, "I can say whether the church should sponsor a Central American congregation – because I've been to Bolivia – and eaten and smoked dope with the natives – and I know their ways."

I bet your teeth are stained, Libby thought. She tuned in elsewhere, trying to get away from work. A woman said, "How the hell am I supposed to know?"

Another woman said, "You're the one who said it was OK in the first place."

An ethical problem that called for a bottle of wine, Libby guessed. This, too, would stain the teeth. She received the next complaint from a condescending sod, who lectured his companion. The crux of his co-diner's crime was that instead of negotiating a win-win, he'd accomplished a "flub-flub."

"Rub-a-dub-dub," Libby said behind her tea glass.

Savoring the meal, Libby accepted the waiter's offer of more soup. Later, he came back beaming, pushing a dessert cart. She didn't want to spoil their new friendship, so she accepted a slice of cheesecake, by her standards, a chocolate-laden colossus. He returned with a steaming hot coffee and the bill. Libby cradled the cup under her chin and inhaled the steam. Watching the tropical fish glide back and forth in the aquarium across the room, she fell into a trance, broken when the wall next to the tank suddenly opened. Four people emerged from a banquet chamber, and Libby realized the door was wallpapered to match the dining room. After the first group stepped out, she saw a cluster of cocktail clothes. A man waved goodbye to the cluster and walked into the dining room. Spotting Libby, he blinked once, gliding toward her like one of the fish.

"Good evening, Dr. Booth," he said, stopping at the table. He clasped his hands behind his back, as if addressing a witness on the stand. Libby stared up at Jed Harkness.

"The Prince of Harkness," she said in hushed tones. "Your Worship."

Jed laughed. His cheeks reddened, and an even row of large white teeth glistened. Libby felt like ground beef.

"Have you dined lustily, madam, or timidly, after your workout?"

"Neither, sire. I have consumed with moderation," she said.

He relaxed his stance and gazed, unblinking. "But madam, one of the prerequisites for residing in Hell – aside from belonging to Me – is doing everything to excess. Are you sure you're not supposed to make the trip 'Up' – instead of 'Down?' "

She shook her head sideways. "Damned."

He smiled. "I rather think, 'Saved.' "

"I must have committed an act of redemption. It wasn't the cheesecake."

"Perhaps you liberated a Faustian hero, or a Flying Dutchman," he said.

"Or freed the slaves," she said.

He raised his eyebrows. "Abe Lincoln, again." He looked behind him, expecting someone. "My driver ran into an old friend, but we should move on."

"Where have you been?" she said.

"That was the fundraiser. About forty people, probably netted fifteen-thousand. The threshold donation to attend was two-hundred and fifty."

Cash for shaking hands at a cocktail party. Libby did a quick calculation. She'd have to encounter a few patients with crooked teeth to make that kind of money.

"Why are people willing to donate that much?" she said, surprised by her own question. But taking no offense, Jed answered in a confidential tone.

"Most of these folks are business owners in Broad Ripple, and they have specific concerns about neighborhood crime, and whether anyone downtown is listening. They think I'm a person they can count on."

"What if they're going to your opponent's parties, too? Wouldn't it be smart to spread their money around?" She couldn't believe she said that.

But again, he met her question. "Some of them do, or they'll send another person from their firm who's a member of the opposing party."

Vulnerable and naïve, she felt like hamburger on an open-face bun.

"Who is your opponent?" she said.

"A Republican by the name of Theo Karnow. He's a good corporate lawyer. The governor has campaigned for him."

"But – no lid on his hamburger." The words came out before she knew what she was saying.

"What does that mean?" Jed cocked his head.

"Well, you know, he's . . . uh . . . too exposed," she said.

"Exposed to what?"

Libby glanced at the aquarium. "You know . . ." The aquatic adventurer was running out of air. Jed warmed her with an admiring look. She appreciated the enticing cut of his black-suited shoulders, and the regal flourish of his purple necktie.

"He's too exposed to failure because of his lack of experience in criminal prosecution," she burst forth.

Jed shifted his weight and winked at her. "That's right, lamb chop."

"No – hamburger," she said.

He smiled at the deliberate evasion. "Libby, when this campaign is over, will you have dinner with me?"

"How did you know my name?"

"It's on the sign outside your office. I notice things staring me in the face. That's one of the differences between Karnow and me."

"Sure, I'll have dinner with you. But are you a Democrat?"

"Are you?" he said.

"Independent."

"Then I still have a chance," he said, regretting he had to postpone such a promising engagement. She was so intelligent.

He received a slap on the back. His driver had arrived.

"Hey," Jed said, acknowledging his six-foot-two comrade, who smoothed one corner of a carefully trimmed gray mustache, a match for his curly gray hair.

"Libby, this is my personal assistant, Gale Mooneyham. He's on leave now to work for the campaign, but he's one of the detectives assigned to the prosecutor's office. Gale, this is Dr. Libby Doherty."

Libby extended her hand, and Gale shook it firmly. "I'm Libby – a dentist, not a doctor of medicine," she said, studying his large brown pupils.

"Good to meet you. I'm Gale, a doctor of the heart." He placed his right hand over his chest.

"Gale is a grandfather," Jed said. "And has arthritis in his left knee." He gave Gale a one-arm hug, pivoting him toward the door. Gale laughed, blowing a kiss at Libby.

"'Bye, love," the driver said.

Looking back, a deadpan Jed echoed, "Yes, 'bye, love."

"Hamburger," Libby said, arching her eyebrows.

The men walked one block south, and Jed was smiling as they reached a black Ford sedan with a V-8 engine. Starting the car, Gale activated the wiper blades. He turned the defroster on low and let the engine idle while Jed made a phone call.

"This is a message for 'Sink or Swim.' I'd like to pencil in a short conference tomorrow. I have windows at nine-thirty and two. Let me know. Thanks." He put the phone back in his jacket.

"Home?" Gale said.

"Yeah," Jed said. Gale drove around the block to an artery and headed to I-465 East. Using this route, he bypassed the stop-and-go grid of Castleton, where in one afternoon, a shopper could buy an Oriental rug, get a Botox injection, and eat from an overpriced grill menu. The worst time to visit Castleton was when traffic backed up two days before Christmas.

Exiting the beltway, he went up to Eighty-Second Street and continued east to Fall Creek Road, where he hung a right, slowed, and turned right again at the entrance to a neighborhood nestled in steep, short hills. He pulled into the drive outside a one-story, white brick house with a black garage door and a curved, paned front window.

Following a routine started after a series of threats, Gale accompanied Jed into the house and checked every room. A dog barked.

"*Los!*" Jed roared in German. A flap in the kitchen door shot open, and a dog ran in from the garage. The salt-and-pepper terrier circled Jed in excitement. Gale nosed around in the garage and the backyard.

"Clear," Gale said, coming in. "Tomorrow."

"Six a.m.," Jed said. The front door closed behind Gale. After enabling the alarm, Jed undressed and put on a flannel robe. "*Los!*" he called again. Scooping up the careening bundle, he hugged the terrier, which reciprocated with tender growls of affection.

Entering the den, Jed deposited the dog on a beanbag chair and poured himself a Perrier from the bar fridge. He placed his glass on the table next to the recliner, where he stretched out with a pen and a legal pad. Trailing the pen in coils over the paper, he let his mind wander, until he took control, sketching a small mound.

***

At home after dinner, Libby put on a soft cotton nightgown and grabbed a multi-colored throw to cover her feet. Sitting cross-legged on the bed's blue comforter, she took a diary and a gold pen from the night table. After long meditation, she made her entry:

Aquarium

Stolen river, boxed fish
Still alive, no danger.
Voyage perfect maiden stares.
Soul afloat in cast iron tub
Pines for tranquil play in glassed-in trouble.

32

Satisfied, she put aside the writing tools and crawled under the covers.

CHAPTER 11
History – April 1921

Mary's favorite instructor at school was Miss Ina Gebhardt, who taught Home Economics and Art. She asked Mary to stop by the art room after school.

The room smelled sour like *papier mâché*. Paint jars stained with green and blue streaks sat on countertops with clay dust.

"I wanted to thank you for being such a good student. You've been a real pleasure, and I'm going to miss you," Miss Gebhardt said.

"Miss me? I don't graduate until next year. I'll be back," Mary said.

"But I won't be, Mary," the teacher said.

"Why? Did you get another job?"

"Not yet. I don't know if I'll be able to get a recommendation from the district," Miss Gebhardt said. "Matters seem to be at a standstill."

"Matters?" Mary said. "What's happening to us?"

"Not to us – to me. I take it you haven't heard the stories. I thought everyone knew."

"Knew what? Why am I always the last to know?" Mary said.

"I'm not being invited back to teach next year."

"Why?"

"The school board decided I'm not suitable."

"How can that be? You're the best. Everyone says so." The girl was disoriented. First, her best friend left town, and now, her favorite teacher was leaving.

"To put it in plain terms, I run around with undesirable men," Miss Gebhardt said.

"Do they drink?" Mary said.

The teacher laughed. "Only Communion wine."

Not comprehending, Mary just stood.

Miss Gebhardt gave her a sympathetic look. "If it sounds silly, it probably is."

Mary felt her chest tighten.

"I had a part-time job in the rectory of a Catholic church," the teacher said. "The two priests needed a cook. Their housekeeper was well-organized, but even she said her cooking was terrible. A friend in their parish told me about it, so I made an offer.

"The priests' favorite meal was supper, and they hired me to fix it. And they always invited me to eat with them.

"So for about year, I went to the rectory every night Monday through Friday. The parish families usually invite priests to dinner on weekends.

"The priests were so interested in what happened here at school, and they reminisced about their boyhoods."

"But what does this have to do with your teaching?" Mary was pleading.

"Nothing. But that's not how some people see it."

"What is there to see?" Mary said.

"Two unmarried men and a schoolmarm having dinner every night. People make of it what they will," Miss Gebhardt said. "I don't know who started the gossip, but one day, I got an anonymous letter in my mail slot in the school office.

"There was no postage. Whoever wrote it called me a harlot for the Catholic usurpers. I laughed it off, but I didn't tell the principal about it, either. Maybe I should have, because he eventually confronted me."

Mary pressed her hands against the sides of her face. She had a feeling she knew what was coming.

"Someone reported me to the school board. I was accused of being a poor example, because of my conduct with the priests," the teacher said. "My conduct. As if making potato cakes was something to be ashamed of.

"Certain members of the board have strong anti-Catholic sentiments, and they believe the Roman church is sponsoring white slavery," Miss Gebhardt concluded.

Mary rolled her eyes. She'd heard the same thing from her mother.

"I'm sorry," Mary said. "I'm so sorry."

"Thank you, Mary. I will definitely miss you."

"But what am I supposed to do? You're the one who critiques – shows me how to be better. I won't have anybody," Mary said.

"Visit the woods. Start a bug collection, and study the fine details, the subtlety of their colors. Draw them, bring them to life. And go on to study human anatomy. With your gifts, you could have a future as a medical illustrator.

"You can do these things without me, but I'll always remember I discovered you," Miss Gebhardt said.

"It's not fair. It's not fair," Mary said, starting to cry. The teacher opened her arms, and Mary cried on her shoulder.

"No, it isn't fair," Miss Gebhardt said.

CHAPTER 12
Present Day – Autumn

Alone on a picnic bench during lunch, Libby sighed, reviewing the morning's events. The shelter at Harrison State Park afforded views of the walnut plantation in the mist. A hawk soared above the red-and-yellow horizon, and she turned to monitor his flight, which continued over picnic groves and the road to Delaware Lake, next to the golf course.

She thought about her staff, and the way they cared for each other, and their loyalty to her. They were flexible, too, and she was grateful for their help on this day. She was hung over from another dream about Teddy.

She reflected on her team's journey. After dental school in her native Iowa, she came to Indianapolis to finish graduate school in pediatric dentistry and orthodontics, after which she bought the practice from a retiring dentist, David Mendelson.

She was alone here, a favorite topic of her employees. Teasing her, they catalogued a list of traits desirable in a swain, but they wouldn't have done so, if they weren't confident of her friendship.

Libby said, "Does he have a hedge fund, and a house on Hilton Head?"

The office manager Libby inherited, Frenchie Stein, shook her finger with delight. "You should be so lucky."

Libby realized her staff was politically incorrect, and deliberately so, but never in front of patients.

Libby enjoyed the occasional drink with Frenchie, a close friend of Dr. Mendelson and his wife. They were actively Jewish and enjoyed teaching the tenets of their religion. While not proselytizing, they alluded to heroes of faith in wide-ranging discussions about politics and art, which Libby enjoyed at the Mendelson's dinner table.

Before retirement, David Mendelson broke his right hand in a fall on the ice while clearing the driveway, a chore his wife had nagged him to farm out. "Ellie, find me a neighbor kid who's not on his computer, and I'll pay him to shovel the driveway."

"But for your information, Hell has already frozen over," he said, heading out the garage door.

Soon after recovering, he missed his freedom. Retiring early, he invested in a small downtown art gallery, which he visited as a breather from the pursuit of his hobby, painting watercolors.

Frenchie remained at the practice, and Libby was happy to retain her. In addition to managing the schedule and keeping the books, Frenchie set Libby's appointments with vendors, who flocked to the office with offers of technology.

The dental assistant who worked with Dr. Mendelson decided to leave when he retired, and Libby hired Drew. Marquita, a registered hygienist, joined with bilingual abilities, because Libby expanded the practice with Medicaid patients, many of whom were Hispanic. Lightening Frenchie's load, Libby transferred the insurance billing and collection duties to Keisha, a new clerk who'd worked for Medicaid.

After their first year as a team, Libby gave the staff a three-day weekend in Las Vegas at her expense, an idea that jelled when she overheard an enthusiastic discussion regarding Vegas attractions. Peddling a story about attending a conference, she asked Frenchie to block out a Friday. Offering airline tickets, Libby stipulated that anyone who accepted the trip had to return with a photo showing her doing something "out of character."

The photos exceeded expectations when Keisha returned with a picture of herself at a "palm-breaking seminar."

"You tried to break your hand?" Libby said.

"No. It was a class on how to break bricks with your palm, like the karate guys."

The picture Marquita took captured Keisha's blurred hand between pieces of flying brick. "You'd be hell on dentures," Marquita said.

They were set in their routine after two years, and they supported her during exasperating appointments, like today's encounter with Danielle Banes.

She kicked Libby in the ribs. The dentist sang, "Ow," in a quick cascade of soft tones. The four-year-old squirming in the chair smiled and drew in her breath.

"No, no, no." Her exclamations mimicked a squeaky dog toy.

"I am so sorry," Mrs. Banes said, grabbing her daughter by the wrist. "Danielle, please stop. We need to peek inside your mouth."

Growling, the child kicked high, exposing pink underpants.

"Can't you give her something?" her mother said.

"I don't use sedatives for routine exams," Libby said. "We could run a video that helps children to get ready for first appointments."

"This isn't her first appointment," Mrs. Banes said, drooping.

Embarrassment will afflict parents from all backgrounds, Libby observed, noting the matron's diamond earrings, and carefully streaked blond hair. Shifting weight nervously, the mother looked down, brushing away fuzzy insults to a silk pants suit in salmon. This parent was anxious, but not about dental work.

Libby tested her. "Do you have a pressing errand for later today?"

"I was hoping to get Danielle to the babysitter by eleven-thirty," Mrs. Banes said. "I need to get the dog groomed before the dog show. We have a Lhasa Apso."

Danielle was pushing her right index finger up her nose, where the digit was held for dramatic effect, but the mother was oblivious.

Breathing slowly, Libby exhaled discreetly, not with vulgar impatience. The Baneses had been late, and with further delays, she would have to improvise to stay on schedule.

Using the intercom, she called Drew to ask if the next patient had arrived. Buzzing back, Drew said, "Marquita has him started."

"OK. I'll go on to him, and you can work with Danielle in the teaching room. She gets the video and the puppets," Libby said.

"And the puppets," Drew said. Dressed in maternity scrubs, she entered, wearing a flushed face and a flowered shirt over raspberry pants.

"I'm gonna burn . . . you . . . up," Danielle said, pointing her ill-used finger at Drew.

"Have her wash her hands," Libby said.

Later resuming Danielle's appointment, she found the child wearing a mask and exam gloves. Drew also dressed her in a disposable clinical gown, trimmed to fit.

"Doctor, I'm ready for my next patient," the child said, muffled behind the mask.

"Very good," Libby said, relieved that play-acting with puppets and rubber instruments had emboldened Danielle, who climbed into the chair and smoothed the hem of the gown.

"Now, doctor, I need to take off your mask for a little while, so I can check inside your mouth," Libby said.

The child's blue eyes widened as Libby slid down the mask. She's on the verge again, Libby thought, but Danielle closed her lids and opened her mouth, like a baby bird expecting food to drop in.

"I just can't believe how you got her to behave," Mrs. Banes said. Libby was certain this mother never played with her child.

***

Finishing her sack lunch, Libby reviewed her dreams about Teddy.

He'd been a fellow graduate student. With a focus on prosthodontics and dental materials, Teddy contemplated earning a doctorate in materials engineering. Libby met him at a school picnic in the fall of her second year, and they joined a group that met for pizza and beer on Friday nights. Slowly, a relationship based on mutual respect allowed them to couple. Nothing interfered with scholarship. Committed and faithful, they never discussed marriage.

Teddy Lee came from a prosperous Asian family in San Francisco and excelled in life to his parents' great satisfaction. When they visited, they barely noticed Libby as they blushed, gazing at their prince, who lacked only purple raiment and gold slippers. She couldn't blame his parents. Suppressing harsh words – and the mean thoughts behind them – Teddy was disarming, and his comic timing, perfect. Despite the innocent expression and smooth, supple skin, he housed a dusty, crinkled soul with the magic of a wizard and the humility of a houseboy.

Teddy lived in a second-floor apartment with a balcony, and Libby thought he'd enjoy a pet. She bought him a cat, which he named Dr. John F. Johnston, after a pioneer in dental research. Dr. John F.'s naughty-puss trick was to jump from the sofa to the hanging shelves and knock down keepsakes and charms. Practical and forgiving, Teddy moved the shelf to the bedroom, where the cat wasn't allowed.

The cat's other habit was to rub against Teddy's ankles. One afternoon, Teddy was carrying a steaming dinner plate to the table, when the cat went for an ankle. Teddy tripped, spilling hot chicken lo mein as he fell through the balcony's sliding glass door. Pressing a hand against a gushing femoral artery, he hobbled to the white-tiled kitchen, soon scarlet and slippery. He managed to dial 911 in the last minutes of his life and tell what happened.

The graduate school held a memorial service, and Teddy's parents established a scholarship in his name. Dr. John F. Johnston went to the pound. Though grieving, Libby studied undeterred, completing follow-up exams on the patients in her experimental trials. But eventually, she let it out.

A group of graduate students made a mid-summer trip to a large reservoir, and she went along. They took picnic baskets, volleyball equipment, and swimming apparel. After lunch, they volleyed for an hour and readied to swim at the public beach. The party charged into the water like animals deprived of drink. When Libby thrust forward at the water's edge, her right leg sank up to mid-thigh in mud. Awkwardly sealed, she feared sinking even deeper if she put too much weight on the other leg to hoist herself up. Her friends entered the water without difficulty and plunged ahead, not hearing her yell. Stopped, she could no longer run from the grief and burst into tears. No one noticed. After crying for two or three minutes, she felt the muddy grip loosen. Raising her arms straight up, she shifted her weight to the left.

"Need help?" a man walking by said.

"Yes, please!" she said. He grabbed her right hand and pulled her up. She thanked him. He looked at her tear-streaked face.

"No problem," he said, moving on.

Surveying the crush of flailing swimmers, Libby was filled with uncharitable assumptions about the coarseness of their sweaty lives, enlivened only by a dunk in a dirty public waterway, where toilet paper would come floating by. She walked back to the pile of beach bags, found hers, and pulled out a T-shirt. She drew it over the swimsuit and put on her shoes.

Locating the concession stand, she bought a soda pop with sugar, a dental nadir. She strode to the edge of a wooded area and paused, her back to the lake. Attacking her legs, mosquitoes left swells, and she stood crying, gnashing her teeth, and accepting judgment from the flying tribunal: Guilty of giving him the cat! With arms wrapped around the ache in her ribs, she stayed, leaving at last when she had to go to the bathroom. At the shower house, she dressed, and on the beach, she waited in a folding chair. Emerging from the lake, the members of the party acknowledged her with querying looks.

"Hi," she said. "Got a leg cramp and decided to go for a walk."

Later that night, she forgave herself, crying until sleep came as she whispered, "I miss you." For the next six months, she cried before sleep, until one night she dozed without the lachrymae.

For the duration of her studies, she avoided intimacy. Now professionally secure at age thirty-one, she was alone. Teddy was on a mission in her dreams, and she had another one last night. She peered up at the hawk, once again circling after his perusal of the soggy golf course. On a notepad from her purse, she scribbled:

> Hawk eye on me, mouse muddy and free,
> Will he shred my dread-bud heart?
> Rain flooding hideaway.
> Golf club, end me; defy ruinous talons.
> By Nicklaus blunt or red-eye sharp,
> Termination is the manly art.

Libby checked her watch, packed her lunch remnants, and went back to work.

CHAPTER 13
History – April 1921

Deck Whittenger was a sympathetic listener, Mary learned.

"What an atrocious thing!" he said, upon hearing of Miss Gebhardt's dismissal from the high school faculty. "I can't imagine anything more ridiculous. The poor lady was just putting back a little money and getting a meal out of it, too.

"It's like Grandfather says – We don't respect self-reliance like we used to."

Mary and Deck were talking during refreshments at Creedmore Hall. He'd asked why she was moping, given that her artwork was quite good. The girls had been sketching a tray of fruit and cheese that Deck arranged.

"What a succulent pear, Miss Mary," Deck said, when he glided up behind her at the easel. "And the holes in the cheese. Most inviting," he added in a lower, suggestive tone.

A naïf, she was tone deaf. "You didn't say what kind of bread would go with the cheese," she said. "It's more inspiring to imagine how the cheese tastes with the bread. But there's no bread."

"You are free to envision the bread in your provocative little mind," he said. "Maybe something with . . . a hard crust."

"Maybe one of those long skinny French things?" she said.

Deck smiled. "One of those long French things," he said, trying not to laugh.

As they chatted later, Deck made a generous offer. "I have a new car – can you believe it? The horn is so loud, I scare myself. And I could give you a ride to a lovely spot where you could collect bugs and sketch until the light fades.

"After all, the best places aren't on the streetcar line."

"Well, I don't know. It's very nice of you, but I'm not sure my mother would approve," Mary said.

"Why not? They pay me to come here and provide instruction. Why wouldn't I be a trustworthy chauffeur?" he said.

"It's not that, it's – it's that she doesn't approve of my going places with – someone – without a chaperone." Mary's face reddened and little beads of sweat formed above her lip.

"If someone is a perfectly nice fellow, I don't see why she should object," he said.

"And you are perfectly nice," Mary said. "But she is a person of firm character, and I don't want to disobey."

"Which makes you all the more admirable," Deck said. "So maybe we could find a way to leave her at peace."

"I don't see how," Mary said.

"Do you visit the public library downtown?" he said.

"Oh, yes. When I want to find out something no one wants me to know, I go there," she said.

He laughed. "Good for you. Then you can see – telling your mother you planned to spend the day at the library would be a nice little dodge – not a lie, really.

"You could go to the library on a Saturday, check out a few books, and then I could pick you up.

"The good lady would be none the wiser, and you'd have a pile of books to take home as evidence."

Mary was shocked. She'd never contemplated an elaborate plan to fool her mother. Until now.

"I don't know," Mary said. "I hate to think of what could happen."

"But what could happen?" Deck said. "Fresh air, the beauty of nature, a picnic lunch, and maybe a sketch will issue from that dainty hand of yours."

"I don't know. I guess I could think about it," she said.

"Those who take action get there first. That's what Grandfather says," Deck said.

As the salon concluded, Deck came up to her and whispered, "Remember who gets there first."

When Mary got home that afternoon, she received a letter from Bina Schwartz, who moved away with her family. As a Jew, Bina was never invited to socialize at Mary's home, but through clubs at school, Mary and Bina had clung to each other as confidantes. Mary was excited by the day's omens – the tantalizing offer from Deck, and now, the letter.

The letter devastated her. Bina wrote to say that in mourning, the family sat *shiva* for her father, who died of a heart attack soon after they moved to live with her uncle.

"Papa's disappointment with life killed him. He lost faith in his fellow man, and he was afraid he would lose the respect of his wife and children. We told him that was impossible.

"We revered him; we revere him, still," Bina wrote.

Sad for her friend's loss, Mary understood the cruelty of the boycotts and smears, and how they ruined the security of the Schwartz family.

She heard her mother clanging utensils in the kitchen. Her own mother was one of the oppressors – someone who didn't want to hear about the hurt she caused. The girl stewed until her anger took hold.

Defiant, she resolved to accept Deck's offer.

CHAPTER 14
Present Day – Autumn

Darla and Trevor were settled in for the evening. Admiring her new haircut, the woman glanced at herself in the dining-room mirror before she turned out the light. A hefty white candle burned on a metal tray on the dining table, protected by a stiff white cloth. She sat down, scooting the padded chair closer to the table.

She lived in a one-story home with a brick façade and a decorative iron rail on the front step. Built in the 1950s, her house was between two century-old homes with generous front porches. In contrast, she had a modest living room, a cramped dining nook off the kitchen, and two bedrooms, one large, and the other, more like a den. The partial basement had a hook-up for the washer/dryer set, and a wooden garage in back shielded the car and the trash cans. The backyard featured a chain-link fence with a locked gate, so Trevor could stay outside when she wasn't home.

"Trevor," she said, and the dog drew near, receiving affectionate rubs between the ears. He relaxed next to her chair. She arranged a notepad and pen in front of her.

"Let's say the Lord's Prayer." She held up her hands, palms out, and after the prayer, she waved her arms as if shooing away pesky children.

"I believe in Jesus Christ – Satan go away!" she said.

She focused on the candle flame. "We call the Holy Spirit to reveal the truth – Lord, we entreat thee – Let these words be yours and yours alone."

46

She wrote random words and phrases without stopping to question their relevance. After scribbling two pages, she felt the letdown of being ordinary. She put the pen aside and considered the writing.

One phrase stood out, "Teddy Bear on the mug, slug."

She murmured, repeating, "Teddy Bear on the mug, slug." It was a warning.

She studied the words before and after the odd rhyme. The word that followed was most important, she decided. Just one word – lawnmower.

"Trevor, I think something's breaking loose at that house we visit – where we see the lady mow the lawn – you know, the one who doesn't know she has company in her house," she said. The dog let out a tender moan.

"I'm hungry. Do you want a big snack?" The dog jumped up.

She turned on the ceiling light and blew out the candle. They stepped into the kitchen.

CHAPTER 15
Present Day – Autumn

When Libby went to the art museum, she would sit on a bench in the gallery and write reflections in a tiny spiral notebook. Her disposition of late had been slurry with introversion, and believing that change was healthy, she attended a preview for museum members in the first week of October.

Extensively remodeled in recent years, the museum sat on property bordered by trees. The new tableau was far more inviting, unlike its former suggestion of a private mental health institution. Arriving after work, she took a quick stroll through a garden, and in the fading light, she paused, looking for the first evening star.

The preview featured a multimedia exhibition exploring themes of violence. Cartoons, oil paintings, sculptures, and film installations comprised a gritty counterculture hidden from the peaceful outdoors.

Finished looking, Libby followed the sound of a piano-jazz combo to a lounge. She bought a drink, and from trays of cheese and hors d'oeuvres, she plucked morsels to enjoy at a shiny black bar table. Soon, two men in sweaters and khakis approached her.

"Hi," she said.

"Hi," the blond buzz cut said. "Jeff Slidell."

"Libby Doherty."

"And this is my friend, Mark Winston," Slidell said. They all shook hands. In her peripheral vision to the right, she saw a brunette woman in a maroon paisley wrap dress. The woman stood alone with her drink as she studied the trio without appearing to horn in.

48

"I don't think I've seen you here before," Winston said. "Our group goes to the summer movies on the terrace, and I guess we're sort of edging our way inside. This was the first preview I've been to –" he ended with a questioning glance toward Slidell.

"Same here," Slidell said.

"I visit the museum often," Libby said.

"The exhibition on violence – I don't know," Slidell said, shaking his head. "It was pretty 'out there.' I did like the metal thing wearing the radioactive-hazard helmet."

"Gruesome stuff," Winston said.

"You know, if you're just getting acquainted with the galleries, you might want to start with the American collection," Libby said. "Everything from frontier landscapes with buffalo to the works of Edward Hopper.

"The preview was thought-provoking, but not something you'd put on a calendar to give to your boss at Christmas."

The men chuckled, and Winston handed Libby a business card.

"I'm a lobbyist for the construction industry, and Jeff is in chemical sales," Winston said.

"I'm a family dentist," she said.

"Oh, cool," Slidell said, backing away just a little. "I hate going to the dentist, but I bet you hear that all the time."

"Sure. It goes with the job."

"You must be pretty smart, then," Slidell said.

What I am supposed to say, Libby thought – no, not really? She hated this game of making men feel comfortable with her accomplishments. She wouldn't play.

"I'm a very good dentist," she said. Still watching, the woman in the paisley wrap dress smiled into her cocktail.

The lobbyist took over. "This is a pretty good jazz group. I've seen them around. It's nice to hear relaxing music after a tough day at the statehouse." Playacting, he rolled his eyes.

"I don't follow politics as much as I should. I only met one of the candidates for prosecutor just the other day," Libby said.

"Oh really? Which one?" Winston said.

Libby wished she hadn't said that. "Well," she hedged, "I believe he's the Democrat."

"Harkness. He's a dirty campaigner, but I don't think he'll make it," Winston said.

"Ah, why is that?" she said, sharing her snack plate. The men murmured thanks.

"For one thing, the governor is staunchly in Theo Karnow's corner, and he can raise more money," Winston said, unimpressed with the neophyte.

"But why do you say Harkness is a dirty campaigner?" Libby said, noticing Slidell was looking around, giving a two-fingered salute to no one across the room. The two pairs of khakis would leave soon, she guessed.

"He's an ambitious cutthroat," Winston said. "The odds are – if elected, he won't finish his term, because he wants to run for Congress. But Karnow's a keeper," Winston said.

"Why is Harkness dirty?" she said.

"Look at the TV ads he's running. He says Karnow is unqualified and compares him to raw meat. That's crass, talking about Karnow while this meat comes oozing out of a grinder," he said.

Meat. Why did that ring a bell? Libby wondered.

"Sounds like he's making democracy-on-a-bun," Libby continued. "Politics is so predictable, anymore – fast-food government sold to the highest bidder." She knocked back her drink.

"I don't know," Winston said. "I find most lawmakers to be very fair-minded, but it probably doesn't look that way to the casual out –" he caught himself, "observer."

Libby smiled. "You almost said, 'outsider.' "

Slidell cut in. "Look, there's Dave Black – we've been looking for him all night."

Winston saw the imaginary Dave Black. "Oh, great! Listen, we'll be catching up with a friend, but it's been great talking with you. Have a great evening." They sidled away.

Libby popped a piece of Monterrey Jack into her mouth, and the woman in the paisley wrap dress stepped closer.

"I counted at least three 'greats,' " the woman said.

Libby laughed. "Would you like to sit down?" she said.

"Yes, thanks." She rested on a stool. "I'm Denise Bookbinder." She pronounced it BOOK-bin-dur. "I may as well give you my card, too." Embossed with floral trim, the card said "PhD" after her name.

"I'm Libby Doherty."

"The scary dentist."

"Very scary."

"I'm a counseling psychologist," Denise said. "You can imagine how people react to *me*. I always say getting the truth out of my patients is like pulling teeth."

Libby's plate was empty. "I'm still hungry," she said.

"Me, too," Denise said. "I was considering a quick run into Broad Ripple for dinner. I started thinking about potato skins. Would you like to join me? I promise not to bring up politics."

"Sure." Libby liked her open and cosmopolitan demeanor.

"How about Zoots?" Denise said. "Not so expensive, and they have really good potato skins."

"I've driven by," Libby said, standing.

"Let's give ourselves about twenty minutes to get there," Denise said.

Zoots, a faux-WW II diner, indeed offered generous portions of potato skins, and Libby indulged, enjoying her new friend, age forty-one and recently divorced. Denise's cosmetics and jewels were hip-just-this-side-of-hard, and she styled her wavy dark hair at shoulder length. She had an attractive brow, a small chin cleft, and dimples. The women exchanged histories – Denise was from Milwaukee – and each explained how she wound up in Indiana.

"My 'ex' got a job here, and I put out a shingle. While I was finishing my doctorate at Wisconsin, I worked at a veterans' hospital, and previously, I counseled youths in drug rehab," Denise said.

"What did your ex-husband do?" Libby said.

"To me, or for a living?"

"For a living."

"He's in the broadcast trade," Denise said.

"A producer?"

"No. Air talent."

"TV or radio?"

"He anchors the news at six and eleven on one of the network affiliates." Denise gave her eyelashes an editorial flutter that said, "Big deal."

"I'm embarrassed to say so, but I don't recall anyone named Bookbinder," Libby said.

"That's because I had the good sense to use my maiden name professionally." After a pause, Denise said, "He's Bob Kring."

"Bob Kring! No kidding!"

"Uh-huh. A real big kidder."

"I'm sorry it didn't work out," Libby said.

"I was sorry, too, for a while."

Libby didn't respond, preferring to let Denise pick her words. The sound system shared an up-tempo Glenn Miller tune. A montage of wartime dance-hall photos and film clips ran on screens placed at different angles around the room. The mounted flat screens were the only anachronisms among the otherwise authentic decorations.

"He left me for a sports and entertainment lawyer," Denise said.

"Oh," Libby said.

"She was doing TV commentary on a big extortion case against a basketball player. I guess it went on for about eight months before I found out."

"The case, or the . . . relationship?" Libby said.

"Their 'thing.' I'm not sure, but I think they started seeing each other right after the trial ended."

"Did he announce one day he was leaving?"

"No," Denise said, "I found out by accident. I went down to Bloomington for a conference at IU, and afterward, I took a pleasure drive along Lake Monroe, where we had a very nice pontoon. It was one of those sunny, breezy days when you think nothing can go wrong.

"I stopped at the store where we always docked to get soft drinks or beer, and the owner asked me what I thought of the tornado on Saturday. I said, 'I don't think I was here for that.'

"He said, 'Sure you were. You were on the dock under your big red-and-white umbrella. The sirens were going off, and Mr. Kring came in and said it looked like the twister was blowing north.'

"I knew right away Bob was cheating. We had a red-and-white umbrella, but I wasn't the one holding it. She probably had her back turned. He'd left early that morning, saying he was going to play eighteen holes and have dinner with a PR guy from the NFL.

"So, I drove to a picnic area and sat in my car and cried. When I thought I could drive again, I went home.

"I knew it wasn't my fault, but it made me feel better to believe the other woman threw herself at him. Then I got mad. I started thinking about all the inconsiderate things he'd done that I let pass, because he was Bob Kring.

"Getting the newscast ready took precedence over everything in our married life, but he still managed to find time for an affair," Denise said, her face reddening. She took a sip of water and a deep breath.

"I confronted him the next Sunday morning after he read his newspaper. I asked him how he liked the tornado that went over the lake, and whether he was afraid he'd lose the boat.

"He just stared at me with his mouth open for a long time. Finally, I said, 'We're finished, aren't we?' He nodded. I just looked at him. Then he asked me, 'What do you want?' " Denise said.

"I said, 'An explanation would be nice, but only for closure. I don't want your boat or your toys. We can do a deal on the house.' So, he gave me a sketch of the affair, and that she was already divorced and eager to get married. And they did."

"Jeepers," Libby said.

Denise smiled. "That's a nice, old-fashioned word," she said, leaning back and giving Libby a new appraisal.

"I'm not so old-fashioned. I might have put little holes in those two with my dental drill," Libby said.

"She was already full of holes," Denise said.

They finished the potato skins, and Denise grabbed the checks. "This has been so wonderful, and I hope you'll come to my house. I'll fix dinner. Can you come next Friday?"

"I'll bring the wine. Red or white?"

"Red, around seven?"

"That's perfect," Libby said. She took down Denise's address.

***

At home, Libby had trouble falling asleep, and she got up to fix a cup of chamomile tea. She pulled a volume of W.H. Auden from the bookcase in one of the spare bedrooms used as a study. She read aloud in the easy chair that traveled with her since college. She paused at intervals, listening, as the grandfather clock struck the quarter hour, then the half, then the hour. It was midnight. She went to the front door and stepped barefoot onto the porch. The night was starry. Something howled like a coyote. The howling intensified and she heard a whirring noise. A bicycling youth wearing a Halloween mask passed under a streetlamp, and she could see his wolf-man get-up. He howled, speeding away.

Libby locked up and went to bed. As she slept, Teddy returned. He was barefoot this time. He stood on the sidewalk in front of her house and waved. The wind was blowing leaves, and he was jubilant, jumping up and down on the cold cement. He pointed to his bare feet and did a little dance. The wind picked up. He tilted his head back to let the wind brush his hair. The wind stiffened, blowing a plastic trash container past him. He laughed, disappearing.

***

Libby listened to the radio as she drove to work. During a stream of commercials, a predictable message came from Jed Harkness, focusing on his experience. She remembered the lobbyist's complaint about the Harkness TV spot. Libby rarely watched television, but tonight she'd look for the ad.

After the evening swim, she forgot to watch TV until eight o'clock, when she turned on the small set in the kitchen. She found a talk show, "Stedlow's Indiana Politics," with an amiable do-nothing serving as host. At age fifty, Bill Stedlow was a former wire service reporter who broke into TV on the assignment desk. He eventually worked his way to the statehouse beat, where his job was to react. He did no digging, except in his pumpkin field, almost as notable as the talk show. This week families were poking around a farm northwest of the city, where he invested in acreage for pumpkins, surely at a premium for the seasonal observances.

Stedlow introduced himself. "Good evening, and welcome to another week in the political pumpkin patch."

"Nothing like a little free advertising," the Republican pundit said off-camera to Stedlow's right.

"I'm saving one just for you," Stedlow said. He identified each panelist. His top story was Jed's TV spot. "The latest from the Harkness camp has Republicans alleging Harkness hit a new low in negative campaigning. A

54

spokesman for Harkness said *this* ad just tells it like it is." The feed switched to a full-screen display of the footage.

The first image showed raw hamburger spilling from a meat grinder. The narrator said, "Theo Karnow is a fresh face in the election for prosecutor. In fact, he's *raw*."

A pair of hands molded the ground meat into a patty and placed it on a grill. A faint sizzle was heard.

"Most criminals aren't raw – They're *well-done*. They know how to *use* the justice system . . . to get what *they* want." The sizzling got louder.

"Theo Karnow has *never* prosecuted a *single case*. He *doesn't know* how to handle *well-seasoned* crooks . . . who pose a *threat* to our city." A hand sprinkled salt on the hamburger.

The grease started to spatter.

A hand holding a spatula turned over the patty. Part of the burger was stuck to the grill.

"Can we afford to let Theo Karnow burn *us*?" the narrator concluded.

The camera was back on the panel, and Stedlow addressed his counterpart from the newspaper. "Did Jed Talbot Harkness go too far with this ad?"

"Well, he didn't lie about Karnow's experience," the newspaperman said. "I guess you could say any objections to the ad would be on esthetic grounds – like if you thought the meat looked stale."

Laughing, Stedlow addressed the Democratic pundit. "Why the comparison to raw meat? It's hardly elevated."

"Neither is Karnow's platform," the Democrat said.

"Now wait a minute," the Republican said. "Theo Karnow is one of the most distinguished attorneys in the state of Indiana – and Harkness is just trying to make him look like he's never been anywhere or done anything. I think people are gonna see though that."

The Republican commentator reminded Libby of a jovial baseball fan who snacked all the time on camera. She thought he should have a hot dog with mustard and relish, then nachos and cheese, and later, an ice cream cone.

The panel members heckled each other until Stedlow switched topics, and Libby shut off the TV. She was titillated and annoyed. Getting up from the kitchen table, she paced around. The night at Big Sal's, she compared Karnow to a hamburger without a lid. Jed agreed with her. Granted, the commercial made a harsher impact than her little comment, but she wondered if the TV spot was made before or after she met Jed.

"Is this politics?" she said, stopping at the kitchen sink. "Is it always about using everyone and everything?" She filled a glass of water and drank until she giggled. Good thing she hadn't said there was no lid on Karnow's toilet. Water leaked from the corners of her mouth, and she swept the back of her hand across her lips. She was beginning to doubt Jed would take her to dinner as proposed.

"Hold it," she said, as if interrupting a dental procedure. "I'm not losing any sleep over this guy." The mention of sleep started a replay of her latest dream about Teddy. She went out to the front porch and sat on the steps. Staring at the sidewalk where he pranced in the dream, she stayed until her rump grew stiff from the cold cement. She finally went indoors for hot cider. The bedside journal required attention. Mesmerized by the purple-and-gold fabric of the cover, she rubbed her fingers along the edges. Writing, she queried:

Fresh insight from stale meat;
Exogenous hormone burns my seat.
Riddle of life on griddle of life:
How to keep fire on low?

CHAPTER 16
History – April 1921

On Saturday, Mary's mother was preoccupied with getting ready for a tea sponsored by the Women's Christian Temperance Union, owner of a big constituency in Irvington. She accepted Mary's fable about her plans for a day at the library.

"Honey, do you have correct change for the streetcar?" her mother said as Mary went out the kitchen door.

"Yes ma'am, just as you always remind, Mother," Mary said, carrying a bag concealing her sketch book and drawing tools.

At the library, she selected books she didn't intend to read, because they were props. She checked out three and went to the curb along Meridian Street.

A horn honked, and a car with a bright red hood drew near, a 1921 Cadillac. Deck waved her aboard, and she got in. He sped away like a bank robber. At the next street, he went around the block and doubled back.

"Where are we going?" she said.

"Bartholomew County," he said.

"What?" she said. "It'll take us forever to get there!"

"Not in this beauty," he said. "The Cadillac gave a perfect performance in the Great War. Ideal for cross-country touring."

"Ye gods!" Mary said. "I'm a doughboy." Deck burst out laughing.

"You are precious, Miss Mary. May I say you're lovely in your blue dress?"

Mary blushed. "Thank you."

"I had the cook throw together a picnic lunch. It's in the basket in back. I hope you like smoked salmon. And a round of cheese."

"Will we stop along the way to buy some pop?" she said.

"With smoked salmon? I brought champagne," he said.

"But that's alcohol. It's illegal, and my mother is in the WCTU," Mary said.

"Are you in the temperance union?" Deck said.

"Not yet. They're having a tea this afternoon. She was taking cookies."

"Then, they can have their tea," Deck said. "We're artists. The sensual life is important, and we need stimulation – for our creative impulses.

"And she'll never know." he said.

"But – it's illegal," Mary said.

"No, it's not illegal to drink it. We just can't sell it. And we had this champagne in our private stock before the law took effect.

"So, let us enjoy it," he decreed.

"Judas priest!" Mary said under her breath.

CHAPTER 17
Present Day – Autumn

One afternoon, candidate Jed Harkness needed a crown, but not of a kingly sort.

For Libby, it was supposed to be a day about the tax code. She scheduled a two-hour lunch with the dental CPA who evaluated the practice before she bought it. She wanted him to look for more deductions.

She returned to the office around three-thirty. As Libby worked on the last scheduled patient, Marquita stuck her head in the door, smiled, and moved on. Moments later, Keisha did the same thing, and then Frenchie, with hands clasped behind her back as she departed. Drew glanced at Libby across the boy she was treating.

"OK," Libby said to the child. "You're done until next time. You can get a reminder card at the front desk." The boy shot out of the chair, and Drew followed him. Libby removed her protective gear, and as she washed her hands, Marquita returned.

"You're not going to believe this, but *El Super Ratón está aquí*," Marquita said.

"What?" Libby said.

"Mighty Mouse is here. In the waiting room. He has a bad tooth," Marquita said, triumphant.

"Mighty Mouse?" Libby realized that Marquita meant Jed.

"There's a big guy with him, too," Marquita said.

Libby guessed it was the driver, Gale. "Let's see what they want," she said, going out. Marquita followed on tiptoes like a cat. At her desk, Keisha

59

was trying to keep a straight face. Frenchie was on the phone, or at least pretending to be.

"Jed," Libby said as he rose to shake her hand. "What's going on?"

"I'm seeking asylum." He rubbed his right jaw. "Yesterday, a filling fell out, and it hurts. I can't concentrate. I'm supposed to be in a debate with Theo Karnow at seven-thirty, but I don't think I can stand it.

"My dentist is out of town, and his emergency guy isn't available until six-fifteen. I'm in big trouble. Can you squeeze me in? Or do I have to be a rug rat?"

"I advertise that I'm a family dentist, so my practice isn't limited to children."

She sucked in a breath and exhaled like a winded sprinter.

"He has a dog," Gale said. "That's a family, right?"

Libby smiled.

"And certainly, this is a very unusual situation," she said. "An electoral debate is a matter of the public good."

A caution about flirting with patients flickered through Libby's mind. "But it's after five o'clock. If you need invasive treatment that's time-consuming, you might not get to the debate in time."

"Is there anything you can do?" Jed said. Libby saw his lonely side. He was like a boy watching a toy fall out of his sailboat and float out of reach.

"I can take a peek and see what's wrong," Libby said. "Maybe we can make you more comfortable."

"I've got dental coverage," he said.

"Forget about it," Libby said. "Just taking a peek."

"Gee," Gale said. "She's taking a peek, and you're too miserable to enjoy it." Jed flashed him a scathing look, and Gale laughed. Libby chuckled, too. She couldn't help liking Gale, droll and intuitive. He also knew when to say nothing.

"Let's go in," Libby said. "I can handle this, so the team can go home," she said to Frenchie, who was smiling like a household goddess figurine.

"I'll attend to my reading," Gale said, sifting through a pile of children's books on an end table. "Over the years, I've benefited from the leadership example of King Babar the elephant."

Swathed in protective gear, again, Libby took Jed's vitals, logged his uneventful health history, and surveyed the dentition. She was seeing him up close. Dark brows over deep-set eyes balanced the proportions of his big forehead, which otherwise would have suggested an egghead. His aquiline nose was a tad long. He had high, ruddy cheeks, and a slightly tapered, strong chin. His wide jaw had plenty of room for teeth, evenly placed by good fortune, and framed by fleshy lips. Straight brown hair, almost black, was parted on his left and freshly trimmed, no doubt in primping before the debate. He was six feet tall with broad shoulders. Perhaps a football player once, he now had the form of someone who lifted weights but skipped the extra milkshakes. The reddened cheeks appealed to her sense of the theatrical, and she envisioned him heavily made up, dressed in a clown suit as Pagliacci.

"Do you sing?" she said, putting tools in his mouth.

"Uh?" Jed gulped. His face showed fatigue brought on by constant pain and multiple worries. She remembered the night he raised fifteen-thousand dollars at the restaurant. It was unlikely the pace of fund raising had slackened.

The filling was indeed gone on a molar in the posterior of the mandibular or bottom arch. Libby tapped the exterior of the tooth with an explorer. Jed issued a loud complaint, confirming the pain lasted for more than 30 seconds after she stopped tapping.

"More than likely, you'll need a root canal," she said. "Let's get a picture." She covered Jed with a protective lead apron.

She blessed the patron saint of digital radiography, whoever he was, and the Deductress on High. The radiograph supported her initial findings.

"You had secondary caries under the filling that fell out – that's new decay after you got the filling." she said. "I'd start the therapy, but this molar has more than one canal. The time required would make you late for the debate. "The cavitation went down to the pulp, and with the pulp involved, you have infection and pain. The pulp needs to be removed, and the root canals, irrigated. If that occurs, you'll get a temporary fill.

"Then you'll need more treatment, maybe several appointments. The dentist will reopen and reshape the canals at least once and clean them. After everything, you'll need a crown." she said.

Jed grunted.

"You're not running a temperature, so you don't need antibiotics. But – the swelling will cause pain. Have you taken aspirin or other pain relievers today?"

"Just aspirin, early this morning," Jed said.

"OK. I'll give you hydrocodone with acetaminophen. That'll take the edge off so you can debate. No alcohol consumption, please." She wrote his instructions for the dosage. "Take it now, and I'll give you enough to get you through forty-eight hours.

"You'll need to see your dentist in the next day or two. Don't put it off – because it could lead to complications."

Jed sighed. "What were the chances this would happen at the worst possible time?" he said.

"Well," Libby said, "I once read a summary of biomedical results obtained from the Apollo missions. The probability of a disabling dental emergency in the astronaut population was one in nine-thousand man-days."

"So I beat the odds," Jed said.

"Only if you're an astronaut," Libby said. "Do you carry an electric shaver?"

"In the car."

"You need a quick touch-up." She poured a cup of mouthwash and raised his chair to an upright position. "Swish this around."

He did so, and she suctioned the wash with an aspirator. She removed his paper bib, and he stood, stretching. As she unlocked the drug cabinet and put pills into small envelopes, he observed a foot-long red toothbrush on a corner table, along with a huge set of plastic choppers with pink gums. He picked up the giant brush.

"I always wanted one of these when I was little," he said.

She handed him two pills and a cup of water. "Take these. I'll be right back."

She went to the supply room and returned with a box sealed in plastic wrap. "You're welcome to this sample. The salesman had too many."

Accepting the package, he smiled at the giant sea-green toothbrush pictured on the box.

"Unbelievable . . . Thank you," he said.

"Here's your med packet," she said.

"Can I pay for these?" Jed said.

"Nah." She looked at her watch. "You'd better be going. I'm sure there's traffic. You don't want to rush in at the last minute. Good luck! Will it be televised?"

"Probably some excerpts on the late news." He took her right hand. "Thanks ever so much," he said, squeezing her hand, perhaps a second too long, and then he was a candidate. "I can see myself out." She nodded a farewell.

She wasn't waiting up to see him on the late news. It occurred to her she forgot to ask about his TV commercial, but her part in the campaign was over. Jed would go on to others. They'd stitch the hem in his pants and check his standing in the polls. She had her own agenda. She was going to the seven-forty show at the movies.

CHAPTER 18
History – April 1921

Deck parked the car along a county road, and they took the picnic basket to the riverfront. The Flatrock River was scenic, and conditions were ideal. Deck led Mary to a wide, smooth ledge overlooking a placid stretch of the river.

The wildflowers along the banks were lush and aromatic under the canopy of silver maple and sycamore trees.

"I think I could sit here forever," Mary said. Deck handed her a small plate with a hunk of brown bread with butter and a slice of softened cheese. She watched Deck use a knife to spread the cheese on his bread.

"Can't I just nibble on the cheese, rind and all?" Mary said.

"Permission to nibble," Deck said.

The flavor of the cheese blossomed in her mouth. Fixing her gaze on a flowering branch, she took another bite, trying to imagine a tree of cheese.

Deck was watching her. He took out his sketch pad and drew her profile in charcoal. Oblivious, she gazed at the pastiche of cool colors along the riverbank.

He tapped her arm and handed her another plate with the smoked salmon and dill relish. He gave her a fork.

"Enjoy," he said. She tasted the fish.

"So refreshing," she said.

"Much better than tea and cookies, don't you think?" he said.

She thought of her mother, stifled in a corset, and helmeted in a hat. She felt sorry for her.

Not answering Deck, Mary bowed her head a little as she worked on the salmon.

CHAPTER 19
Present Day – Autumn

The morning after Jed's emergency, the staff lined up behind the front desk to wait for Libby, who found their smiles unbearable.

"You don't get extra points for being saccharine," she said, as the women followed her to the private office.

"*¡Díganos!*" Marquita said. "Tell us."

"Did he act like a big baby?" Keisha said.

"My husband acts like one," Drew said. "He hates the shots." Libby noticed Drew's lips and face were swollen, not a good sign in pregnancy.

"His assistant was very charming," Frenchie said. "He wanted to know all about the office, how busy we were, and how long I'd worked here. We talked for about ten minutes. So warm and solicitous – you'd think he was selling jewelry."

They stared at Libby. "I hope you like to watch me dress," she said, changing into scrubs.

"You're doing this on purr-puss," Marquita vamped.

"OK," Libby said. "I told him he needed a root canal, and I gave him pain pills. Then he had to leave for his debate."

"I saw it on the news last night. He looks 'fine' on TV," Keisha said.

"He really was in a jam," Libby said. She clapped her hands.

"Let's get our game going," she said, and they dispersed to their workstations.

After business, she went to dinner at Denise Bookbinder's in a neighborhood east of North Meridian Street near the White River. Denise lived in a secluded block near a nature walk along the water. Libby missed the turn-off and had to double back. Mature tree growth and big lawns put an aloof distance between the homes and the street. Denise's neighbors included a surgeon; an heir to a natural-gas fortune, and an antiques dealer. Denise owned one of the smaller properties, a one-story brick house renovated in the 1980s to include a skylight and a back terrace with a privacy fence.

Greeting her with a hug, Denise ushered Libby into the sunken living room, plush with red upholstery, red carpet with patterns, and red wallpaper with cream-and-gold trim. Padded with red damask seats, the wooden side chairs matched the glossy corner tables, which held miniature lamps. The bases were of Limoges crystal, and each wore cream-colored shades with ruffles.

"Wow," Libby said.

"I toured the White House and liked the Red Room," Denise said. "I moved here after the divorce. Bob would never have gone for 'all red.' But you'll see the rest of the house is very casual, like a different person lives here."

Carrying the bottle of wine she brought, Libby followed Denise to the dining room, and they opened the bottle, left to sit for a while. From the kitchen, Denise produced a basket of warm French bread wrapped in a starched white towel, and making another trip, she came back with a purple crock of onion soup. Seated, the women ladled soup into purple bowls and tore chunks of bread for dipping. After demolishing half the loaf, they poured the first toast. Warmed by the soup, they downed more drink, and then Denise brought in steak salads tossed with tenderloin, veggies, grated fontina, and vinaigrette dressing.

For dessert, they enjoyed baklava and mint-flavored cocoa. Libby was comfortable in the dining room, a long, narrow space enhanced by the skylight. Defining the room's simplicity – a bare wooden floor; a suspended lamp with a gold shade; a wall of bronze tiles with irregular borders of brown and pink; and a row of undraped windows with stained wooden frames. At one end of the room, a large hanging canvas featured an array of flowers depicted in black against waves of pink and yellow. Outdoors, a soft light bathed the back terrace, visible from the dining room.

"Now that we're sated," Denise said, "I'll break out the snacks." With more wine, the women settled in the den, casual with suede furnishings in tan, hanging quilts in desert colors, and Navajo blankets draped over chairs. A flat-screen TV was mounted on a brick wall, and magazines sat on the floor in nooks away from foot traffic.

"This is the contrast, backstairs at the White House," Libby said, and Denise hooted.

"A little more wine?" Denise said. Libby held her left thumb and first finger slightly apart, and Denise poured a few swallows from the bottle on the coffee table. "*Salud*," Denise said. They clicked their glasses together. Libby stopped drinking after this last serving and concentrated on the crackers.

"Did you start seeing anybody after your divorce?" Libby said.

"Oh, yes, ma'am," Denise said, rolling her shoulders. "I found a younger man."

"How much younger?"

"Seventy-two hours," Denise said. "He was all right. We shared a birthday party."

"You're not seeing him anymore?"

"No. He wanted a deep commitment. I had mildew from my divorce, so I ended the relationship. I did him a favor. What about you? Anyone special?" Denise said.

"No, I . . . um . . ."

Denise leaned over. "You 'um'?"

"I haven't been involved for a long time," Libby said. Denise waited. "He died."

"I'm very sorry," Denise said. "When did he pass away?"

"Almost five years ago, but it seems like yesterday."

Denise said nothing. Libby continued.

"He fell through a glass door and bled to death."

"That's a terrible thing. What was his name?"

"Teddy."

"How was your last conversation before the accident?" Denise said.

"It was positive. He spent the night at my place and left early. I watched him go." Libby paused. "He did something weird. He stood next to his car for a long time and stared at the apartment building. He looked at my window, and I waved. He waved back, and then he left. The accident was that afternoon."

"Sounds to me like he had a premonition," Denise said. "I hear about these things. Was he a spiritual person?"

"I guess. He kept his grandparents' Buddhist relics, partly as a reminder of the family, but I believe he perceived divinity in the objects. Even so, I think his parents were members of the Disciples of Christ."

"So he had this 'thing' going with the universe?" Denise said.

"Yes."

"What about you – you have a 'thing'?"

"I believe in God, but I have a struggle putting it together," Libby said. "I don't know how to accept the phrase, 'No one gets to the Father except through Me.' I believe in Jesus' divinity, and I believe in his teachings.

"I just find it hard to believe that non-Christians don't have a way to know God through eternity. But maybe one's faith affects the quality of the afterlife, sort of like flying coach instead of first class."

"And maybe some people never get a boarding pass," Denise said. "I've met quite a few self-proclaimed Christians who should be locked in the airport toilet."

"Yes. But Teddy was a good person," Libby said. "I don't like the idea of Teddy not going to a good place, but I don't know where he went."

They were silent. After a minute, Denise said, "Did you pick your own way to say goodbye?"

"How so?"

"Like planting a tree in remembrance. Others get together at a place the departed person enjoyed. Did you do anything like that?"

"No," Libby said. "We had a memorial service, and that was it."

"Sounds kind of impersonal. Did people recognize your grief, and how special he was to you?"

"Our circle of friends."

"So did you do anything as a group to remember him?"

"No. One night we ordered pizza and got around to talking about him, but it was spontaneous. We didn't stay on the subject too long."

Denise swished her wine around in the glass. "It's not too late to do something. I think it would be good for you. You don't have to look up the others.

"You can be creative and say what you always wanted to say to him, but never got the chance."

Libby looked at the neutrally shaded carpet.

"Do you know what you would have said?" Denise said.

"I don't. We were so busy all the time."

"Deep down, you do know, or you'd have found someone new," Denise said. "A woman as feminine and caring – and as smart as you – deserves a little fun, and maybe it turns into something else."

Libby was quiet. Denise watched her, finally asking, "Do you think you owe it to him to be alone?"

"No."

"Then what are you holding on to?" Denise said.

"I don't know."

"You do know, Libby. It's right in front of you."

"What do you mean?"

"Did you ever say the words, 'I love you,' to each other?" Denise said.

"No. It would have made our lives too complicated."

"But you loved him anyway."

Libby looked up at Denise. "I did – I didn't know how much until he was gone, and then I couldn't do anything about it."

"No, sadly, you could not," Denise said. "But you can do something with your own life. I think it's important that you speak to Teddy – unload everything.

"You could make a ceremonial dinner, bless each dish, and say something like, 'With this bowl of soup, I honor the healing we did for each other. And with this chicken, I honor the meat of our friendship.' And so on.

"But that's just an idea, because I like to cook. Then you should start socializing more," Denise said. "You'll meet someone."

Thinking about Jed, Libby dismissed him as a flight risk, and she didn't bother to mention him to Denise, who furrowed her brow. She was watching Libby think – or struggle, really.

In her years with Teddy, Libby granted him physical intimacy after they established an abiding friendship. Their frank encounters were carefree, and the relationship lacked drama, except when he died. Then, the loss of a great love sobered her, and now, she was having to speculate whether he believed in the existence of an afterlife. They'd never talked about it.

Studying the perforations in a cracker, Libby brooded.

"Do you fear losing someone, again?" Denise said.

Libby was sheepish. Denise sipped her wine. "I think it would kill me," Libby said.

"But you already know that it won't," Denise said. "You've built a career – you're self-sufficient. If you find someone who respects you, and who gives more than he takes, then only the wheel of fortune can spin to your detriment – and none of us has control over that," Denise said.

"I don't think I could stand losing another person to the 'wheel of fortune,' if that's who's in charge," Libby said.

"How many men do you think are going to die on you?" Denise asked.

"They don't have to die. They can be thieves and charlatans."

"Where did that come from?" Denise said.

"A movie?" Libby said. They laughed.

"Speaking of movies, Hitchcock's *Spellbound* is on tonight, with Ingrid Bergman and Gregory Peck. Would you like to stay?" Denise said.

Libby looked at her watch. It was nine-forty-five. "I wish I could, but no. I've never seen it, though."

"That's the one where the leading and supporting characters are shrinks. Terrific movie, great theme music," Denise said.

"Sounds like fun, but I have a huge day tomorrow. I work three Saturdays a month. Can I help with any dishes?"

"Oh, no," Denise said. "I'm going to finish this wine, and if the dishes get done, they get done."

CHAPTER 20
History – April 1921

Mary greeted a grasshopper as she and Deck sat along the riverbank.

"He's such a polite little man," Mary said. "He looks like he should be sitting behind a desk." She began to sketch him in charcoal. Deck leaned over to watch her quick work.

"Very good, Miss Mary. I'm envious of your ability to see the character in such a small creature," Deck said. "Do you want to take him home in a box?"

"Oh, no!" she said. "I don't want to kill him. I just want to remember him the way he is, so erect and noble, and gentlemanly."

"Not a bad way to be remembered," Deck said. His late father's words of disapproval came back, "Do you want to be remembered as a gentleman, or as a disreputable bastard?"

Deck stared at the river, and then he shrugged as if casting off a bug about to land on him.

Mary paused sketching. "You looked sad just then."

"Did I?"

"You were remembering something," she said.

He looked her full in the face. "How did you know?"

"I just did."

"Don't trouble yourself about it. Have some champagne to celebrate your masterful sketch of Mister Grasshopper," he said, taking glasses and a bottle from the picnic basket.

"I'm not finished," Mary said, focusing again on details. She picked up the grasshopper as if he were a fragile glass bauble and placed him in the palm of her left hand. The grasshopper nuzzled her skin as if bestowing a kiss. She turned her hand so she could look him in the eye. She felt loved.

She heard a mighty popping sound and saw champagne froth flowing from the bottle. Deck filled a crystal flute and handed it to her. She had a grasshopper in one hand, and a serving of champagne in the other.

Deck poured himself a flute. "To art," he said, toasting.

"To art," she mimicked. The grasshopper loped from her hand and landed on the flat rock where they sat.

They stayed for another half-hour. Deck tried to talk her into a second glass of champagne, but she refused, saying she was light-headed and might pitch over into the river.

They packed their supplies and went to the Cadillac. As they headed down the county road to pick up the main route, she felt queasy and apprehensive. Maybe she went too far that day.

"I feel a little strange," she said. "Do you think we might stop for a bottle of soda pop? I have change. I can pay for it."

Deck stared straight ahead. "I'll buy it for you," he said, after a beat.

Finding a small general store at the next junction, they stopped and got out. A Model T was parked there, in addition to a horse and buggy.

A young man exited the building and was going to his Model T when he recognized Deck.

"Old fellow!" the man said, stopping.

"Hello, Charlie!" Deck said, striding to shake hands with him. Mary hung back.

Charlie glanced past Deck's shoulder at Mary and gave Deck a knowing half-sneer.

Deck stepped sideways to block Charlie's view of Mary, who returned to the car. At the passenger door, she stood with her back to them. Her cheeks were hot, and she was a little relieved, but confused about why Deck hadn't introduced her to Charlie.

Laughing at recollections of school, the men spoke for a minute, and then Charlie went to his car, and Deck, into the store. Charlie drove off without giving Mary a second look.

Deck came out with a bottle of pop, open, but warm. Thanking him, Mary took it and got into the car.

CHAPTER 21
The Present Day – Autumn

Calling a Buddhist temple, Libby reached a message recorded in what she guessed was Vietnamese. She planned to visit and pray for closure. Teddy never said he was a Buddhist, but she was going, anyway.

On a misty Saturday morning, she found the temple behind a fence on the edge of a neighborhood filled with warehousing operations. The gate was open, and she veered into a gravel lot giving access to three outdoor altars and several fishponds. Already in sacred territory, she was careful not to slam the car door.

Facing west, she felt compelled to view the altars in clockwise fashion. At nine o'clock, the largest altar sat between two trees strung with colored lights and beads. On a path of textured bricks, she approached the altar. A fishpond was on the right.

A yellow cloth covered the altar's first shelf. From left to right, the shelf held a bright-orange pyramid of Clementines on a platter; three glasses of water in a row; a pot of sand with a stick of incense; and a heavy vase of yellow and violet flowers. Pink candles stood in front of the fruit platter and the flower vase.

The altar's top shelf supported a four-foot-high, ivory-colored statue of a fat, smiling advisor in a robe. Maybe this is Buddha, or one of his cronies, Libby thought. Glancing across the fishpond next to the altar, she saw a rough-granite statue depicting a woman with an infant.

The smaller altars at two o'clock and four o'clock displayed similar elements. The statues were smaller. Goldfish ponds separated these altars, also accessible from brick paths.

Obviously, the Clementines were an offering, and nothing was arcane about the accessories. The garden's pleasing layout filled Libby with a sense of discovery, renewed as she noticed details upon closer inspection.

Nervous like a debutante approaching a ballroom, she walked toward the white cement-block temple, a two-story building likely built 60 years ago as an appliance-repair shop. A garage resembling an aluminum boathouse faced north. The garage door was open. Walking into the dim shelter, Libby saw the entrance to the temple was behind closed red doors. Several pairs of shoes had been left in front of the entrance. Their owners had small feet.

She paused in front of the red doors. A drumbeat and rhythmic chant were audible, and she bobbled her knees in time with the beat. A pleasant, low tone with a slow vibration sounded. Maybe it was a gong.

Why not just open the door? She listened, interpreting the chant as "Kam-ram-sing-song-tick-tock-ding-dong." The drumbeat went on, BUMP-bump-BUMP-bump-BUMP-bump-BUMP-bump.

A little panicked, she was afraid to walk in. She looked down at the row of shoes. Next to the divine Buddhist slippers, which were size five HushPuppies, her shoes would be like the feet on the mascot at a football game. Her shoes were for an ignorant tourist. She needed authentic piety, not big feet. But she'd done her homework and was determined to finish.

Studying at home, she'd learned a Tibetan Buddhist will offer a gift when he visits a religious statue. The worshipper places the gift, called a *kata* – usually a white scarf – on the altar. The nearby temple was probably Vietnamese, not Tibetan, but Libby thought it didn't matter. Generally, the gift is to signify the purity of the seeker's motives. But in one legend, the *kata* was used to sanctify the sudden death of a wealthy man, who keeled over in front of his servant. Improvising a ritual observance, the servant tied a cow's woolen halter around the corpse's neck. Teddy should have his own cow halter, Libby decided.

From a photo album, she selected a snapshot of Teddy taken at Navy Pier in Chicago, where they went for a Fourth of July. At a discount store, she bought a white ribbon; a palm-sized, plastic cow from the toy aisle, and a picture frame for the snapshot. Last among the errands, she checked out a book on Buddhism from the public library.

She read nightly for a week. A fallen-away Lutheran, she lost interest during her late teens, when pizza parties and lock-ins at the church constituted youth worship. For many years, her spiritual life was largely about celebrating her self-sufficiency.

Then just before Teddy died, one thing happened she couldn't explain. A birthday card mailed to her grandmother came back stamped, "No such address." Baffled, she called her grandmother to ask if the street had been renumbered. It had not.

Libby re-mailed the card, which was returned, again, stamped, "No such address." Miffed, she called a toll-free number to complain about the Post Office in Mason City, Iowa, where her grandmother still flourished after decades in the same house. The complaint was investigated, and a supervisor consulted with the carrier, who assured him he knew exactly where Mrs. Bertha Doherty lived.

Libby sent the card a third time. The mail was not returned, but two weeks hence, she checked with her grandmother, who said she never got the card. "But lately, I've heard from you more than I did in the last year," her grandmother said.

Two months later – on the day of Teddy's memorial service – the card, again bewitched with "No such address," finally appeared in Libby's mailbox. This time, there was no postmark. Observable phenomena had gone on strike.

Gradually, Libby's skepticism was replaced by a voluntary engagement in mystical thinking. She hadn't gone back to church, though, and now she was rusty, requiring preparation for the foray into the temple. The jewels – the Buddha, the Dharma, and the Sangha – stood for the person of Buddha, the teachings, and the spiritual community, respectively. These reminded her of the person of Christ, the Gospel and the church.

Libby couldn't disagree with Buddhist precepts – You had to revere life, be generous, be sexually responsible, eat wholesome foods, and live in the present moment. She thought she did all that.

But the Buddha wasn't a savior, and according to his system, Libby would have to live many lifetimes until her soul was ready to reach Nirvana, an extinction of suffering. Not quite Heaven.

But what did Jesus mean when he said if you don't forgive, you'll pay every penny? Was this a hint about reincarnation?

"Pay every penny," Libby mouthed, as she sat alone in her study.

***

Now she was at the red doors. She removed her shoes and went into the temple.

A giant bell with a rough surface sat just inside the entrance. The bell reminded her of a sea turtle guarding the shore of an island. She found two altars, the larger of which supported a golden Buddha flanked by red candles.

The Buddha gleamed, smiling at the novice, suddenly heavy with unnecessary togs and hair clips. She wondered if she should shave her head. Confusing her, the smiling Buddha filled Libby's mind with aphorisms like, "You can practice being bald without losing your hair."

"Your bundle looks intriguing," the Buddha said, and then Libby realized a slim white woman with an ivory complexion was talking to her. Though middle-aged, the gray-haired stranger had the creamy skin of someone who meditated her wrinkles away. She wore a pink-and-white silk tunic over a filmy black skirt.

"Hi," Libby said. "I hope I'm not intruding."

"We welcome visitors," the serene woman said. "I'm Carnation. Today was my turn for housekeeping. Do you have any questions?"

"All seekers of truth have questions," Libby said, stoned on aphorisms. "That's a big bell. Do you ring it often?"

"We don't ring the bell. We invite the bell to sound," Carnation said. "Did you bring an offering?" She nodded at the bundle Libby held.

"Yes. I was hoping to say a prayer for a close one who died."

"The shrine for the deceased is in the other room. I'll show you," Carnation said, walking to a side door.

By coincidence, Libby had brought the ideal props. In the small room, glints of candlelight bounced off picture frames. Photos of the dead were lined up on shelves above the shrine. The pictures appeared to be listening to the chants playing from a small boom box. Libby guessed they were prayers for the dead to reincarnate.

"Do you have any questions, or would you like to be alone?" Carnation said.

"I think I'm ready. But I would like to know, were you raised a Buddhist, or did you convert, if that's not too personal a question?"

"I converted when I married a Vietnamese doctor. I was a nurse, and I met him at a clinic in Los Angeles. He was taking care of the immigrant community."

"I see. Thanks for sharing the shrine with me."

"You're most welcome," Carnation said. "I hope to see you again. I'll pray for the soul of your loved one. You can pray for yourself, too, by saying, "Let me benefit all.""

Once alone, Libby put Teddy's picture and the toy cow on the shelf. She was glad she could leave the items. Down on her knees, she held out the white ribbon before the Buddha figure and recited a short appeal, not to the Christian saints, but to the Bottisavas, archetypal figures who represent Buddhist ideals:

"Dear Master, I come to you with a clean heart and ask for your blessing, and I pray to the Bottisavas that they intervene on Teddy's Lee's behalf. Grant him a quick reincarnation, so he may continue to live a life of compassion. Grant him a joyful progress toward Nirvana. Amen."

She tied the white ribbon around the plastic cow.

From her handbag she retrieved a poem, written the evening before. She read aloud:

> You had to prove The First Law.
> Not destroyed,
> You dance in nimble state.
> I tried to carry your atomic weight,
> But I'm not you, Moo Cow,
> You boo-hoo cow.
> Milk for a dead bull?
> My udder shudders.
> I need to do
> What a milkmaid should.

She picked up the picture frame and kissed it. "I loved you," she whispered.

In the outer room, the giant bell was invited to ring. She listened, a native hearing the call of a huge reptile from the other side of the island.

CHAPTER 22
History – April 1921

Mary took a streetcar from the point where Deck dropped her off downtown. When she arrived home, she could smell the dinner her mother was fixing.

Stopping under the arch between the dining room and the kitchen, Mary said, "I'm home."

Mrs. Hobson's back was turned as she peeled potatoes on the countertop. "What did you read today?"

She caught Mary by surprise. She hadn't bothered to come up with phony details about her day at the library.

"I read about bug collections," Mary said, remembering the grasshopper.

Her mother stopped peeling and turned her head sideways to speak over her shoulder. "Bug collections? Whatever for?" She spit the word "bug" as if she'd just seen one.

"The book just jumped off the shelf," Mary said. "And then it was in my hand. So, I sat down and read it."

"Hardly useful. Were they at least pretty bugs, like butterflies?" her mother said, skinning the hapless potatoes, again.

"Beautiful and elegant," Mary said, pleased with her fib. "Shall I set the table?"

"Please, after you scrub the streetcar off your hands," her mother said.

Dinner consisted of homemade noodles and butter, boiled cabbage with potatoes and onions, and a salad of pickled tomatoes. Careful to compliment her mother's cooking, Mary was otherwise quiet during the meal. Her mother filled in the blanks.

"You'll never believe who's going to be in Cincinnati this year," Mrs. Hobson said.

"Laurinda, I probably won't believe it," Mary's father said.

"The Reverend Billy Sunday! He's holding a crusade, and the women from my church are planning to go on the train."

"One more reason for me to be a sinner who stays home and reads," he said. "Maybe I'll read about the city election, if I don't fall asleep."

"Barker," Mary's mother said. "You men take it all for granted because you always had the right to vote. But we ladies are just getting started."

"Is there a dessert this evening," he said, trying not to smile.

"We're having your boxed ears for dessert," she said, trotting to the kitchen and back. She presented a platter of sour cream thumbprint cookies with little wells of apricot preserves.

"These are left over from the batch I took to WCTU. Do you want them with a glass of milk or a steaming cup of coffee?" she said.

"Both," Mr. Hobson said.

"Oh, you!" Mary's mother said.

"May I try a cup of coffee, please?" Mary heard herself say.

Her parents looked at her and then at each other.

"It has no alcohol," Mary said. Her father laughed.

"Since you're washing the coffee cups, I don't see why not," her mother said.

Alone in her bedroom later, Mary pulled out a diary, the last gift Bina Schwartz had given her. It had a strong spine and a leather cover in olive green. Bina was her keeper of secrets, and now in the diary, Mary would pretend to tell Bina in coded terms what she'd done that day with Deck. Referring to herself as "Selma," she told the story in the third person, in case her mother found the diary.

After she finished the entry to Bina, Mary started a new page by sketching a grasshopper. She named him Clay Zell, a dapper man with spats and a watch on a chain. She decided he needed an office, and she drew him a desk with a typewriter.

She regarded her hero with pride and the relief of intimacy. A hero, and a new friend who could keep secrets.

CHAPTER 23
Present Day – Autumn

Frenchie dropped an envelope marked "Personal," on Libby's desk during the lunch hour as Libby read the newspaper. The missive was a thank-you card with two tickets to an event at Standage Performing Arts:

> Dr. Booth,
>
> I followed your advice and sat through a root canal. Do you people enjoy that? The pain has subsided, and I thank you for your kind intervention.
>
> I spoke to the High-Altitude Civic Club at its luncheon yesterday. I bought two tickets to a show the club is presenting Saturday night.
>
> Of course, there's no way I can attend, but I thought you could use the tickets or give them away. It's for a worthy cause. The proceeds go to a scholarship fund. Again, thanks ever so much!
>
> Warmly,
> Jed

The tickets said, "High-Altitude Civic Club presents Frederick Fontine."

She'd never heard of him. She went to the front desk and asked about Fontine.

"Isn't he some kind of mind reader?" Frenchie said. "I think I've seen him on a daytime talk show."

Back at her desk, Libby surfed the Internet. Frederick Fontine had a home page. He billed himself as a psychic. The evening could prove amusing, but Libby thought she'd go alone, in case she wanted to walk out early.

Standage Performing Arts was a professionally run venue on the far-east side. Originally part of a magnet high school for the arts, the theater still flourished after the campus became a center for vocational education.

The High-Altitude group rented the auditorium and provided ushers. A friendly, burly gentleman accepted Libby's ticket. With the suntan of someone who spent too many hours on a bass boat, he pointed a freckled hand to the aisle Libby should take.

Water stains afflicted the walls and the carpeting, she noticed, but the shopworn areas were not prominent. A few ceiling tiles were missing. But with soaring, curved walls like sheer cliffs, the theater's grandeur signaled big-time intentions, and she understood why the well-worn venue was popular. Easy to get to, it had a sizeable parking lot and a spacious lobby. Wooden fixtures in the theater baffled noise. The patrons were talking, but she didn't hear an annoying hubbub. She judged the attendance at fifteen hundred, a competitive turnout against the city's attractions.

Not only that, but the patrons weren't sitting with arms folded in skeptical anticipation. They were eager. The audience came to see Frederick Fontine because they believed he was genuine. And each ticket was twenty-five dollars. Checking her watch, Libby was ever more curious.

An emcee wearing an official High-Altitude jacket appeared on the apron of the stage at curtain time. Acknowledging the purpose of the fundraiser, he thanked the audience for its support. After reading a list of Fontine's accomplishments as a public speaker and author, he welcomed him to the stage. The audience received Fontine as a TV star, and a man in the back of the hall shouted, "Oh yeah!"

Fontine, a flabby, clean-shaven man of medium height and curly dark hair, described his childhood in Savannah, Georgia, and how he realized at the age of ten he was receiving "information from spirit."

"Down in Georgia," he said, "The only spirits you talk about are in a beer cooler in the back of your truck."

He kept his talent a secret, until he envisioned a car accident on Johnny Mercer Boulevard. His family was about to go to a restaurant, and he begged his mother to pick a different place. He finally told her why, and she said, "OK, if it'll make you feel better."

And sure enough, he said, "That very night, a car hit another one broadside as it turned onto Johnny Mercer from a parking lot. Two people were killed. After that, my mama didn't argue with me."

Audience members shook their heads in agreement, and Libby could see he was establishing authority with his anecdotes. The old "one-two" was coming.

"I'll never forget the time I met this Norwegian ship captain when I was tending bar in Savannah," Fontine said. "We've got a lot of great restaurants, by the way. The captain told me he was thinking about taking a new job. I said, 'For some reason, I'm seeing a bunch of dead birds, but I don't know why.'

"He said, 'I don't either.' Well, you know, he came through Savannah again about seven months later. He came to tell me he hadn't taken the job.

"He said it would have been on a tanker that wound up having a big oil spill. Killed a bunch of wildlife. Dead birds," Fontine said, punctuating the air with his index finger.

"So then I got serious about using my gifts, and I met other spiritual people across the South who had the same 'perspective,' if you will, and I knew I could do a whole lotta good.

"I guess my moment came when I was in Selma, you know, where they had those civil rights marches. I was working as a medical supply salesman, and I stopped at a nursing home.

"While I was waiting in the lounge for the director, I noticed an old African American woman who was missing part of her nose. I thought maybe she'd been in a fire. She was sittin' in a wheelchair in front of the TV, and every so often she'd cry, 'Oh, Lawd, Oh Lawd.'

"Well, I just couldn't watch this for too long. So, I went up to her and said, 'Ma'am, is there anything I can do for you this morning?'

"She said, 'Baby, ain't nothin' you can do.' Her boy did a robbery at Mobile, and the gas station clerk shot him dead.

"I said, 'Mother, take my hand.' She took my hand. I said, 'Mother, it's all right. Your son went to be with Jesus. And there's someone else with him, too. Did you have another son who passed?' She said, 'Uh-huh.' I said, 'He's wearing a military uniform.' She said, 'My boy Lamar. Died in Vietnam.'

"I said, 'He's fine, too, and he wants you to know he's looking after your other son.' And she said, 'Hmm.' And I said, 'Lamar is telling about the sweet potato pie with marshmallows.'

"She said, 'Praise Jesus! His favorite dish.' And I said, 'Ma'am, you have nothing to worry about, because you'll see both your sons again in glory.' And bless her heart, she cried for joy and kept squeezin' my hand and sayin', 'Angel send you, baby, angel send you.' And I cried, too.

"After that, I knew I had to start helpin' people full time. I gave myself about six months to put some money back, and then I went to hotels and conventions and gave readings.

"So let's get to know each other," he said.

Here it comes, Libby thought, noting his Southern accent came and went as he clipped the endings of words. He was trying a little too hard to sound folksy at times.

"Can I take some questions?" Fontine said.

Hands shot up. "The lady in the yellow sweater — yes, you darlin'. You wanna stand up, and the fellow with the microphone will come over."

"Yes, thanks, Mr. Fontine," she heaved, leaning too far into the mic.

"Please, everybody, call me Freddy."

"Thanks, Freddy. I'm Susan. I have to ask about something that's been bothering me for some time."

"Stop right there," Fontine said. "I don't answer medical questions, like, 'Do I have cancer, will I have a heart attack?' and so on. You were about to ask me a medical question, weren't you?"

"Oh, my gosh, yes," Susan said. "It wasn't that serious. I just wanted to know if it was inherited."

"Well, yes, it was, I can tell you that much. Your grandmother is here now, and she's saying she used to complain about the same thing."

"Thanks." Susan sat down.

More hands waved. "The gentlemen in the Colts jacket, please," Fontine said. The inquirer stood up.

"Hi, Freddy, I'm Joe. My brother is missing – about fourteen months. He went out West to trade antique farm implements and never came back. The police haven't been able to find out much. Can you help us?"

Taking out a white cotton hankie, Fontine wiped his face and put away the hankie. He looked at the man and said, "Your brother is here now, and he wants me to tell you he was robbed at gunpoint outside his hotel. They forced him to drive to a spot out in the country.

"He was shot and killed, and they took his identification when they stole the truck."

The audience was still.

"His body has not been found, I'm very sorry to tell you. But – he is at peace, and he wants the family to accept what happened," Fontine said.

"Thank you," the inquirer said hoarsely. He sat down, covering his eyes with his hands. Fontine gazed at him.

"That's very tough to hear, but God has blessed him," Fontine said. "And your brother wants you to remember the time you swam in the river, even though your mother told you not to."

Joe's explosion of sobs was audible, and many wiped away tears. Libby didn't know what to think, but she felt sorry for Joe. She began to resent Fontine, who had complete credibility with the mob. He was making good money exploiting private pain. Maybe she should get up, examine his mouth in front of the audience, and see how he'd like it.

Fontine continued to answer questions about lost pets, long-dead relatives, and bad financial deals. Nearing the end of his show, he said, "It's time to take the Silver Cord Challenge."

Carrying a silver rope with tassels, the emcee reappeared on stage from the wings. "Bill, you wanna explain to the folks what we're gonna do?" Fontine said.

Bill the Emcee announced the rules. "Four of you will be chosen at random. Two will go backstage with Freddy, and they'll wait with him in the dressing room.

"The other two will take this silver cord out to the audience and pick a married couple. The husband and wife who are picked will each take an end of the cord, and they'll pull on it a few times, like a tug of war."

The emcee removed an index card from inside his jacket. "Then, the husband and wife will sign their names on this card, which will be returned to me.

"Now, when Freddy comes back, he'll take hold of the silver cord, and using his talents, he'll find the same couple. When he thinks he's found the husband and wife, he'll ask them to stand and state their names. Using the information on the card, I will tell Freddy whether he is correct.

"If he succeeds, one of our sponsors will double his contribution to the scholarship fund we're supporting. So let's get started." Bill the Emcee scanned the audience. He pointed to a woman in an aisle seat about six rows back. "Ma'am, the lady with the red hair, would you be kind enough to join us on stage?" She came forward, looking for steps. The emcee pointed to the spiral stairs below stage right, and she bounded up.

"How 'bout a fella'?" A waving hand near an exit caught the emcee's eye, and he said, "Sir, come on up."

The lucky one lunged forward, and when he arrived, Bill said, "Now, to keep this fair, have I ever met either one of you?" They shook their heads in denial.

"And are you acquainted with Frederick Fontine?"

"No," they said simultaneously.

Then Fontine said, "Y'all don't know each other, do you?" The audience laughed.

"OK," the emcee said. "Next, I'm going to let each of you pick one person, a perfect stranger, please. We'll let the lady choose first."

The redhead picked another woman, who gave high-fives to the man sitting next to her and ran up to the group.

The male guest on stage had the final choice, and faced with dozens of gesturing wannabes, he settled on someone sitting still. Pointing at Libby, he said, "The blond lady in the Iowa sweatshirt."

Libby didn't catch on, until the folks in front of her turned to stare. An old man said, "Well, go on." In a few minutes, she would wish she'd ignored everyone, but in the spotlight, a place she rarely sought, she didn't want to appear rude. She floated out of her seat and up to the stage. Face to face with Fontine, she felt like a hologram.

"Now that we've assembled our team, it's time for introductions," Bill said, beginning with Libby. "What's your name, ma'am?"

"I'm Elizabeth." Libby could see Fontine's eyes gleam at the ruse. Her name was Elizabeth, but she never used it.

"Thanks for helping tonight, Elizabeth. What do you do for a living?"

"I'm a health-care provider," she demurred. Fontine smiled.

"Thanks. Now to our only gentlemen," the emcee said.

"I'm Gary, and I work in a lumberyard."

The redhead was Gina, housewife and mother. The last volunteer, a bleached blond with shaggy hair, was Annette, who worked in a tanning parlor.

"Wonderful!" Bill said. "OK, now Elizabeth and Gina will go backstage with Freddy, and Gary and Annette will take the cord and choose the married couple. When they're finished with the task, Gary and Annette will return to the stage, and we'll bring out Freddy and the others."

Fontine exited stage right, and Libby and Gina followed him to a tiny dressing room. The countertop held a plate of peanut-butter crackers and an empty glass next to a large pitcher of orange juice. Libby guessed this was Fontine's pick-me-up after the show. His manager, Brownie, introduced himself, and the quartet waited awkwardly. How long could it possibly take for the others to accomplish the chore and get back on stage? Fontine was quiet, but Brownie made small talk about the limo service from the airport and how friendly the driver was. When Fontine smiled, Libby observed his teeth had veneers. Finally, someone knocked on the door, and they exited..

Fontine accepted the silver cord and took over, asking Libby and Gina, "Will you attest that we never left the dressing room until we were advised to return to the stage?"

"Yes," they said.

"All right, you can go relax in your seats now, and thanks for helping. And one more thing, Elizabeth," he said. "I know this sounds funny, but I'm supposed to tell you that your suspicions about the hamburger are correct."

The audience laughed. Libby sucked in air, nodding once in acknowledgment before fleeing the stage.

The audience rustled, muttering, and Libby didn't know what they were talking about. The old man appraised her as she sat down.

Fontine paused, trying to pick which side of the auditorium to work. Finally heading down, he snaked through the crowd. Several times he stopped but changed his mind about the couple. His confusion was obvious.

He wiped his face with his hankie. Amid the noise of the crowd's speculation, Fontine forged along his miserable, serpentine path through the hall. The old man in front of Libby whipped around, asking, "Did you plan it?"

"What do you mean?" she said.

"They let a bunch of people pull on the cord, including some little kid."

The implications sunk in like cans of food breaking through the bottom of a grocery sack. Gary and Annette had rigged the experiment to fail.

"Were you in on it?" the old man said.

"I most certainly was not," Libby said evenly.

After twelve minutes, Fontine was no closer to the couple in question than Libby was. Bowing his head, he appeared to pray. Finished, he walked to the front and stood below center stage. The body microphone amplified his dejected tone.

"Ladies and gentlemen, tonight a light has gone out of my life. For some reason, I cannot use my spiritual gifts. I don't understand why, but I don't think I can go on with the show."

The crowd gossiped, and Fontine started to leave. A legion of High-Altitude officials greeted him at the base of the spiral stairs. "Frederick," Bill the Emcee said. "We believe that in all fairness, we should tell you the rules were not observed."

Fontine lifted his arms heavenward.

"The two volunteers with the cord did not follow instructions," the emcee said.

The crowd booed. Libby slumped in her seat. The old man snorted, tossing his head. She could see the smirk in his profile.

"Therefore, we'd like to start over with new assistants," the emcee said.

Whooping, the crowd applauded.

Fontine shook the emcee's hand and ran up the stairs. The emcee chose all four participants this time, and the two who picked the married couple obeyed the rules. A confident Fontine strode into the house. The crowd noise tipped him when he was getting hotter, Libby suspected. Whispers matured into groans as he moved closer to the husband and wife who tugged the cord. Fontine got a standing ovation when their names matched those on the emcee's index card.

After the show, a woman recognized Libby as they filed out. The woman smiled like she was confronting a con artist. "For real, did you have it all set up?" she said.

"No, ma'am," Libby said.

Driving home, she reviewed the last few weeks. Jed Harkness imposed on her, and she did him a favor. She accepted a thank-you token, and then she wound up looking foolish. She admitted Fontine's message about the hamburger was intriguing. Perhaps a pound of conceptual hamburger dwelled in the refrigerator of her mind, and Fontine raided the fridge. All because of Jed and his burgers.

CHAPTER 24
Autumn – The Present Day

Darla had taken Trevor to the vet for a routine exam and shots. Heading home on East Washington Street, she drove west past the intersection with Bolton Avenue. On the southwest corner, a man in a bowler hat stood, beckoning to a boy with short, greased-down hair. The child wore knee-length pants and a buttoned, long-sleeved, yellow-green shirt with an open collar. Instead of gym shoes, he wore dark leather shoes with laces and no socks.

The man with the bowler also wore a belted, double-breasted wool coat that fell below his knees. His curly hair was dark, and he had a thick, carefully trimmed mustache. He was dapper, but when he gazed at the dog walker as she drove by, she saw white rays like lasers beam from his eyes. Hitting the accelerator, she passed the usual turn-off. Doubling back on a side street, she reached home five minutes later.

"The village idiots who walk here from the homeless hideouts are always overdressed for the season," she said, helping Trevor out of the car. "That wool coat was too hot for sixty-eight degrees.

"He probably wears the only wardrobe he's got every single day."

But the man's eyes. And it troubled her the coat looked so clean and expensive. Also, weird -- the boy's archaic haircut and slick hair tonic.

About two weeks later, she was watching a TV documentary about Indianapolis neighborhoods, when a segment on Irvington began. Paying close attention, she turned up the sound.

The town had been the temporary base of Herman W. Mudgett, alias H.H. Holmes, who confessed to twenty-seven killings, although a factual number was not established. A widely traveled swindler, Holmes attempted to cover up the murder of his partner in an insurance fraud. The killer arrived in Irvington in 1894, where he murdered his partner's young son, who'd been in Holmes' company. The child's remains were found in the cottage Holmes rented.

Strong evidence also pointed to Holmes as the killer of the boy's father, Ben Pitezel, and two of his daughters. In the end, Holmes was tried, convicted, and executed for Ben's murder in Philadelphia, Pa.

The dog walker felt dizzy during the description of Holmes' crimes, but she slid off the sofa to her knees, when the TV displayed a vintage photo of Holmes wearing his bowler hat and a healthy mustache. He was the man she saw on the street corner. The next photo was of the boy he presumably murdered, but he wasn't the boy she'd seen with Holmes. Had he killed someone else? Or were they a pair of lost souls strolling the streets of Irvington?

She shut off the TV, lowered the lights, and lit a candle. Praying for safety, she asked God to protect her from evil energy. She recited the Lord's Prayer several times. After the fourth recitation, Trevor barked, and she realized he needed to go outside. Practical matters are for the living, she thought.

CHAPTER 25
History – May 1921

Deck whispered to Mary at Creedmore Hall that they should plan another Saturday trip. He stood so close, and she tingled as his breath cooled her ear. He suggested they visit the countryside around the West Fork of the White River.

"The West Fork is nice," Deck said. "All the artists in town have pretty much overdone the best vistas in the city. But you'll see new places.

"And there's local history that's inspirational."

The first ruse worked, so Mary gave the same story about going to the library. Her mother, heating up the phone lines with Klan smears, waved goodbye as Mary poked her head into the kitchen that morning.

"And that's just what I thought, too," Mrs. Hobson was saying.

Mary wore a blue gingham dress with a frilly collar and gold buttons. She hid a bottle of pop and an opener in her book bag with the art supplies. That way she wouldn't have to ask Deck to get her something to drink.

He picked her up in the Cadillac once more. He swerved recklessly through town, as if late for an appointment. He drove them south for the better part of an hour, and they pulled into a small town on the steep banks above the river.

"You know, a few miles back, we crossed the Ten O'clock Line," Deck said.

"What's that?" Mary said.

"The boundary line of a treaty with the Indians. They gave up three million acres. That's how Indiana got its present shape on the map," he said, stopping

94

the car in the town's business district on a side street. A man coming out of a general store admired the Cadillac.

"If it hadn't been for the Ten O'clock Line treaty, old Abe Lincoln wouldn't have been able to come up here with his family from Kentucky," Deck said. "And Grandfather wouldn't have his vacation cottage overlooking the Ohio River." He laughed.

"One winter when I was about twelve, I threw a fresh bone from a roast way out onto the frozen Ohio.

"Grandfather's hunting dog ran out on the ice to get it. He got back, for sure, but the ice was thin and watery where the bone landed. Dogs can't tell whether ice is safe. That was the only time Grandfather smacked me. He really loved that dog," Deck said.

"My father was a lot calmer. He just said, 'Your grandfather hit *you*, but my knowing that you did it on purpose punched *me* in the face.' "

They got out of the car.

"We can walk down the hill to the river," Deck said, pointing. "You see a few blocks down, how the street ends way at the bottom?" he said, taking a blanket from the car. Mary noticed he didn't bring a picnic basket this time.

As they reached the foot of the steep hill, the White River came into view. The banks were like small cliffs. Deck motioned to the left and she followed him into a grove of trees and tall grasses. As they walked, the ground sloped downward until they were level with the river.

Mary was ecstatic. Running between sumptuous, green tree lines, the sparkling river was broad, flowing with a tantalizing current that offered a massage. No factories or smokestacks marred the horizon, and no ugly pipes dumped sewage.

"Good thing it hasn't rained lately. Dirt is nice and firm," he said.

Mary looked at the bright blue water seared with sunlight. The view made her thirsty. Deck spread the blanket on the ground.

She was about to open her book bag to get the pop bottle, when he grabbed her from behind around the waist.

He kissed the back of her neck.

"Oh," she said, like she'd sunk her bare feet into a tub of icy water.

"Oh!" Deck mimicked her in a falsetto. His hands cupped her breasts under the frilly dress collar. He squeezed, and she squirmed to get away, accidentally rubbing against his crotch in the attempt to flee.

He hardened, pushing himself against her over and over, and she could feel his hardness visiting her tailbone.

"Don't, Deck, don't! I shouldn't behave this way," she said, gulping for air.

"But you are meant to be this way, Miss Mary," he said, practically bouncing off her backside.

"Please, I'm not. I can't do this," she said, almost in tears.

"In a minute, you will," he said, biting the back of her neck.

"I'm just in high school. Please don't make me change so fast," she said, pulling at the hands that imprisoned her breasts.

"Then we'll go slowly," he said, pushing his right knee into the back of her right leg. She lost balance and he toppled her to the blanket.

He threw himself on top of her. She was pinned to the blanket. He forced his tongue into her mouth, and she felt his fierce breath flowing into her nostrils. She relaxed, limp, hoping he would get bored.

But he stopped only to say, "You see," he said. "I can tell you see."

"See what?" she said in a thin voice. Her arms were numb.

"That there's no going back, not when you've had the pleasure," he said, pulling the hem of her dress up to her neck.

"No, please don't," she said, filling with shame as her strength faded. He pulled down her bloomers and pushed his hand into the crease between her thighs.

Terrified, she screamed. He stifled the scream with another engulfing kiss. She thought she might pass out because she couldn't breathe. But he reared back on his knees and pulled off her bloomers. He tossed them aside.

She was powerless. "Please don't hurt me. I've never done it. Please, please don't hurt me!" she said, shaking with fear that idle fishermen were watching.

Deck laughed. "Oh, this is not going to hurt." He grabbed her wrists.

To her utter mortification, his face disappeared between her legs. She couldn't believe this was happening to her. A flock of ducks flew overhead. A turkey vulture circled high above the two on the blanket. What this must look like from way up there, Mary thought, before Deck unleashed her hollers of humiliation as she felt intense pleasure against her will.

His mouth forced her a long time, and with each spasm, she screamed, "Oh no!" It was the same cry of alarm she gave as a youngster when she threw up on the floor at school.

He tightened the grip on her wrists. She feared her screams would summon the whole town to gawk. Gritting her teeth, she kept emitting a stifled yelp.

Trying to disappoint him, she couldn't regain control. She imagined someone standing on the opposite bank as a spectator, clucking at the squirming, soiled body. Her degradation was complete.

Deck drew himself up on his knees and loosened his belt and pants. He pulled out his swollen organ. Bracing for the pain, Mary closed her eyes and whispered, "God help me."

"You should be ready now. It'll just be a tight squeeze and then it'll break. And you'll be glad it did," he said, guiding himself into the crease. She felt pressure and searing pain, and she cried, "Ow! Stop, stop!"

She sobbed. Merciless, he shoved harder, and the pressure collapsed in a flood of warm wetness she thought was blood.

"Ah!" he said. "There's no going back." Deep inside her, he began thrusting in the direction of the sky. And gritting her teeth, she would not give in. Her throat was dry, and her eyes, blurred with tears. "No . . . No," she croaked in time with his thrusts.

He shoved like he was trying to break down a door, and in pain, she cried out, "Not so hard." Deck laughed. The turkey vulture circled high above, and Mary saw him glide through a ray of sunlight as she passed out.

CHAPTER 26
The Present Day – Autumn

The Capital Cabaret and Playhouse sent Libby an invitation to a fundraiser. Recalling her distress at the Freddy Fontine show, she didn't want to attend, but as another week waned, she decided to go. The Saturday event featured cocktails, a five-o'clock preview, and dinner at seven.

The theater was in the Wholesale District downtown in an old department-store building. The cabaret on the first floor had a small stage, linen-covered tables, and dim lighting from electric lanterns. Patrons could enjoy a dinner show. On the second floor, a wooden cathedral ceiling was suspended over the stage for acoustic enhancement. A fly space was created behind the stage by cutting a hole in the building's third floor. In the hall, terraces with carpeted risers supported rows of wooden chairs with arms and padded seats. The terraces creaked every so often, but footfalls were muffled. Dinner would take place in the cabaret room after a performance of *The Batter-Fried Bulgarian*, a new work by a Missouri author who won the theater's playwriting contest.

Libby showed up in a form-fitting, long-sleeved burgundy dress sprayed with tiny blood-colored sequins around the neckline and cuffs. Carrying a black velvet clutch purse that matched low-heeled pumps, she walked with her raincoat slung over an arm. Her blue-gray eyes widened as she took in the etched marble around the entrance to the old building.

A spicy aroma passed her as the elevator rose to the second floor, and she tried to guess what they might serve at dinner. Upstairs, she checked her coat and declined offers from waiters bearing trays of drinks and plump little appetizers. She located the board member who sent the invitation and they chatted about their common interest, a photography club. About ten minutes before the show, Libby entered the theater. At her level of donation, she had reasonable choices between spots close to the stage or midway up the terraces, but the only seat close to the aisle was in the front row, where she ended up.

She read the program. The playwright was a Kansas City bus driver, a collegiate cross-country champion before he started going to poker tournaments. He dedicated the play to his brother, a chef in San Francisco. She turned to the director's biography. This was his third production in the Midwest. He began his career as a set designer, and in his spare time, he played the mountain dulcimer.

Still reading at one minute to show time, she paid no attention to the man who was removing the cord that reserved the aisle seat to her right. He sat down. The lights dimmed. In the darkness, a bright spotlight appeared in front of her below the stage. The man in the next seat stood up, walked into the light, and faced the audience. Raising his right arm in a declamatory gesture, he shouted in an Eastern-European accent, "I tell you, I have no knowledge of the crimes you accuse me of!" He held the pose, and a voice offstage said into a microphone, "Next." The man lowered his arm and walked into the darkness.

Emerging from the dark at Libby's right, another man walked into the spot. He, too, raised his arm and spewed an accent combining several nationalities. "I tell you!" he cried. "I have no knowledge whatsoever of the crimes you accuse me of." The offstage voice said, "Next." The man slumped and exited.

A third man stepped into the light, shook his fist, and shouted in the least credible of the three accents, "I tell you, I have no knowledge at all about . . . anything, about these crimes – "

"Next!"

A fourth man, heavier than the others, stepped up. Raising his right arm, he opened his mouth for the bombast, but changed his mind and raised the left arm, instead.

"Thank you – Next," the off-stage voice said. The audience laughed.

The spotlight faded, and the stage brightened to reveal a group sitting on a movie set. Gesturing with pens and notebooks, they began to comment on the auditions. As it turned out, *The Batter-Fried Bulgarian* was a fictitious, independently produced film. The movie's hero was a humble short-order cook suspected of identity theft. The characters in the play were the film's cast, crew, and financial backers. The plot consisted of their predictably dysfunctional relationships and arguments over how to end the picture.

The pratfalls provoked sufficient belly laughs, and the audience returned the favor with a standing ovation that Libby took part in. She enjoyed the show, not a flawless production, but if she alone remained seated, it would be a perverse snub of the playwright, who was taking a bow right in front of her.

At the buffet downstairs, she selected baked tofu with ginger; Cajun mashed potatoes, and baked zucchini. A waiter offered a glass of white wine, but she declined, looking forward to a simple strawberry ice for dessert. Libby was eating when two men approached, carrying appetizers, salads, and wine. The pair was a couple, she perceived. Wiping her lips with a napkin, she pointed at the empty chairs at her table.

"Please join me," she said.

"Oh, thanks," the shorter one said, placing the armload of food on the table without mishap. "I guess all the time I spent as a waiter was good for something." He helped his companion settle and then took a seat. "I'm Kerry Wittenhouse, and this is my partner, Tony Dreisen."

"Libby Doherty. Good to meet you. If you were tempted by the Cajun mashed potatoes, they're worth trying."

"We sampled a lot of Cajun when we went to New Orleans after the Katrina flood. We met right after the flood. We'd only been out of school a few years, and we wound up going to the same church," Tony said.

"So our church did a mission to rebuild a house in New Orleans, and one house was all we had time for. Everybody used vacation days to go.

"I was a little worried about the stories – you know, the ones about turtles in the bottom of sealed coffee cans, and I drank only bottled water, especially after the corpses marinated in the flood. But the food was out of this world," Tony said.

"And the jazz. And the strippers," Kerry said.

Tony laughed. "We went to a strip joint, because we'd never been to one. Call it a sociology class."

"One stripper we saw left her hat on," Kerry said. "I did like the hat."

"What was so neat about the hat?" Libby said.

"It was a giant hot dog on a bun."

Libby burst out laughing.

"Her act was comic relief, and the others were elegant," Tony put in. "She'd turn sideways and do this nasty bump and grind – and the hot dog would wobble – and she'd reach up and squirt mustard and catsup on the hat in time with the bumps. I thought I'd die."

"And she didn't get any on her," Kerry said.

Libby liked the pair, guileless and open. Kerry was from Fort Wayne, and Tony, from Lafayette. Kerry was the sales director of a surgical supply company, and Tony, a technician in the nuclear medicine department of a hospital. They were both close to forty.

Sensing once again how circumscribed her life had been, Libby was excited when they asked her to join them for Sunday brunch at a downtown hotel. They said goodnight as the men left to check on their pets.

Libby stayed to mingle, getting a glass of sparkling water from the bar.

A man she estimated to be age sixty approached her. "Wally Friedline," he said, pronouncing it like "Freed-line."

"Libby Doherty." They shook hands. He had wavy gray hair and a closely trimmed gray beard. He wore a navy silk suit, a tan shirt, and a cream tie. "Did you like the show?" he said.

"Yes, I did. I was little surprised. I must have been more skeptical about new plays than I thought."

"That's understandable," Friedline said. "I've been on the board for two years, and I haven't liked all the plays we've done. But if there's one thing the artistic director keeps telling us, the public's curiosity will be rewarded more often than not."

He held up two fingers. "I don't mean to sound like an expert. I operate a chain of pubs, so that doesn't make me a cultural lion. I got interested in the playhouse after we came to a show with some friends of my wife, who was divorcing me at the time, but I didn't know it. What do you do?" Friedline said.

"I have a dental practice at Fifty-Sixth and Post," she said.

"Wow! I just opened another pub around the corner from you." He took out a business card and a pen.

101

"I'd be really grateful if you'd stop by there for something on the house –
take one friend, eat and drink as much as you like – and then give me a call
about the food and the service." He scribbled his name and "Code 53," on the
back of the card.

"They'll know it's on the house when you hand in this card with the tab.
Just call me at the cell number and tell me how it went. Anything out of place,
I want to know."

"That's very kind of you," she said. "What's the pub's name?"

"Wally's Millenium."

"OK. I saw the 'Grand Opening' banner. I'll try to get there next week
and give you a report," Libby said.

"Don't put yourself out, and by all means, have fun." The cell phone rang
inside his blazer. "Maybe some feedback from my other places." He pulled
out the phone.

"I'll let you take that," Libby said. "Thank you. I'll be in touch." She
handed her glass to a strolling waiter. Friedline gave a friendly salute. After
she got back to her car in the parking garage, she made a note on her scribble
pad:

> Mystery shopper at dramatic premiere
> Finds barkeep needing mystery boozer –
> Surplus for fishing in playwright's drink.

***

Libby turned on the late news when she got home from the theater. She
caught the end of a report.

"A spokesman for the Harkness campaign said Karnow's accusations are
unfounded and disturbing. This is Caleb Tremaine reporting. Back to you,
Bob and Deena."

"Back to you, Jed," Libby said, laughing, but curious.

Sunday morning Libby found an account in the newspaper. Harkness
misled a judge into issuing a search warrant for evidence, Karnow alleged.
The case involved the attempted murders of three children. The suspect was
the children's mother. Evidence against her was obtained improperly because
of Jed's mistakes, his opponent charged.   The children were shot and
critically injured after they went to bed, but all survived. At a pretrial hearing,

the charges against the mother were dropped after the judge excluded the evidence.

The Harkness campaign offered its version of the foul-up.

"It was an unfortunate miscommunication between the police department and the prosecutor's office. As a result, the prosecutor's office set forth new procedures for the review of evidence, and the police department ordered retraining on evidence collection," Harkness said.

"This was an isolated incident that occurred more than six years ago, and on the whole, metro police are outstanding in their handling of evidence.

"In no case would we ever attempt to mislead a judge," Harkness said.

A spokesman for the Harkness camp called Karnow's allegations "desperate and seedy." Karnow retorted the city had to pay the mother $175,000 to settle a lawsuit filed after her release from jail.

Libby let go of the story, because it was time to go downtown for brunch. Kerry and Tony greeted her in the lobby of the Morton Plaza, one of the newer hotels built to accommodate the city's convention traffic.

Libby regarded the couple anew. Topped with a reddish-blond crew cut, Kerry shone with the finish of a regular visitor to manicurists and skin consultants. Tony had longer hair, black and curly, now missing the hair gel from the other night. He'd also sprouted a shadow beard. His nails were clean and trimmed, and not one flake of dandruff fell on his black sweater. Nonchalant and ready with jokes, the men spoke and moved with economy and athleticism.

The hotel had several restaurants, and Sunday brunch was served in a dining room heavily camouflaged with greenery. On the wall behind the buffet was a giant black-and-white photo of Hoagy Carmichael. The picture revealed the Indiana composer as a perfectly groomed, dapper celebrity. Hoagy's eyes were on the three friends as they moved along the buffet.

Business was slow, and the dishes and trays were amply stocked with sliced fruits, oatmeal, bagels, fried potatoes, scrambled eggs, steamed vegetables, and different meats, including sausage links, meat loaf, and turkey and dressing. The waiter brought coffee, orange juice, and a small platter of doughnut holes.

"You can order toast if you want," the waiter said.

Kerry picked up a doughnut hole. He placed it on his plate. "If I study it, it'll feel like I've had more than one."

Guiltless, Tony and Libby sampled the doughnut holes and enjoyed their coffee. Eventually, the trio filled the buffet plates, scarce of pork and festive with fruit.

"We're of one mind when it comes to food," she said.

After an interval of chewing and swallowing, Kerry said, "We're dying to ask you something." Tony sat back and folded his hands.

Libby swallowed the last tablespoon of her orange juice. "Go ahead."

"We'd really like your opinion, because you're a dentist around kids all the time. To put it bluntly, we want to adopt a child, but we're weighing the pros and cons," Kerry said.

"In other words, we don't want to mess up the kid," Tony said.

"Right," Kerry said. "Having two dads might be difficult for a little one, especially in a place like Indiana."

"Have you considered moving to another state?" Libby said, already regretting the question. Kerry was disappointed, she could see. "Never mind," she said. "You shouldn't have to leave good jobs and a nice home."

"We could move if we had to," Tony said.

"I'm not a psychologist," Libby pointed out. "I think you should take my opinion as that of a new friend." She looked around at the room's décor. The number of plants was oppressive. Why was Hoagy surrounded by all this shrubbery? She focused on the men.

"If you can get your children to brush their teeth, you'll be way ahead of some heterosexual parents I've met." She had little more to offer. She fell back on an old excuse. "I'm from Iowa," she said, shrugging.

Tony's eyes watered. Libby thought Kerry would have been the one to show his emotions. Libby searched for words of comfort.

"I mean, look around. Hardly anyone's here today, and the buffet is ready to collapse under the weight of the food. We certainly can't eat it all. But so many children have nothing, and their lives are over in a blink.

"Who is to say that two men couldn't provide them with a better future?" she said.

"We can offer a loving, two-parent household with religious training, civic involvement, and educational opportunities," Tony said. "I believe in a loving God, who knew me before I was in my mother's womb, but that's the line the anti-abortionists use.

"It happens to apply to gays as well as fetuses."

"Eloquently stated," Kerry said like a vice-president complimenting the company CEO.

"Then you know what you need to do," Libby said. She would wiggle out of giving them permission, which she had no authority to give. "Let's go back to the trough."

They returned to the buffet under Hoagy's constant gaze. He appeared to be fascinated with their conversation. Eventually, he caught Kerry's eye, when the sound system played the Largo from Dvorak's New World Symphony.

"I just realized how this piece could have inspired 'Georgia on My Mind,' Kerry said. He drank a little coffee. "I work to support my soon-to-be growing family. But music is my mistress," he said.

"Uh-oh," Tony said. "He's going to spend the afternoon at the piano."

Later, a call from Denise jarred Libby out of an after-brunch haze.

"Hey girlfriend – just got in from Chicago. I want to show you these suede boots I bought."

"I was going to call you today," Libby said.

Denise's answer was muffled. "I'm sorry – I'm eating a bagel and schmeer. I had the best trip. I brought you a knick-knack," she said.

"I love presents," Libby said. "I've got a present for you, too. How 'bout dinner at this new pub in Lawrence? It's on the house. Owner said, 'Bring one friend, eat and drink as much as you like.' "

Denise's laugh was raucous. "You're on."

CHAPTER 27
History – May 1921

Mrs. Hobson was organizing friends to go see the Rev. Billy Sunday in Ohio later in the year. She was making herself a new dress for the event. Mary was expected to make the train trip to Cincinnati for the crusade.

The journey was several months away, but the girl was reluctant to go. Now deflowered, the only self-image she viewed in her lonely struggle was "hypocrite," and it never occurred to the child that others were hypocrites, too, even bigger ones.

And she couldn't sift through the differences between rape and seduction. She only saw she failed to maintain a standard of decency upholding Christian morality. She confused Deck's responsibility with the exercise of privilege, and the unfairness of it had yet to sink in.

She feigned illness on the days of his art lessons at Creedmore Hall. She worried about seeing him laugh as he remembered how she tried to fight him off.

The public way he removed her clothing under the bright sun made her fear that everyone looked at her, now. To be safe from speculation, she spent a lot of time in the attic, where she kept a bug collection. Armed with her diary, Mary slipped upstairs in the afternoons to sketch the insects as her mother worked in the kitchen.

However, not even sketching could keep Mary's thoughts from replaying the incident with Deck. When he'd finished with her, he stripped and waded into the river. Rinsing, he dunked himself and returned to the river's edge where he stood, drying in the sun.

When she came to, Mary sat up on the blanket and cried into her hands. She felt greasy, and she was parched. Finding the pop bottle, she downed most of the drink in less than a minute. A little remained. She looked at the flowing river. She drank the rest of the pop and scurried downstream to get away from Deck.

She found a spot where bushes would give privacy. She took off her shoes and stockings, and she waded, rinsing and filling the pop bottle. Behind the bushes, she lifted her dress and poured water down her mound and inner thighs. Filling the bottle again, she rinsed some more.

Shaking, she tossed the bottle into the river and climbed to the shroud of bushes. She held her dress up by the hem until she was dry. When she returned to the blanket, she saw a large, damning blood stain, and she found her underwear in the grass a few feet away. She shook out the bloomers and put them on.

Deck was getting dressed. She wadded up the offensive blanket. Running downstream, she hid the blanket behind a fallen log.

Returning for her bag of art supplies, she said, "I'd like to go home now," surprised at the firmness of her voice.

"As you wish," Deck said, shrugging. The walk up the steep hill several blocks to the car felt like mountain climbing, and when they passed houses, she imagined people peeked through the curtains. Saying almost nothing on the trip home, she kept her head turned away from him. He dropped her at the streetcar connection, and she said nothing as she climbed out of the Cadillac.

The attic gave her privacy, so she could be disgraced in seclusion. Deck picked his spot because it was far from home, she realized. And he could walk into the river and rinse off, without being carried away by the current.

All his big talk about the history of the area and the build-up he gave describing the scenery – just a cover for his plan to get her to the perfect place.

Oh, yes, she was taken in. Fretting about it, she balled up her fists, and her chest tightened with panic. Sometimes she paced, going from one end of the attic to the other.

Mary's footfalls from above provoked her mother's curiosity, and one morning she went to the attic while Mary was gone. At first, all her mother saw was a wicker chest full of Christmas decorations, and a small wooden bookshelf stacked with her husband's math books.

But then she noticed a dress box. She didn't remember it, so she bent over and removed the lid. Shrieking, she jammed the lid back on the box, full of carefully mounted insects, and kicked the box to the stairwell. She tilted the box and sent it like a sled down the stairs to the bedroom closet.

She took the box out the back door to the trash can. Her husband burned garbage every night, and the box and its magnificent, lifeless captives went up in smoke.

CHAPTER 28
Present Day – Autumn

The week of the excursion to Wally's began with Libby having to arrange Drew's maternity leave. Drew looked like a blowfish, shocking her co-workers. In her seventh month, she retained too much fluid, so Libby sent her to the doctor, who ordered complete bed rest.

Libby powwowed with Frenchie, and they interviewed candidates from a temp agency. They had positive feelings about the second person they met, Claris Ridge.

The next day Drew called from the hospital. She was admitted with pre-eclampsia after her blood pressure went up. The women gathered around the front desk as Libby spoke.

"It's a dangerous situation, but they've got a treatment plan. Let's just hope for the best," Libby said. "Claris will start tomorrow."

"I've been a temp, and I always felt like an outsider. I'll bring a coffee cake," Keisha said. Libby asked Frenchie to order flowers for Drew.

Ready to play mystery shopper with Denise, Libby met her in the parking lot at Wally's. Denise showed off her multicolored suede boots.

"You look like the Pied Piper," Libby said. "I should have more fun with my clothes. I'm not going to ask how much you paid."

They entered Wally's Millenium. In the foyer, the specials were listed on a clear plastic panel dangling from a pair of chains. Scrawled in bright blue ink – "Brats and Sauerkraut," and "Rib-Eye Dinner."

The women pushed through a swinging saloon door into the dining room. Seating themselves, they chose a booth along the far wall opposite the bar, where several patrons watched television.

The wait staff and bartenders wore Bavarian alpine hats with feathers in the spirit of Oktoberfest. Beer glasses sported tokens hanging over the rims. Libby would order a beer to get whatever the toy was. Signs in German decorated the walls, and Denise translated them to indicate, "The Free State of Bavaria."

The room had an antiseptic feel. Not that Libby wanted to eat in a dusty, lawless saloon. One could see the expanse of the rectangular room, although accent lighting created softer contours removing the industrial feel. The tables and chairs in the center of the room were occupied, and about half the booths were filled. A vintage jukebox stood at the far end by the entrance to the restrooms. A few feet from the jukebox, a grandfather clock ticked with each authoritative swing of the pendulum.

A sloped wooden awning over the bar gave the counter a cloistered appearance. Behind the bar, decorative clocks showed the time in New York, London, Paris, Berlin, Moscow, and Tokyo. Glowing green letters spelled the city's name under each clock.

Astronomical themes continued throughout the décor. A framed sidereal chart hung next to the entrance. Most distinctive – a real sundial with a granite base on a platform in the middle of the pub. The timepiece was aged from outdoor use. A soft spotlight focused on the sundial, aloof in its universe. Libby wanted to ask Wally where he got the sundial.

Heralding Oktoberfest, each tabletop had a miniature chalet housing a plastic coo-coo, stuck in apoplexy as he poked out of his hutch over the toy clock.

The waitress took their beer order and returned with filled mugs, small empty platters, a basket of taco chips, and a squeeze bottle of salsa.

The token on the beer glass was a tiny fuzzy bear, whose right arm clung to the rim, while the left arm raised a Bavarian flag on a toothpick. The bear wore an Alpine hat.

"Nice detail," Libby said. "I wonder what they'll do for Christmas."

Denise sampled a taco chip. "It's warm -- that's a plus." She squirted a pool of hot salsa on her platter and dipped the chip. "Huh," she said after another bite. "My sinuses just opened."

Taking to the role of critic, Libby surveyed the menu. The specials didn't interest her, so she asked for the Reuben sandwich. Denise ordered Caesar salad and the soup of the day, cream of broccoli.

The waitress was asking about dessert, when bullets were served. Three men in ski masks entered through the swinging door. One of them sprayed the jukebox and the grandfather clock with automatic gunfire, shattering the glass. Diners screamed and dove under tables. Dropping to her knees, the waitress crawled under the table and clung to the center support as if it were the slippery edge of a pier. Libby and Denise threw themselves down on the booth seats, and they could see each other under the table. She locked eyes with Denise, who pressed a napkin over her mouth.

"Don't nobody move!" the bandit in charge shouted. While the other two held weapons on the diners, he approached the cash register and instructed the bartender to open the cash drawer. Expressionless, moving slowly, deliberately, the bartender emptied the contents into the gym bag the robber held. Hands atop their heads, the drinkers at the bar lowered their faces to the counter like pathetic sots throbbing with hangovers. Hushed sobs came from under the tables.

"Sweet T," the leader shouted. "Move out." Still training his gun on the patrons, Sweet T backed up and held the swinging door open with his shoulder. The leader with the cash ran out, and the third swept his gun across imaginary checkpoints before he and Sweet T took off.

Libby and Denise stared at each other. The room was still, except for the ticking of the grandfather clock, missing its glass window, but breathing.

Finally, the bartender relaxed, walking from behind the counter. "It's OK now," he said, leaning to reassure the guests under the tables. People hoisted themselves into seats, and husbands and wives and companions reached for one another. Libby and Denise stood, joining hands with the waitress, who needed help getting to her feet. The three passed reassuring squeezes.

A woman cried, "Call for an ambulance. My husband can't breathe!" Several guests grabbed cell phones and dialed.

Libby dropped the waitress' hand and looked to the source of the outburst. A woman in her fifties stood over a balding, flushed man of some girth, who sat like an exploding frog in his green turtleneck. He crossed his arms over his chest and fell unconscious against the table. Libby sprang like a creature of mythical power and grabbed the man under his arms. "Pull the chair away," she said to the wife. Despite his weight, Libby managed to lower him to the floor without dropping him.

Forcefully tapping his shoulders, she asked him to respond, and he failed to. The grandfather clock breathed, but the lifeless man didn't. Humming to herself, she pumped his chest with compressions to the beat of the BeeGees "Stayin'Alive," a tip she learned in CPR class.

The bartender appeared with a mini defibrillator. "I don't know if it's charged," he said, "But it's brand-new."

"Hand me the scissors in the kit so I can cut his sweater," Libby said. She prepared the fat man's chest and applied the defibrillator pads.

"Please, God," she said. "Everyone clear!"

The device delivered a shock, and she resumed the compressions. The diners were quiet, except for the man's wife, who prayed in a low voice. The grandfather clock ticked.

Libby's knees bore into the carpet as she leaned, giving him two quick breaths. Finally, the ambulance arrived, and she scooted away as the crew took over. Resting her palms on the floor, she leaned back with her legs stretched out. The bartender asked if she wanted a drink, and she said no. He wiped his face with a napkin.

The patient was unresponsive to shocks, and doubting he'd survive, Libby tricked herself into analgesic detachment. As minutes passed, the back chatter of paramedics blended with murmurs of disbelieving pub customers. The attendants transported the man, and as he passed by, she saw the swell of his gut, once covered by the last green sweater he owned.

City police arrived, securing the site. and poking about with latex gloves. Witnesses took their turn. "All I know is, when I heard the shots, it was nine-thirty in Tokyo," a man at the bar told a cop.

Another cop studied the likely trajectory of the bullets toward the jukebox. He stopped, fascinated by the sundial. He looked closer, motioning for a colleague to join him. The colleague put a numbered evidence tag on the sundial. The sundial had been shot, and a bullet was lodged in the weathered base.

The bartender pointed out Libby to a detective, who took her statement and thanked her. She gave the officer a business card. She looked around for Denise, who was patting the arm of their waitress as she recounted the robbery to another plainclothes officer. Libby hung back, not wanting to repeat the story to anyone else. The detective thanked the waitress, and Denise returned to the table to get her purse. Approaching Denise, Libby took her by the elbow.

"Let's get out of here," Libby said.

"Right," Denise said, following her. Slipping over to the bartender, Libby handed him the bill, her own business card, and Wally's card with Code 53 written on the back.

"I'm too worn out to call Wally with my critique," Libby said. "Eventually, I'll be in touch."

"I'll tell Wally what you did," the bartender. "You ladies have a better evening."

At the cars, Denise grabbed Libby by both arms. "Are you OK?" Denise said.

"No, but I'll be able to drive home."

"Will you call me when you get there?"

"Yes," Libby said. "I'm sorry I got you into this."

"Don't start that. Hey! I almost forgot," Denise said, opening her large handbag. She pulled out a small gift sack padded with protective tissue. "Open it later." She hugged Libby. "Call me," Denise said, emphasizing each word.

"Thanks," Libby said, accepting the gift.

***

Skipping the ritual of checking the closets, Libby went to her bedroom and sat on the edge of the bed in the dark. Dry-mouthed, she reflexively licked her lips, those lips applied to the man at the pub. The scents she ignored during the emergency now came to mind. The man's breath had smelled like pastrami and peppers. He'd probably almost vomited before the heart attack, and as he lay there, a slow, foul breeze had wafted from his bowels. Picturing herself bent over him, Libby retched, running to the toilet to throw up, resting afterward on the side of the tub. After a minute, she rinsed her mouth with water, brushed her teeth, flossed, and gargled. She peeled off her clothes. Each garment felt like a paper wad stuck to the teacher's blackboard. She was ready to start the shower when the kitchen phone rang. She sprinted, naked. She forgot to call Denise.

"I'm sorry," Libby said. "I got sidetracked in the bathroom."

"You all right?" Denise said.

"Uh-huh."

"I'm a shrink, but I've never been in an armed robbery or watched a man die. Would you call me tomorrow night?"

"Sure. I didn't have those on my resume, either. Why don't you drink some of the mint cocoa we had at your house?" Libby said.

"That's a good idea."

"I'm jumping in the shower, OK? Talk to you later," Libby said. After they hung up, she remembered the gift bag on the kitchen counter. She sat at the table and opened the sack. Her naked bottom stuck to the chair. A shaded lamp on a rung over the sink provided a soft yellow glow, highlighting tufts of lavender tissue paper concealing a hard object. Pulling away the tissue, she uncovered a small plate, five inches in diameter, wedged into a packing panel. She removed the cardboard stays and appraised the plate.

In the technique of cloisonné, green leaves, orange fruits, red rubies, and yellow flowers bordered the rim. Against the faintest of blue glazes, calligraphy in darker blue said in the center: "Let me benefit all."

The guide at the Buddhist temple had spoken the same words. Either the room disappeared, or Libby's conscious mind dwelled in a circle of showering crystals. She felt someone tap her on the shoulder. She held the cool plate to her bare breast for a long time.

Gradually, she was aware the nipple touching the plate had hardened. She tugged on the other nipple, until it matched its mate. She stretched her limbs and ran the soles of her bare feet along the chair legs at the other side of the table. The cool, hard surfaces of the furniture disciplined her senses in a way she'd forgotten how to enjoy. She studied the decorative tiles on the wall above the stove. Tiles depicting roosters. Strutting red roosters. When had she last strutted? She should crow, "I'm still here!" She imagined herself naked on a runway before an audience. Putting the plate aside, she stood, peeling her bottom from the vinyl chair surface. She massaged her buttocks. She walked to the dining room and struck a lewd pose like an exotic dancer. Enticing the imaginary fatheads in the dark living room, she sashayed, bumping and grinding into their midst.

"Still here – a-three-four, still here – a-three-Boom! A-Boom-two-three-Boom!" she chanted. Backing against a wall, she slid to a raunchy squat like

114

a pole dancer and then sprang upward, exploding into a fierce samba. "One-and- two-and, still . . . here, and still . . . here, and still . . . here," she croaked, jiggling her body at double the tempo of the chant. She slowed, swaying her hips in a rumba. "Stil-l-l here, stil-l-l here." She bent low at the waist and swung her torso around and up. Pointing her toes, she took a couple of dainty steps. Leaning, she perched on all fours on the arms of an easy chair. She wiggled her bottom. She'd never done anything like this before. She always behaved like a guest in her own home. Her pleasure was building, competing with the horrific tension of the evening. She hopped off the chair. "I will not be miserable anymore," she shouted to the imaginary crowd. "I'm a good person . . . I am a *good person.*"

A cold draft swept across her backside in affirmation. She stopped in mid-swagger. A frigid little breeze played around her mid-section.

"I *have* to call the heating and air-conditioning guy," she said.

She went to the shower.

CHAPTER 29
Present Day – Autumn

Before work on Monday, Libby browned chicken breasts and placed them with vegetables in a slow cooker set on low. Eager to test the results, she came home for a quiet dinner with cherry pie and a glass of milk for dessert. The doorbell rang as she sat down at the kitchen table. Grousing, she ignored the bell, which rang two more times after short intervals. Poised to eat a chicken morsel stuck on her fork, she heard a forceful rapping on the back door.

"Quoth the raven, 'Nevermore,' " she grumbled. At the wooden door's window, she pinched the edge of the terrycloth curtain to see out. A dark-haired man in a black leather jacket was aiming his knuckles to rap again on the storm door.

"Who is it, please?" Libby said.

"Sergeant Davis, Indianapolis Police." He displayed a badge. "I need to speak with Dr. Libby Doherty."

I would like to have a nice, quiet dinner, she wanted to say, unlocking and speaking through the glass in the storm door. "I'm Libby. How can I help you?"

"My name is Ken Davis. I apologize for coming at the dinner hour, but I'm very pressed for time. You spoke with Officer Crotty at Wally's Millenium. I need to ask you a few more questions."

"OK." She let him in. He saw the supper cooling and apologized again.

"No problem," Libby said. "I didn't make coffee, I'm sorry. Can I offer you a piece of cherry pie?"

"No, thanks, but that's kind of you. This won't take long, and then I'll leave you to your meal."

"Let's talk in the living room," she said, planning his exit through the front door.

Crossing to the front room, she motioned him to the sofa. His black leather jacket was like a marker-pen slash on the sofa's gold Italian leather. "I'd just like to know if you remember whether the robbers spoke to each other or called anyone by name," Davis said.

"One of them said it was time to leave."

"Do you remember the words?"

"To 'clear out,' " Libby said.

"Was there anything else?"

She'd locked eyes under the table with Denise and had no visual details to share about the assailants. Her memory replayed the audio portion of the robbery. One of them shouted, "Sweet T, move out!"

"Um . . . I just remembered he said, 'Move out,' not 'Clear out.' And one of them was called 'Sweet T,' " Libby said. "I don't know whether it meant Sweet T with a capital T, or Sweet Tea, as opposed to unsweetened tea. But that's what I heard."

"Did the others talk to each other?" Davis said.

"I don't think so."

"Do you remember details about the gang? It could be anything at all – like mismatched socks, distinctive jewelry, a wristwatch," Davis said.

"My head was under the table. I hid when the shooting started. Did anyone else see something?"

"We're still comparing notes," the officer said.

"What was the final disposition of the man with the heart attack?" she said.

"His funeral is next Thursday. I understand they're waiting for relatives from out of state," Davis said.

"Oh," she said. They were quiet for a moment.

"Those are all the questions I have for now, but you'll probably be contacted by the prosecutor's office if charges are filed," he said.

"Will the robbers be blamed for causing the heart attack?"

"That's a legal question I can't answer. We're just trying to make an arrest as soon as possible."

"Thanks for stopping by," Libby said, half-sincere.

"Sure. We'll be in touch if we need anything," Davis said.

Libby returned to the kitchen and slapped the countertop in frustration. The prosecutor's office. Rummaging through a cupboard, she found a small bag of chocolate-covered peanuts. She took out several and put the rest away. Saluting the assailants, she spoofed Denise's example of a litany with food.

"I eat this peanut in memory of the mismatched socks you wore to the robbery." She chewed and swallowed. "I eat this peanut to honor the urine you spilled while making your escape." She ate another one. "And – I eat this peanut to sanctify the STD you caught from your girlfriend last week."

She washed down the snack with water and consecrated the awaiting meal with a moment of silence. She allowed herself one chicken breast and refrigerated the others, destined for chicken salad with grapes. The cherry pie from the grocer's bakery was fresh enough, though the crust was a little doughy, and she warmed a slice in the microwave.

After supper, she cleaned house. One of her dental professors had rhapsodized the morphology of a tooth was "just like a big house with a lot of rooms." Thus, the "enamel" of the house was dusted, vacuumed, and polished.

She took out the trash at ten-thirty and relaxed in the kitchen. Up later than usual, she found the local news at eleven. A live stand-up report was in progress:

"Bob, the word tonight from the Harkness camp is – they had nothing to do with the release of the video."

The picture cut to a shot of Theo Karnow walking his dog. The reporter, Kevin Kirby, paused for emphasis several times.

"Karnow, who lives in a downtown condominium, is shown walking his golden retriever. The video was provided by another downtown resident, Jeff Sonavich, who was using his cell phone camera to document skateboarders trespassing in the private lot reserved for his apartment building.

"Sonavich said Karnow stopped along the curb next to McMurphy's grocery and allowed his dog to leave excrement on the sidewalk."

The video showed Karnow's dog squatting.

"Next," the reporter continued, "The video shows Karnow waving at a driver who honks and rolls down his window. The car stops momentarily, and the two have a brief conversation. Karnow then leaves the dog excrement, instead of cleaning it up."

Concluding his report, Kevin Kirby was back on camera. "Bob and Deena, Sonavich said he thought the public should see how a candidate behaves when he thinks no one is looking. Sonavich said he doesn't plan to vote for anyone who puts himself above city ordinances. Karnow's spokesman, Duff Turley, said the candidate had a waste-disposal sack with him, but forgot to take along the scoop. Turley compared the oversight to leaving the house in a hurry and forgetting your wallet, and not realizing it until you're at the checkout. This is Kevin Kirby reporting."

"Thanks, Kevin," Bob said. "We have breaking news on the south side tonight as a police chase ends in a traffic fatality. We'll have more on this story when we come back."

The promotional theme music roared, and the voiceover snarled, "You're watching the Final Report with Bob Kring and Deena Ramirez." A commercial for a trial lawyer began, and Libby ran to the bathroom. She came back as the newscast resumed.

Deena fired away. "One robbery suspect is dead, and another in the hospital, after a police chase ended in a fatal crash tonight. You're looking at live pictures from I-65 near the Southport exit, where highway crews are cleaning up wreckage. The chase began when police attempted to pull over the suspects' car.

"Police say the two were wanted in connection with an armed robbery at a pub in Lawrence. A third suspect was already in custody. The driver apparently lost control of his car and hit the wall of the underpass. The car spun back into traffic and collided with a semi rig.

"The driver of the suspects' vehicle died at the scene but has not been identified pending notification of relatives. Police say the truck driver was not hurt. The suspect in the hospital is Dante Hopkins, listed in fair condition. "Earlier tonight police arrested Jaden Wheeler, who's in the Marion County Jail on a preliminary charge of armed robbery. Police say right after the robbers left the pub last week, a customer died of an apparent heart attack."

"I would like a nice, quiet evening," Libby said. The phone rang.

"Yes?" Libby said.

"They got 'em," Denise said.

"I know. Did the police come to see you today, too?"

"No. Did they visit you?"

"Yep," Libby said.

"What did they want?"

"It was a 'he,' and he said they were comparing notes. Book us a cruise so we can escape this."

"You mean those cruises where everyone catches a virus?" Denise said.

"Yes . . . No."

"Get some sleep," Denise said. "I'll call you about getting together this weekend."

Later, Libby skulked under the blue-and-white checked throw and made an entry in the bedside journal:

> Kring-cast exposes Karnow as Krap-now.
> Is Sweet T[ea] on ice in morgue or still straight up?
> Plaque and film at eleven.
> Don't turn that dial!
> If anchor had diamond tooth stud –
> Kring-bling.

***

Across town, Gale Mooneyham perched on the edge of the desk Jed slumped behind.

"You're sure Sonavich has nothing to do with our camp?" Jed said.

" 'Sink or Swim' ran a check on him. They can't find any campaign contributions or obvious ties. I think he was doing exactly what he said he was doing – filming the skateboarders, and Karnow just walked into the picture." Gale said.

"Six months ago, I wouldn't have said I wanted to win by a pile of dog poop. Now I just want to win. I'm so tired, I don't think I can stand it. What was the poor dog's name?"

"Marbury."

"And he has a little cat friend named 'Madison,' " Jed sniped, straightening his posture. Gale raised an eyebrow. "You know – the case they made you learn in the eleventh grade, *Marbury v. Madison* – 1803," Jed said, raising his right arm in a dramatic gesture.

"The United States Supreme Court is not bound by an act of Congress that is repugnant to the Constitution," Jed said, rolling the 'r' in repugnant.

"In other words," Gale said, "They weren't taking any crap."

"Worthy Mooneyham -- you are correct -- but most important, the court reserved the right of judicial review over crap. The Rehnquist Court oversaw many piles," Jed said.

"You're not so tired," Gale said.

"I guess not. Let's make popcorn."

CHAPTER 30
History – June 1921

School was out for the year, but Creedmore Hall ran year-round. Mary couldn't keep pretending to be sick on Thursday afternoons.

She had to summon the courage to face Deck. On the next Thursday, Mary looked for him, but he never arrived. She finally asked a student where he was.

"Oh, him!" Millie Jenkins said. "He never came back after the lesson a few weeks ago. He just vanished, and they didn't tell us why.

"So my mother asked the minister if he knew where Deck went. The minister said Deck's family always goes to Lake Michigan for the summer and he went so he could paint undisturbed."

Undisturbed. Deck was not to be disturbed. Mary stood staring at the stage curtain, which was closed, just as Deck had drawn a curtain.

"Lordy, Mary! You're pale. I don't think you got well. I hope I don't catch whatever it is," Millie said.

"Just stay off the riverbank," Mary said, in a fog. Millie gave her a quizzical look and stepped back.

"I think I'd like another glass of punch – excuse me," Millie said, leaving for the refreshment table.

CHAPTER 31
Present Day – Autumn

Darla fell asleep on her sofa after supper on a Saturday night. A client was at the house in the afternoon, and the reading was about the traumatic injury that killed her son. The grieving mother brought his framed picture to the appointment. The psychic was able to summon the adage, "Neither a borrower nor a lender be," and the mother was satisfied that her son was in touch. The saying had been a joke between them whenever he asked for his allowance.

A passenger on the back of a motorcycle, he was thrown during an accident and died of a head injury. The psychic offered the phrase, "Lantern Lake," and the mother said it was the riders' destination when the accident happened.

"He says he wants you to forgive him for the pain he caused, and he wants you to know that he's OK, and that he is with Carlton, whoever that is," the psychic said.

"Oh, my God!" the mother said. "He was our neighbor about fifteen years ago. He had a stroke and died at a bowling alley. He used to come over on Friday nights and bring beer and pizza. Oh, Carlton!"

The mother burst into tears, and the hostess ended the reading to fix a pot of apple-cinnamon tea.

Later, the dog walker took Trevor for exercise. They neared the special bungalow and stopped as Trevor made friends with an inviting bush. The wind picked up for a moment, and then the air was still. The earth and sky were hushed, waiting.

Sobbing. She heard sobbing, just as before, and the female voice wailing, "I'm sorry, I'm so sorry."

Darla led Trevor home, and she prayed for advice. Relaxing on the sofa after dinner, she fell asleep.

When she awoke, she knew what to do. Darla lined up carved relics and picture frames on her dining table. She lit the white pillar candle and turned out the overhead light. She sat at the table and Trevor came over, sitting on his hind legs at attention. He knew when she lined up her toys, as he thought of them, he needed to watch over her.

She picked up a gilt-edged frame shaped like a church window. It displayed a lithograph of the Virgin Mary. The woman kissed the frame.

"Mother Mary, help us to relieve the unhappy spirit in the house we visit. Please intercede on her behalf to help her find eternal peace."

The woman closed her eyes. "I smell flowers," she said.

She picked up a framed photo of her late great-grandmother on her mother's side. "You prayed for the souls of the dead. A girl who died needs your help. She is at the house we visit. Please help with your powerful prayers."

The candle issued a sputtering sound. The flame bowed ninety degrees in the seeker's direction and then straightened, as if in agreement. Trevor released a tiny whimper.

The woman picked up a framed print of Jesus walking on the water. It was an old print that her great-aunt bought from a door-to-door salesman during the Great Depression.

"Lord Jesus, Trevor and I know you see us visiting the house. That poor girl is stuck. Your healing power can fix all. We pray for your intervention, for her soul, and for ours."

The candle flame shot up, doubling in size, burning with fierce energy. Trevor barked, standing on his hind legs while balanced with his front paws on the edge of the table. The woman and her dog watched the candle for a long time.

CHAPTER 32
Present Day – November

Jed Harkness sat alone in his suite at the Morton, where the Democrats were watching election returns on a giant screen in one of the ballrooms. He called out for his dog as if he were at the hotel with him.

"*Los!*" Jed hurled from the gutter of his throat. "It's almost over. When I get home, we'll watch a little TV."

If he won – and he was going to – many people would surround him, but none would understand him as well as the dog.

Jed got up to put on a tie, most of which would stay hidden under a pullover of purple cashmere, chosen to convey a relaxed royal mien. A pale-blue dress shirt provided the collar. Knotting the tie, he wished for feminine help, an adjustment by slender fingers on a graceful hand. He imagined the woman's arm, and his eyes followed the firm muscle of the limb to a desirable shoulder. The crown above the shoulders was Libby's.

The hotel line rang, and he answered.

"Mr. Harkness – Duff Turley with Theo Karnow. Mr. Karnow would like to speak with you."

"Of course," Jed said.

"Jed? – Theo. Here it is: I'm conceding the election. Congratulations." Karnow sounded a bit clinical, like someone reporting the albumin level in a urine specimen.

Jed's pores secreted a smelly glaze. He needed more than his little dog, right now. "Theo, I'm grateful for the call," he said. "You ran a commendable campaign."

"You ran a more effective one," Karnow said. "We probably underestimated you."

"I don't know that," Jed said. "What are your plans after tonight? A vacation, I hope."

"You bet. Chelsea decided six months ago that win-lose, we'd be heading for Venezuela. We're leaving next week."

"Please give her my best. I think I should let my staff know you were so kind to call. Thanks very much, Theo."

"Certainly. Take care. See you later."

Jed was tempted to pour a small shot glass of whiskey from the bar in his room, but he'd shake hands with hundreds of people and couldn't smell like booze. He would tipple as he relaxed with the dog.

Using his cell phone, he left a message on someone's voicemail. "This is for 'Sink or Swim.' I just got the concession call. Thanks for your help. We'll talk soon."

He dialed again, this time for Gale Mooneyham. "Theo just called. We'll need the stage right away. Is Tom somewhere nearby?"

"Right here. Put him on?"

"Please," Jed said.

"Jed?" Tom Shelton, the campaign manager, said.

"Tell the TV people to get ready for the live feed. I'm coming down for the acceptance."

"Jed, this is great. I'm very happy for you. Anything else?"

"Yes. You can give yourself a ten-percent bonus. You're one hell of a campaign manager."

"Are you sure you can afford it? We spent like crazy in the last two weeks," Tom said.

"I've already checked. After we both get some sleep, we'll talk about your plans." Jed spied his bottle of aftershave on the hotel bathroom counter. "Listen, I need to freshen up. Just go ahead and give Gale his phone."

Shelton scanned the ballroom. He caught the eye of his media coordinator and motioned him closer. "It's time," Shelton said.

"Right." Alerting field producers, reporters, and photographers, the campaign assistant lined up interviews for after Jed's speech, and then he called the ballroom's sound manager. "Start the CD – loud."

126

The music kicked in like a bold fist pounding on a bar countertop, and elated supporters of every size, color, and creed began dancing. Jed ran to the platform as the frenzy peaked, and the crowd erupted into an ovation.

***

At home, Libby was asleep. After ingesting the toxin of violence at the robbery, she imposed a regimen of exercise and healthful eating to flush out the effects of fear. Before bed, she admired the plate Denise gave her, and after lights-out, she finished a whispered prayer with, "Let me benefit all."

The election was far from her thoughts. Her mind slumbered under a heavy tarp. Awake before the alarm sounded, she was renewed, exuberant, and sheepish, as if someone had kept watch while she was having a sexy dream. The bedclothes were intact, and the only sound was the efficient hum of the furnace. But it was freezing in her room, as if the window were open. She lay still with her hand over her mouth.

The alarm blared, and she shut it off like she was smashing a bug. She bounded to the kitchen for food. She noticed the rest of the house was comfortably warm, unlike the bedroom.

The coffee, more aromatic than usual, evoked the burro that carried the beans. The cinnamon on the toast must have arrived on a vessel sailing from China. Her meander along commercial trade routes of antiquity came to a halt when she turned on the TV.

A newscaster chirped under big hair that looked like a forsythia bush, likely to be trimmed under orders from the executive producer. "Harkness won by fifty-two percent. Our news analyst, Dr. Charter Hemingway, is a political scientist at Dale Methodist College. He's here this morning with an overview of the Harkness-Karnow contest. Dr. Hemingway?"

"Thanks, Jordan. It's clear that Jed Talbot Harkness benefited from the organization built by his mentor, Armistead Hauser, but at the same time, the association likely cost him a bigger margin of victory," Hemingway said.

Libby didn't know what to make of the political scientist, whose wide, square face was shaped like a data graph. His left eyebrow arched higher than the right, and a curl of gray hair flipped up over the left eyebrow, as if a line plotted with data points started on his chin and ran right off the edge of his forehead.

Hemingway continued his analysis. "Voters in several strongly Democratic precincts went for Karnow by split-ticketing.

"The exit polls at precincts in Warren and Wayne townships revealed that Karnow was able to make inroads with his message. Some voters said the Hauser machine had been there too long, and this statement validated the Karnow strategy, which was to remind people that Harkness was Hauser's protégé.

"Even though Armistead Hauser retired as prosecutor and took over as US Attorney eighteen months ago, Harkness was stuck with his old boss' baggage, including the firing of two assistants who allowed a casino operator under investigation to cover their betting losses. Voters we interviewed said the 'change' message from Karnow was appealing.

"Ultimately, Harkness prevailed. Voters who indicated they chose Harkness said Karnow was inexperienced at criminal prosecution, and indeed, the police union endorsed Harkness for that very reason. In addition, Harkness benefited from the dominance of the Democratic Party in Center Township.

"Here's the final thing to remember: To get to 52 percent, Harkness simply outworked everybody. He was everywhere for the last six months – at softball games, church picnics, bicycle races, and he impressed party leaders with his fundraising ability. He's no longer regarded as a political insider waiting to take over. Jordan, Jed Harkness was on the street from Day One, and it paid off yesterday."

Libby rinsed strawberries, topped them with yogurt, and rolled each one in her mouth, like a child dangerously sucking on a small toy. Crushing a berry, she enjoyed the tingling sensation from the fruit's frosty interior. She considered the latest about Jed. He wanted to have dinner after the election. She would wait for him to call, although she was free to call him. No, he knew where to find her, and he would have to exert some effort. As Dr. Charter Hemi-demisemiquaver had said, Jed was on the street.

He could call her. He could stop in with another dental problem, but that would betray a masochistic streak. She laughed, picturing herself poised with a dental drill over a trussed-up Jed begging for more. He could send a note to invite her for drinks, and then they'd decide where to dine. She was sure of one thing: They would be friends, first, and she would wait to see how the permanent dentition grew in.

CHAPTER 33
Present Day – November

Jed was wearing a gray sweater, gray trousers, and a brown suede bomber jacket. He entered the historic Birch Bayh US Courthouse and Post Office from Ohio Street and passed through the security checkpoints. Though trained for any contingency, security staff had the relaxed demeanor of people working the big time, like ushers at the Metropolitan Opera.

To Jed, the courthouse's Classical Revival architecture of 1905 proclaimed the majesty of the law, unlike the City-County Building, which reminded him of black and gray dominos. His own office was a few blocks away in a rented suite big enough for his department. But the county courtrooms were farther away, now, at the new Justice Center, in gleaming facilities that left him uninspired. When it was under construction, he chuckled at the campus looming at night on the plains of the city's southeast side. The luminaries on the steel skeleton blazed like the lights on a casino.

However, in the old federal building, one could find marble columns, gold leaf, and murals – oh, the murals! – and Van Ingen's painting, *Appeal to Justice*. The historical courtroom featuring this work was Jed's destination, arranged with the archivist for a private showing. Meditating alone in the chamber, the prosecutor-elect would renew his commitment to the administration of justice.

He entered the courtroom, stepped past the bar, and sat at one of the tables facing the bench. The campaign took him from trial duty, which he'd miss for years. The preparation for trial could interfere with Jed's oversight of his

129

office, and fulfilling the duties of such could jeopardize the quality of a single case's prosecution.

Jed sighed. The courtroom was an energy field, and though alone, he felt a presence. He remembered the archivist's story about an autistic boy who visited the room. In a group of elementary school students touring the building, the autistic child sulked for most of the trip, but upon entering the William Steckler Courtroom, he said, "It feels different in here."

The boy pointed at Van Ingen's painting of her ladyship Justice, presiding as usual on the wall behind the judge's bench. And then the child fell silent. Staring at the mural, he put his hands over his ears and moved his lips, as if whispering.

Jed rubbed his palms together. A chill enveloped him as a presence came closer. The ghost of Milligan? An accused insurrectionist during the Civil War, Lambdin P. Milligan was scheduled to be hanged on May 19, 1865. His appeal was adjudicated in the old federal courthouse that was once down the street.

A civilian, Milligan was arrested by the military commander of Indiana and tried by a military commission. Found guilty of wicked plans against the US, he was sentenced to death.

The noose loosened, when Milligan successfully argued that as a civilian, he wasn't under the rule of military judges. In fact, a civilian grand jury convened in early 1865 without returning a bill of indictment against him.

Just days before the scheduled execution, Milligan petitioned the US Circuit Court for the District of Indiana to set him free. Still seeking to hang him, the government's counsel argued for an exception to the Constitution, on the grounds the necessities of war justified conviction by a military tribunal. Divided in opinion, the local judges sent the case to the US Supreme Court, which sided with the condemned man in *Ex parte Milligan*, 71 U.S. (4 Wall.) 2 (1867). Jed revered a passage from the opinion of Justice David Davis:

> The Constitution of the United States is a law for rulers and
> people, equally in war and in peace, and covers with the
> shield of its protection all classes of men, at all times and
> under all circumstances. No doctrine involving more
> pernicious consequences was ever invented by the wit of

man than that any of its provisions can be suspended during any of the great exigencies of government.

Every so often, a prosecutor was tempted to suspend the Constitution for the sake of expedience. Jed maintained his self-discipline by reciting Davis' phrase, "at all times and under all circumstances."

Propping his elbows on the table, he rested his chin on his hands.

Jed looked at the courtroom's paneling, high ceilings, and glimmering fixtures. The elegant room was more like a rich man's personal library than a courtroom. The building was solid, and Jed wished some of his colleagues could be as solid as the courthouse foundations. His thoughts now focused on personnel.

They were Armistead Hauser's people, hired by him, sometimes about to be fired by him. Jed owed Army a lot, but he didn't have to keep his people forever. Still, he liked them. Jed could reassign duties, too. For a start, he would enlist an outsider, Jim Phillipi, a friend from his days clerking in Chicago, to join the executive staff. This addition would give Jed the flexibility he needed to reorganize.

Ron Rable had been the interim prosecutor after Hauser resigned. Rable declined to the run for the job and threw his support to Jed, who was serving as chief deputy, until he took leave to run the campaign. Rable was returning to private practice after the first of the year. Though grateful, Jed measured his loyalty, because Rable was dating the mayor's tourism director.

She was a political aspirant, and a mannequin in the mayor's department store, as far as Jed was concerned. The lovebirds tried to be discreet, but few secrets eluded the ubiquitous Gale Mooneyham. He was loading sacks of diapers for his grandbabies into the trunk of his car, when he spotted the couple getting into a Jeep outside the dry-cleaner next to the supermarket. As they walked to the vehicle, Rable was cupping her elbow with one hand, and with the other, carrying her plastic-draped suit on a hangar.

Jed thought back to Army Hauser's tenure. Although of the same political faith, the mayor sandbagged Hauser's expansion of public-safety initiatives by getting the City-County Council to vote against the funding. Army then obtained grants from state and federal sources, but he could afford only one program, instead of the proposed three. Army shrugged off the mayor, who was simply padding his budget for tourism and conventions.

But with Jim Phillipi on board, Jed would have a confidante to keep an eye on the mayor. And then, Jed could elevate Fabiola de Torre to chief deputy, a role she took on an interim basis during the campaign. Jim would move into Fabiola's previous job as associate counsel to the prosecutor.

Beginning her career in Porter County in Northwest Indiana, Fabiola moved to Indianapolis and impressed Hauser with a string of convictions. After three years, he promoted her to head the sex crimes division, and she managed the team well. Fabiola was politically talented, Army said, promoting her again to his executive staff. As associate counsel, she oversaw community prosecution, legislative affairs, and human resources. From time to time, she was entertained by scouts from the top legal firms in the state, Perlmuter Hoffman, and Dunwoody Schiff. They were looking for lobbyists, and for stray dogs to rummage in the bin of their insurance defense work, but Fabiola stayed with Hauser.

Jed truly liked Fabiola, a black-haired electric current from Michigan City. Her mother, a hotel housekeeper, had commuted to Chicago on the South Shore Railroad six days a week, and her father was a truck driver. The family of nine lived in a three-bedroom house, and the children often went to the library to enjoy the space. As a teenager, Fabiola worked in restaurants, competed on the speech team, and started a neighborhood improvement association. With scholarships to Valparaiso University, she stayed through law school. She was intense, candid, and skilled at asking for favors.

Jim could step into the role of associate counsel and be exceptional at legislative affairs. Jed reckoned Fabiola would be relieved, because she'd been doing two jobs for the past year.

Although practicing in Illinois, Jim was admitted to the Indiana bar right after finishing Indiana University Law School at Bloomington. He met Jed at a bar association mixer in Chicago when Jed was clerking, and they became close friends.

Their paths diverged when Jed introduced himself to Army Hauser at a legal convention in the Loop. Army invited him to dinner at a hide-away pub near the top of the John Hancock building. After a spirited, two-hour exchange, Army said Jed was a "natural," and that with Army's guidance, he could have a political career back home.

Ever the policeman's son eager to serve and protect, Jim was in Chicago as an assistant in the Cook County State's Attorney's Office, which had over eight hundred lawyers. After seven years in Cook County, he caught wind of sizeable budget cuts. His record was outstanding, but he was among the last 10 percent hired before a multi-year freeze. Always looking to the future, he'd made friends with a contact at the special office that argues appeals on behalf of Illinois' local state's attorneys. Eventually, Jim got a job as an appellate prosecutor.

Last weekend in Terre Haute, or "Terrible Hut," as Jim called his hometown, he met Jed for dinner. Over drinks, Jim said that he was skilled at scraping "appellate crust."

"How about a change of crust?" Jed hinted.

Jim winked. "Crust and soda, on the rocks, lime twist."

Jed predicted his friend would welcome the chance to earn an administrative credential, if the financial compensation was adequate. Frustrated with the low pay for prosecutors, Hauser had sworn barnyard oaths in the names of various livestock. At times, the turnover rate in the office was 25 percent.

Yet, Jed picked up on Jim's loneliness, and that he hadn't met anyone he wanted to settle down with. He'd probably benefit from a change of scenery. And certainly, the job duties would broaden his contacts. Using the Web on his phone, Jed looked up pay for Illinois appellate prosecutors. He smiled at the empty chair behind the judge's bench.

Two other executive staff slots remained – trial coordinator, and chief of investigations. Ray Stonehill, the coordinator, could stay in his position, reporting directly to Fabiola and supervising activity in all courts. Probes into white-collar crime were overseen by the chief of investigations, Karen Cranley-Garner, and Jed wanted her to stay.

Fabiola, Ray, Karen, and Jim. Jed had his inner circle.

***

Jed stared at the vacant judge's bench. His late father wanted him to be a judge. An auditor with the Finance Center at old Fort Ben, Jed's father died of a heart attack shortly after his sixty-seventh birthday. Jed agreed with his sister, Melanie, in urging their mother to move to a retirement community in Tallahassee, where Melanie lived with her family. Alone in Indianapolis, Jed went back to the family home, still furnished and in good repair. He made use of his father's tools and toys, including a ping-pong table in the basement. Although she took paintings and photos from the living room, his mother handed down the durable sofa, the matching wing chairs, and the piano. Jed permitted his terrier to roam the house, modified only by the installation of a swinging flap in the kitchen door, which allowed the pet to visit a doggie toilet in the garage.

Remembering his father's final birthday, Jed swallowed. His father would have cheered the election victory, but with humility. A devout Catholic, he sent Jed to Cathedral High School, on the condition Jed volunteer to help people nobody gave a "flying rat's ass about." Henceforth, Jed supervised after-school gym activities for children, taught reading to adults, and stocked shelves at a food pantry. During the Christmas season, he visited nursing-home residents. He was ordered to ride the city buses to develop habits of conservation.

"You can see the cost of snobbery and myopia in terms of gas and gridlock," his father said.

Jed got an education on the bus lines. One rider was outraged at needing to deposit the fare before picking a seat. "The people of God are gonna rise up!" she proclaimed. The "people" continued her rant through several stops, until a tired man boarded the bus during the tail end of an outburst. Rolling his eyes, he announced, "Ridin' the bus makes my feet stink."

Another rider would have traded his own affliction for smelly feet. He lost control of his bowels. Jed couldn't figure out where the smell was coming from, until the hapless transit customer stood to leave. The evidence had stained his pants and was running over the top of his shoes. Jed heard the woman next to him mutter, "He boo-booed on hisself." Given the biohazard on the seat, the driver called for a replacement vehicle and the riders had to move to the new bus.

Hearing this story over dinner, Jed's father said, "This shall be known forever as the 'boo-boo on the bus.'"

"At least Melanie will benefit from college," Jed's mother said.

As a teenager, Jed didn't always know what came over him. "I'm glad you didn't fix beef stew," he said.

"Another word – and your dinner is over," his mother said.

Laughing and lighting a cigarette, his father said, "You got to your destination, but the lessons on the way were probably more important."

Taking one last look at the courtroom, Jed focused on the Van Ingen painting. It would have been on the book cover, if Louisa May Alcott had written about the law. Painted in the last hours of the Victorian era, Justice wore brunette hair clasped behind her in the style of the day. To Jed, the figure's broad shoulders, billowy garb, and thoughtful bearing suggested both a scholar and a colleague of Mother Earth. Presenting his complaint, the petitioner was humble, but Justice listened, absorbed, and without condescension.

Each time he saw the painting, he wished he could leave a message the way Jews in Jerusalem left prayers on paper stuffed in the holes of the prayer wall. This was when politics and ambition fell away.

"Jed?"

Approaching from behind, the tall, lanky Armistead Hauser stepped into the courtroom. In his late sixties, he still wore the stiff collar and conservative tie required during his days as an FBI agent.

"Army!" Jed shook hands with his close friend. "When did you get back from Michigan?"

"Last night. I talked to Sheri, and she wants the job. She'll be down here to look for an apartment before Christmas. I told her we'd get together for drinks."

"That's great. I need to put my executive staff together, and then I'll let the new associate counsel invite Sheri for orientation after New Year's. She understands her start date will probably be toward the end of January?"

"Yes. Your new associate counsel?"

"I'm promoting Fabiola to chief deputy. I'm bringing in a new associate, Jim Phillipi. We go back to my days at the Seventh."

"An excellent decision. Have you told Fabiola? Army said.

"Not yet. I'll call to see if she has dinner plans."

"She may very well have plans. I hear she's been around with Perry Montana."

Jed feigned confusion. "Perry Montana, the abstract title researcher, or Perry Montana, the manager of the baseball team down the street?"

Army snickered. "I don't think she's into real estate."

"I'll be dogged. Are you free for lunch?"

"I'm always free for lunch. Anything special bring you here today?" Army said.

135

Jed nodded toward Justice in the mural. "On a date with my girl."
"When are you going to pop the question?" Army said.
"She's a lousy cook." Jed said.

CHAPTER 34
Present Day – November

The dog walker had gone to the grocery to get a chuck roast and a bag of potatoes. Driving home, she again saw H.H. Holmes, this time, walking east on Washington Street toward Arlington Avenue. She went home and prayed.

***

Libby listened to Marquita translate for a patient's Hispanic mother. The toddler's alarming and unsightly brown tooth decay, early childhood caries, was preventable. Marquita was asking about the mother's nutrition during her pregnancy. The mother said she was on the move to different cities and didn't take vitamins. She listed a diet of beans, tortillas, cereal, canned fruit, and when affordable, fast food.

Marquita asked how often sweetened drinks like pop or fruit juice were in the baby bottle. Holding up her hands in a defensive gesture, the mother admitted the boy drank a lot of colas, chocolate milk, and fruit juice.

"Please tell her, first, that we're not judging her. Then explain that the baby teeth keep a space in the jaw for the adult teeth," Libby said. "If the baby tooth comes out too early, a tooth beside it could drift into the empty space, and then, when the adult teeth come in, they could be crooked." Libby waited for the translation.

Perplexed, the mother put a hand to her forehead.

"Therefore, we can't expose baby teeth to the acids that attack them. Some things the baby needs, like milk or formula, contain sugars. The sugars meet the germs in the baby's mouth, and the sugars change to acids.

"So – we want to make sure we're not using the baby bottle at the wrong time, like when you put the baby down for a nap. Please don't put him in the crib with the bottle. The milk is soaking the teeth, and the acids are attacking," Libby said.

To represent a tooth, Marquita held out her left hand with the fingers pointed at the floor. With her right hand, she tickled the left to illustrate the acids attacking the tooth. The mother watched, wide-eyed. She was an illegal entrant to the US, Marquita said, but the baby was born here, entitling him to full Medicaid coverage.

"He might be president someday," Libby said. "But not if his teeth are missing."

Late in the morning, Claris answered a phone call from Drew's husband, who reported Drew delivered a baby girl just under five pounds. Both were in stable condition after an emergency Caesarian section.

It was a day full of challenges in the clinic, and after her swim at the Y, Libby was sleepy on the way home, longing for the warmth of her quilt. The drowsiness reminded her of how she felt after Thanksgiving dinner, soon approaching.

***

Driving to see family in St. Louis on the Wednesday night before Thanksgiving, Libby pulled off the highway for coffee and a stretch. After closing the office at two, she went to the bakery to pick up a chocolate cake, elaborately decorated with vanilla icing and red leaves of confectioner's sugar and butter. The cake was for people who didn't like pumpkin pie.

She thought the cake box would slide around in the trunk, so she placed the box on the back seat of the Volkswagen and strapped the seat belt around the box. "Better safe than sorry," she muttered.

Arriving at Terre Haute when the sun was low in the sky, Libby wanted a break. Restaurant signs in toy-box colors loomed on pillars. Not picky, she turned into the first lot on the right. She went inside to place an order.

"Good evening, Dr. Booth."

Reddening, she turned around. "Jed." Oh, that man, she thought, where does he come from?

He was smiling like a friendly interloper. "I know I asked you to postpone dinner with me until after the election. I still envision something fancier," he said. "Not to abridge our agreement, you understand – but can I buy you a sandwich now?"

"No, thank you. I'm just getting a coffee for the road," she said.

"I take it you have plans for tomorrow?"

Before she could answer, they heard a crash of metal and glass. Customers rushed to the east bay of windows and gawked. Jed and Libby turned to look, but the patrons blocked their view.

The store manager went outside and returned. "Call the police," he told his assistant. "This guy coming in hit a car that was backing out of a parking space, and that car got pushed into a parked car."

"A parked car," Libby said, heading outdoors. Jed followed. "Oh, gosh!" she said, stopping in mid-stride. The Volkswagen's back fender was dented, and the taillight housing reflector on the right rear was broken. Glass from the other two cars littered the parking lot.

"Let me check it," Jed said. He examined the wheel housings and pushed on the fender. "It's ugly, but roadworthy," he said. "The main thing is to back out of here without getting a flat tire."

Despite the cool air, a mustache of perspiration formed over Libby's lips. She wiped her face with the back of her hand. "I guess I should call my insurance agent."

The store manager approached them. "That your car?" he asked Jed.

"No, the lady's. As soon as the police make their report, we need to clean up the glass."

"We'll take care of it, sir."

Libby fumbled, looking in her purse for the insurance ID card. She dropped the purse. "Oh, darn."

Jed picked up the purse. "I'll hold it for you," he said.

"Thanks." Finding the card, she called the 24-hour claims number. Jed zipped up the bag and held it close like a football. "Thanks," she said again. He relinquished the purse. The two waited for the police officer as the wind picked up. Cloud cover moved in.

"I hope it doesn't rain," Jed said.

"Me, too," Libby said.

After they talked with the policeman, Jed said he'd wait with her inside while the parking lot was cleaned, and he and Libby found a table near the window. The manager presented them with a free tray of food and asked what they wanted to drink. Jed thanked him, and Libby said, "Coffee black, please."

"I'll have the same," Jed said, adding, "Nice fellow," after the manager left the drinks.

"Do you want the fries?" Libby said. "I quit them a long time ago."

"Yes, thanks." Jed squirted the pile with catsup.

Libby bit into a burger. Jed concentrated on the greasy sticks. After a few minutes, she said, "What were you doing here tonight?"

"I just checked into the budget hotel down the street. I was hungry," he said. "I'm spending Thanksgiving with an old friend and his parents. He's coming to work for me after the first of the year. And you?" he said.

"I'm going to St. Louis to my sister's. All of a sudden, I'm really tired. It's tempting to turn around, but I haven't seen my family since Easter."

"You could stay at the inn and leave early tomorrow," he said.

"No. I'm the potato peeler and masher."

"A scullery maid after all. The other side of dentistry," he said.

"She has two preschoolers who get into things. It's easier for me to cook and let her deal with their escapades. I'll make deviled eggs, too," she said.

"I love deviled eggs. My mom usually makes the purple ones with beet juice," Jed said.

"Does she live in Indy?" she said.

"No," he said. "She moved to Florida to be near my sister. For five seconds, I thought about going down there, but I'm still tired from the campaign. I didn't want to spend the weekend in airports. Mom understood. I'll see her at Christmas."

"Congratulations on your victory," Libby said.

"Thank you. Did you remember to vote?" he said, not playfully.

"I did. I thought I wouldn't be able to, because the voting machine wasn't working. I was about to leave for the office, but they said we could drop paper ballots into a storage hole in the machine."

Jed sighed. "Trouble all over town. We heard a complaint that a precinct opened late, because they had to appoint a new inspector at the last minute.

"The original inspector called from jail. The inspector's supplies were in the trunk of his car, which was at the impound lot," Jed continued.

"The police had the car towed, because the inspector was drunk and got pulled over the night before. So, one of the county clerk's people went to the impound lot with a cop to retrieve the election materials from the trunk."

"Gee," Libby said.

"Nothing like playing with the peanut politicians," he said.

Libby saw how tired he was, and she refrained from asking if he were the "Correlative Cashew."

Intuiting each other's desire for calm, they limited small talk. When they finished their coffees, Jed said, "Will you be OK on the road tonight?"

"Oh, yeah. I'm only falling an hour behind schedule."

"I'd feel much better if you'd call me when you arrive. Here's my cell number." He jotted his private number on a business card and handed it over. Still poised to write, he took out another card. "Would you mind giving me your number, in case I don't hear from you?"

She gave it, and they went out. Escorting her to the Volkswagen, he kicked away stray fragments of glass in the lot. Something in the back seat caught his eye, and he looked closer.

"Is that a cake in the seat belt?" he said.

"Yes. Chocolate."

Shaking with silent laughter, he brushed the smile off his face with his right palm. "You've given me a story for the dinner table," he said.

"That's something," she said, opening the driver's door. He walked around to her.

"Call me when you get there," he said. She saw that when he smiled, his nose flattened, softening the angles of his face.

"I will, Jed. Thanks for everything." She shook his hand. "Have a good time tomorrow. Try to take it easy."

"Planning on it."

Libby got into the car, and Jed stepped back. She waved. He watched to make sure the taillights worked as she drove away.

For the first half-hour, Libby enjoyed music from an oldie's station, but the signal grew weak as she pushed through Illinois. She scanned the frequencies. Country music prevailed, but some ballads held her attention.

She marveled at the coincidence of seeing Jed. Once again, he precipitated a crash. First, he begged for emergency treatment; then, he gave her tickets to a show that caused her an embarrassing incident. Tonight, he materialized, and in less than a minute, her car was dented. What would happen if they went on a date?

She relented, admitting that she, not Jed, picked the fast-food place. Second, he was not responsible for the Freddy Fontine fiasco. Jed gave her the tickets, but he didn't make her use them.

She listed his good points. He didn't ask if she voted for him, but only if she voted. He wasn't condescending, just helpful. He held her purse un-self-consciously, instead of making a show of dangling the bag away from him, as if it were contaminated. And he let her in. He referred to his mother as "Mom," instead of the more distant, "my mother," and he gave Libby his private cell number. Marquita would be on the ceiling if she knew Libby had *El Super Ratón's* private number.

***

Back in Terre Haute, Jed stretched out on the hotel bed. The TV set blared. Life was comical. He sat up grinning and called Gale Mooneyham's cell, programmed with a special ringtone that activated when Jed called.

"Now what?" Gale said with a good-natured sigh.

"I saw your girlfriend tonight," Jed said.

"My girlfriend," Gale said. "I just came back from getting another package of diapers for a grand-child, and I'm about to start wearing them, too."

"Your diaper runs are an important exercise in field intelligence. See anything I should know about?" Jed said.

"There was one thing," Gale said.

Jed laughed.

"Larry Averitt, who ran for City-Council," Gale said.

"He won," Jed said.

"Yeah. He was at the drug counter yelling at the Chinese pharmacy tech. Averitt called him a 'stupid chink.' "

"Oh, dear," Jed said. "Any insight into what caused the outburst?"

"Averitt is a 'stupid jerk.' "

"Careful, Gale."

142

"I know. That comment just went around the world, and to the nosy hump in the beat-up Buick parked down the street."

"How long has the hump been there?" Jed said.

"Off and on for a day or two."

"Did you run the plate?" Jed said.

"No record. 'Sink or Swim' doesn't know him, either. If he sticks around, I'll ask the police to tell him to move on. Now, about that girlfriend," Gale said.

"Oh, yes. Your favorite dentist turned up here. She was on her way to St. Louis." Jed described the mishap in the parking lot.

"I missed the fun and the free food," Gale said.

"I'm all in. Have a good holiday with your family. I'll call you when I get back," Jed said.

"Tally-ho." Gale said.

Reclining again on the coarse stiff bedspread, Jed stared up. Holidays were for families, but he had to borrow one. The failed rocket test of his love life stymied further research. He rehashed the past.

His girlfriend in law school, Cynthia, was from Seattle. At the University of Michigan, they relaxed by camping on weekends. In wintertime, they bet on how long each could stay outside the tent naked. He usually won, and she called him, "Metallic Rooster." He assumed they'd stay together and pursue their careers. But cloaking her plans until the last minute, she dumped him after graduation to pursue an MBA. Cynthia moved to New York and never contacted him after she said goodbye. He didn't blame her for being ambitious, but he never trusted another woman.

He studied the granular swirls in the off-white ceiling tile. He didn't grovel, but he was deeply hurt by Cynthia's calculation. Maybe he'd been so wrapped up in himself he wasn't worth the trouble. From then on, he doubted his appeal, and he doubted the sincerity of women who found him appealing. He attributed their interest to the aura of power that surrounds a politician.

However, Libby was exceptional. She radiated warmth and interest without clinginess or desperation. Although perhaps bored by politics, she regarded voting as important. She gave away her French fries. Gale liked her. The Gale Scale was a trustworthy index. He could estimate someone's character as accurately as Jed's late father, who predicted the eventual fall of Jed's scoutmaster.

"A phony bastard," Jed's father said. Eventually, the scout leader was arrested in his basement, a profit center of narcotics distribution.

Jed sat up on the hotel bed. "Phew!" he sent forth. The first Sunday in Advent was coming, portending a month of shopping for dog toys. Undressing, he pulled back the bedspread and lay on the blanket in his shorts and T-shirt, but the synthetic fibers in the blanket irritated his skin. He slid under the covers. He would prefer a firmer mattress. The television now carried a Thanksgiving special about miracles, and he watched the entire show. The most intriguing segment was a survival story about a man stuck on a mountain ledge. Injured in a fall, he waited in sub-zero temperatures for fellow climbers to bring help. He was about to fall unconscious, but he kept his wits by counting in decimal points, "Zero-point-zero, zero-point-one, zero-point two," until he was rescued, when the count reached two-hundred-thirty-seven-point-five.

After the show, Jed donned his bathrobe and stepped outside to the walk leading to the swimming pool. Under an awning, he found a vending machine and bought a diet cola. He ventured out to the fence around the pool. The air was damp, and the wind, from the south. The cloud cover hid the stars.

Going back inside, he pulled the chair away from the desk and sat, propping his feet on the bed. The current TV show was featuring cases of anorexia among celebrities. He shut off the set and browsed through the local paper he bought at the front desk. The city of Terre Haute needed more money for sewers, he read. As a flippant high-school journalist, he would have proposed a headline using the Latin word for sewer: "Cash for *Cloacae*?"

In Indianapolis, he lived in the *Cloaca Maxima*. The people elected him prosecutor, and he would put on his toga and go downtown and stroll among the food vendors at the City Market, and leer at the village jokers, and – the cell phone rang, interrupting his triumphal procession.

"I made it," Libby said.

"*Mirabile dictu*," he said.

"I used to know what that means."

"Something like, 'Miracle told, or wonder to tell,' " he said.

"Oh, that's right," she said. 'The ship was foundering, when, *mirabile dictu*, a pterodactyl appeared, picking up the captain and dropping him gently to land.' "

"Your usage is correct," Jed said. "However, the state is not willing to stipulate the existence of the pterodactyl."

"The state is an ass."

"You mean the law is an ass. Mr. Bumble said the law is an ass," he said.

"Don't get your Dickens in a twist," she said.

"This talk of knickers and Dickens – I'm not sure I can know you," he said.

"Must our acquaintance now sink?"

"I have an image to protect," he said.

"Front or back?"

"Dr. Booth!" Jed couldn't wait to see this woman, again.

"We're going in circles. I said the state was an ass," she said.

"I'm going to ask the court for sanctions," he said.

"Then you're sanctimonious."

"I'm certain I can't know you," he said. "However, when I take you to dinner, I'll pass you off as my guardian. That would imply I'm not responsible."

"I'm sure you're not responsible," she said. "I'll be happy to explain it to anyone who asks."

"I'm sort of glad your fender was bashed in. I was more than happy to check your fender," he said.

"Heaven for-fender," Libby said.

"*Mirabile dictu*," Jed said, after a beat.

They bid each other good night. Jed darkened the room. A troublesome shaft of light from the parking lot pierced a thin gap between the curtains, and he adjusted the drapes and rolled into bed. At peace, he murmured, "Two-hundred-thirty-seven-point-five." He fell into the sleep of a thousand decimals.

CHAPTER 35
History – July 1921

The Fourth of July was at hand, and Mary's mother wanted the family to spend the day in Greenfield, her hometown. She was making a picnic basket for them to enjoy at a band concert on the courthouse square. Early in the evening, Mr. Hobson would drive them to a relative's farm, where they'd set off firecrackers and eat cherry pie and homemade ice cream.

That evening, Mary's uncles and cousins were blasting the farmland with tiny explosions, and Mary was enjoying it, but needed to visit the bathroom. Entering the house through the back door at the kitchen, she stopped, hearing her name invoked by voices in the dining room.

Deep in conversation, her mother and her great-aunt were having coffee at the dining room table.

"Mary seems to have done very well over the years," Aunt Myrtle said. "After where she came from, I confess I had my worries."

After where she came from? Mary froze.

"That's why we had her examined by the doctor before we brought her home. But he said she was perfectly normal," Mrs. Hobson said.

Compared with what? Mary wondered.

"But we watched her very closely for the first few months – to look for any sign she might have her mother's falling sickness," Mrs. Hobson said.

My mother's sickness? Mary clutched her chest at those words. She wanted to scream, "You're my mother. You don't have falling sickness."

Aunt Myrtle said, "I made your husband's brother swear he'd never tell his children their cousin was adopted. And he's kept his word."

Mary's bladder was ready to burst. She couldn't face them, so she ran out into the darkness. She missed overhearing her mother say, "I knew when I looked into those beautiful blue eyes, I had a perfect baby – and I was the luckiest mother in the world. And I still feel that way.

"I've kept a beautiful sachet – a new-mother's gift. My cousin gave it to me when we came home with Mary. I have it wrapped up in my dresser, and every so often, I take it out and smell it.

"The scent is faint, but it's there. It reminds me of how it felt to hold my baby."

The firecrackers were even louder than before. Hiding behind a bush, Mary stepped out of her underwear and squatted. The urine stream flowed forever, and she fretted. The earth was soggy when she finished.

Dressed again, she wanted to run as fast and as far as she could. She bolted down the gravel drive to the dusty county road and ran to the left along a cornfield. Winded, she ducked into a corn row and crouched. Her sobs broke the breezeless air, punctured by the firecrackers.

She wept for about fifteen minutes, until she heard a rustling sound. She hopped up, looking, holding her breath, until a raccoon emerged from between corn stalks as he went to cross the road.

She exhaled. Gazing at the twinkling stars, she wanted to be one.

The firecracker explosions stopped, warning she needed to rejoin the others.

The night was still. She was feverish. Of late she'd been warm and queasy a lot. She didn't know where the fever came from, and the upset stomach.

Returning to the farmhouse, she ran to use the water pump out back. She splashed a few handfuls of water on her face and dried it with the hem of her dress. She took a slow, deep breath. Chattering, dark figures moved closer, and the family would be upon her in a minute.

And they're not even my family, she thought, resolving to make a secret visit to the doctor's office to find out the truth.

CHAPTER 36
Present Day – November

In the spring, Kerry and Tony were to bring home their new daughter, Evelyn Carter Horatio, to be known as Evvie.

"We couldn't agree on whose last name to give her," Tony said. "The minister at our commitment ceremony was Hal Carter, so that's how we got the middle name. And we tried combo last names, but they didn't work – Dreisenwitt, Witten-Dreisen – too Hanoverian."

"You could always name her after your lawyer," Libby said.

"His name is Finkel." Kerry said. "So far, he's been perfect. But the name – not so much. 'Evelyn Finkel' sounds like the dean of a girls' college."

"We'll have a party," Libby said. "Give me a list of people you want to invite. I have a good friend, Denise, who wants to meet you. She'll help with the party. But where did you get the name 'Horatio'?"

"A Purdue alum by the name of Horatio Chang introduced me to Tony," Kerry said.

Finishing pie, the friends were in Libby's dining room after supper on Saturday night. She'd driven back from St. Louis that morning. Using Thanksgiving scraps the men brought, she made grilled turkey sandwiches with bacon and avocado. Leftover stuffing was heaped on their plates. With white wine, the trio toasted the new baby. They were having after-dinner coffee.

"I got us fifty-yard-line tickets for the Bears-Packers game," Tony said.

"You didn't," Kerry said. "You must be somebody's kept man."

"One of our mutual friends at Purdue sold them to me. Remember Craig Neuss? He's a stockbroker in Chicago. He's going to Hawaii on game day. He sent out thirty-five e-mails advertising the tickets, and I was the first to answer."

"I didn't get the e-mail," Kerry said. "Of course, I need to check my calendar to make sure I won't be backpacking in Europe."

Tony snorted. Libby topped off their coffee.

"Should we leave her a tip?" Kerry said.

"She'll just spend it," Tony said.

The three talked about their plans for Christmas.

"My folks finally accepted us as a couple, after all these years, so we're having our first Christmas with them," Kerry said. "My sister Kathleen isn't so accommodating, but she'll be there."

"How many siblings do you have?" Libby said.

"Two. Kathleen is younger," Kerry said. "My other sister, Rhonda, is five years ahead of me."

"Kathleen will come around eventually. She's mad, because you found someone – and she hasn't." Tony said.

"She's very attractive and vivacious, but she lives in Logansport," Kerry said. "I don't think she's going to meet anyone there. Maybe she should move to Chicago."

"Maybe you should give her the Bears tickets," Libby said.

"No!" the men said in unison. They all laughed.

Tony stood, stacking the dessert plates and utensils. "I'll take these to the dishwasher," he said.

Hugging her goodbye, Kerry said he and Tony needed to go home to Woodruff Place near downtown, because an old buddy would stop in. Leaving, the men walked through a matrix of evening mist and the smell of pizzas a deliveryman carried down the sidewalk.

The weekend of rich food would exact a payment unless Libby started to move. She thought twice about walking too far at night. She could walk at the mall, probably open late for the seasonal kick-off. On the way to Cumberland Century Market, the car hit chuckholes on Tenth Street. Libby made malicious comments about the city administration, and immediately, her cell phone rang, as if a censor listened. The phone was mounted on the dashboard, in compliance with the ban against holding the phone while driving.

"Hello?" she said, bewildered.

"Libby – Jed."

"Oh, hi," she said.

"Everything all right?" he said.

"Why wouldn't it be?"

"That's the sort of answer I expect from someone being held hostage," he said.

"The night's not over," she said. "But at present, I'm at liberty on Tenth Street."

"You're back. Good! No more mishaps with the vehicle?"

"Not unless you count the chuckholes. Do you know who's in charge of chuckhole-ery?"

Jed cackled. "I'm sure I've been a called a 'real chuckhole,' from time to time. You can try a number for city government in the phone book. It's listed under 'feudal estate.' "

"Thank you, Worship."

Jed smiled to himself. "Would it be predatory of me to ask where you're going, Little Red Riding Molar?"

"To the mall. I need to walk off supper. A couple of guys came over, and we had a huge meal."

Jed paused. "A couple of guys."

Libby smiled, wiggling her eyebrows in the rearview mirror. "Yes, very nice guys."

"Did you talk football?" he said.

"As a matter of fact, we did."

"So," Jed said, pausing, "Are they fellow dentists?"

"No. One is a nuclear med tech, and the other sells surgical supplies."

"Any ho-hum chats about root canals?" he said.

"I ho-hum myself all the way to the bank," she said.

"Independent lass, and one who will undoubtedly bristle, if I ask whether she's going out with one or both of the guys?"

"Both? What do you take me for?" she said.

"So far, you've shown yourself to be a model of efficiency. It would make sense for you to have two men, in case the one gets boring."

"And when we go out, who will be coming with *you*?" she said.

"My ventriloquist's dummy, Chuck Hole, but I should warn you, he likes to titillate."

"I imagine so," she said. "Hold on, I'm getting to the turn-off now, and I need to watch." She swung the car into the mall lot and found a space close to the building. "OK, I'm back."

"Enjoy the walk," he said. "I'm ordering a pair of tickets for the symphony's holiday extravaganza. I thought we'd have dinner and see the show. I'll call you when I find out about the seats, OK?"

"Sounds like fun," she said. "As long as Chuck Hole turns off his phone in the theater."

CHAPTER 37
Present Day – December

On the first Monday of the month, Frenchie told Libby, "I've got some things to share with you. Can we have a drink after work tonight?"

"Sure. The usual place?"

"That'll be fine," Frenchie said. The "usual" was King's Kosher, a grill pub and catering service. Frenchie asked for a booth in the back corner, and she and Libby ordered martinis and breaded zucchinis and mushrooms. It occurred to Libby that Frenchie was fortifying herself.

"I'll be sixty-eight soon enough," Frenchie said. "I've thought a lot about the Peace Corps lately."

Libby sipped her drink as if it were lighter fluid.

"Paul isn't well." Frenchie said. She ate the olive from her martini. "I don't think he'll be able to travel again, so I'm going by myself."

Libby was trying to put things together. "When do you want to join the Peace Corps?"

"I think I'll be ready in a year. I'm going to need a while to sort things out."

Libby was silent. She didn't want to appear rude by asking what Paul was going to do while Frenchie was gone. Frenchie held her glass close to her chin and stared at the ice cubes. Libby waited.

"Paul isn't well," Frenchie said, again. "It's the kind of thing that has an unknown timetable." She swallowed some of the drink.

Timetable, Libby thought. She decided to take a chance. "Does he need surgery?"

"No. They said it wouldn't do any good." Frenchie said. "It's more about making him comfortable."

Libby chewed a mushroom and swallowed. "Frenchie, what are you trying to tell me?"

"Paul is dying," Frenchie said, looking down.

"I'm very, very sorry," Libby said, leaning forward.

Frenchie rubbed her forehead. She looked embarrassed, like someone who'd admitted her car had been repossessed.

"How much time off do you need?" Libby said.

"Oh, it's permanent. When I leave, it'll be for good."

Pausing first, Libby said, "I guess what I really need to know is, when?"

"Two weeks."

Libby sucked in her breath. Whatever Paul had was progressing rapidly. She ate a zucchini morsel, a sorry sponge on her tongue.

"Pancreatic cancer." Frenchie said. "They're giving him some chemo to stretch out his life, but it won't be much of a life. He'll have to quit smoking. That'll be horrible enough." She was far away in the past. "I told him to stop smoking."

Libby's eyes watered. She made a stage business of sipping the martini. She knew Frenchie wanted friendship, not pity. Just then, a Kosher waiter stepped toward the table. Gesturing to hold him off, Libby smiled. "Could you come back in about ten minutes, please?" she said. The cheerful waiter pivoted on tiptoe and headed back to the bar.

Frenchie's eyes followed the waiter. "I'm OK," she said.

"I'm not," Libby said. "Have you told David and Ellie?"

"I'm stopping by their house, later. The rabbi will be there."

"Is Paul going with you?" Libby said.

"No," Frenchie said. "We put a hospital bed in the living room. Makes it easier for me to help him. He asked me to tell the Mendelsons. He said David will rush over, anyway."

Indeed, Libby thought. She didn't know Paul well, but David certainly did. In fact, she hadn't seen Paul since last Christmas, when she threw a holiday dinner for the staff at a restaurant. She hadn't gotten around to planning this year's shindig, likely to be more subdued than the last.

Frenchie spoke up. "I think you should ask your CPA to help you outsource the bookkeeping. You don't need a full-charge bookkeeper right now. Instead, I think you'd benefit by having another dental assistant."

"You're way ahead of me," Libby said.

"I don't know how you feel about Claris, but if you like her, now would be the time to ask her to stay," Frenchie said. "Drew won't be back until March, remember? After that, you'll need an assistant when she's taking her baby to the doctor and doing all the things mothers do. Having two assistants would give you more flexibility."

Drew had asked for additional leave. Libby wanted her to come back for sure, but Libby also liked Claris and found her competent.

"We should settle with Claris immediately, because if she doesn't want to stay, we'll need to run down someone else," Libby said. "I'd prefer she take the job."

"I have a feeling she will," Frenchie said. "She's been talking about a private school she wants her kids to attend. But – she must stay on the agency's payroll for at least four months, so you don't have to pay a penalty for hiring her direct."

Libby sipped her drink. Another martini would be nice, but she had to drive.

"OK. So we're outsourcing the bookkeeping. I'll ask the CPA to recommend a vendor, and you and the vendor can meet.

"But how does all this tie in with Keisha's role as the billing clerk?" Libby said.

"It involves a safe and practical method of data transfer," Frenchie said. "I extract data from Keisha's work, when I'm doing the books. The vendor would be doing the same thing.

"I would discourage you from using an outside billing firm at this time. Part of what Keisha does is financial counseling, and she's very good at contacting accounts that are at ninety days. She keeps a good percentage out of collections.

"You don't need an outsourced clerk in the Pacific Rim trying to coax money out of a working mother in Indianapolis," Frenchie said, with a gleam in her eye.

Libby gave her a sad smile. She was going to miss seeing Frenchie every day. "What about job titles? You've been the office manager. What about

Keisha? Does she have ambitions to do more, or something different?" Libby said.

"I don't know," Frenchie said. "You should ask her what she wants."

They said nothing for a few moments.

"I'm sorry to do this to you at Christmas," Frenchie said.

"You have nothing to apologize for," Libby said, and she finished the martini. The Kosher waiters sang "Happy Birthday" to a middle-aged man surrounded by co-workers. As she listened, Libby decided the CPA should configure the best way to help Frenchie retire with extra compensation. Libby wanted to declare a bonus, but bonuses were taxed at a higher rate. The financial oracle would be consulted.

Frenchie looked at her watch. "I should be going. I don't want to make the rabbi wait." Libby reached over and held out her hand. Clasping it, Frenchie released it after a few moments.

"I'll sit here for a while," Libby said. "Maybe they'll sing again."

"OK," Frenchie said. After she left, Libby ordered coffee. Clearing her throat, she chose Claris' number from her phone list. Libby disapproved of making calls in a restaurant, but she felt threatened, as if some dentist could make Claris a better offer at that moment.

Claris answered, and Libby gave only a few details to explain Frenchie's retirement. Optimistic about the offer, Claris said she wanted a day to think about the salary she'd expect. Libby said they had plenty of time, and to let Frenchie announce her retirement when she was ready.

Libby finished her coffee. Mulling over the challenges of the coming year, she resolved to cut back on restaurant food. Tonight, she'd step up her physical training with another workout.

She'd forgotten to turn off the phone. Jed called, disrupting her plans.

"Hi," he said. "I'm calling the symphony box office back in a minute. They have two seats in dress circle for the eight-o'clock show on Friday. I thought we'd have dinner at six-thirty at Coleridge, around the corner from the hall. Is that too soon after work?"

Libby laughed to herself. She still had at least one more restaurant meal coming.

"I live in Irvington. You'll have to pick me up by six," she said.

"Can you do it?" he said.

"Think so," she said.

"Good! Maybe after the show, we can have a glass of wine?"

"I'll bring ID," she said.

"A good thing, considering you'll be out with a Cub Scout," he said.

She pictured Jed as a boy, leading a pack of friends behind bushes concealing a tiny shack. "By chance, did you have a clubhouse with a sign that said, 'No Girls'?" she said.

"Girls were always welcome. Adults were the problem. They kept interrupting the physical exams," he said.

"Did you harvest any body parts?"

"My specimens lived. They are fiercely loyal to this day," he said.

"I don't doubt it," Libby said, letting her mind wander to Frenchie's predicament.

"Everything all right?" Jed said, after a short silence.

"No. I just got some bad news – "

"Not about your family!"

"No. An illness in another family is forcing one of my people into retirement." She sighed. "It's just been one thing after another. First, the robbery, now this."

"Robbery?" he said.

"I guess we never talked about it." She rehashed the events.

"I'm going to assign Mooneyham to follow you around," Jed intoned, as if tucking a child into bed.

"Oh, I can take care of myself."

"As you have demonstrated," he said. "I'm getting a beep. It's probably the office. Could you hold for a minute?"

"Sure." The waiter came by, and she turned down more coffee. When Jed returned, she gave directions to her house.

"A pilgrimage I anticipate with great pleasure," he said.

156

CHAPTER 38
Present Day – December

Jed answered the summons that interrupted his call to Libby. Armistead Hauser wanted him to stop by to meet his niece, Sheri Neulander, who just passed the bar exam and was joining the prosecutor's office. Giving her a job was one of the favors Jed was doing to thank his mentor. Army lived on North Illinois Street about five miles from downtown in a two-story brick home with a gated drive. Tall maples and oaks filled the front yard like a small forest.

Jed pressed the intercom button at the gate. Army's voice crackled, "Who goes there?"

Jed answered like an amateur actor delivering his lines in a monotone, "Everyman, thou art mad."

"It's my Dad?" Army shouted.

"Open the damn gate, Army."

Once inside, Jean, Army's wife of forty years, took Jed's coat and asked if he wanted brownies. Hugging her, he declined, and she told him to go to the family room. He found Army showing his niece photos on the fireplace mantle.

Sheri Neulander was a trim five-foot-six, with auburn hair styled under at the shoulder. She wore a winter white ensemble – a cashmere turtleneck over pants, and low-heeled dress boots to match. A delicate gold necklace with a diamond chip complimented the sweater. Her handshake was firm, and her expression, serious. Speaking in well-modulated tones, she avoided the use of distracting or awkward facial expressions and gestures. Jed bet she'd gone to finishing school. Such poise would serve her well, but he wanted to see the instincts needed to win criminal prosecutions.

Always skilled at low-key hospitality, Army offered a shot of smooth whiskey, and Jed accepted. Sherry was nursing a glass of tonic water, and Army, a murky liqueur. They sat in leather club chairs upholstered in a shade of burnt orange. The stone fireplace, dark wood paneling, and shuttered windows suggested a lodge. After a few visits, Jed commented that the manly chamber differed from the rest of the house, full of light and airy spaces in Country French décor, and Jean said, "I control everything except the family room."

Sheri placed her drink on a coaster on the table at her right and crossed her legs at the ankles. In white against the burnt-orange chair, she was like the center of a flame. Jed settled back in his chair and tasted the whiskey. He let the sensation in his throat calm down.

"Sheri, tell me about yourself," he said.

"Of course, I'm delighted to have passed the bar exam, "she said. "I was a social worker for the state of Michigan, and I developed an interest in the law after working with child-abuse victims.

"I found that even though classes and therapy can help offenders to 'unlearn' abusive behavior, some people are evil. They just need to be locked up."

One of Jed's eyebrows arched. Some people are evil. Maybe the white outfit was her uniform in the contest between the forces of light and darkness. He swallowed the rest of the whiskey. Army held up two fingers as a question, and Jed nodded. Army refilled the shot glass.

Sheri continued. "I got very angry after one case blew up. We had serious concerns about the boyfriend of a mother. She was leaving her two-year-old son in the boyfriend's care while she was at work.

"The case came to us after police found the child in the middle of a busy street. He was skipping down the center line.

"We recommended foster care, but the mother promised the judge that from then on, her own mother would baby-sit. The judge allowed the boy to remain in the home."

Sheri recited the facts as if summarizing the performance of an investment fund. "We found out much too late the boyfriend was a heavy drinker. He had a history of getting drunk and coming over to beat up the victim's mother. She never called the police.

"One night after the first investigation, he came over drunk and tripped on a toy in the living room. He threw the child against the wall several times. The boy's brain swelled, and he died."

Sheri let out a lady-like little sigh. "Right then, I wanted justice for that child, and I didn't want to be a social worker, anymore. When I found out the mother had covered up the boyfriend's history of violence, I wanted to make an example of her.

"If she liked having the daylights beaten out of her, that was her problem, but she put the child in jeopardy." Again, these sentiments were delivered coolly, like a recitation of a European travel itinerary.

"Humph," Army said, echoing his niece's sentiment.

"What was the disposition of the case?" Jed said.

"The boyfriend entered a plea of guilty to manslaughter, and he was sent up. The mother also plea-bargained and did eighteen months. Then, she was dismembered," Sheri said.

"I beg your pardon?" Jed said.

"She was dismembered," Sheri said. "When she got out, she took up with another boyfriend, who was the jealous type. He thought she was looking around, and she wound up in garbage bags at the county landfill.

"They found her head and one arm," Sheri permitted her hands to make a sylphlike wave of indifference.

Jed never blinked, but he straightened his posture at Sheri's dismissive gesture. She took another sip of tonic water and smiled.

Jean popped into the doorway. "Need anything from the kitchen?" she said.

"I think I just changed my mind about the brownies," Jed said. Jean raised her arms in triumph.

CHAPTER 39
Present Day – December

In the dark, Jed and Gale stood at the corner of Market and Alabama outside the City-County Building. Just out from a meeting with the Democratic members of the City-County Council, they'd run into former Congressman Joe Hobbs, who began his career as an activist for the NAACP. Hobbs said he'd been up to see the mayor on a social call. Jed wanted to hear Hobbs' views on strengthening state gun-control laws.

Jed voiced support for more restrictions on gun sales, while knowing that many elected officials, including the governor, were tight with the gun lobby, and that they considered Hobbs a relic.

"We could try for a state law on gun sales, but 'activism' and 'Indiana' are not synonymous," Hobbs said. "The gun lobby knows how to get the vote out."

"Apathy is a problem. The check-out lady at the grocery told me she doesn't register to vote, because she's afraid she'll get jury duty," Jed said. "I should have stuck to two topics, the weather, and if the potato salad from the deli was good."

Gale had come along, too. He was back on the job as an investigator for the prosecutor's office. Once Jed took office, his new associate counsel, Jim Phillipi, would be going to political meetings, which Fabiola de Torre currently handled. Fabiola was on vacation, so Gale accompanied Jed this time to gather intelligence.

As the two men stood on the corner after Hobbs departed, Gale turned up his coat collar against the surging wind.

"I went to his last concert," Gale said, jerking his thumb toward the new buildings east of Alabama Street.

"Whose?" Jed said, pretending not to know.

"Elvis, you child – nineteen-seventy-seven – in the old Market Square Arena." He pointed to where the arena had once been. "I think our seats were in the section right there, above where that Buick SUV just went by." He returned his gaze to Jed. "Oh, hell, the plates on that SUV were expired.

"Anyway, the timing was creepy," Gale said. "At the end of the show, Elvis introduced everybody in his life – like he knew he was about to check out." Pulling his collar even closer, Gale stared ahead, as he envisioned the decades of his own life. He was vulnerable, Jed thought, deciding not to tease him.

"Are you up for a beer?" Jed asked.

"That's too far to walk," the older man said.

"Around the corner?" Jed said.

"In the frisson of life, we can't know what's around the corner," Gale said, like he was delivering a fireside chat.

"Free-SAWN? Free-SAWN? Did you just pull that out of your ass?" Jed said.

"More than likely," Gale said.

"And they said you were high-class," Jed said.

"That was just a lie," Gale said. The wind picked up. "I'm going home to my wife. I'd like a piece of pie and a cup of coffee waiting on the TV tray next to my recliner. At some point, I'll speak to my wife."

Jed smiled. He knew Gale would read the paper aloud and editorialize. His wife, Lee Ann, would laugh, and eventually, they'd watch a movie channel until bedtime. One night the couple viewed a double feature, the first of which had Bonita Granville as Nancy Drew, and the second, Chester Morris as Boston Blackie. The next morning, Gale held several court bailiffs under his spell as he retold the stories. During the campaign, Gale missed many such evenings, and he was glad to resume the routine. Gale had given up more than Nancy Drew, Jed realized.

Saying good night, he squeezed Gale's shoulder. "Enjoy your evening, Worthy Mooneyham."

"Thanks," Gale said, like a tired bum accepting money from a stranger.

161

CHAPTER 40
Present Day – December

The big date night arrived, and the tap-dancing Santas were warming up at the symphony hall. Libby selected her clothes that morning and lined up cosmetics, jewelry, and hairpins on the dresser. Her makeover had to be done quickly to accommodate Jed's timetable, threatened throughout the day with otherwise tolerable interruptions. At the office during the last appointment, the patient's mother asked questions, and Marquita wanted to know about a new brand of sealant. Libby stopped her with, "Tomorrow, please, and many thanks."

It was a polite deferral, but one that alerted Marquita. "Ah!" she said, tiptoeing in her idiosyncratic way. If she'd been a cat, she would have had black legs and white paws.

Libby laughed as she fled the building. Marquita must have smelled *El Super Ratón.* Libby had another surprise for Marquita. At the holiday gift exchange, she would receive a Betty Boop lava light.

Traffic slowed as Libby was a mile from home. She tensed, wondering if she should have postponed the dinner until Saturday. Making it home by five-thirty, she allowed herself three minutes in the shower.

After pinning up her hair and applying make-up, she zipped herself into a slinky indigo velvet dress that fell just above the knee. The straight, full-length sleeves were mesh and showed off her arms. The tiniest bit of cleavage was expressed at the base of the V-neck. She put on a sliver-thin necklace with a tiny diamond-chip pendant. She sprayed the air in front of her with Chanel and stepped through the mist.

It was five minutes until six. She exchanged her house slippers for indigo stiletto pumps and transferred her comb, wallet, and keys to a matching clutch purse. Finally, she put on the lipstick, which trended toward pink rather than red. She admired the blotted imprint of her lips on facial tissue, a detail she hadn't fussed over in a long time. Amid the traces of Chanel, she felt like a model pictured on the scented insert in a magazine.

Her dress coat was double-breasted wool in camel. Until now, she'd never thought of owning a fur coat, or more humanely, one of fake fur, but on this occasion, a shimmering silver fur would have completed the ensemble.

Coat in hand, she stopped in the middle of the living room. She was losing her mind. Dentists don't daydream about fur coats – do they? The doorbell rang. Her heart pounded. A voice whispered from somewhere in the house, "Let him help you put on your coat."

In confusion, she looked around, resting her gaze on the painting over the gas fireplace. The auction in the tableau was in progress, as always. She could hear the auctioneer's non-stop chant, "Five-thousand-dollar bid on the coat, now six, now six, will ya gimme six? Six-thousand-dollar bid, now seven, now seven, will ya gimme seven? Seven-thousand-dollar bid, now eight, now eight, will ya gimme eight?" The doorbell rang again.

Libby shook herself. The auctioneer in the painting was holding a dining room chair, not a coat. She had lost her mind. She rushed to the door and flung it open.

"Sold!" she said. Jed laughed.

"Come in!" Libby said. The grandfather clock in the corner began its hourly chime.

Jed was still laughing. "You must be hungry," he said.

"Oh, yes," Libby said. He held the coat while she wrapped herself in it. "I'm ready," she said, smiling.

"And lovely," Jed said.

"Thank you," she said. "I'll just lock up, and we'll be on our way," she said.

"I guess Washington Street is the quickest route, because it's the only one that goes under the train tracks," Jed said, as he drove them downtown in his Nissan.

"Yes. I've gotten stuck at the tracks on Michigan a few times," Libby said. The businesses on Irvington's main drag flashed by, and judging from the view through the storefronts, the restaurants were doing brisk Friday-night service. Lights burned in the sanctuary at the Catholic parish, and she wondered what was going on. When they got to Emerson Avenue, a caravan of high-school basketball fans crossed in front of the car.

Leaving Irvington, the ride continued west on Washington toward Sherman Drive, the entrance to the "Swamp," as the police called it. This stretch from Sherman to College Avenue was typically referred to as the Near-Eastside, home to middle- and lower-income citizens, hookers, drug dealers, and addicts of all types – plus the preservationists who moved in around the time the city hosted the Super Bowl. At the corner of LaSalle Street, a T-shirted man without a coat swayed in a drunken stupor as a bus driver refused him a ride. On side avenues and parallel thoroughfares like Michigan and New York streets, the process of gentrification stood out, with sizeable homes undergoing renovation. Yet setbacks were predictable, like arson fires and killings.

The car reached the intersection with Rural Street, and if one were seeking the frisson Gale talked about, this block offered a midway of perils. But hope of salvation flourished in the Rural neighborhood, as shelters dispensed job training, food, clothing, medicine, and good tidings, even when someone drove into the glass storefront of a mission. In fact, the Holy Spirit blew life into the stale air of the neighborhood, and one still could hike from downtown to Irvington and pass safely through this gate.

Used-car lots lined both sides of Washington. Libby wondered about the reliability of the vehicles – cubes of red, gold, blue, and white – priced at $2995. She didn't know that the mechanics at Burt's Bonus-Buy were among the best that Kentucky exported, as a tow-truck driver told Gale, when he was stranded with a dead alternator.

"If you want, I can take you over here to some hillbillies," the truck driver said. "Their office isn't too clean – but they'll do a real good job for you." Gale let them do the repairs, and after that, he stopped by every so often to say hello.

Defunct factories that graced the tour with broken windows and smudged exteriors were being rehabbed or torn down, replaced by gleaming commercial entities or apartment complexes. Green space could be found at a park with a swimming pool next to a firehouse. Closer to downtown, aggressive marketers found their headquarters in old brick buildings.

Turning right on College Avenue and then left on Market Street, Jed drove west to Pennsylvania Street to a parking garage. Dining would be at Coleridge, on the third floor of a building down the block. They exited the garage and strolled down Penn past a slumbering wino, who'd propped himself against the garage. He had a sign that said, "Help. I need help." An old coffee cup held financial donations. He sat next to a rolled-up sleeping bag, a bulky laundry sack, and an aluminum pail. Libby was grateful it was empty.

Jed dropped a ten-dollar bill into the coffee can. He shook his head as they walked. "He probably worked on my campaign," he said, looping his right arm around Libby's left as they approached their destination. In the elevator going up to the restaurant, he detected the scent of her perfume, and he looked sideways and smiled.

They stepped into the foyer of Coleridge. The owner was there, talking to the headwaiter. "Jed!" the owner said. "Nice to see you again. I'll take you to your table." The *maître d* gave Jed a friendly nod.

The campaign probably held a fundraiser, here, too, Libby thought, remembering the night at Big Sal's. Were fundraisers ever held at Burger Mope?

***

They arrived at the table, and Jed shook hands with the owner, who placed the menus and seated Libby. She thanked him, and Jed sat down.

The restaurant's décor was opulent. The stiff tablecloths and napkins were crimson. Each table had a polished-brass Victorian oil lamp with a five-inch base, and a frosted glass shade etched with a floral design. Overhead lights were dimmed, and reflections of lamplight flickered on the ceiling's dark wooden panels and crossbeams. Below, laurels stitched in gold decorated the cream-colored carpet, thickly padded to silence footsteps. Set against crimson walls under accent lighting, elements of chinoiserie were present, including a mural of a village next to a creek. The depiction, rendered in light blues, yellowish greens, and faded reds, summoned a fantasy world of pavilions suspended over water by bridge supports. Hand-carved wall sconces shaped like jack-in-the-pulpits cradled bulbs of nominal wattage.

Unlike the tableau at Wally's, there were no clocks – a good omen, Libby thought.

A faint accompaniment of chamber music was heard over the sound system. The tables were far enough apart to accommodate discreet conversation. After assessing the patrons – sleekly tailored and full of sang-froid – Libby thought that discretion was advised. They were comfortable with taking and using power, and they all had something on each other. A shadow must have crossed her face, and Jed raised his eyebrows. Catching his look, Libby smiled to allay any disappointment.

"You've obviously been here before," she said. "Why don't you order for both of us? My only desire is, no seafood," she said.

"Dr. Booth, I shall be only too glad to arrange your dinner." He smiled. "Can I have your fries?"

Of course, no fries were on the menu. "By all means," she said.

The waiter appeared, promising bread as he poured wine.

"Thank you," Jed said. They sipped their wine, and Libby, who hadn't eaten since lunch, began to feel warm.

"This is intriguing," she said.

"The wine, the company, or the experience?" he said.

"All of it. The sun never sets on the empire of the people here tonight," she said.

"That's probably true. That guy sleeping against the garage will never be here." After a moment, Jed said, "Does this place turn you off?"

"Oh, heavens no. I keep waiting for King Bertie to walk in."

Jed smiled. "You watch too much public television."

Libby, warmer than ever, cast Jed a radiant, appreciative look.

"Are you on public TV very often?" she said.

"No, but who is, between all those shows about antiques?"

"Do antiques turn you off?" she said.

"Only when they hold public office."

Returning with bread, the waiter asked if they were ready to order. "We'll have the Chateaubriand with portobello mushrooms and madeira wine jus," Jed said.

"Of course," the waiter said. "I always enjoy lighting the brandy for the flambé at the table. After that, we let it simmer in the wine sauce for about a minute. Some people say that's the longest sixty seconds of their lives."

166

The waiter returned with salads of romaine and iceberg lettuce and cherry tomatoes, topped with artistically carved, colorful raw vegetables. He also produced a plate with two servings of smoked Scottish salmon on Russian pumpernickel.

Libby tasted the salmon. "That's wonderful," she said.

"I thought you didn't like seafood," Jed said.

"I do. I just eat very small quantities, because of the pollution. But let's not spoil our fun. It's terribly glamorous," she said.

Yes, you are, Jed thought, momentarily losing his nerve.

Libby picked up her wine glass. "*Salud*," she said.

"*Salud*," Jed said, lifting his, also.

Jed's words about antiques holding public office came back to her, and in a confidential tone, she asked him about the campaign.

"You know, I was listening to a political commentator – Dr. Charter Human-Sacrifice, or something like that – "

"Charter Hemingway," Jed said.

"Yes. He seemed to think that your predecessor left you with a lot to overcome. Not to suggest that it was true, but how did you get around whatever happened during Hauser's tenure?"

"Well, I almost didn't," Jed said, confidentially as well. "Our polling data showed that my affiliation with Army was my highest negative. And that's a shame, because he did a fine job with limited funds, and a police department that lost a good many experienced investigators to retirement.

"The turnover in police ranks caused some potentially good cases to be botched," he said.

"That one story about the woman who supposedly shot her kids – the Karnow people said you misled a judge. Did it harm your campaign?" Libby said.

"The campaign, no, but at the time, I thought I'd die," Jed said.

He shook his head. "The case fell apart, because the chain of custody was broken for the key piece of evidence, a Cyclops mask."

"What is the chain of custody?"

"That's the paper trail showing the seizure and disposition of evidence. Every transaction involving the evidence has to be documented, and the fewer transfers, the better. We must be able to prove that an unauthorized person didn't handle it.

167

"Otherwise, we can be accused of tampering with evidence. At the very least, the defense could move to have the evidence declared inadmissible," Jed said, continuing.

"A bloody knife entered as evidence has to be the same bloody knife found at the crime scene, and there can be no chance that the knife was substituted or tampered with."

"So what happened to the Cyclops?" Libby said.

"In Homer's Odyssey, he was blinded. But in this case, the Cyclops went to Kokomo."

"I know I shouldn't laugh," she said, laughing.

"It's OK," he said. "What happened was this: The mother of the three victims had taken her boys to spend the night at her ex-husband's house. He and his new wife and her daughter from a previous marriage were living in a modest home on the southwest side, where the people breathe a very modest amount of clean air.

"The house had only two bedrooms and a bath upstairs, so when the boys stayed over, they slept on the living room floor. The shooting occurred around three a.m. in the living room.

"The mother sent them over to the ex-husband's, because she'd gotten a prescription for sleeping pills. She complained for weeks before the shooting that she couldn't sleep.

"Then, when she got the pills, she told her ex-husband she was afraid something would happen to the kids while she was conked out.

"So, he agreed to keep them while she got a good night's rest. The oldest child said he woke up when he heard someone walking around, and then he heard a thud, like someone throwing a bean bag. And then, one of his brothers moaned.

"Next, the witness said he saw someone wearing a mask with one eye in the middle and a horn sticking out of the top. Like a Cyclops. The masked figure pointed at him, and then he heard a popping sound and was in a lot of pain. He didn't remember much after that."

"So the Cyclops had a silencer," Libby said. "But how would she have gotten into the house?"

"We think she made a copy of the house key when the oldest boy was taking care of the pets, while his dad's new family was out of town."

"So what happened to the case?" Libby said.

"Unfortunately, when the mask was turned over to police, it was already inadmissible. But they used it as the reason to obtain a warrant to search for more evidence. The items seized during the search implicated the mother, but the evidence was thrown out," Jed said, shaking his head with regret.

"Of course, when the charges were dropped, the public was curious for about five seconds, but during the campaign, the issue was about whether we tried to dupe the judge," he said.

"Karnow didn't make a fuss about the charges being dropped, because it would have implied the woman was guilty. She could have sued him. Instead, he tried to make me look unethical, by raising the issue of how we obtained the search warrant.

"But Karnow miscalculated. Most people don't know enough about the rules of evidence for the allegation to matter. It would only matter to other lawyers," Jed said, stopping to enjoy a little more salad.

Libby finished her portion of salmon. "I guess I'm with the majority in the dark. I don't understand why things got all mixed up in the first place," she said.

Jed nodded. "The mother's sister was the one who found the Cyclops mask in the attic of the suspect's house. She was up there collecting stuff for a rummage sale and found it by accident.

"But instead of calling the police right away, she removed the mask from the house and gave it to police later. A detective briefed one of our trial assistants on the evidence collection.

"Our assistant was unscrupulous, and he withheld from me that the evidence was tainted. The case was high-profile, and there was a lot of pressure on us. He thought he was doing us a favor.

"So based upon the presence of the mask in the house, I requested a search warrant so police could go through the home, and eventually, the gun was found."

Jed stopped long enough to sip his wine. Enthralled with the narrative, even more compelling because of Jed's unblinking gaze, Libby couldn't remember eating the salad.

Jed continued. "When the suspect's lawyer talked with her sister, she told him she took the Cyclops to her place in Kokomo before she called the police."

169

Jed shook his head. "Gale knew the defense lawyer and bumped into him at the county building. The lawyer asked Gale if he'd heard much about the detective who made the arrest.

"The lawyer said the officer wouldn't know chain of custody if it were wrapped around a certain body part.

"Gale told me what really happened, and I was in disbelief – trying to figure out what to do next. The gun was inadmissible, because it was found with a search warrant based on tainted information."

"Why?" Libby said.

"Because the mask was obtained improperly, and therefore, so was the evidence leading us to the gun. Fruit of the poison tree."

"The voters would never figure it out," Libby said.

"I agree," Jed said, sipping the wine. "And it happened so long ago. The judge quashed everything, and there went the case."

"What did Mr. Hauser say?" she said.

"Oh, pretty lady, you don't want to hear that. Let's just say someone on his staff was fired. And please believe I don't want to insinuate that Indy cops aren't good at what they do.

"This was just one of those times when an inexperienced officer and an unethical trial assistant were collaborating. It was – underscore – horrible," Jed said.

"It's my turn to talk," she said, "So you can finish your salad. One of my staff is leaving for good, and I've shifted duties around. I wound up with an extra dental assistant. I guess if I don't find ways to increase business now, I won't do it later."

Jed took a bite, studying her. "You don't look happy about it," he said after swallowing. "Are you sure you want to?"

"Oh, yes. I'll still have one Saturday off. But I need to add more patients, if I want to take on an associate."

"If," Jed said. "You're not sure yet."

"It's a big decision. I'm comfortable managing the staff I have now. I guess I'll just take incremental steps to grow."

She drank some wine. Jed appreciated a garnish, a rose carved from a radish.

"What do you like to do when you're not drilling?" he said.

Libby smiled, now a fiend. "For one thing, I like to write poetry." Right away, she was surprised she confided in him. Nobody knew about her journals. Jed's eyes softened, and then they twinkled.

"A defense of poesy," he said.

"I don't know if I try that hard," she said. Jed consumed more lettuce and then offered an insight.

"The poet is the 'least liar,' as Sir Philip Sidney put it. You don't have to scavenge for facts, because you're not purporting to give a factual account. Ironically, the finished product manages to tell 'a' truth, if not 'the' truth," Jed said. He dug into the salad.

"I think it's just 'my' truth," Libby said. "I usually react to little things going on around me, or fleeting images. I wrote a poem once about a leaky hose in the kitchen sink. I got interested in the fine jet of water that shot out of the tiny hole."

"I found it symbolic of how life begins to change – with a small leak." She paused a moment. "I'd forgotten about Sir Philip Sydney.

"The fun in keeping a journal is that it's for *me*," she said. "If I want to fling around some free verse and then toss in a few heroic couplets, I can. I'm not writing for a critical audience, so nobody's wagging a finger." She sipped the wine to give him time to swallow. "You're full of surprises," she said. "Did you major in English?"

He wiped his lips with his napkin. "No," he said. "Medieval Studies."

"Of course," she said. "A good prosecutor should be familiar with the rack, the pincer, and the flame."

Jed laughed.

"I guess you must have studied Latin, then? I studied French," she said. "Of course, the language I needed for dentistry was Spanish, it now seems. It's a good thing my hygienist can translate. She was born in a Texas border town to Mexican immigrants."

Jed admired the yellow squash carved in the shape of a crescent moon. He pushed it aside in favor of a carrot nugget. "Sounds like you have a lot of Hispanic patients," he said.

"Increasingly so. But the greatest increase, to my accountant's delight, is in the number of orthodontic patients.

"People said I was crazy because I accepted a Medicaid panel, which is a roster of patients on public assistance. I stipulated the number I would accept, and then I closed the panel to more enrollments.

"Many of my colleagues will use their vacation time to give free treatment on Native American reservations or mercy ships, but they won't take Medicaid in their practices. The dentists say they're not reimbursed fairly for their time and expense.

"I'm sure they're not – but I don't like spending my vacations doing dentistry. So, I just absorb the low-income patients into my business plan."

Jed winked at her. "I have never practiced law on a beach," he said, growing more curious about the woman and less so about the salad. "Where did you go to dental school?" he said.

"Iowa. I got my bachelor's at Grinnell." She drank some more wine to create another pause. "I hadn't planned to stay here after graduate school at IU, but when the practice went on the market, it was too good to pass up.

"Where did you go to school?" she said, after he'd swallowed.

"I went to the University of Chicago, and then to Michigan for law school," he said.

"Wow!" Libby said. "Chicago. Why Medieval Studies?"

"I went to a Catholic high school, and one of my teachers was a medievalist. When I said I was interested in law school, he gave me some things to read about Salic Law."

"Which is?" Libby said.

"A fifth-century legal code for the Salian Franks. Articles governing property, community life, the relations between the Romans and the Germans.

"But chiefly, Salic Law is remembered for the rule prohibiting women from inheriting Salic land. The law was later expanded to allow inheritance if there were no male heirs," he said.

"And this made you want to major in Medieval Studies?" Libby said.

Jed smiled. "I was intrigued with the social contracts, and the emotional responses to spectacle in the Middle Ages. And I liked the tapestries and illuminations. Plus, I always wanted to be a knight."

"Were you knighted?" she said.

"Still waiting for the phone call."

172

The waiter arrived with the Chateaubriand, and he prepared the brandy flambé with a flourish. After the flame subsided, he let the meat simmer in the wine sauce as promised. "Do you want me to time it for you?" Libby joked, looking at her watch.

"By all means," the waiter said. When she whispered, "Stop," he carved the beef, topped it with mushrooms, and made a drizzle with the wine jus. Jed asked for sparkling water to accompany the meal, and for coffee with their dessert.

The side dishes were mashed potatoes piped into rosettes and browned; asparagus au gratin, and a red pepper soufflé with onion marmalade.

Savoring the beef, Jed and Libby dined in peace, occasionally chatting, and at ease in the crimson room. As they nearly napped over coffee and pineapple sherbet, Jed looked at his watch. "If we leave in about five minutes, we can get to the theater without rushing." He settled the bill, and the couple was on its way. Libby cast a last glance at the Victorian lamps, the paneled ceiling, and the mural of the Chinese village.

CHAPTER 41
Present Day – December

The symphony hall was once a movie theater, now a densely atmospheric auditorium, cleaned and lacquered to abolish all traces of spilled colas, crushed popcorn, and mysterious body fluids. The upholstery and carpeting gave the hall a rosy hue, and mirrored tiles lent the walls near the proscenium a palatial effect of dubious acoustical value. Additional lobby space was acquired through expansion to the building next door, and lines queued there for refreshments and receptions.

As Jed and Libby entered the lobby, she observed the contrasting levels of the patrons' self-awareness. A man of cadaverous color clung to the arm of a woman in her fifties, likely his daughter. Both were dressed in black slacks and turtleneck sweaters. She guided him to the coat check as if it were the front closet at home. An acquaintance waved hello, and the daughter nodded a cursory acknowledgment. Libby and Jed stepped up to relinquish their coats. As they turned toward the bank of entrances to the hall, another pair caught Libby's eye – a young woman in a bright red sheath, and her tuxedo-clad date. Entering the auditorium through the center-aisle door, they smiled at each other, as if waiting to be announced.

"Jed! Good to see you!" a man boomed. The shiny-faced greeter was a former linebacker, with thinning, reddish blond hair brushed back from the peak on his forehead. He wore several diamond-encrusted rings, a hunter-green wool jacket, a light-gray button-down shirt, gray trousers, and a gray silk jacquard print tie.

"Clarence, how are you?" Jed said.

"Just great. We got back from San Francisco yesterday after a week with our son and his new wife – she's Polynesian. She cooked the best meals I've ever had," Clarence said.

"Sounds like fun." Jed placed his hand on the Libby's shoulder. "Clarence, this is Dr. Libby Doherty. Libby, this is Clarence Hamerton, one of our crafty local attorneys."

"Nice to meet you," she said, yearning to bolt.

"Doctors or lawyers, we all bill by the hour," Clarence said.

"Actually, Libby is a dentist," Jed said, "And a very good one, I might add."

"Still a lot like being a lawyer," Clarence said. "We're always pulling teeth."

Who else said that? Libby wondered. Oh, it was Denise, who hadn't been clued in about Jed. Maybe the disclosure was at hand.

"Our seats are in Dress Circle, so we'd best be going," Jed said, shaking hands with Clarence. Upstairs, an usher, a young man with pierced ears, assisted them. Heads turned as they crossed the balcony. A local celebrity, Jed was accustomed to the attention. Libby was glad she'd worn the indigo dress, and then she was miffed that it mattered. She was a dentist, not arm candy. Denise would have to be clued in.

Finally seated, her mood swung again, as a trombonist warmed up. The thrilling sound poked through the fibrous wall around her emotions. She willed a silent benison for the sumptuous dinner, the brisk weather, the dress, and incidentally, the mirrored tiles she caught sight of. Peripherally to the right, she spied a woman who leaned forward to take in a view of the glam couple. As if by accident, Libby rotated her head a little and granted the woman a smile, which the matron returned. Libby started leafing through the program as Jed watched her.

The man was a mind reader, Libby decided, after the evening was over. He'd whispered to her as the house lights dimmed, "You handled that very well."

She looked him full in the face, in the darkening room amid silhouettes. "It was too far down to leap," she said, under the music of the overture.

"Of course, Dr. Booth. That's why I picked these seats," he said.

In a relatively shallow staging area, the holiday troupers presented strolling quartets, slapstick humor, sentimental arias, and ballads sung in a cabaret style. A thin story line, barely a libretto, nonetheless connected the running jokes and reappearing characters. Scene changes and special effects updated the format, which had gratified audiences since the days of operetta and vaudeville.

Ultimately, as if he knew what he came for, Jed sighed as the tap-dancing Santas presented the finale. "I always wanted to do that," he whispered to Libby.

As they approached the staircase after the show, Jed and Libby encountered Mr. and Mrs. Rigby Conover, now elderly, who were still dispensing the sizeable fortunes they'd inherited as young people. For some reason, performing good works with great endowments had failed to enhance the couple's demeanor, dour in aspect. Jed recognized the husband, who sprang forward and gave Jed a friendly slug on the arm.

"Young man, good to see you," the husband said, brightening and fading just as quickly. "We're having a little cocktail party for Rudd Kellaway," referring to the symphony's newly appointed general manager. "Why don't you folks join us? It's around the corner at the Guild."

The Guild was a private club dating back to the 1920s, and its members treasured the Art Deco furnishings and autographs of celebrities invited to leave notes on the bar walls over the years. In the club's heyday, many were invited to visit the Guild, but few belonged. As the grand old families of Indianapolis began to die off, club membership dwindled, and it was opened to the professional class, and then – alas – to anyone who could afford the dues.

"That's very kind of you, Rigby, but Dr. Doherty and I already have another engagement," Jed said. He introduced Libby.

Once again, perfecting the gracious salutation, Libby shook hands with them.

"So glad to meet you, my dear," Mrs. Conover said, with a fleeting lilt in her voice.

"We should be whisking away," Jed said. "Enjoy the party. Very nice to see you." The Conovers said good evening, and Jed and Libby descended the stairs.

"We should be whisking away?" Libby said, as they put on their coats.

"You didn't want to get stuck going to the cocktail party, did you?" Jed said.

"No – but whisking? Don't mice whisk away when they see a cat?"

"Yes. If you'd stayed, you'd have been a couple grand lighter when you got home. Rigby is the fundraising supernova on the symphony board, and you have 'doctor' in front of your name. And the Conovers know they're fading, so they're looking for people to take on their roles."

Libby sighed. It was always about the fundraising.

***

They walked arm in arm around Monument Circle, admiring the holiday lights. The loop around the Soldiers and Sailors Monument was the hub of an annual lighting ceremony during which strands of bulbs cascading from the top of the monument were switched on to the cheers of thousands. This evening a horse-drawn carriage went by with a family of four enjoying the festive decorations.

Jed and Libby completed their circuit and turned south on Meridian Street. "Let's duck in at The Blue Sedan. Things have probably settled down, and we can have a quiet drink," Jed said.

Jed found a corner booth affording privacy, away from the blue neon 1950s auto with yellow headlights that lit up the wall behind the bar. The waitress was prompt, and they settled on two shot glasses of bourbon. Libby rarely indulged in such, but so far, the evening had been notable for its string of exceptions.

"Can I tell you something?" Jed said when they were alone.

"Uh-huh," she murmured.

"It's been a very long time since I've had this much fun, or felt so lucky," Jed said.

Libby weighed his comment. It was a compliment to her, or an indirect statement about the drudgery of his life. She chose to embrace the compliment.

"Me, too," she said. "I truly enjoyed the show – and the Santas."

"Will you write a poem about them?" he said.

"A lot has been said about Santa. I'm not sure I have anything to add."

"I don't know – maybe I should give it a try," Jed said, beginning a limerick. "There once was a tap-dancing Santa, who left the North Pole for Atlanta."

"That's not bad," Libby said. "But you're already in a corner. The next two lines can change the scheme, but the end has to rhyme with Santa."

Jed thought about it for a moment. "Raved and rant-a," he said.

"It must have been about Mrs. Claus," Libby said.

Jed studied her with his unblinking gaze. Although glib, she had a secret, but not one that would hurt him, he decided. He was tempted to probe, but he knew embarrassing questions were better left to depositions. Someday, she'd talk about her past, and then he'd talk about his. Maybe when they were finished, they'd decide their regrets had gone stale, or so he hoped.

"You write poems – are you musical as well?" he said.

"I was. I played the violin until I was a senior in college. Once I began my professional training, I didn't play."

"Do you still have your instrument?" he said.

"Oh, sure. I take it out every so often. What about you?"

"I took piano lessons though the tenth grade, and then Mom let me quit," Jed said. "I like playing, but I don't like to practice. I moved back home after Mom went to Florida, and since then, I've taken out a few Lennon-McCartney tunes and hacked around on the keys. But that's it."

After a beat, Jed said, "Perhaps we should attempt a duet, just to see how bad we are."

And after another beat, Libby said, "Or how good."

They emptied the shot glasses in silence. Although drowsy, Libby was aroused. She would let things simmer for now. Too many changes had rained on her, but she was enjoying the renewal of desire. Feeling shy, she looked at framed pictures of vintage autos on the wall of the booth.

Jed was nearly undone with longing, but he knew not to take her for granted. He was terrified he'd botch the friendship. If he did get close to her, it was because he'd earned her trust.

Later as he walked her to the front door of her house, he said, "We'll do this again, won't we?"

"Only once a year at Christmas?" she said. "I was hoping to see you much sooner."

"Much, much, sooner," he said. At the door, they enjoyed a long kiss, but not one that was impossible to get out of. Jed looked into her eyes, said good night, and gave her one last peck on the cheek.

CHAPTER 42
Present Day – The Same Night

The dog walker was out later than usual with Trevor. They almost never went out after 10 p.m. But tonight, Darla was restless, and all day she'd been thinking about the bungalow. Convinced she was supposed to see something, she put on a down jacket and earmuffs. Trevor looked at her with wonder as she connected the leash, and on a treasure hunt, he trotted and sniffed as they headed toward the bungalow.

They were rewarded. The porch light was on, and outside the front door, a man stood chatting with the homeowner. The wooden door was open, and a warm light shone through the storm door. The lady was wearing a dress coat and high heels.

Darla tugged on the leash, and Trevor stopped. He was watching, too.

They saw the man grasp the woman's shoulders as he leaned to kiss her.

Trevor let out a whimper and his mistress cupped her hand under his jaw. He was quiet.

The man and the woman stepped apart, and the man started down the steps. Going to the curb, he got into a sedan and took off. The woman went inside.

Excited, the watchers turned for home. Trevor slowed their pace as he stopped twice to wet some bushes, and the dog walker was chilled by the time they arrived.

She made herself hot cocoa and gave him a biscuit. Skipping the candlelight ritual, she jotted on her notepad at the table. Just a few phrases this time, but loaded, in her opinion.

She read aloud. "Bird soars, tumbles, hatches."

"Huh." She sipped the cocoa, interlacing her fingers around the mug.

She read the next line. "Big chief watcher visits girl."

She laughed. "Sounds like Tonto talking to the Lone Ranger."

Nestled in his bean bag in the corner of the dining room, Trevor rolled his head.

She knew it all meant something, but it would be a while before things played out.

CHAPTER 43
Present Day -- December

Frenchie unwrapped the farewell gift from Libby. Silver foil with bright green ribbon concealed a flat gift box holding a black silk scarf.

"It's for you to wear to temple, if you want," Libby said.

"Thank you, it's lovely. I've been wearing the same black scarf for 20 years," Frenchie said. She unwrapped a large box sitting on the lunch table. "Oh, my goodness, you shouldn't have, but I'm really glad you did," she said, smelling the calf leather tote.

"It's from everybody. Keisha went shopping for us." Marquita said. "I might have picked out a laundry bag."

"I could use one of those, too," Frenchie said. Over turtle pie, her favorite, the group chatted, putting off the inevitable. Keisha broke up the party by saying she had to pick up her nephew from basketball practice.

"I should be going as well," Claris said. She hugged Frenchie. "I wish we'd been able to work together a little longer."

The others took turns hugging Frenchie, who collected her gifts and departed. Libby was the last to go. She looked out her office window at the Friday night sky. The holidays were pressing, and she hadn't scheduled the staff party. Frenchie already said she'd pass on the event, because she didn't want to leave Paul alone at home. She privately thanked Libby for the cash given to her off the books, and the two had wept together.

Libby reviewed her evening with Jed. The symphony show was well-executed. Maybe she should buy tickets for the staff, instead of having a party. She called the box office to ask about availabilities and blushed when she found out what Jed spent, when she added the cost of the elaborate dinner. No one ever spoiled her like that, and with such nonchalance. Perhaps he entertained women all the time. Anxiety began to interfere with her common sense.

Perturbed, she made herself decide. She'd give the staff a catered luncheon for their holiday party at the office, which would be closed for the afternoon. Her surprise would be cash tucked into each Christmas card, in addition to wrapped presents and generous gift baskets loaded with cheeses, cookies, and crackers.

She was restless. Harrison State Park was closed\at night. She could drive to Brown County to look at the stars, but fog often crept across the foothills. Tonight, it was unreasonable to drive for almost an hour and possibly encounter mist, instead of meteors. A better plan would be to travel south on the weekend and stay after dark. An outlet mall was in the vicinity; maybe she could go shopping and finish the day at the state park. Denise wanted to go shopping, but Libby didn't know if Denise was in love with the woodlands.

Libby called her and proposed an excursion for Saturday to include lunch, shopping, and stargazing.

"We can find a vista in the state park. I thought we'd find a deserted place where we can talk. I've got some things on my mind," Libby said.

"Deserted," Denise said. "Are you going to rob me at gunpoint?"

Libby laughed. "We've done that, remember? I just don't want anybody to overhear what I'm going to tell you."

"Are you in some kind of trouble?" Denise said.

"No. But I've gone out with a 'person in the news.' I'm just starting to get to know him," she said.

"He's not married, is he?"

"Oh, no, he's *El Super Ratón*," Libby said.

"What does that mean?"

"Mighty Mouse."

Denise said nothing.

"It's a long story," Libby said.

"And I thought my last appointment was weird. So we're doing this tomorrow?"

"At your earliest convenience," Libby said.

Denise laughed. "Who is this guy?"

Libby swallowed. "Let's just wait until tomorrow."

As they headed south on I-65 the next day, Denise avoided asking questions. A snow flurry began, lightly dusting the road. Libby activated the windshield wipers.

"I hope the front moves through, so we can see the sky tonight," Libby said.

They went to an outlet mall. Lunch and shopping lasted several hours. By four o'clock, the friends were exhausted, and they witnessed the arrest of a portly shoplifter, struggling with sheriff's deputies who forced him to the ground. On his belly, the man squirmed and grunted like a hog. A woman in plainclothes knelt and cuffed the detainee's hands behind him.

Libby's expression soured. Denise turned her back to avoid the scene, a vignette for shoppers who stopped and stared.

"Whatever happened to the kind of Christmas where each person gets one gift, and maybe some candy in the stocking, and then the highlight is Christmas dinner?" Denise said. "This is crazy. Do you realize we have to wrap all this stuff?"

"I have to go to the bathroom, and after that, I'm thirsty," Libby said.

"There must be a better way," Denise grumbled as they searched for restrooms. "And did you see those children ordering their parents around in the toy store? It was a complete role reversal. When those kids are teenagers, that family is going to explode like a boiler."

The restrooms were out of paper towels, and only one electric hand dryer was functional. "This is what I like," Denise said. "All the amenities."

Denise's mood improved during the drive to Brown County. The rural scene erased thoughts of a retail Christmas. At the turn-off to the state park, the layered hues of sunset drew exclamations from the women, and they stopped at an overlook and watched until dark. They dined at the park lodge, and then Libby drove them up a winding road to Hoehn Point, facing the southeastern horizon. Clutching cups of coffee, they sat atop a picnic table and watched the moon.

"That's a nice sliver of a moon. Here comes part of Orion . . . no, I think not. Whatever it is just moved. So what's on your mind?" Denise said.

Libby told her about meeting Jed and their subsequent encounters, which culminated in the elaborate dinner and the holiday show.

"It was all very recherché," Libby said.

"I think I know what that means," Denise said. "Do you want to see him again?"

"Yes," Libby said.

"Then what are you doing up here with *me*?" Denise said.

Libby couldn't resist. "You . . . me . . . the moonlight." Denise laughed.

"That's Orion," Libby said, pointing. Denise looked up.

"If you're not bringing him here, then where would you like to take him?" Denise said.

"I'm not sure. Do you think I should get involved with a politician? I mean, they're so 'out there.' Do they have any privacy?" Libby said.

"Has he complained about the lack of it?" Denise said.

"Not yet. But he just got elected. I wonder how he'll feel about things later."

"Or how you will feel about things." Denise said.

"What do you mean?" Libby said.

"I think you like him a lot, but you're very private. You know if you allow the relationship, you'll have to be seen in public. He's not going to downplay his public life, because he can't let people forget about him," Denise said.

"And if I don't want to get used to it?"

"Then he's not the guy for you," Denise said. "But I'm not telling you to stop seeing him. I think you should give him a chance."

"Why?"

"For one thing, it was possible that you'd lose interest, because you had to put off your date until after the election. But when the time came, he asked, and you were available.

"So he's persistent, and a little vulnerable. For another, the guy lavished attention on you. My ex-husband never treated me with such care, and sad to say, I'm almost jealous," Denise said.

"Do you think Jed's attention could have been a front?" Libby said.

"Did you think he was a phony at the time?" Denise said.

"No. It felt really good," Libby said. "Really, really good."

"Then I'd say, give yourself some credit. He probably doesn't know anyone as intelligent as you," Denise said.

"He must know plenty of female attorneys," Libby said.

"Was he escorting them during the campaign?" Denise said.

"No. He was single-minded about winning the election."

"But later on, the first person he called was *you*." Denise said.

"I don't know that I was the first, or the only," Libby said.

"But so far, you don't have the 'right' to be the 'only,' " Denise said. "So even if you weren't, it shouldn't matter, any more than it should matter to him if you dated others during his campaign."

After a pause, Libby was crabby. "I don't like to be thrown off balance. I like to be in control. Jed makes me feel tipsy, even after only one drink."

Denise guffawed, and the folks down at Horseman's Camp probably heard it. "Now we're getting to the good stuff," she shouted. "He makes you hot!"

Libby blushed and looked up at the sky. "I guess so," she said.

"You guess so," Denise said in a deep voice like a professional wrestler issuing a challenge.

Libby sipped her coffee. "He's very attractive," she said.

"Do you want to tell me how the evening ended, or do we need to put up a privacy screen?" Denise said.

Libby laughed. "He walked me to the door, and we kissed. It was a good kiss."

"How long has it been since you went out?"

"A week," Libby said.

"Have you talked with him since then?" Denise said.

"Nope."

"Well, I would call him next week and invite him out," Denise said. "What is he doing over the holidays?"

"He'll be in Florida visiting his family," Libby said.

"What about New Year's?" Denise said.

"I don't know if he'll be back by then. I don't even know when he'll be sworn into office, come to think of it," Libby said.

"Give him a call. Find out about his travel plans, and then improvise. Maybe you could get some pizza," Denise said.

"I don't know. He's pretty busy," Libby said.

"And that's the drawback. People in the news or covering the news always have something else to do," Denise said, rolling her eyes. "Remember, you've got your own priorities. You can't just drop everything and perform for him."

"That's true," Libby said. "I guess I was lucky our date wasn't canceled because one of my patients had his two front teeth knocked out."

"Right," Denise said. "And here's something else to consider. Look at it from Jed's point of view. He knows you don't need a man for financial reasons. That's intimidating to a lot of men.

"Believe it or not, some men hide behind their wallets, so you won't notice anything bad. And Jed could have been hiding, so to speak, by giving you the ritzy treatment."

"In fairness to Jed," Libby said. "He'd been to those places before. It was more like he was in his element."

"And is that such a bad thing? Would you prefer his element to be a twenty-four-hour truck stop?" Denise said.

"Truth told – he probably lives in those."

"Then maybe you can visit one together, and avoid the limelight as well," Denise said. "Who knows what it might lead to?" she said, wiggling her eyebrows.

Libby frowned.

"What's the matter?" Denise said.

"Can I tell you something?"

"Of course," Denise said.

"You know, when I look at magazines at the drug store, the headlines scream, 'Head-Banging Sex, Page Twenty-Seven,' or 'Ten Places He Wants to Be Touched.' It pisses me off." Libby said, resorting to a phrase she seldom used.

"Why?" Denise said.

"Because it's pressure to make sex the centerpiece of relationships and self-esteem. Whatever happened to friendship and courtship? And what about the death of childhood? If I had a ten-year-old, I wouldn't know how to shield her from all the pressure," she said.

"I'm not sure it's possible," Denise said. "Did Jed do or say something to make you feel pressured?" she said.

"No."

"Not to resurrect any heartache for you, but looking back, did you and Teddy have a conflict about intimacy?" Denise said.

"No."

"Do you remember the first time you had sex with him?"

186

"Yes."

"How was it?" Denise said.

"It was a logical conclusion to the day. We finished semester exams, and then we went to my place and stripped."

"You make it sound like players going to the locker room after the big game," Denise said.

"No. It was super-fast and super-erotic. I was dressed; then I was undressed; I was standing up; then I was on my back; then Teddy was running his tongue down my front; then I was satisfied."

Denise swallowed a sip of coffee. "If Jed heard that, he'd be breaking down your door. You know what? He's just trying to catch his breath, keep himself grounded.

"He's not ready for you, I think. You're borrowing trouble. You'll have plenty of time to be alone with your dirty thoughts, if you haven't censored them completely."

"I haven't stopped fantasizing," Libby said. "What I'm trying to say – I look at what I can do, and what I can't do. I guess I wonder what Jed wants out of life, and if I could give it to him," Libby said. "If he's looking for a big family, and for someone to put her life on hold during his campaigns, I'm not that person."

"So maybe what you're afraid of," Denise said, "Is that if you become intimate, a break-up later could be very painful."

"Yes." Libby said.

"Then take it slowly. But I've got news for you. Two people can destroy each other without ever having sex. Just don't give up on him before you get to know him. You can still be hard to unbutton," Denise said. "Ugh! Did I really say that? I sounded pretty medieval just then."

"That's OK. He majored in Medieval Studies," Libby said.

"Good. You can turn on together by reading *The Canterbury Tales*," Denise said. "As I recall, some kisses landed in some very interesting places." She sipped from her cup. "My coffee is getting cold."

Denise looked at the clear sky. "What is that? It goes back and forth." They stared at a transient object blinking in the heavens.

"I'm not sure I want to know," Denise said at last.

CHAPTER 44
Present Day – December

Libby was getting ready for a swim at the Y, when her cell phone rang.

"Dr. Booth – you summoned me."

"Hi, Jed." Libby blushed as she stood topless in the otherwise deserted locker room.

"Thanks for your message," he said. "You mentioned getting together."

"Yeah," she said, with a slippery touch of irony. "Yes, I was thinking we might celebrate your swearing-in. Isn't it scheduled for New Year's Day?"

"Indeed. But after I take the oath, I have long-standing plans with a group of five buddies to watch football at somebody's house. The women usually flee, because of the grotesqueries. Belching – and worse."

"Oh," she said, deflating. "I remembered you were going away. I wasn't sure if you'd be around much."

"Actually, I will," he said. "I'm leaving on the twenty-third and coming back on the twenty-seventh."

"Would you like to come to supper one night?" she said.

"My schedule isn't very predictable right now. I'd hate to say that I'd be there and then cancel at the last minute. Maybe we could catch a late show at the movies Saturday night?" Jed said.

Libby was disappointed, because she wanted to take the lead. She wasn't used to this. "That sounds like fun," she heard herself say. "Did you have a movie in mind, or shall we wing it?"

"Wing it. Drop by at eight-forty-five? That'll give us time to pick the show, get there, get the popcorn," he said. "If you want to hide cans of pop in your handbag, I won't report you to the authorities."

"Yessir," Libby said. "Down jackets also conceal contraband."

"Don't cross an important line. You can carry things in your purse for medicinal reasons, but a coat is where you hide the pot roast," he said.

She laughed. Her belly had gooseflesh, and she rubbed it. She wasn't used to this.

Jed said he had to run, that he was "needed" somewhere. Afterward, Libby realized he hadn't bothered to ask about her own plans for Christmas, even though she knew all about his. She was closing her office for five days to go home to Des Moines. She'd already wrapped and shipped Christmas gifts, now under the tree at her parents' house.

A moderately heavy snowfall decorated most of Iowa on Christmas Eve. Behind a city-owned salt-spreader, she rode with her parents in their SUV to the midnight service at the Lutheran church where she was raised. After the benediction, the chancel choir entertained with secular carols. Despite the warnings about drifting snow, Libby's family and many parishioners stayed to enjoy hot chocolate and doughnuts.

After Christmas, the appointed evening arrived, and Libby wore a rib-knit burgundy sweater with a mock turtleneck; blue jeans, and tennis shoes, easily cleaned after bonding to trash on the movie house floor. The time crept toward nine o'clock, and Jed hadn't shown up. Finally, he called, describing a meeting that ran late in the back room of a steakhouse. He promised to arrive in ten minutes.

Later, escorting her to the car, he said, "You'd think people in politics would relax between Christmas and New Year's, but I think those guys were actually trying to get away from their families."

"It's OK," Libby said, imagining Denise saying, "They've always got somewhere they've gotta be."

Libby told Jed to pick between the two movies she described.

"Ladies and gentlemen, tonight, we are pleased to present – Comedy!" he said, imitating Zero Mostel.

Driving, he said, "Hey! Did you ever get your car fixed?"

"Oh, yeah. But I flew home for Christmas." she said.

"How is your family?" he said.

"Just fine. We enforced a rule this year: No TV on Christmas Day. The kids didn't like it – but they found things to do – and then they forgot all about TV," Libby said.

"We observed the season for centuries before the advent of television." Jed said. "TV is very boring, compared with pagan festivals and royal events of antiquity.

"In December, the ancient Romans observed the feast of Saturnalia – several days of public merrymaking, even nudity. Then there was Sol Invictus on December twenty-fifth, to celebrate the unconquered sun, reborn after the solstice," he said, beginning a brief chronology.

"In the year eight hundred, Charlemagne was crowned on Christmas Day, and King William I of England on Christmas in ten-sixty-six.

"As the Middle Ages flowered, the Yule festivals were known for 'misrule' – drunkenness, promiscuity, gambling. Revelers knocked on doors and demanded hospitality. If they were turned down, they'd get even."

"Sounds like trick-or-treat with mistletoe," Libby said.

"And the occasional bludgeoning," Jed said. "I like the term 'misrule.' I'd like to be able to charge somebody with that. Anyway, later, the Puritans almost killed Christmas, but pro-Christmas rioting broke out -- a positive use of 'misrule,' in my opinion.

"And in America, after the Revolution, Christmas fell out of favor, because it was an English custom. Luckily, your local hero was a champion of the holiday in the eighteen-twenties."

"My local hero?" Libby said.

"Your town was named after him, as your historic district propaganda teaches," Jed said.

"Oh, you mean Irvington. Washington Irving!" she said.

"The very. If you read *The Sketch Book of Geoffrey Crayon*, you'll find his depictions of 'Old Christmas.' "

"I'll have to walk over to the library and get a copy. How come you know so much about Christmas?"

"I love it. The more I learn about it, the more I enjoy it," he said.

"Misrule," she said.

"During Yule," he said.

The movie was a dark comedy about a prosecutor's personal conflict with a racketeer. Jed chuckled throughout the film, but Libby noticed he tussled with dozing off. About twenty minutes before the end, he lurched forward and grabbed his phone, clipped to his belt. "I'm being vibrated," he muttered, going out to the corridor.

"I'll try to keep my eyes averted," Libby said. He came back somber. After the show, he hurried Libby into her coat and said in a low voice, "We need to get out of here." When they got to Jed's car, he took her by the shoulders and kissed her.

"I'm sorry to end our evening, but I got a bad call," he said. "I need to run you home and get downtown. Five kids were killed after a holiday basketball tournament, and police think they were mistaken for gang members."

"That's awful," Libby said. En route, she said, "What do you need to accomplish right after a crime like this?"

"Visibility is important. The community will react badly, and it will expect statements from its leaders. I wouldn't be at all surprised to run into the mayor at the crime scene. I'll probably spend tomorrow expressing condolences. These families are going to bury children. Not one of the victims was over fifteen," Jed said.

"And you haven't even been sworn in," she said.

CHAPTER 45
Present Day – The New Year

Darla was invited to serve as the paid entertainment at a New Year's Eve bash for a group of singles in their late twenties. They reserved a party room at a downtown hotel and enjoyed a catered buffet and cash bar. For a group fee, the psychic gave a reading to anyone who requested it. She agreed to stay for three hours. When finished, she strolled to Monument Circle to wait for fireworks at midnight. As the crowd counted down, she noticed the back of a bowler hat covering curly dark hair – the ghost of the killer Holmes, again. He disappeared into the crowd at the stroke of midnight.

She ran to her car, went home, and read from the book of Psalms aloud for about a half hour before going to bed.

***

Valentine's Day was coming, and Libby had gotten only a few calls from Jed since their movie date in late December. Understanding the weight of responsibility on him, she desired to be a reliable friend. If she offered to make dinner on Valentine's Day, it could seem oppressive, like saying the way to a man's court docket was through his stomach. But if she offered to treat him to a casual night out, he might welcome the distraction.

Skimming news briefs in the daily paper, she found notice of a lecture on forensic medicine. This would be of interest to both, and in a gremlin-like way, she anticipated his amusement at her choice of a morbid subject for

Valentine's Day. They could have dinner downtown, maybe pasta, and walk to the lecture.

During lunch at work, she dialed his number and got voicemail. "Hi, it's Libby, calling about Italian food." Sounding out of breath, he rang back in twenty minutes.

"Where is it?" he said.

"Where is what?" she said.

"The Italian food."

"Ah, yes," she said. "Unfortunately, it's not for immediate consumption." Making a blithe proposal for the evening of the fourteenth, she concluded, "In other words, a post-mortem with Parmesan."

Jed chuckled. "You're edging toward that jump off the balcony, Dr. Booth. It sounds like fun, but I'm going to have to decline.

"I'm breaking in new staff, and the General Assembly is in session. We have to attend a number of get-togethers to push our legislative agenda."

Libby was silent. Jed pressed on. "But I'm so glad you called. I've thought about you a lot lately, especially when I went to the dentist to get my tooth crowned, per your instructions. That certainly was a drawn-out affair."

"I was afraid it would be," she said, relieved he changed the subject. "Is the 'permanent' on, or just the 'provisional'?"

"The permanent. The provisional kept popping off, and it drove me crazy. I found it stuck in a peanut butter cup," he said.

"That happens," Libby said. "I'm glad it's done."

"With your help, milady," he said. His voice was tender. She heard someone in the background speak to him.

"OK, I'll be there in a minute," he said, muffled. He hung up telling her, "You made my day."

She attended the lecture, anyway. Beforehand, she dined on spaghetti in her cozy kitchen, filled with a radio broadcast of the Tchaikovsky Symphony No. 5. She wore a gray knit turtleneck over dark green wool slacks. After dinner, she went out sporting a copper-colored down jacket with faux fur trimming the hood – a good coat for the night, which brought a sharp wind.

At the historical society, the lecture was on the ground floor in a meeting room, where forty or so had gathered. A colleague hailed her; he was known for his work in dental forensics, or forensic odontology, and they chatted about his recent collaboration with archaeologists in Mexico.

A few stragglers arrived, and the program began, presented by two educators from local universities. Designed for a general audience, the lecture highlighted notable events in the state's history of forensic medicine. Libby heard a little about everything, including the invention of the field sobriety test by R.F. Borkenstein of IU, and the coroner's role in sensational cases like that of Madge Oberholtzer, murdered by the Ku Klux Klan leader D.C. Stephenson in 1925.

Remembering the tour guide's commentary during the ghost walk through her neighborhood, Libby knew that Oberholtzer and Stephenson had lived a few blocks apart in Irvington. Tonight's review of the post-mortem confirmed Stephenson's long-standing reputation for savagery.

On the way home, she stopped behind a line of buses at the traffic light on Ohio Street at the state capitol's north entrance. Visible under the lights, a man and a woman emerged from the building and started down the steps. In fact, the landscaping was such that one could see the north doors from a block away.

Libby recognized the man as Jed. He conversed with the striking, dark-haired woman, whose excellent posture enhanced the svelte lines of her winter white coat. More people came down the steps behind them, and he guided her by the elbow to negotiate the last step to the parking lot. The traffic light changed, and Libby resumed her trip east.

Something gnawed at her, and she impulsively turned north on Illinois and went up to Vermont, where she doubled back to the west and turned south again on Senate. This time, she waited at Senate and Ohio as a black limo pulled up shy of the driveway to the capitol lot. Jed and the woman were waiting at the curb. The driver helped the woman in, and Jed disappeared into the limo, which pulled away and turned south on Capitol Street.

Libby's heart sank. No doubt this was one of the get-togethers. Smarting during the ride home, she experienced the range of feelings from jealousy to embarrassment. Why would a politician forgo an evening of deal-making and schmoozing with attractive women, just so he could hear about insect larva associated with the decay of remains? Libby felt by turns unimportant and defiant. She'd set herself up. Yes, the legislature was in session, but if not, then something else would take precedence. As Denise had warned, these people always have somewhere they've gotta be.

And then, as Libby drove up the last incline into Irvington, she admitted she was jealous – jealous of the woman, and jealous of everyone claiming a smidgen of Jed's courtesy and the whole of his ability to render aid. He is a helper – just like me, she thought. This quality sanded the abrasive edge of his competitive nature. He knew his moral purpose for competing, and he slowed down for people deserving his attention. Libby's defiance returned as she refused to qualify herself as deserving. She thumped the steering wheel. She wasn't going to ruin the pleasure of a quiet dinner and a provocative lecture by being mad. A walk in the bladder-poking wind would take her mind off everything.

***

Jed climbed into the limo, chartered by Jim Phillipi, his new associate counsel. Waiting inside with Jim were Warren Stuckey, the chairman of the Indiana House Committee on Courts and Criminal Code, and Fred Knutson, the director of the prosecuting attorneys' council. They'd been to dinner at an exclusive restaurant near the airport, and Jed and his new hire, Sheri Neulander, were joining them for drinks. The nightcaps were served in the limo as the driver cruised around downtown and up Meridian Street.

Sheri had been on the job for two weeks, and Jed took her to the capitol to meet the local legislative delegation. Later, the two shared an elevator with the state's attorney general, Bill Clayton, who invited them to his office and served bottled water. The AG welcomed the distraction. Although touted as the two-term Republican's likely successor, Jed had an easy rapport with Clayton. After about twenty minutes, Jed rose and thanked the AG, and the visitors went downstairs, where they waited for the limo.

Jed's confidence in Jim rose even more when he observed how well his friend related to Stuckey, whom people called "Warren Stuffy." Well-respected, he was a small-town lawyer whose dying declarations could convict a number of county officials in Southern Indiana. Stuckey insisted that things be done properly, and some of his legislative colleagues and the omnipresent ring of lobbyists resented his persnickety side. Jim, however, was persnickety in his own way, and he soothed the elder's nerves. The council director, Knutson, was busy serving drinks.

Stuckey perked up when Jed mentioned that Sheri was Armistead Hauser's niece. "On Army's side, or his wife's?" Stuckey said.

"On his. His sister is my mother," Sheri said.

"Army's quite a fellow," Stuckey said. "My wife had a slight stroke, no permanent damage, but it sure scared the dickens out of me. She's only sixty-three. Passed right out in a restaurant. Army heard about it, sent flowers. He met her at the Speedway only once during the race, and he always asks about her. Quite a fellow."

Sheri smiled. "Thank you. I think so, too."

The party lasted for a half-hour, and then Jim checked his watch. "Everybody ready to call it a night?" he said. The others agreed, and he instructed the driver to return to the capitol. As they parted, Stuckey said to Jim, "Young man, I'm very glad you decided to come back from Illinois."

On the way home, Jim called Jed. "The mental-health lobby and the public defenders are pushing for an interim study committee on issues involving mentally ill defendants," Jim said. "Stuckey is supporting it. Knutson would be our link to the committee.

"But we have only two weeks before the midway point of the session, and the bills on child molesting aren't moving. They need to get third reading by the twenty-seventh," Jim said. "Stuckey said he might be able to push one bill, but not all."

"Have you met with the victims' advocates?" Jed said.

"Yes. They want a hearing on the bill to move child seduction to a higher class of felony, if the offender is a guardian, custodian, adoptive parent, or a teacher, and if the victim is between sixteen and eighteen years of age."

"These cases with older teens happen more often than people realize," Jed said. "When I was in high school, I knew a guy from another school who got taken to bed the day after his sixteenth birthday, as a present from his forty-year-old English teacher. She really worked on his mind – even after he graduated."

"What finally happened?" Jim said.

"I'm not sure. He quit college in his sophomore year to backpack through Europe. We didn't stay in touch," Jed said.

"Maybe he met another teacher of *inglés*," Jim said.

"That's perverse," Jed said.

"So are two lonely guys like us talking to each other on Valentine's Day," Jim said.

Jed was quiet.

"You still there?" Jim said.

"Yes. Reception must be cutting out," Jed said. He was thinking about Libby.

"If you don't need anything else, I'm going to stop at the grocery and pick up my breakfast," Jim said.

"OK, buddy," Jed said.

Jed checked his watch. It was ten-thirty. Maybe it was too late, but what the hell. His call went to Libby's voicemail. He left a message.

"Dr. Booth – it's late, but I wanted to wish you a Happy Valentine's Day. I'd like a rain check on the Italian food, if that's possible. Maybe you could toss a salad, and I'll bring the breadsticks. I could help with dishes. Sleep tight."

CHAPTER 46
Present Day – Late February

During the lunch hour, Libby was picking up clothes from the drycleaner, when Jed called.

"Are you available on Thursday the twenty-sixth for dinner?" he said. "The United States attorney general is coming to town."

"Are we roasting him on a spit?" she said, surprised by how relieved she was to hear from him.

"With pineapple," Jed said. "Stanton Marshfield, who's now at Dunwoody Schiff, was a deputy AG for a time, and he arranged for his old boss to address the bar association after dinner," Jed said.

"I guess that means we can't leave right after dinner," she said.

Jed burst out laughing.

"Actually, it sounds intriguing," Libby said. "What do I have to do?"

"Be your lovely self," Jed said, smiling like he'd birdied on the eighteenth hole. "We'll have a table near the front, probably. Stanton said he'd arrange the seating so we don't have to sit with Theo Karnow, although it wouldn't bother me if we did. We always get along."

"How do you want me to dress?" She was horrified at once that she'd uttered those words.

"Business attire is fine – that is, for a lawyer. I guess you wouldn't wear scrubs," he said.

I ought to, she thought. "Some dentists dress like lawyers all the time," she said. "Can I just meet you downtown?"

"If that's all right," he said. "Cocktails are at six-thirty, dinner at seven, and the speech at eight."

"That's fine. Where do you want to meet?"

Jed suggested the lobby of the Morton Plaza, where the association would convene.

When Libby arrived at the hotel, Jed was engrossed in the comments of an elderly legal sage, who leaned on a wooden cane. Taking off her coat, she folded it over her left arm. In a black dress suit with a teal blouse, she stood back, not wanting to interrupt. Jed motioned her forward, introducing her to Brenton Haverly, a retired appellate judge.

"Young lady, if you argued a case in front of me, I'd be struck dumb by those wonderful eyes," Haverly said.

"Why, thank you," she said.

"Your honor, Libby is a dentist," Jed said. "She's my guest."

"Ho-ho – a dentist! Now there's a twist – 'The quality of justice is not strained, except through my dentures,' " the old jurist said.

"Would you indulge in a cocktail with us?" Jed asked him.

"A glass of sparkling water is my limit, but if I enter the room with this young woman on my arm, I'm sure I will be quite intoxicated." He extended his free arm, and Libby took it as he steadied himself against the cane. Jed walked a little ahead of them, and Libby paced herself to avoid dragging the old man. They stopped at the coat check, first.

More than a little like royalty, they appeared in the banquet hall, and heads turned. Jed glowed as he shook hands with members of the legal community. Libby escorted the judge to the bar, and she ordered their beverages.

Strolling away from the bar, she and the judge encountered a barrel-chested man about twenty years younger than the judge. The younger man gave the judge a bear hug. The judge introduced Libby to the chief justice of the Indiana Supreme Court, Harry Holloway.

"Brenton was my mentor, when we were on the appellate court together," the chief justice said. "I was trying to decide whether to accept an appointment to the Supreme Court, or to be general counsel for an engineering company, which was unquestionably more lucrative.

"Brenton told me, 'A bridge can always be blown up, but a good ruling lasts a long time.'

"I told Brenton one of my law professors said a ruling could be blown up like a bridge. The very next day, a bridge collapsed somewhere down South, and twelve people were killed. It was all over the news.

"Brenton poked his head into my office and said, 'Now do you believe me?' I needed to give the governor an answer, so I took the court appointment," Holloway said.

"But you miss the money," Haverly said.

"Every judge in Indiana misses it," the chief justice said, eyeing Jed, who noticed him and immediately came over. The group talked for a few minutes, and then the chief justice spotted US Attorney General Richard Kampagner. He entered the room with his host, Armistead Hauser.

"I guess I should go say hello to Dick before the throng reaches him," Holloway said, leaving.

A thin, bespectacled man full of energy and good humor strode up, and Jed shook hands. "Theo, good to see you. How was Venezuela?" Jed said.

"Fabulous. I should have skipped the campaign and gone directly to South America," Theo Karnow said without guile. He shook hands with Judge Haverly, who said, "Youngster, we need you on the court."

"I hope you mean the tennis court," Karnow said, not twitching a muscle. "I don't see any vacancies on the Supreme Court."

"You and Holloway would make good colleagues," Haverly said.

"I'd rather play tennis with him. I've beaten him," Karnow said.

Jed introduced Libby to Karnow. "I'd also like Libby to meet some of my staff. Would you excuse us?" Jed steered Libby in the direction of Sheri Neulander.

Libby recognized her as the woman who left with Jed in the limo. Jed explained she was Hauser's niece, and Libby blushed, hoping she wasn't turning bright red. Sheri was very charming.

"You'll have to meet me for lunch sometime," Sheri said. "That is, if you own a treadmill. The food downtown is very fattening, but delicious."

"Surely they have some things that aren't so laden," Libby said.

"They do, but they're not nearly as much fun to eat," Sheri said, winking. "Would you rather have a salad – or two eggs, toast, hash browns and bacon, and a strong cup of coffee?

"No contest," Libby said.

Libby also met Fabiola de Torre, the new chief of staff, who impressed her as a high-energy power source. Jed also pulled his friend Jim aside, and he hovered near Libby like a defensive linesman while Jed went to speak with Hauser and Kampagner.

After the dinner of chicken cordon bleu, the lawyers and their guests rustled, waiting for Kampagner to speak. Jed whispered to Libby that Kampagner told him the topic of his speech would be the theft of intellectual property.

"Not my favorite subject," Jed said. "But there's a lot of legal business here with pharmaceutical companies and medical device makers, and they deal with intellectual property all the time.

"By the way, I haven't steered you to meet Army, because Kampagner is his boss. Knowing Army, he'd want to sit next to you, but he must focus."

Libby just smiled.

Jed was attentive during the address, which piqued Libby's interest when the AG brought up a case involving the distribution of counterfeit toothpaste. Up to now, she'd felt like arm candy with a DDS, but she developed an authentic interest in the speech as Kampagner listed examples of counterfeit drugs and point-of-care devices. He was humorous, expressing puzzlement at the choice of luxury items purchased by counterfeiters, including one who bought his own ambulance.

As the speech bloated with a summary of Justice Department accomplishments, Libby examined her attitude. Why couldn't she just enjoy being with Jed, instead of resenting her role? If she invited Jed to a dental convention, would he feel like arm candy? He'd probably be bored, but maybe not – he exercised his intellect. And what was wrong with her? She met the most powerful members of the judiciary, and it wasn't as if they were coming to her office for braces. Jed had given her an opportunity to stretch. She looked around. Several TV crews were recording the speech, and they panned cameras across the audience. This was where the action was.

She heard Kampagner say, ". . . and may God bless America." The audience rose, showering him with applause, and she stood. As the crowd thinned, Jed asked where she parked.

"In a garage."

"I'll walk you over," he said. "We've had a wave of muggings."

He held his arm around her as they walked down Illinois Street. "You were very sweet to Judge Haverly," Jed said.

"He's a sweet old guy," she said.

"And still with it. He retired after a stroke, but his legal acumen is intact. He teaches continuing-ed, and those seminars are always sold out."

Stepping over a patch of frozen soft drink on the sidewalk, they reached the garage and went to the elevator. She pressed the fourth-floor button, and they went up.

"I'm going to feel terrible if you get mugged after I leave," Libby said.

"Then you'd better kiss me now," Jed said, pulling her close. She was surprised by his ardor. The door opened at the fourth floor. Jed hit the "Close Door" button and held it down. He pulled her tighter with his other arm. Libby returned his energy, but upon hearing voices outside, she whispered, "I think somebody's trying to use the elevator." She gently swatted his hand off the control panel. The door opened, and an elderly couple stared, unsmiling.

"Excuse us," Jed said as he and Libby hurried from the elevator car. "The button gets stuck sometimes," he called over his shoulder.

Libby laughed and punched Jed in the arm. He laughed like a schoolboy. She stopped short. "Where's my Jetta?" she said.

Jed laughed harder. "Think, think," he said, like a hypnotist. "When I count to three, you will remember."

She saw the Jetta near the end of a row. "There it is." She scurried toward the car, and Jed trailed.

As she unlocked the door, Jed stuck his finger in her back. "All your money – now!" he said in a low voice.

"I have friends in powerful places," an imperious Libby said.

"The tooth fairy?" Jed said.

"Among others," she said.

Getting in, she started the car and unrolled the window. He leaned in and kissed her on the cheek.

"Thanks for coming down here tonight," Jed said.

"Thanks for inviting me," she said. "See you soon?"

"You bet," he said, kissing her lips. He stepped back, and she eased the car out.

At home, staring at a blank page in the bedside journal, Libby relived her evening. She twirled her pen in concave doodles. A rap came to mind:

> They call me Lib tell a fib so fly ruff bid
> Got Jed no lead he fine go to –

She broke off, tossing the pen up in the air. The pen hit the ceiling and fell on the quilt.

CHAPTER 47
Present Day – Spring

Jed called Libby on a Saturday in mid-March. "Where are you?" he said.

"I'm at home. It's my weekend off." She was nonchalant, because he'd called only a few times since the bar association event.

"Good! Can we go for a drive this afternoon and get dinner?" he said.

She let herself say, "You can pencil me in?" She was sorry right away for her tone. After a moment, Jed's voice quivered.

"Uh, I thought we might unwind a little with a ride in the country, and then try this Italian place up by Zionsville," he said.

Libby knew he rarely said, "Uh," and she sought to doctor their rapport. "Yes, turtledove, we can fly to the Zion-zenith."

"OK if I come by around two-thirty?" he said, relaxing.

"Yes. What should I wear?" Blast it! She'd said it, again.

"The restaurant's pretty casual from what I hear. It's up near a borrow pit," he said.

"Casual it is," she said. "I'll be ready."

Jed arrived wearing his suede bomber jacket and sunglasses, and a black turtleneck sweater with a pair of casual slacks.

"You look like you should be in a cigarette advertisement," she said.

"Unwholesome?" he said.

"No, you know, just, I don't know. Never mind," she said. The corners of his mouth began to twitch. He wasn't going to let up.

"I obviously don't resemble a cowboy. Maybe a hit man?" he said, helping her put on a navy pea jacket.

"No," she said. He followed her out the front door.

"So you admit that you've seen a hit man?" he said.

"Of course not," she said, locking the door.

"Then how would you know whether I look like one?" he said.

She hurried down the steps to the car. "It just occurred to me that I'm trying to get away from you, but we're getting into *your* car," she said. Jed laughed.

"What was it you called me earlier – turtledove?" he said with mock disbelief. He opened the car door for her.

"Yes. They leave sticky droppings," she said.

He almost skipped around to the driver side. "So – first you call me a hit man, then a bird turd," he said, getting in.

"No. What I said was, you should be in a cigarette ad," she said.

"Which you have yet to explain," he said.

"Lawyers!" she said.

They drove west on all the way to Plainfield. Jed received three phone calls, which he took using a hands-free headset. During the third, he pulled a pen from the nook under the radio. Gesturing a charade of taking notes, he handed the pen to Libby. She had no paper. He pointed to the glove compartment, but it was locked.

"Carey, just a minute," he said. "I need to write this down, but I have to pull over." Jed drove into the lot of a gas station. He rummaged around in a box in the back seat and found a legal pad. Winking at Libby, he took the pen back.

"OK, go," he said. After jotting a few items, including a phone number, he thanked the caller and hung up.

"Sorry about that," he said, tossing the pad onto the back seat. "We resume our journey."

"Why didn't you have him send you a text message?" Libby said.

"Paranoia," Jed said.

She looked at him. He wasn't smiling.

"A politician's list of appointments, phone numbers, dinner reservations – all very useful," he said.

"To whom, aside from the press?" she said.

Silent for a moment, he answered then. "Hackers. Private investigators."

"What?" she said.

He moistened his lips. He wished he could postpone this talk. "Libby, I'm under surveillance by any number of interested parties – my own allies, even. It's a fact of life in politics.

"The average citizen hears about investigators all the time, but it's always in the context of something happening to a big fish, not a local person."

"How do you know you're being watched?" she said, appalled.

"Several means. My office is swept weekly for bugs. My phones are checked. The underside of my vehicle is searched for stuff attached with magnets, and the inside of the car is examined, too," he said.

She squirmed a little in her seat.

"It was gone over yesterday," he said.

"That's awful. What are you doing that's so bad?" she said.

"Nothing. That's the funny part. Some people are just addicted to collecting information. They're not targeting for a specific purpose; they're casting a broad net. Power brokers are always interested in finding bombs they can drop, even if they decide to wait ten years to use them.

"Case in point – a local legislator sired a couple of children out of wedlock. His mistress moved to Wyoming with the kids. That was fifteen years ago. Before the last Congressional primary, he declared his candidacy, but pulled out of the race. His opponent threatened to disclose the existence of the guy's second family," Jed said.

"How did *you* find out?" she said.

"Army was at the meeting when the bomb was dropped. And that's just between you and me, turtledove," he said.

Libby mulled it over. "So the blackmailer knew all along, but kept it until he needed to use it."

"Yes. And it was a 'she.' She had photographs of the children taken at different ages," Jed said.

Libby's eyes filled. She looked straight ahead. A single teardrop escaped and trickled. She wiped it away. Jed sighed with deep resignation.

"The good news is, the tooth fairy is real," he said.

"Was Army at that meeting, too?" she said. Jed laughed. He reached over, stroking the side of her face with his index finger. He changed the subject.

"Saint Paddy's is next week. I get to march in the parade because I'm the prosecutor."

"I'm sorry I can't go to the parade, for once," Libby said. "It would be fun to shoot photos of you. I normally don't care about the holiday, but when you know somebody . . ."

He began looking for a county road on the right-hand side as they passed out of Plainfield. "This is it," he said, turning north. "I've been driving out here since I was in high school. When my best school buddy's grandfather died, I went to the funeral. He was buried up the road in a little cemetery that dates to the Civil War.

"If you look on maps on the Web, you can find the town marked with a dot. But when you drive through it, you don't know you were there. No vestiges."

They rode in silence, and after a minute, she cleared her throat. "Jed, do you spy on people?"

"No," he said. "But I will defend myself against threats."

"Such as?" she said.

"Threats. Verbal, physical, all kinds. Sometimes you need an edge," he said.

"How have you been threatened?" she said.

"Well, for one thing, after the May primary, somebody sent me a photo – of me. I was sitting alone in a fast-food restaurant at night. You could see the French fries."

His jaw stiffened. "Then I got a photo of my dog and me in the backyard at home."

She shook her head in disapproval. "What was the point?"

"Intimidation. Whoever sent them was saying they knew where I was all the time. I don't believe they did know – but we took those incidents seriously. I took certain precautions. And Gale was a big help. I never entered the house at night during the campaign without him escorting me."

"I would just hate having to worry about going into my own home," Libby said. "I don't ever want to live that way." Jed looked crestfallen, but she didn't see his expression as she watched the road.

A snow flurry began and stopped after a few minutes. "No trace of a town, but a trace of winter," she said.

"Yeah," he said. Just when he was allowing himself to be happy, his spirit weathered a trace of winter. He brightened when he came to the bend in the road just before the cemetery.

"You probably wonder about a guy who visits cemeteries on a cloudy day," he said. Slowing and signaling a left turn, he waited as two vehicles passed by.

"Not really. Cemeteries are works of art. They make interesting photos," she said.

He turned into the horseshoe-shaped drive arching around the burial ground. "That reminds me of what happened the time I brought my camera out here," he said. "I was working on the high-school paper, and I had the use of an expensive camera the school owned.

"I thought it would be neat to practice black-and-white photography of highly textured surfaces.

"I came about an hour before sundown. I got very wrapped up in what I was doing, and I put the lens cap on a headstone.

"When it was time to go, I'd forgotten which headstone I'd put the cap on. The light was going fast, and I couldn't see very well. I was walking over graves and feeling the markers, and then a bunch of stray cats appeared out of nowhere.

"I mean, poof – they were all around me, meowing, rubbing against me. It was creepy. I kept saying, 'Go away – go away.'

"I got really frustrated. I didn't want to go back to school and say that I'd lost the lens cap. And all these cats kept circling and rubbing. I could swear I heard the faint echo of laughter.

"I finally found the cap, and I couldn't wait to get out of here. After that, I gave myself plenty of time to leave before sundown." he said, parking the car.

***

The cemetery was on a ridgeline, and the steep, tree-lined, south face of the hill dropped to a creek bed not visible from the lot. Jed first showed her where his friend's grandfather was buried. As she looked around, Libby was impressed with the fealty of living descendants who still left flowers for relatives they'd never met – people who died a century ago.

"My buddy said his granddad thought it would be an honor to be buried alongside Civil War veterans," Jed said.

"What made you want to come back?" Libby said.

"The first time, it was because I needed to write a theme for English class. We had to describe a true incident, and the exercise was about using metaphors.

"I remembered this place and thought the funeral would be a good subject. I'd just gotten my driver's license, so I asked to use the car. My Dad was reluctant, but he gave in."

"When I got here, it was bright and sunny – a Saturday. I started walking about, just reading the markers.

"After a while, I started making a list of comparisons. Tombstones were like the headboards of beds; the flowers were like gifts left by fairies during the night. And then I realized these were similes, not metaphors," Jed said.

"A mighty fortress is our God," Libby said. "That's what I memorized as an example of a metaphor."

"Right," Jed said. "So then I had to start over. It was hot – and I sat on the ledge of a tombstone and drank a can of pop. Then it came to me that I'd have to rename some of the dead.

"I started with my friend's grandfather. He never served in the armed forces, but he wanted to be near his kin. He carried their flag, so to speak. So I called him the 'golden pennant marking the campsite of souls.'

"But that wasn't enough. The teacher said he wanted at least three metaphors. Coming up with the second was easier – the mourners at the funeral were 'muted cannons.' I was stuck on the third. I started viewing more tombstones, and I got fascinated with the giant, reddish-pink one over there," he said, pointing.

They walked to a big slab. The woman's epitaph said, "A Mother to Orphunts."

"When I saw this, I was moved. I could just see all those urchins scrambling up the steps to her house, where she was waiting with outstretched arms. Standing here, I felt like I was on her front porch.

"I said that in life, one of the grandfather's new neighbors had been a front porch for lost and lonely children."

Libby saw the idealistic boy in front of her. "That's lovely," she said. She leaned over, kissing him on the cheek. "Show me more," she said. They walked arm in arm around the cemetery, and then a stiff wind chased them back to the car. Thunder boomed in the west.

CHAPTER 48
Present Day – The Bug Juice Guy

Jed and Libby arrived at the restaurant on Main Street in Zionsville in Boone County on the northwestern fringe of Indianapolis. The town kept its brick street in the old village, but the Italian eatery was on the paved road leading into town. Judging from the quickly filling parking lot, the Etruscan Mode was serving dinner to an early crowd.

Rain eased from torrential to sloppy, and Jed and Libby darted to the entrance, where a vigilant host held the door for them. "We're getting a canopy soon," the host said. He checked Jed's name off the reservation list and escorted the couple to a table near a potbellied stove, which cradled a gas flame. Accepting the offer of a glass of wine, Libby picked chardonnay. Jed preferred a light beer.

"I think it's your turn to choose for both of us," Jed said.

She ordered risotto with red radicchio and onions in balsamic salsa, and for the main course, herb-crusted rack of lamb with Mediterranean vegetables in rosemary sauce. The waiter suggested a red wine with dinner, but the couple settled on iced tea. Dessert was dark chocolate shortbread with vanilla ice cream.

"Wow," Jed said, leaning back in his chair as he drank the after-dinner coffee.

"Yes, wow," Libby said. They eyed the pizza being delivered to the next table.

"No imagination," Jed whispered.

Comfortable with gaps in their conversation, they contemplated the meal and each other. When dessert was brought, Jed shifted in his chair. His left calf came to rest against Libby's right leg, and she nuzzled him back. They sat connected, enjoying the shortbread, and then Libby excused herself for a few minutes to visit the lady's room. The coffee and mints arrived while she was gone, and so did a visitor. Seeing him, she sagged a little and then pulled herself up.

"Oh, Dave, this is Libby Doherty," Jed said. The visitor shook hands with her.

"Dave Black," the visitor said.

Dave Black? *The* Dave Black? She remembered the night last fall at the art museum, when the two nerds – the lobbyist and the salesman – excused themselves to join their imaginary friend, Dave Black.

"Nice to meet you," she said. "Are you a lobbyist?" she said. Jed gave her a look that said, "What brought that on?"

Dave laughed. "I'm an exterminator. I lobby to get rid of bugs," he said.

Libby saw how dumb the question was. "Oh, well, I just wondered, because, uh – I did know of a Dave Black who represented – an industry at the statehouse," she said. "I guess we could use an exterminator at the capitol, come to think of it."

Dave laughed. "I don't think I have enough canisters for that outfit," he said. "I'll just stick to residential and commercial pests."

"I take it you're here for dinner, and not to exterminate?" Libby said, winking at Dave. Jed turned red and started to laugh.

"This is a pretty nice place, but I've seen a few where I could have earned a quick buck," Dave said.

"It's nice to meet you. Enjoy the dinner. Ours was wonderful," Libby said, sitting down. Dave left to join his party.

After a beat, Jed repeated, deadpanning, " 'Are you a lobbyist?' I was about to object to the line of questioning as lacking foundation, but you established relevance quickly enough."

"It's a long story," she said.

"I have no doubt," he said.

After they finished the coffee, Libby said, "Do let me leave the tip this time," and she glanced at the bill to calculate twenty percent. She left a stack of bills on the credit-card tray. As they walked out, she said, "You never did say how you knew the exterminator."

"We went to high school together. At first, he started his own bug business. It fizzled, and he bought a franchise of a well-known exterminator. Things took off for him because of the chain's marketing program. He does quite well," Jed said.

Sunset was in forty-five minutes, but cloud cover hid the display. The wind blew heavily, drying the earth from the earlier downpour. "Let's take the local streets instead of the highway," Jed said.

As they neared 71st and Spring Mill, Jed pointed toward the south. "Gale lives back in there. He almost moved when he got his property tax bill. He said if his wife hadn't been a teacher all these years, they never would have made it this far uptown.

"He was from Beech Grove, and there's nothing wrong with that," Jed said. Remembering something, he started to laugh. "Gale!" he said.

"What about him?" Libby said.

"One time, we were working on a case, and the defendant's lawyer pursued a complaint that the arresting officer roughed up the defendant.

"Gale saw the video of the interrogation, and he didn't think any brutality was committed. I forget what the lawyer said to set Gale off, but Gale got really flustered – one of the few times I've seen that happen.

"He said, 'That's the way the mop flops,' and he meant to say, 'And the cookie crumbles.' But what came out was, 'And the cookie craps,' " Jed said, dissolving into laughter. Libby laughed, too.

"I told Army Hauser about it. He couldn't wait for an excuse to say to Gale, 'That's the way the cookie craps,' " Jed said.

CHAPTER 49
Present Day – Their Night

Libby fingered the cover of the bedside journal. It shouldn't be visible, provoking his curiosity. She dropped the book into the top drawer of her dresser. Jed was freshening up in the bathroom. He would come down the hall soon.

When they arrived at the house, she'd said, "Why don't you pull in the driveway and park in back?"

They came in through the kitchen door. She took his coat to the front closet, while he poured a glass of water from the pitcher she'd taken from the refrigerator. He leaned against the kitchen counter and drank. She returned, beckoning.

She clasped his hand and stepped back at arm's length. She pulled him like a kite to the living room. As they sat down, she twirled like a dancer, landing with his arm comfortably around her. She kicked off her shoes, and he did, too. The grandfather clock struck the quarter hour. She closed her eyes and leaned against his shoulder. She fell asleep.

Jed listened to the steady rhythm of her breathing, slightly out of sync with the tick of the clock. He couldn't decide whether she breathed behind the beat, or ahead of it. He studied the painting above the gas fireplace. The languid mood of the picture belied the activity in the auction scene. He saw the mattress in the pickup truck. He let out an involuntary sigh, which woke her up.

"Asleep . . . Stupid!" she said.

"Perfectly natural," he said, kissing her forehead. Watching the pendulum, they felt the potential of energy build with each tick. Exactly on the beat, Libby stood up, pulling Jed to the side hall and pointing him toward the bathroom.

"You first," she said, releasing him. She headed to her room, turned on the overhead light, and pulled back the bedcovers. She took her robe out of the closet. Spying the bedside journal, she concealed it in the dresser. Her hands shook a little, and she relaxed, taking a deep breath. The clock struck the half-hour. She felt like she'd walked through an invisible door to a vast plain, where she now surveyed a vista of bright sunlight. She didn't hear Jed come down the hall in his stocking feet, and suddenly, he was next to her.

"You can put your things on a hangar in the closet," she said, picking up the bathrobe. "Be right back." A few minutes later, she returned, tossing her clothes onto the wooden chair. Already under the blankets, Jed had hooked his hands behind his head and was staring at the ceiling. Seeing her, he pushed down the coverlet and slapped the empty space on the mattress to welcome her. Facing him, she slipped out of her robe and tossed it onto the chair. Naked, she stood at the foot of the bed. He inhaled and let out a long sigh. She made a slow turn, letting him see all of her, and she reached for the wall switch to shut off the overhead light. In the dark, she raised the window shades a quarter to let light from the street through the filmy drawn curtains. She stood next to the bed and looked down at Jed. He reached with warm hands for the mid-section of her silhouette and toppled her into bed.

Sunday morning brought clear, cold weather. Through the window over the kitchen sink, she watched birds line up along the peak of the garage roof. The basement door was open, and she kept one ear perked for the buzzer on the clothes dryer. Drinking coffee and chewing a bagel and cream cheese, she let the crumbs fall into the sink. Gray sweats and slippers kept her warm against the cool air from the crack where the storm door was propped open.

Barefoot and wrapped in a towel, Jed padded into the kitchen. "The floor is freezing," he said, taking pains to rub the soles of his feet against Libby's pant legs. He wrapped his arms around Libby from behind. "Do you know what my dad would have said about leaving the door open on a cold day?"

"Probably the same thing my dad says," Libby said. "I'll shut it now. I just wanted the outdoorsy smell." She closed the storm and wooden doors.

"I favor the outdoors, but usually when I'm dressed," he said, forgetting the stay-outdoor-naked contests he'd held with his old girlfriend, Cynthia. In fact, in the last twelve hours, he'd forgotten Cynthia. "Where are my clothes?" he said.

"Right where you left them," Libby said.

Vulture-like, he swooped from behind and grabbed her. He muttered in her ear. "Madam, I file a protest in earnest. My underwear hath fled," he said.

The dryer buzzer sounded. "Follow the trail of lint to the basement, and you'll find your underwear," she said.

He muttered into her other ear. "I don't want to walk in the moat slime in my bare feet."

"Oh, all right," she said in mock martyrdom. "The basement is dry, but I guess I can fetch your underwear." She went downstairs and emptied the dryer. Noticing the yardstick on the tool shelf, she made a flag with plastic clothespins attaching the shorts and T-shirt to the stick. Going upstairs, she halted short of the top step and waved the stick around the corner of the doorframe.

"Worship, I greet thee with all deference and good will, and hereby submit, authentically, thy undergarments," she said.

"They'd better be authentic," he said, snatching the warm clothes from the pins. She came into the kitchen. He slipped on the T-shirt. "Smells good," he said. He dropped the towel from his waist and hopped into his shorts. "That's much better," he said. He handed her the towel. "I thank you, milady, for thy personal care of my shorts."

Smiling, she gave back the towel. "Please hang this up in the bathroom." He answered by kissing her delicately on the cheek.

"Anon, madam," he said, turning to go. She tapped him gently on the rear end with the yardstick.

"I'll get you, Little Red Riding Molar," he said, not looking back.

She threw together a bowl of sliced oranges and bananas and toasted another bagel. "Butter and cream cheese?" she said, when he appeared.

"Just the cheese, thank you," he said.

She poured his coffee. "Do you want eggs, or cereal?" she said.

"No, this is fine," he said, sitting down. "After I go to Mass, I have brunch with a group that hits a different restaurant after church every week."

"Ah," she said. She leaned against the kitchen counter and drank some more coffee.

"I never miss Sunday Mass," Jed said. "I often go on Saturday night, because it fulfills the obligation. But as you recall, I was busy last night," he said. "You were overbooked as well," he said.

She smiled. "Did I mention I was raised a Lutheran?"

"I'm told it's Catholicism without the middleman," Jed said, between bites of fruit.

"The middleman being the priest?" she said.

"Yep," he said.

"I guess so. We didn't confess to the pastor, unless we had no one else to tell," she said. "But you'll have plenty to tell." She leaned down and whispered into his ear, and he blushed.

"Also," she said, "I should point out . . ." She uttered a few more details into his ear.

"Dr. Booth, that's not how I remember things," he said. "And you were pretty loud."

She laughed, sitting down across from him.

"One of these days, you should come to Mass with me, and we'll compare notes on men of religious authority," he said.

"Will the priest be wearing a Notre Dame jersey?" she said.

"Nah," he said. "But we might strip you, ravish you, and sacrifice you at the altar. It's what we Catholics do. But at the last minute, we might sell you into white slavery," Jed said.

"I'm going to burn a Cross on your lawn," Libby said.

"And who said girls from Iowa don't know how to have a good time?" he said.

CHAPTER 50
Present Day -- Pizza

The lawn of Jed's one-story white brick home, with the curved, paned front window and the black garage door, was immaculately kept. The condition of the adjacent properties also reflected pride of ownership. Libby parked in the driveway and approached the front door. As she neared the stoop, she heard furious yapping. Jed shouted "*Los!*" and opened the door. He was in jeans and a T-shirt.

"Hi," Libby said, smiling at the college boy in front of her. She, too, was wearing jeans and a T-shirt. She stepped inside, and the dog skidded up to her.

"This is *Los!*" Jed said.

"Los?" she said.

"No, no," Jed said. "*Los!*" he barked from the gutter of his throat.

"It sounds like a command of some sort, like, 'Sit!' " she said.

"You're close," he said. "Have you ever seen *The Enemy Below*, with Robert Mitchum and Curt Jurgens?"

"Can't say that I have," she said.

"It's a World War Two story about a sea battle. The German U-Boat commander, played by Jurgens, is giving the order to fire, and he says, "Torpedoes – *Los!*"

"*Los!*" Libby said, more like an angry schoolteacher, and less like a German.

"No, no," Jed said, repeating "*Los!*" as if a party noisemaker had unfurled in his throat and fired out of his mouth.

"I'll work on it," Libby said. "Why did you name your dog that?"

"Because I like the way it sounds. *Los!*" The dog raced to the end of the hall and turned around, racing back.

"Rather like a torpedo," Libby said. "But one that comes back."

"Yes," Jed said.

Jed took her to the kitchen and offered a low-calorie beer.

"Split it with you," she said.

"OK," he said. "I knew you'd enforce health standards, so I ordered half-veggie, half-pepperoni. It should be here anytime."

He expertly poured the beer to reduce the volume of foam. They clicked their mugs together. "Cheers," he said.

"Curt Jurgens," she said.

She studied the kitchen, redecorated in the early 1990s. Jed's mother had labored many hours in a comfortable niche. Abundant countertop space would allow for an assembly line of mixing bowls and cookie sheets. The wallpaper theme in gray, gold and salmon with a blue-gray trim gave the room a peaceful aspect. Facing south, windows over the sink would let in the mid-day sun as a homemaker went about her chores. A single window, also facing south, was opposite the table, which sat near the arch to the hallway. In the northeast corner, a cupboard towered, painted blue to match the trim. On the other side of the cupboard, an arch opened to the formal dining room, adjacent to the garage. The door to the garage was at the east end of the utility room adjoining the kitchen. One could walk a complete circuit from the foyer to the kitchen, then into the dining room, and back through the living room to the foyer. Libby looked down. Flecked blue and gray, the floor tiles were clean, but dull.

"Do you keep house, or do you have a maid?" she said.

"I have a housekeeper who comes in once a week to dust and vacuum, clean the kitchen and bath, and mop the floors."

But not wax, Libby thought. The maid service probably charged extra. Had Jed entertained her on his floor-waxing budget? Surely the prosecutor received compensation adequate for a bachelor.

The dog barked just before the doorbell rang. Jed went, coming back with a sixteen-inch box.

"Wow," Libby said. "You'll have leftovers."

"If you weren't here to hold me in check, I could eat the whole thing," he

218

said. They ate over half of it.

"Let's stop," Libby said. "Put the rest in the freezer."

Jed wrapped the leftovers and tossed them onto a stack of super-sized frozen dinners. He has no homemaking talents, Libby realized.

"Easter is coming. If you're not visiting your family, I hope you'll let me make Sunday dinner," she said. "Do you like ham?"

"Yeah. I actually don't go to Mass on Easter Sunday. I attend the Great Vigil on Saturday. Do you know about the Vigil?" he said.

"Some Lutheran churches offer it, and others don't," she said. "Mine at home didn't."

"It's the best night," he said. "The service starts with a darkened church, and the procession brings in candlelight. Later, we receive new members, and we give them a chorus, 'You have put on Jesus Christ,'" he sang, intoning a little running melody.

"And my favorite part is the litany of saints – a long one, and a little hard on the knees."

"How long does the service last?" she said.

"At least two hours," he said.

"Then you'll need a ham," she said. "I think cherry pie is in the offing."

She pondered the Easter story, including the mob shouting "Crucify him!" This reminder of state-ordered executions made her apprehensive. Jed sensed her mood shift.

"You want some sparkling water?" he said.

"Sure."

He fixed a couple of glasses.

"Thanks," she said.

"What's wrong?" Jed said.

Libby stared at the floor tiles. "You know your case about the man who killed the hardworking Haitian immigrant?" she said. "I've been following it on the news."

Jed's unblinking gaze arrested her. She had to tell the truth.

"Does it have to be the death penalty?" she said.

"It could be," he said.

"What would change things," she said.

"Many factors. To date, the defendant has proclaimed his innocence. He hasn't cooperated with the police or the prosecution," Jed said. "So, one strategy is to threaten with the death penalty, but take it off the table if the defendant will enter a plea of guilty."

She took a sip of water. He watched, sobered.

"Jed, if you're a Catholic, how can you seek the death penalty for anyone?" she said.

"The cop-out answer is that not everyone is Catholic. There are Jews, Baptists, Methodists, Presbyterians, Lutherans, and atheists who believe the death penalty befits certain crimes," he said.

"These people vote. They support legislators who keep the death penalty on the books. They expect the prosecutor to function within the context of community standards, and according to the criminal code of the state of Indiana.

"In sum, it's not all about me," he said.

"But some of it *has* to be about you," she said.

He was very calm. "And by extension, are you saying that it's also about *us*?"

She drew in her breath sharply. "*Los!*" she said softly.

He finally smiled but said nothing.

"Why can't you just file for life without parole?" she said.

"I would like to, but people need to have confidence in the criminal justice system. They need to know that if someone on probation commits a murder – as the accused did in the case of the Haitian immigrant – the system comes down hard." he said.

"I don't disagree it was a heinous crime," she said. "But you already said your answer was a 'cop-out.' If you really think so, how do you go through with it, if he does 'get' death?" she said.

"Because I'm not the only player here," he said. "The trier of fact, the appellate courts, the US Supreme Court, and even the governor, have roles to play. Not everything gets filtered through the underwear of Jed Talbot Harkness."

"I heard about a poll that said half the people would rather support a sentence of life without parole," she said.

"I've read all the surveys," he said. "If you ask a general question about capital punishment, the majority support using it. But when you ask people to rate life without parole versus the death penalty, then the numbers break evenly," he said.

"I'm not in favor of doing my job according to polls," he continued. "But what they do show me is that both constituencies, for and against, need to be accommodated. The system, and not the prosecutor alone, can provide checks and balances."

"If the system is wrong, don't you have an obligation to try to change it?" she said.

"Within a certain context. Don't think these things are water under the bridge. My parish priest is on my case all the time.

"Personally, I hate the death penalty. However, the adversary system must work properly. It's the defense attorney's job to save his client's rear end. The judge and the jury can show clemency during the punishment phase," he said.

"But Jed, would you be willing to witness an execution?" she said.

Alarmed, Jed looked at her as if she were someone he'd mistaken for Libby. "Why would I go up to Michigan City and watch an execution?"

"If you're defending the system – right to the end – then why don't you have to watch?" she said.

Suppressing an outburst, he exhaled. "If I absolutely had to, I would witness an execution. But so help me, I would do everything I could to get out of it."

Libby didn't know what to make of him.

Passionate, he leaned forward. "That doesn't mean I'm a chickenshit – It means I'm human."

Libby said nothing.

"I'm in love with you, and I'd appreciate hearing, 'Jed, you're not a chickenshit,' " he said.

Her eyes widened. "You're not," she said.

He stood, extending his hand. "I can't defend my honor on a full stomach. Let's go for a walk. Why did we eat so much?"

She rose, accepting his grip. Nearing the front door, Libby noticed the keypad. He punched in a code before they stepped out. She remembered the story he told her about the surveillance pictures he was sent.

They headed west. The night was comfortably cool. As they rounded the first corner, she said, "Stop!" She turned to face him.

"You're not a chicken, or its excrement. I just want to be sure I know you. You said you were in love with me. I believe you, but I'm afraid," she said.

"Of what?" he whispered.

"Retractions," she heard herself say. "Mine and yours."

"I'm not retracting anything." He held her in place with his eyes. "Are you intimating you're in love with me, too, but that my political decisions could change your feelings?"

"Not that you would do it to hurt me on purpose," she said in shaky voice. He wrapped his arms around her waist.

"So, if a chunk of meteor hit me on the head and I woke up a Republican, you'd have to take it all back?" he said.

"That wouldn't be enough provocation. Labels don't matter," she said. "But I will tell you – It scares me that politics could make you cross a line, and that we'd lose each other."

"You mean that I could lose *you*," he said. "Because I'm not going anywhere."

"I have to be honest," she said.

"The tricky ethics of politicians and lawyers are about as inviting to you as a mouthful of cavities," he said.

"I know what to do with the cavities," she said.

"Then regard me as an equal," he said. "I know what to do with the tricksters."

Libby realized if she acknowledged Jed's skills, she could better respect his position.

"Let me say," he began, "You're not a lawyer. You're a voter. So if you don't like the job I'm doing, don't vote for me. But you can still bake the ham."

She was mildly embarrassed. She wasn't a lawyer. She'd be angry if he questioned her own ethics as a dentist.

She certainly could vote against Jed. A sudden insight about the late Teddy infused her mental vapor: The first man she ever loved was a fellow dentist who never antagonized her. However, he died prematurely before declaring his stance on a lot of things. His record was frozen because he had no chance to offend.

As for Easter dinner, how many defendants – One? Ten? Fifty? – would Jed need to spare from capital punishment, before he could earn a single baked ham?

"It occurs to me I don't know everything," she said. While the self-deprecation was intentional, her load lifted.

"Torpedoes -- *Los!*" he said.

CHAPTER 51
The Present Day – Spring Weather

The dog walker woke up during a thunderstorm as Trevor hopped onto the bed. He whined. Hearing the peal of the storm siren, Darla swung her legs to the floor and wiggled her toes into slippers. Putting a sweatshirt over her nightgown, she snapped her fingers, and Trevor followed her to the basement. The overhead light was on, but she had a flashlight ready. She rested in a lawn chair with her feet propped on an overturned laundry basket, and Trevor sat facing her.

As the wind picked up, the overhead light went out, but the flashlight wouldn't turn on. "It's OK, baby," she said, stroking Trevor's chin, and he licked her hand. She shivered. She recognized the sensation as the onset of a message. The turbulence outside was bringing news, whether she wanted it. The low voice in her head was masculine. He was amused.

"You picked a good one, but you ought to watch more TV," he said. "And read the newspaper."

"Uncle Ray," she said, nodding.

The wind blew with greater force, and she could hear debris smacking the side of the house.

"It's only loose tree branches," Uncle Ray said.

"I picked a good one – do you mean the mass murderer I saw last autumn? Because I don't want any part of him," she said.

"Don't bother with him. He likes to be seen because he's a show-off," Uncle Ray said.

"But I picked something?" she said.

224

"You and the dog are fascinated," he said.

"The special house, where the trapped girl is?"

"She *is* trapped," he said.

"You said follow the news," she said. "What am I looking for?"

"You'll feel the coming negative energy," he said. "You'll be tempted to intercede, but don't try. There's nothing to be done."

The basement light came back on, and the flashlight started working. The siren had shut off, and so had the message.

After a few minutes, the wind subsided, and the furious wash dwindled to a steady rain.

"We can go up, Trevor," and they climbed the steps. As they passed through the kitchen, she noticed the digital clock on the stove was undisturbed by the power outage. In the bedroom, her alarm clock showed the correct time. Usually, during an outage, her clock would blink on and off until she reset the time.

She sat on the bed. The batteries in the flashlight were new. She tested it again, and this time, it worked. Perhaps the electromagnetic energy of her uncle's spirit interfered with the lights.

"I guess we'd better pay more attention to the news," she said to the dog. Very tired, she crawled under the covers, and Trevor curled up next to her.

Before she went back to sleep, she said, "I'll be tempted, but there's nothing to be done."

CHAPTER 52
Present Day – A Visitor

Libby heated leftover chili in the microwave. From the window over the sink, she watched the rain. As the earth drank, she downed a pitcher of lemon water.

She was depressed after attending a funeral. And she hadn't spoken with Jed since their pizza dinner, but why should he call after she challenged his ethics, and maybe his manhood?

Refilling the filtered pitcher, she placed it in the fridge. She let the chili bowl sit in the oven after it shut off.

Returning to her post at the window, she reviewed the funeral for Paul Stein, Frenchie's husband. The rain began just as the mourners finished the burial service.

David Mendelson had called to inform her of Paul's death and the funeral plans.

"One more thing I'll mention, to save you the trouble," David said. "The Jews don't do flowers. And we don't view the body. If you want, you can make a memorial contribution to an art museum. Any museum was a temple to him.

"I know the service will be on the Christian Sabbath, and you could have other plans. Please understand – we never issue invitations to a funeral.

"But you're a non-Jew, and I wasn't sure if you understood it was OK to attend," David said.

Libby's staff assembled at the temple, and she represented them at the burial. The sky held its display of emotion until everyone dropped a shovelful of dirt on the grave.

David's wife, Ellie, called her to the passenger window of their car. "Do you know about sitting *shiva*?" Ellie said.

"No," Libby said, opening her umbrella.

"The mourners stay inside for seven days, except to go to temple on the Sabbath," Ellie said. "If you come by today, you'll wash your hands outside the front door. Someone has set up a basin and towels.

"Today we're serving a meal of consolation. If people stop by later in the week, they should bring their own food and drink. The family isn't supposed to fix anything for guests," Ellie said.

"Usually, a mourner sits in a short-legged chair close to the floor. This is to show that grief 'brings you low.' But Frenchie won't be sitting that way because it messes up her back," Ellie said.

"I have bagels from the staff. I was wondering if you could take them." Libby said. "I thought maybe I'd wait a few weeks before I visited."

"Bagels are perfect," Ellie said, and Libby went to her car to get them.

Jolting her into the present moment, the doorbell rang. Half-dreading, half-wishing it was Jed, she was surprised to find Gale Mooneyham.

"Get in out of this rain," she said. He stamped water on the doormat.

"Sorry to bring the weather in," he said.

"Come on back and have some chili," she said.

"Chili! Now that is tempting, but I didn't invite myself to dinner. I just wanted to find out how Barbara Stein was doing."

Libby was flabbergasted. Surely, he and Frenchie had met only once, when Jed came by with a toothache.

"I'll tell you all about it, if you'll have some chili." He followed her to the kitchen.

He saw the table setting. "Shoot, I didn't mean to barge in," he said. "My wife and I eat a big lunch on Sundays and then we have popcorn and milkshakes for supper. I should have called."

"I'm very glad to see you," she said. And she really was.

Using a hot pad, she put the steaming bowl at the place setting. "You'll need a glass of something cold, like iced tea?"

"Tea sounds good. This looks like all your dinner," he said.

"No. I have a quart left. If you don't help me, I'll just freeze it." She prepared another bowl and put it in the microwave.

She poured his tea over ice in a tumbler, and he sat down. His eyes gleamed like the gold chain peeking from the unbuttoned collar of his short-sleeved, pale rose dress shirt. His thick gray hair was tousled, and a recently acquired tan complimented his gray mustache. He'd been to Florida for a short vacation.

"Go ahead and eat, and I'll do the talking," she said.

"Cops like to eat. Especially old ones," he said, digging in.

Libby sat opposite him. For the moment, curiosity suppressed her appetite. She wanted to know more about his acquaintanceship with Frenchie. Libby described the funeral, and he listened, interrupting only once with, "Good chili!"

"Thank you," she said.

"It's too bad she's alone now," Gale said. "Barbara is very nice."

"I thought you met her at my office," Libby said. "Did you run into her later?"

"I sure did. My neighbor to the east is an elderly Jewish lady by the name of Myra Himmel – a widow who needs help with chores and things. Myra broke her hip last fall, and Barbara came over with soup and sandwiches while I was there vacuuming on a Saturday.

"So the three of us sat down and ate. The soup was delicious, with all these little potatoes floating around. And we talked for a long time. Finally, my wife called to see if something happened to Myra, and I realized we'd been sitting there for three hours.

"So that's how I knew Barbara, and then it got to be a regular thing, when I'd be working on something – and she'd come by. And then as her husband got sicker, she couldn't drop in as often.

"She was over there last week, and she said her husband was way gone on pain meds. I figured this was coming to a close, and then I saw the obituary," Gale said. He finished his tea.

"You need a refill," Libby said. "I used extra chili powder." She poured another glassful. The microwave had sounded, but she ignored the bowl.

"You would have been welcome at the funeral, but Frenchie knows that non-Jews are relaxing on Sundays." Libby said.

Gale nodded. "We had a big dinner with the grandkids."

Libby was proud to know this man. He was the campfire meal in people's lives.

"You know," Gale said, "She introduced herself to me as Barbara, and Myra calls her that, too. Everybody else uses the nickname. I wonder why."

"She let you into an elite circle," Libby said.

"That's nice to think so," Gale said. "Get to that chili, Libby." She obeyed. They discussed his day with the grandchildren, and Libby recalled that he lived seventy blocks away. "What brought you down here?" she said.

"I had to make a quick run to Beech Grove to deliver a bottle of pills. My brother and his wife came up for lunch, and he takes diabetes medication at mealtimes. He left the bottle at my house." Gale rolled his eyes. "Zero refills." He shook his head.

"Coming back, I thought I'd stop by," he said.

"How did you know where I lived?" Libby said.

"Been here several times," he said. "Jed said you witnessed an armed robbery. I made a few sweeps through the neighborhood, just to make sure nothing came home with you."

Libby swallowed a spoonful of chili and cleared her throat. "You didn't have to do that." she said.

"Jed told me about that mess up in the pub in Lawrence, so I read the case reports. I called Ken Davis. He and I go way back. I told him, 'So much as a falling leaf lands on that woman, I want to know,' " Gale said.

Libby reddened. "You don't have to worry about me."

Gale regarded her sternly, but with favor. "I want you to understand something. In law enforcement, we take care of our own." He took a business card from his wallet. "Keep this in your purse. Just call me and say, 'I've got a problem.' I'll take care of it, and nobody needs to know why."

"Gale!" she said, softly, accepting the card.

"Jed prizes you," Gale said. "I've told him many times, 'Don't let that one slip away.' " Gale's eyes had a faraway, but satisfied look. Turning somber, he took deep breaths. His shoulders rose and fell with each breath. He folded his hands.

"Oh! I almost forgot!" Libby said. "You can visit Frenchie while she's sitting *shiva*."

"Is that painful?" Gale said. "It sounds like something with rotating knives."

Libby recapped Ellie's brief explanation. "You could stop by, take some food. Maybe Mrs. Himmel would go with you," Libby said.

Gale cocked an eyebrow. "That might be a way to get Myra out of the house. She's terrified of falling and breaking the other hip."

"If you stop by a kosher bakery, you'll find what you need," Libby said.

"That's a good idea. I'll call Myra when I get home. She'll be impressed when I talk about sitting *shiva*," Gale said.

Libby chuckled. "I hadn't heard of it until today. I was raised Lutheran. What about you?"

"Methodist born and bred," Gale said. He looked at his watch. "My wife probably thinks I got engrossed in a TV show at my brother's. I should be going," he said, standing.

As they reached the front door, Libby said, "If you drop by accidentally-on-purpose, I might have some homemade pizza with artichokes."

Gale's eyelids fluttered. He mopped his brow with his fingertips. "Nighty-night, you temptress!" he said.

CHAPTER 53
Present Day – An Introduction

On Good Friday, Libby closed her office at noon. She had not observed Holy Week in many years, but seeking a refuge that fostered peace and meditation, she decided to visit a church. She had a rekindled heart for religious celebrations.

On her way to the car, she looked at the sign in front of the office building. The upstairs tenant, Shoemake & Higbee, was still listed, and she recalled first bumping into Jed after he visited them. She never asked him what they did.

She went back in, going upstairs for the first time. Occupying the entire second floor, the suite was laid out with the foyer in the center, and office space on either side. As she reached the landing, she faced windowless wooden double doors. They were closed. Chrome lettering on the wall to Libby's left said "Shoemake & Higbee, Suite 200."

She stood, considering excuses for going in. Perhaps she could introduce herself, saying it was important to know the other tenants. She was acquainted with the engineering consultant from the suite next to hers, but only because he stopped in, asking about dental work for his children. She wouldn't recognize either Shoemake or Higbee, assuming they were alive.

Her debate ended when the doors opened. A middle-aged, tautly muscled fellow with curly, reddish-blond hair stepped forward. He wore a crisply ironed blue-and-white striped shirt, and stone-colored jeans.

"Can I help you?" he said.

"No . . . well, I mean, yes," she began. He scrutinized her without seeming impatient. "I'm Dr. Doherty, from downstairs, in the dental office."

"Hi." And that was all he said.

"I moved the practice here about a year ago, but I never met the tenants above me. I closed early today. I thought I'd introduce myself." she said.

"OK," he said. "I'm Mike Higbee."

Alive! She extended her hand, and he shook it.

"So, you have a partner, Shoemake?" she said.

"Yes, but he's not here. He's on a boat somewhere near the Yucatan Peninsula."

"Wow," she said.

He didn't offer more.

"I imagine that whatever you do professionally is quite demanding, so a vacation was probably in order," she continued.

"It was," Higbee said. He was making it hard. Standing at ease, she put nervous hands behind her, like a mere corporal addressing the visiting brass. "My neighbor downstairs is an engineer," she said. "What do you do?"

"We're a security firm," he said.

"A very important function. Do you install alarms?"

"We can," he said.

She nodded, as if hearing something profound. "So, if I needed one for my office, you could put one in?"

"Sure. But we'd assess your security needs first. It might be you needed something else even more."

"Like what?" she said.

"Protection against computer hacking, theft of confidential data. Or even background checks on prospective employees."

"All valuable services," she said, deciding to go for it. "Do you ever check out things for non-profit organizations . . . or political campaigns?"

Higbee was expressionless. "I guess that's always a possibility," he said.

"What about . . . uh . . . surveillance? I mean, if somebody were concerned about crank calls or stuff like that, would you be able to help him? Or her?" she said.

Shifting his weight, Higbee tilted his chin upward. "Are you having some kind of trouble?" he said.

"No, not at all. I was just trying to envision everything that a security firm might do," she said, feeling queasy.

"It would still depend on the assessment. We try not to prejudice our thinking about what a client may need," he said, looking at his watch. She took this as her cue.

"It's nice to meet you," she said. "I guess I should be going – Have a nice Easter."

"Same to you, Dr. Doherty." He watched, not moving, as she went downstairs. She faked serenity on the way to her car. But she wasn't sure she could drive, so she gave herself a minute before she started the engine.

"Oh, crap!" she said.

At home, she paced to and fro in the living room. Right under his private detectives all along! Dammit! Why didn't he tell her? Was he having her watched? And the creepy way Mike Higbee just appeared. He must have seen her standing like an idiot in front of a security camera.

It was almost one-thirty. She didn't want to miss the church service, but she wanted Jed's explanation. She called his cell.

"Yes, turtledove?" he answered.

"I met Mike Higbee today." Jed didn't respond.

"Aren't you going to ask me what we talked about?" she said.

"No, but I will discuss it with you later. In person. Can this wait until Sunday?"

"No, it really can't. I'm pretty upset," she said.

"OK. We're expecting a verdict in a child-murder case. I don't know how late it's going to be, but I imagine we'll hear from the jury today. Can you go for a ride after lunch tomorrow?"

"No, I don't want to wait that long," she said.

***

In church Libby grew more resentful, unable to concentrate fully on the message of Good Friday. She slipped in as the service started, sitting near the back of the sanctuary. She guessed maybe forty worshippers were in attendance. Jed agreed to stop by her house later, and she couldn't relax.

The sermon conveyed a cautionary insight about acknowledging the presence of light in each soul. Christ's tormenters didn't see his light, and every day, we don't even see the good in ordinary people, the minister said. Libby wished she could x-ray Jed's soul. Light was important in the production of x-rays. Interpreting the dense images in a dental x-ray was crucial to understanding the whole picture. Where enamel and dentin were broken down, the image was denser. Healthier teeth allowed light to pass through the crystalline structures.

Was it thus with the human soul? Had she failed to recognize a dense area in Jed's soul? She prayed for help.

Around eight-thirty in the evening, Jed called to report a guilty verdict. "This one grabbed a kid outside an after-school program," he said.

When Jed arrived, he had circles under his eyes. He wore the prosecutor's gray pinstripe suit and forgettable tie. Unsure of what to do, he stood in the center of the living room. Seeing his confusion, she motioned him to the kitchen.

"Something to drink?" she said.

"Water's fine," he said, yearning for the recliner in his den. She pointed at a chair and he sat down at the table. She filled their water glasses and joined him.

"When I met you, you'd just been up to see Shoemake and Higbee. You had a bunch of thumb drives," she said. "Financial reports, you said. I believed you. I thought maybe the guys upstairs were accountants.

"Then later, you told me about having to check your office, your phones, and your car for listening devices. I wanted to know if you spied on people, too. You said you didn't," she said.

"And I don't," Jed said. "But I also told you I would defend myself against threats. First of all, from now on, let's refer to the security firm as 'Sink or Swim,' instead of using the corporate name."

Libby exploded. "Oh, please!"

"I'm serious, Libby. They're the ones who asked me to call them that. They know their competitors will use any means to traffic in confidential information."

"Collected right above my office," she said. "Do you have them keep an eye on me?"

Jed sounded like he had a hole in his diaphragm. "No," he said. "Why would I have them watch you?"

"You tell me!" she said.

Getting mad, he scooted his chair back from the table. "I would no more invade your privacy than I would my own mother's. What's wrong with you?"

"What's wrong is that I feel compromised. You should have told me straight out that your private investigators were housed in my building," she said.

"I don't see what difference it would have made. They were there before you moved in. Would you have moved your dental office, again, if I had told you?" he said.

"Of course not. But I would have felt better, like maybe you trusted me, and that maybe I could trust you, too."

"I didn't go out of my way to conceal anything," he said. "I just didn't think it was important."

"But it was important, Jed. Security is so important, that you worried about the safety of your dog. You needed to find out who was hanging around your house. And the day we met you acted like you were handling business about financial reports.

"What were you really doing?" she said.

"Having them check financial reports," he said, laughing. "They run a screen using databases to see if a contributor has a potential conflict, like pending charges for a DUI.

"And 'Sink or Swim' did handle the security issues around my house. They installed the alarm system, and during the campaign, they had people parked around the neighborhood."

"But I still don't see why you didn't tell me?" she said. "We were talking about all that cloak-and-dagger stuff, and it was the perfect time to say, 'Those guys above your office are my consultants.'

"It would have taken four seconds." she said.

His eyes watered, and he stared across the room at the stove. His lower lip almost caved in. "I guess I thought it was too much for you right then," he said. "You were so disgusted."

"Jed, don't try to decide what's too much for me," she said.

"Then I guess you can put a note in my personnel file. I'm tarnished now," he said.

"I don't like the sound of that. I'm not making hash marks every time you screw up," she said.

"Aren't you?" he said, leaning forward a little, like he was taking deposition.

She leaned back. "No!"

"It sure as hell feels like it," he said.

"My office is my life," she said, emphasizing each word. "I like to control my environment."

"I like to control mine. That's all I'm doing," he said.

"But your environment overlapped with my environment," she said.

"That generally happens when people sleep together," he said.

"Jed, I can't be intimate with someone who hides things. Maybe we should take a break . . . which sounds strange, considering we spend so little time together."

Jed felt his insides disintegrate, but instead of pleading for mercy, he stood up.

"I'll make this easier for you." he said. "My church throws Easter brunch in the fellowship hall. You don't have to fix lunch on Sunday."

She was disappointed he agreed, but she wouldn't back-peddle. "OK," she said. "Maybe we'll call each other in a few weeks – see how things are going?"

"I'd like that," he said. "I guess I should go home."

At the front door, they hugged, not clinging too long. After Jed was gone, Libby broke down and cried.

At the white-brick home on the city's far-northeast side, Jed cuddled his dog in the leather recliner in the den. "*Los!*" he whispered. "I wouldn't spy on you, either."

The dog growled as if to say, "I know."

CHAPTER 54
Present Day – Good Friends

Libby baked a ham with honey, brown sugar, cider vinegar, nutmeg, cinnamon, and cloves. For the appetizer – toasted baguette slices topped with goat cheese, cream cheese, and olives. Next, she'd serve a salad of broccoli and zucchini with vinagrette. For side dishes, she planned a casserole of potato, turnip, and celery au gratin, and buttered green beans with sun-dried tomatoes.

Denise came to Easter lunch with a bag of chocolate eclairs. "Not a creative choice, but they're fresh," she said.

"You hit the spot," Libby said. They enjoyed their meal at the dining room table, decorated with the centerpiece of yellow flowers and candles she'd picked out for Jed.

"Zowie," was Denise's review of the meal. "Dammit, anyhow," was her review of Jed.

"He's not so bad," Libby said.

"There you go, defending him. But high-fives for drawing the line! He probably told the truth, when he said he thought you wouldn't want to hear about his security firm. But yes, he was silly not to tell you their office was directly above yours – made it look like he had something to hide.

"I'll give him credit, at least, for having the sense to fall in love with the right woman," Denise concluded.

"Did he?" Libby said. "He was eager to leave, after I suggested we stop seeing each other for a while."

"Don't read too much into that. For one thing, he was embarrassed. For another, men flee."

"I don't know what to do, except wait a month or so, and then give him a call," Libby said.

"If you still care. As time passes, I think you'll start to miss him, and he, you. You already said this was a tiff over control. So, you need to find something else to do. When did you last take a real vacation?" Denise said.

"I went to Iowa for Christmas."

"That sort of counts. I recommend a spring get-away – to a beach," Denise said. "How far ahead do you schedule your patients?"

"They're packed tight. I could leave on Friday and come back Sunday on my weekend off."

"By all means, do so." Denise raised her wine glass. "To drawing the line, and to having a good time."

It was three weeks before Libby could get away, but she experienced euphoria during a trip to Key Biscayne, where she learned to windsurf. At an outdoor cafe next to her hotel, she watched a sunset. She didn't notice the man observing her from across the dining area, and then someone sent her another glass of wine with an unsigned note that said, "I loved the sunset, too."

Trying to figure out who ordered the wine, she scanned the room, and when her eyes landed on a distinguished-looking African American, he nodded and waved. She mouthed the words, "Thank you." As a question, he gestured as if getting up from his table to join her, and she waved him over.

"Please sit down," she said.

"Derek Barnhouse," he said, producing a business card with the logo of a well-known life insurance company. "Don't worry," he said. "I'm not in sales. I'm an actuary."

"How interesting!" she said. "I'm not carrying my cards today, but I'm a dentist from Indiana. Libby Doherty."

They talked for an hour about their mutual interests in math and science. From Hartford, Conn., he'd been to a conference of actuaries in Miami. Libby judged him to be about forty, highly intelligent, and extremely well-mannered. She found him attractive, and he could see it in her eyes. As the hour passed, she realized he wanted a sexual encounter. She was turned on, but it wasn't in her nature to pick up a stranger.

They took a short walk along the beach and returned to the veranda outside the hotel. She let him kiss her goodbye, and she enjoyed it. Then, she released herself from his hold and said, "Good night." She walked away without looking back. In her hotel room, she stretched out on the bed.

Someone besides Jed could tempt her, but she wasn't ready to invest in a new relationship. It wasn't because Derek lived in Hartford. She wouldn't bed Derek if he lived in Irvington. She thought about Jed while windsurfing high above the water. She wanted to look down and see him waving to her from the boat. She wanted him in the hotel room now. Calling him, she reached his voicemail and hung up without leaving a message. That brought her down to land. She didn't know what to say.

She didn't notice that a man with a cell phone camera was taking photos of her as she walked with Derek and kissed him. She would never be told that a manila envelope containing those pictures was mailed to Jed. He didn't think she'd believe he didn't order the surveillance. But someone had – just more psych-outs intended to demoralize him. Now, he was keeping a secret to benefit himself, because he truly feared she'd never give him another chance. He wanted to be worthy of her. He wondered if anyone in politics could ever be worthy of a woman like her.

CHAPTER 55
Present Day – Rain

On a Saturday after work, Libby went to a downtown pub for dinner. Her mood turned to despair, and she hid behind the menu a couple of times to wipe away tears. While she ate dinner, the skies unloosed heavy rainfall with dangerous winds. A person caught in the downpour would have compared it to being hit with a stream from a fire hose. The city's century-old storm sewers often failed on these occasions, and one had to know the trouble spots to avoid stalling the car in floods. Unfortunately, on the way home, Libby forgot about one vulnerable block, and she drove into a few feet of water. The automobile stalled. She stepped out and waded to higher ground. She called the auto club, and the agent said the wrecker might take an hour to arrive.

Tired, tense, and soggy, she looked around. If she waited at the nearby burger place, she could see when the wrecker was coming. She bought coffee and sat at a table with a hard bench. She called Jed.

"Dr. Booth," he answered. Despite the humidity, she felt cool and dry now.

"Jed," she said, letting herself be tender. "How are you?"

"OK. What are you up to?"

"Coffee. I'm waiting for a tow truck."

"Where are you?" he said.

"Somewhere on East Washington. I'm at Tower Burger. My car's stuck in high water, so I came here to wait. They said it might be an hour."

"Stay put. I'll be over in a few minutes." He hung up before she could argue.

He must be in the office, she thought.

"Couldn't you at least get stranded in a half-way decent neighborhood," he said, coming in. "There's a crack house around the corner."

"I hear crackheads don't like rain," she said.

Sliding in next to her on the bench, he put his arm around her and kissed her cheek. "I always take the opportunity to rescue a dentist," he said.

"I've missed you," she said. "I went to Florida last weekend. I wished you were there."

"That's more than I deserve, probably," he said. "I owe you an apology. I made light of your concerns. I was out of line. My dog and I have thoroughly hashed this over, and we don't want to be without you."

"The dog is smarter than both of us," she said.

"No truer words," he said, kissing her hard on the lips. She was aloft again, windsurfing.

They waited an hour and twenty-five minutes for the wrecker. She tried starting the car after it was yanked from the water, but no go. The truck driver jump-started the car, and she let it idle for fifteen minutes.

Jed followed her home to make sure the Volkswagen didn't stall again. "Come in," she said at home. "The first thing I need to do is wash off the water I waded through," she said.

Catching her off guard, Jed picked her up and whirled around. Half-screaming, half-laughing, she said, "I almost kicked over the lamp!"

"I've got you now, Little Red Riding Molar," he said, as he carried her to the shower.

Much later, after they dozed, she massaged his shoulders.

"Gale is having a Memorial Day cookout, and he wants to know if we'll attend," Jed said.

"Yes, we will. I've got a party to plan, too," she said.

"Is your birthday coming?" he said, alarmed.

"That's not until August," she said. She kissed the back of his neck. "No, this is to celebrate an adoption. Two guys I know brought home a little girl from China."

"Two guys?" Jed said.

"That doesn't bother you, does it?"

"It better not. I got elected by gays," he said. "And one of my deputies is gay. He's very low-key about it, but I can tell."

"The Church is a little sticky about it, wouldn't you say," she said, kneading his back.

He let out a contented sigh. "'Sticky' makes the Church sound like it has strong opinions about paper versus plastic. 'Paranoid' would be a better description, in some rectories, but the Vatican is crawling toward tolerance, believe it or not."

"These guys are harmless. They just want to be a family," she said. "Will you come to the party if I give you enough notice? I thought maybe a Sunday would work out for everybody."

"Yes, I'll come to the party, and you don't have to give me sufficient notice. It's not like you're trying to get out of a lease," he said. Rolling from under her, he pushed her onto her back and slid on top of her. He held her tenderly by the shoulders.

"I know I can't have everything, and be all things to all people," he said. "But I will be there for you, one way or another." She held him tightly, as if he were the rope dangling from a helicopter. They swayed in the wind.

CHAPTER 56
Present Day – Home Plate

The Mooneyham cook-out was a family affair. Libby and Jed were the only outsiders. Flipping hamburgers, Gale listened to his wife comment on the hot dogs and chicken breasts. "Aren't they too black?"

"Stick to your potato salad," he said. She blew him a kiss.

Jed refereed a kickball game among the grandchildren, coached by their parents, while Libby talked with Gale's brothers and sisters.

"If you don't get enough to eat, it's your own damn fault," Gale said. He popped open a beer can and guzzled. Libby enjoyed watching him chug it like a fraternity boy. He eyed his wife and let out a belch on purpose.

"Gale!" his wife said, looking sideways at Libby.

"That was good – but a little louder next time," Libby said. Gale laughed. Thoughtful, Jed watched them from afar, behind home plate.

As they grazed at the picnic table throughout the afternoon, Gale hovered, making sure Libby was having a good time. During a lull as the women put away perishables, he perched next to Libby and patted her knee.

"Full?" he said.

"You bet. It was wonderful."

"Thank you. I love the first cook-out of summer," he said.

"Your grandchildren are beautiful. Such healthy teeth," she said. "Your daughter said they go to a dentist on South Madison."

"We took our kids to him, too," Gale said. "I'm surprised he hasn't retired."

She looked around the backyard, shielded by a wooden privacy fence

243

attractively aged by weather. A line of carefully trimmed shrubs bordered the fence, and near the back of the house between the east end of the patio and the fence, a small rose garden flourished.

"Do you spend a lot of time working in the yard?" Libby said.

"My wife and I trade off. She likes pushing the manual mower, and you don't have to mow as often as you do with a gas mower."

"I have a manual mower, too," Libby said. "I'm very jealous of my time in the yard."

"Jealous of time," Gale echoed. He was somewhere else. Libby wondered if he'd had too many beers, but then Gale tuned in.

"Barbara Stein is doing pretty well, from what I can see," he said.

"I think so. It must be hard. I think grief sneaks up and pulls on you, like when you walk past a doorknob and get your clothes stuck on the knob."

"That's a good way of putting it. Or like getting duct tape stuck to itself when you're trying to pull off a clean strip," he said. He looked at her. "I've always thought you knew something about grief."

"I do," she said, wilting under his policeman's eye. "When I was in graduate school, I was involved with another student who died in a household accident. He fell through a balcony door and bled out right away."

Gale looked down. "That must have been pretty rough," he said.

"It was. I didn't perceive until recently that I'd only just begun to heal."

He looked up. "That boy working wonders?" he said, winking.

Libby giggled. "When I give him a chance," she said.

"He's still young, testing his limits. I'll put a bug in your ear. He's got people working on him to challenge Trinity Weatherstaff for her Congressional seat."

"I thought parties liked to rally around one candidate to save money," she said.

"They do, but Trinity, if you'll pardon my saying, is a first-class sterilizer. She's de-nutted a lot of people, and some of them are talking about forcing her to retire."

"She's only in her fifties." Libby said.

"Fifty-two, to be exact, but if she keeps doing like she does, she'll be lucky to see fifty-three."

"Jed hasn't told me, but that doesn't mean he's not interested," Libby said. "We don't spend a lot of time talking politics."

Gale allowed himself a leer. "If I were Jed, I wouldn't waste any time on talk," he said. Libby blushed.

"Maybe you should ask him about it," Gale said. "You can tell him I told you."

"I'll bring it up," Libby said. "But I think he'd wait for this Trinity person to self-destruct. He's not the type to go storming into somebody's mess."

"That's a very good point," Gale said. "Jed doesn't like other people's messes."

"But politicians are ambitious for something, if they want to stay alive. Isn't that so?" she said.

"Sure. Jed's probably trying to figure out what he's ambitious for. I think I'm looking at her."

"I don't know that I could replace the thrill of winning an election," she said.

"Depends on how you get your thrills," Gale said. "Speaking of that clumsy lout." he said as Jed approached.

"You talking about me, Mooneyham? I can't do anything right," Jed said. Libby felt a rush of affection for Jed, and a cascade of pity for herself. She was starting to want to be enough for him.

On the way home, Jed stopped at a gas station to fill the tank, and he went inside to get fountain drinks. As Libby waited, she steeled herself to ask about his ambitions.

"I thought I drank enough at the cook-out, but I'm still thirsty," he said, getting behind the wheel. "And this shirt is rank." Airing his neck, he tugged at the collar of his gold-and-white striped polo shirt.

You'll always be thirsty, Libby thought. "Gale said I should ask you about Trinity Weatherstaff. I understand she's a first-class pain in the pulp."

Jed's eyebrows shot up and stuck there, as he turned the car back into traffic. Safely in the passing lane, he said, "Trinity represents tooth decay in politics."

"Do you want to replace her?" Libby said.

"No," Jed said.

"Will you ever want to?" she said.

"Probably not."

"That easy?" she said.

"That easy."

"Well," Libby said, not sure of what to say next.

Jed helped her. "I've been approached more than once about challenging Trinity. In fact, Gale and I were at a vending machine in the new court building last Friday, and one of the judges came up. He said, and I quote: 'I hope the rumors about the impending demise of the un-holy Trinity are correct.' "

"A judge said that?"

"A judge," Jed said.

"What does Trinity do that's so bad?" Libby said.

"Use people in an obvious and demeaning way. But the public hasn't made a case for her replacement. Voters think she's a hip, visionary populist."

"I've heard the prosecutor is a hip, visionary populist," Libby said.

"Without the dominatrix boots," he said.

"Are you sure the antagonism toward her isn't just plain old sexism?"

"Some of it. But Trinity snuffs out the light in people. I beat Theo Karnow, but I didn't destroy him. You met him; you saw he's very much alive. But with Trinity, it's lights out."

"What happened to her last opponent?" Libby said.

"He's the one exception. A sterling person, who hasn't made the proverbial 'regrettable mistake' she's so fond of exploiting. And he has a wife who saw right through Trinity. I think the wife kept his head together during the campaign.

"It's the behind-the-scenes stuff that Trinity does." Jed said. "She's an extortionist. Eventually, you demean enough people, they'll talk about getting even."

"So," Libby said, "They want you to be the avenger."

"Yep. And that's not a good reason to run for Congress. You have to want to be in Congress."

"Do you?"

"Not now. I'm a lawyer. I like practicing law. If you listen to all the rumors, you'll hear I might run for attorney general."

"Will you?"

"Depends on a few things," he said, gripping the steering wheel as if to brace himself.

"Like what?"

"Like you," he said, staring straight ahead.

"What have I got to do with it?" she said.

Looking sad, he resolved not to give up. "I might need someone to keep my head together," he said.

"You? Captain Fundraiser?"

"That's not what I meant, Libby." He wasn't joking. He turned down a tree-shaded side street and pulled up to the curb. She swiveled in her seat to face him.

"You can fix some kid's tooth without my help," he said. "And you can manage your own practice. I can prosecute a case without your assistance, and I can run a campaign.

"I'm not talking about what each of us does alone. I'm talking about what we can do together," he said.

"Such as?" she said.

"We can get a life," he said.

"I thought we were getting one."

He didn't blink, but he took a tiny breath.

She could see a moving van pull up in the opposing lane. "Not here, not at somebody's curb," she said. "I'm not ready to talk about this yet."

Maybe he was still in the hunt. "OK," he said. "Some other curb."

CHAPTER 57
Present Day – News Junkie

Since the message from Uncle Ray, Darla had been a diligent patron of television news, and she read the on-line daily newspaper during her lunch hour. One night she set up a TV tray in the living room and brought in soup and crackers to eat during the local broadcast.

She got goose bumps when Bob Kring did a feature on the county prosecutor, Jed Harkness. He was talking about programs to get guns out of the hands of teenagers, when she heard a high-pitched tone in her ears. The tone changed pitch, and then her ears popped. The prosecutor's voice was louder now.

"This is it," she said. "Something about *him* . . . Oh, God! . . . Oh, my God! . . . Oh, God!" She squeezed the cracker in her hand until it broke into crushed meal.

But Uncle Ray had said she mustn't interfere.

She was angry now. "Why am I shown this, if I'm not supposed to do anything?"

She prayed. "Lord, help me to be patient as You reveal my purpose at the proper time."

CHAPTER 58
Present Day – Summer Living

The party for Evelyn Carter Horatio was on the second Sunday in June. In Libby's kitchen, Denise mixed apricot and pineapple juice with ginger ale to serve in the crystal punch bowl she brought.

"This was a wedding gift from the Kring cousins," she said. "I never, ever used it."

"I'm honored to be the first beneficiary," Libby said. "Just don't pee in it."

Denise laughed. "One divorce fantasy that never occurred to me."

The dining room table was covered with a mint green damask cloth. White carnations in a glass vase with gold trim graced the table. On a platter matching the vase, tea cookies glistened with mint icing. Serving trays held finger foods – pastry rolls filled with provolone and prosciutto, and bite-size sandwiches of roast beef and Roma tomatoes on cocktail rye. Crackers, fresh veggies, and spinach dip were available, along with refried beans and sour cream in tortilla logs. For Evelyn's family to take home for left-overs – a bakery-decorated cake. Green icing on stiff vanilla frosting said, "Welcome, Evvie," ringed by pastel flowers of sugar.

In a corner of the living room, Libby placed a coffee warmer and paper cups on a wooden serving cart.

The grandfather clock struck the quarter hour, and someone rapped at the back door. Recognizing Jed, Denise ushered him in, introducing herself.

Crossing into the living room, he gave Libby a peck on the cheek.

Libby suppressed a smile as Denise studied him.

"Why don't you carry in the punch for Denise and test it?" Libby said. "She's a perfectionist."

"Gladly," he said, going back for the crystal bowl, filled with fizzy, orange liquid. Denise patted the space on the table for the bowl, and he set it down. She ladled Jed a serving.

"Very nice," Jed said. "All I need is a quart of this and a recliner, and I'm set for the afternoon."

"Speaking of seating," Libby said, "You can help me put these in the living room." Her kitchen and dining-room chairs were disguised with decorative slipcovers.

Jed busied himself arranging the chairs. Removing her apron, Denise straightened her sleeveless, lavender knit dress, accented by dangling silver earrings. Libby wore a yellow pantsuit with roll-up sleeves, and Jed, a light-blue dress shirt with khaki pants. The three were attired to fit in with the guests coming from Evvie's baptism.

A gray compact car pulled up in front, and a slender Chinese man got out. From the front window, Libby watched him come up the steps. He tossed his head to get his bangs out of his eyes. How like Teddy, she thought. A baptism marked a beginning, and maybe an ending. She met the stranger at the door.

"Horatio Chang," he said. "I'm with the baptism party."

"Of course," Libby said, waving him in. "Didn't they name the baby after you?"

He giggled like Teddy. "Just for the last name, I hope."

Quickly explaining Horatio's importance in the selection of Evvie's name, Libby introduced him to Jed and Denise.

"And the baby's middle name, Carter, came from the minister who celebrated her fathers' commitment ceremony. He did the baptism, too," Horatio said, accepting a glass of punch from Denise. On the sofa, he talked sports with Jed.

More cars lined the curb, and eventually seventeen guests arrived, including Kerry Wittenhouse's parents. Reverend Hal Carter, from the United Church of Christ, offered a toast. The cups of fizzy orange liquid jiggled slightly as the celebrants laughed at his remarks.

"Kerry and Tony debated whether two guys hooked on sports could raise an effervescent little girl, who looks so ethereal in this lacey, white dress.

When I see these three together, I have no doubt they'll make it – although it's pretty obvious she's the one with the brains.

"So as God continues to bless us, let us raise our cups and give thanks. Cheers!"

"Cheers," the group answered.

Denise held the toddler on her lap, but just barely. At twenty-four months, Evvie was interested in Denise's hand-crafted earbobs. She fingered one, and Denise said, "Oh, no, no, darling." Reluctant to relinquish the child, Denise took off the earrings and gave them to Libby for safekeeping.

Jed circulated, making sure he met everyone, before he engaged in a long talk with Kerry's parents. Just before they left, Kerry's mother squeezed Libby's arm. "Thank you for being such a wonderful friend to my son and his partner," she said.

"They make it easy. I'm very glad you could be here today," Libby said.

Mrs. Wittenhouse leaned closer and said in a faint voice, "I wouldn't let Jed out of my sight."

Libby just smiled. She could hear Horatio giggling like Teddy in the background.

When the guests were gone, Libby chased Jed out of the house, although he offered to help clean up. "Go take a walk," she said. "Denise and I put all this out, so we'll just do everything in reverse."

Jed strolled down to Audubon Circle and continued south across Washington Street. Passing the public-library branch and the back lot of the Presbyterians, he eventually paused in front of the Italian Gothic mansion known as the Julian House. Resuming the walk, he came to the park on Irving Circle, where the fountain gurgled. Jed stopped in front of the pedestal supporting the bust of Washington Irving, who now wore lavender eyeliner and lavender post earrings. The historian, diplomat, and father of the American short story lacked only a faded, denim jacket. The vandalism occurred a while ago, Jed thought, because the lavender was partially worn off.

Admiring the bust, Jed felt a kindred spirit with Irving, the underappreciated apostle of Christmas traditions in the new America. "Thanks," Jed said in a low voice.

"You're most welcome," a voice said. "Do you think you could get someone to wash off these cosmetics?"

Electrified, Jed looked around. He was alone on the circle. In awe, he regarded the bust for a few minutes, until a car engine alerted him to witnesses. He stepped back and watched as a sedan rounded the circle and went north on Audubon.

A snide young man stuck his head out the driver's window and drawled, "You *know* he's not real?"

Remaining deadpan, Jed began his return trip. After the car was up the street, he retorted.

"That's what you think," he said.

He found Libby alone in the kitchen. Claiming first dibs on the leftover cookies, Denise had gone home.

"Whadya see on the walk?" Libby said.

"Oh, nothing," he said.

"Ready for your recliner?"

"You have one?" he said.

"A lawn chair, in the garage. There's also a folding chair with a canvas seat. Why don't you get those out, and I'll bring the punch."

She joined him in the backyard. They sat, holding hands and sipping punch.

"This living?" she said.

"I believe so," he said. She kicked off her shoes and draped her right leg over Jed's left. Pretty soon, Jed was asleep on the lounger. To keep away the bees, she dumped his cup on the gravel drive. Rejoining him, she listened to the birds.

CHAPTER 59
The Present Day – July

The summer passed. Libby intended to close the office for two weeks in late July to give her staff a vacation before their children returned to school. Later, she'd grant a long weekend for Labor Day, when she could see Jed between the traditional political gatherings.

Libby looked forward to her itinerary. She would spend two days on home improvement, and then fly to Chicago for a two-day tour of museums. After that, she was heading to Milwaukee to stay with Denise and her family for a night. From there, she'd fly to British Columbia, a place she picked at random by closing her eyes and stabbing a pen on a map of North America. She'd return to Indy to rest with Jed before resuming her practice.

On the second day of vacation, the heat, humidity, and ozone provoked TV weathercasters to beg people to mow only after six p.m. Feeling superior, Libby guffawed, because she used a manual mower without exhaust fumes.

In the morning, she trimmed hedges and washed windows. After a light lunch, she napped before starting to mow. She was content.

Downtown, the City-County Building was sufficiently cool, but malodorous. Jed and Gale had walked over from the prosecutor's office to pay political visits. Jed was in a good mood, because that morning, the homicide team negotiated the plea agreement for Mahlon Dinwiddie. Striking a bargain at last, the state would recommend Dinwiddie for a sentence of life without parole. In exchange, he would plead guilty to th murder of Haitian immigrant Raoul Duvalier, the innocent who caught a bullet in a drive-by shooting.

Relieved that Dinwiddie had taken his lawyer's advice, Jed praised his prosecutors for their work. In private, he thanked God for listening to his prayers so he could drop the request for the death penalty.

And he wanted to tell Libby, because she'd brought up the case during their tense discussion about capital punishment.

Unknown to Jed, a certain malefactor, Malik Thresher, was lurking outside the building. Alluding to an issue regarding "home bidness," Thresher vowed to friends he would take care of that "Mo-Fo 'Harness.' "

He slouched across from the City-County Building at a vantage point on the plaza outside the City Market. Thresher always carried a gun and wouldn't pass the security check on the first floor of the government center. In baggy clothes hiding the weapon, he looked like any other loafer.

"Everybody know he eat at Egyptian food truck," Malik said. "He got to come out sometime."

Around one o'clock, Jed and Gale exited the government building from the north door on Market Street. The bright sun and high humidity challenged the men's alertness as they walked to the traffic light at the junction with Alabama. At mid-block, workers rolling a giant spool of cable made a slow passage, and Jed and Gale went by them on the way to the corner.

Thresher murmured, "He come out." Pacing himself to match Jed and Gale, Thresher walked east on Market parallel to the men on the other side of the street. They reached the opposing corners at the same time. Thresher pretended to look at something to the east. The light changed, and Jed and Gale began to cross the street. Thresher turned, showing them his left profile, and with his right hand, he pulled the gun out of his pants under a billowy T-shirt. He held the weapon next to his right hip.

Jed and Gale were fifteen to twenty feet away now. Thresher pivoted on his left foot and fired. The bullet tore through Jed's upper left extremity. Jed fell to the street, and Gale threw himself on top of Jed.

Malik Thresher's second shot hit Gale in the neck.

Thresher ran across Alabama toward the overpass of Interstate 65. Onlookers froze, trying to comprehend what they'd seen. A sheriff's deputy on a break outside the government building sprinted toward the bodies as she radioed for help. Sirens pealed from all directions.

At home, Libby was cutting grass. Across town, Myra Himmel listened to a public radio show. Frenchie was working in the garden. Gale's wife was at the bank. Armistead Hauser was having lunch with his niece, Sheri, downtown. It was a miserably humid day in "Little-Green-App-polis."

***

Sheri's phone rang, and Jed's chief of staff, Fabiola de Torre, relayed what happened. She was on her way to a hospital north of downtown. Army Hauser saw the horrified look on his niece's face.

Sheri handed him the phone.

Listening, Army's face crumpled. "All right," he said, hoarse. "I'll meet you there."

Sheri went back to the prosecutor's office. Meanwhile, the City-County Building was in an uproar, and citizens having business with the government were diverted to the south entrance of the building away from the crime scene.

Libby had no idea what was happening. Two officers and a chaplain were waiting for Gale's wife, Lee Ann, when she returned home. Informed of the shooting, she kept insisting they contact Libby. The chaplain gave tender assurances as they helped Lee Ann into the back of a squad car.

Sheri wondered about Libby, too. Fabiola called, instructing Jim Phillipi to contact Jed's mother in Florida, and then, per Mrs. Mooneyham, to call Dr. Doherty. He tried, but the message at the dental office said the practice was closed for two weeks. He found her home number, but the land line rang over to voicemail. Libby was outside, hand-trimming the corners of the yard where the mower didn't fit. With the air conditioner running, the windows and doors were closed, and she didn't hear the phone.

Sheri volunteered to find Libby. At the bungalow, Libby was sweeping grass clippings off the front walk when Sheri's car pulled up, and it was a few seconds before Libby recognized the driver as she got out.

"Hi!" Libby said. "What are you doing in my neck of the woods? You look so nice in that white suit. I'm a mess from the yard work." She was wearing navy shorts and a gray T-shirt.

Sheri paused at the bottom step of the walk to Libby's porch. "Libby, if you would, please, I'd like you to come downtown with me," Sheri said. "There's been an incident, and Jed and Gale Mooneyham have been taken to the hospital."

Amid the roar of locusts, Libby smelled the cut grass. An incident. "What kind of incident?"

"They were attacked by a gunman."

Libby threw down the broom. "Let me lock up." Her ears rang. On wobbly legs, she ran inside for her purse. She had to grab the banister to make it down the porch steps, and getting into Sheri's car, she banged her knees on the dashboard.

As they drove, Libby's throat tightened. Hearing the sore, crispy sound of her own voice, she asked what happened.

"We're not sure. Jed and Gale were crossing the street at lunch, and this guy shot them. He ran, and as far as I know, we haven't caught him. But we will," she said.

"How seriously were they hurt?" Libby said.

"Gale is critical," Sheri said, trying to control the emotional level of the conversation while she drove. "Jed was going into surgery. My uncle went to meet Fabiola at the hospital.

"Gale's wife insisted we call, but I guess you were outside."

So Jed didn't ask for me, but maybe he couldn't talk, Libby thought. "Where was he hit?" she said, her voice cracking.

"I don't know," Sheri said.

When they reached the emergency room lobby, Libby saw police officers of all ages and ranks. Hushed and despondent, they hugged each other, wiping away tears. Libby dreaded what was coming next. As she pushed forward, her knees buckled, and she caught herself. She turned to Sheri.

"Where are we going?" Libby said.

"To find my uncle."

"Where is Gale's wife?" Libby said.

"I truly don't know," Sheri said. "Army will have all the information."

"We need to find her," Libby said. "Excuse me," she asked a uniform officer. "Have you seen Gale Mooneyham's wife?"

The officers standing nearby stopped talking. The policeman shifted his weight.

"Ma'am, are you with the family?" he said.

"No, but she asked someone to find me," she said.

"I believe she is still with the body. We're waiting to give him an escort to the coroner's office."

"No! My sweet friend!" she said, dissolving into tears. Sheri took her by the arm. The police officer looked down.

"Let's try to find my uncle. He'll know more," Sheri said, turning to the cop. "Do you know where the surgery waiting room is?"

"I do not, but the people at the desk can help you." Assisting them, a clerk tracked down Jed's whereabouts, and the women found Fabiola and Army in a waiting area near the operating suites.

Libby had never spent time with Army, and despite all she'd heard about him, she was suddenly formal, brushing away tears and shaking hands.

"I just can't believe Gale is gone," Libby said in a whisper, which was all she could produce.

Army answered, "I think Emily Dickinson said, 'Parting is all we know of heaven, and all we need of hell.' "

"How about a cup of coffee, Libby?" Fabiola said, returning from a vending machine a few feet away. She gave Libby the cup.

"Thank you," she said. The hot liquid coated the dry gully in her throat. She needed to blow her nose. She poked around in her purse, but there was no tissue. She sniffled.

"Hankie?" Fabiola said, taking a package of tissue from her purse.

"Yes, thanks. I'm usually better prepared," Libby said.

"There's no way to prepare for something like this," Fabiola said. "I still can't believe it." She reminded Libby of a more consciously stylish Marquita, made up with a conservative application of eye liner and a muted shade of red lipstick. Upswept, Fabiola's black hair was carefully pinned into place. The trimly tailored gray dress suit was flecked with lilac threads, and her shoes and handbag were of light gray leather. She was sinewy, strong, and self-confident, the person Libby wanted to encounter at such a time.

"Why don't we sit down for a while?" Army said. He looked tired and old, not like the suave manipulator, or the starchy ex-FBI agent. Libby saw that he didn't want to rest alone, and she sat with him.

"I just thought of another one: 'Poetry is about the grief. Politics is about the grievance,' " Army said.

"Who said that?" Libby asked.

"Robert Frost. He was correct. I've spent my life juggling grievances, and looking back, it was pretty easy. But this . . ." he said.

"How did you come to memorize quotations about grief?" she said.

257

"One of my tricks as a novice prosecutor. I'd spice up my closings with these poetic sayings. I'm out of tricks, now," he said. "Would you think it rude if I closed my eyes for a minute or two?"

"Not at all," Libby said. Shutting his eyes, he leaned back, resting his head against the wall.

Libby took the scratch pad from her purse and began to toy with lines. Soon, she wrote:

> The good ship Gale has sailed.
> Grief, washing the coast, sent us home
> Hungry to the breadbox of verse, where
> We found the burned toast, the poet's curse.

Armistead Hauser sat up. He glanced sideways at her notes. "A little Frost in the freezer?" he said.

"Yes," she said.

"Would you share it with me?" he said.

She handed him the pad. He read it under his breath. She watched his lips move.

"God, that's so true," he said.

"Thanks. I never show anyone my poems."

"Sometimes it's better to keep the window shades down," Army said.

"Yes! I could use another cup of coffee. Can I get you one?"

"I'm buying," he said, handing her change from his pocket. "Black tar."

"Will do, thank you," she said, rising. She came back with the coffee, and they sat in silence. To her, it was like resting next to a venerable tall tree in winter. She could picture Army dusted by snow swirling around his long arms and legs.

Two hours passed. Finally, a surgeon appeared, and he'd apparently spoken to Army before the surgery. "He's stable. Any family here?"

"No, but this is his companion, Dr. Doherty," Army said.

"I'm a dentist," Libby said.

"Nice to meet you. I'm Dave Black. Mr. Harkness is in recovery, and it'll be about an hour before they take him up. You can ask the unit secretary where he's going. I'll be up to fill him in later."

"Thank you, Dr. Black," she said.

258

The surgeon excused himself, and they stood, panting, as if they'd finished running a race.

"I should get back to the office and make sure no one has gone crazy," Fabiola said. She and Sheri had paced the halls while they waited.

"I'll be going, too," Sheri said. Libby thanked them, and Army said he was going to the men's room.

Libby was alone. "Dave Black," she said aloud.

***

Jed woke up in the recovery room. A nurse stood over him. She said his name. He grunted. She removed a tube from his throat and went away. Soon, another nurse appeared, feeding him ice chips. He could barely move, but he could see other beds, one flat, another filled with a lump under a blanket. His plane of vision didn't permit a view of anyone's face. He was sleepy. The nurse went away.

He kept his eyes closed as someone wheeled his bed to an elevator. Cool air brushed his face as the bed traveled. The elevator noise was loud and irritating. Now he was in another hallway. Peeking as the bed rounded a corner, he shut his eyes, like a boy on a ride at the county fair. Voices bothered him, and he withdrew into himself. Eventually, the rolling stopped, and he peeked at his surroundings. Someone put tusks in his nose. They were oxygen lines, a nurse said. He focused on the room, bland, hideous – was he back in the City-County Building? He closed his eyes.

A warmth exuded from someone nearby. He opened his eyes. Libby.

"Hi," she said. "The doctor is coming by to explain things. I don't know anything."

He looked at her. "Dr. Booth. We both can't be dead."

"You're alive, Jed," she said, trying not to give away more.

Dave Black appeared. "Mr. Harkness – good to see you responding – OK if we include Dr. Doherty in our talk, or should she come back in a few minutes?"

"She needs to stay," Jed said.

"That's fine," Dr. Black said. "How much do you recall about the attack on you?"

"I got hit. Gale fell on top of me. I passed out."

259

"You had a missile injury to the left brachial plexus," the doctor said. "In other words, you were shot in the shoulder."

"I won't be wearing any off-the-shoulder-gowns for a while," Jed said.

"Probably not," the doctor said, glad his patient's sense of humor was healthy. "We'll monitor closely for infection, but it could be a few months before we know if you sustained any vascular injury or loss of function."

"Great," Jed said in monotone. "Where's Gale?" he said.

The doctor glanced at Libby. She nodded her head to mean that Jed should be told.

"Mr. Harkness, I'm very sorry, but Mr. Mooneyham passed away from his injuries."

Jed was shot, again. Trying to comprehend, he stared at the ceiling.

"Gale," he gasped, disbelieving.

"I'm very, very sorry," Dave Black said.

Jed started to cry. "That's the way the cookie craps," he said. Concerned, the doctor gave him a sharp look.

"Don't worry," Libby said. "He knows what he's saying. I'll stay with him."

"Sir, I'll be around tomorrow," the doctor said. "Again, I'm very, very sorry." The doctor stepped out, and Armistead Hauser appeared in the doorway.

"He knows," Libby said. Slumping, Army gave the doorframe a single rap with his fist. Tears flooded Jed's face, contorted, with the corners of his mouth turned down.

CHAPTER 60
Present Day – Bad Weather

At home on medical leave, Jed stopped answering his phone. Libby couldn't understand why he wasn't taking her calls. He developed severe bronchitis with fever after the surgery and had to stay in the hospital longer than expected. Now home, he was getting nebulizer treatments from a visiting nurse, who also checked his wound. After three days of leaving messages, Libby took action on a Sunday.

She called Denise for advice.

"A home-cooked meal would be an appropriate gesture. You could take it over. I bet he'll answer the door if he looks out and sees you." Denise said.

Libby prepared a thermos of tomato soup, chicken-and-noodle casserole, green beans, and rolls. She also packed a banana and a fresh pineapple core, and a tray of brownies. As she loaded the items into the car, the humidity overwhelmed her. Like the drops of condensation on the windshield, beads of sweat broke out over her mouth. She ran the air conditioner on high.

On the way to Jed's, she saw spurts of water making splats on the windshield like something from a squirt gun. The sky looked like a pencil sketch drawn by a depressed third grader. Indianapolis was a great city when the sun was out, but on a day like today, every pothole, broken sidewalk, abandoned house, and untrimmed hedge offended the eye.

She turned into Jed's drive. Unloading the food, she heard the terrier bark, but no one opened the door or rustled the curtains. Nervous, she rang the doorbell with her elbow. The dog barked. No one appeared. She rang again. Finally, Jed unlocked the door, which creaked like the entrance to a dungeon.

Unshaven, with deep circles under his eyes, he wore an open bathrobe over pajama bottoms.

"Hi," she said. "I brought you a meal. Will you let me serve it to you?"

Wordless, he used his good arm to prop open the storm door while Libby slid by. He reset the alarm. *Los!* trailed her to the kitchen. She found an empty pizza box on the floor next to the sink. Used paper plates covered the table, along with a sour glass of milk. Empty pop cans overflowed from the wastebasket.

"Nutrition City," she muttered.

"Sorry," Jed said sarcastically from behind. She turned around.

"Why haven't you returned my calls? I've been worried about you," she said, cranky.

"I had nothing to report," he said.

"That's not the point, Jed. You don't have family looking after you, so when friends try to help, you should at least let them know you're OK."

"Sorry again," he said lightly.

"Jeez!" she said. "I'll warm up your lunch." She cleared a place on the countertop for the containers of food. Rummaging in the cupboard, she found a clean coffee mug and filled it with tomato soup from the thermos.

"Please, sit down and drink some of this. No, on second thought, I'll serve you in the dining room. This table needs to be wiped off." Listless, Jed followed her to the dining room. Cloth placemats that had waited too long for a dinner party were on the table. She pulled out a chair and pointed at the seat. He sat.

"Sip slowly, it's hot," she said. "I'll get you some ice water." She came back with a glassful. "I'll cut up some fruit." Staring at the table, he said nothing, making no effort to taste the soup. A few minutes later, she brought the fruit and a spoon.

"You didn't have to do this. I'm not hungry," he said. The soup along the rim of the cup gave evidence that he'd taken a sip.

"You need balanced meals to heal," she said. "This is important."

Returning to the kitchen, she warmed a serving plate with the casserole and green beans in the microwave. She'd forgotten to bring butter for the rolls, but no butter was in the fridge. In the cupboard, she found a jar of peanut butter and spooned some on each roll. She took the food and cutlery to the dining room. He'd consumed about half the soup, but the fruit was untouched.

"Try a little fruit, Jed. You need it," she said, coaxing.

"I don't want it," he said like a child.

Not recognizing him, Libby pretended not to notice the abusive tone. "OK. You might want it later," she said, taking the bowl to the refrigerator. Returning, she sat at the head of the table, next to the corner where he hunched over his meal. They were silent for a long time. Ignoring the rolls, he finished the casserole and most of the vegetables, and she rewarded him with a brownie.

He swallowed a drink of water. "I'm never going to accept it," he said.

"Accept what?"

"Not what. Why."

"Why it happened?" she said.

"No." he said. "Why it happened to Gale, and not me."

He paused, coughing a stretch before sharing information. He drank some water.

"The police were here Friday with some mug shots. They picked up a quirk by the name of Malik Thresher," he said.

"Did he do it?" Libby said.

"Bastard bragged he was going to do it. Undercover guy heard it from a snitch," Jed said.

"And the police followed up," she said.

"They brought me a stack of pictures of no-goods. I spotted him right away. It's not like I was going to forget that face," he said. "But the outdoor cameras on the buildings caught the whole thing."

"I haven't heard anything about him on the news, yet," Libby said.

"You will. Trust me."

"What's causing the delay?" Libby said.

"They're moving carefully. The cops are certain he did it, so they don't want to blow it by rushing. Not this time." He bowed his head.

Absorbing this, Libby finally said, "So . . . you have closure, at least."

"I do not," he said, swelling with rudeness.

She was getting tired of his tone. "Do you want to explain, or should I stop asking questions?" she said.

"Dammit!" he shouted, throwing a dinner roll. It bounced off the wall after leaving a smudge of peanut butter.

"Jed, get a hold of yourself!" Libby said. "I'm trying to understand your feelings. You don't have to be so nasty."

"My feelings? *My* feelings? What about *Gale's* feelings? He's not feeling anything. What am I supposed to say to his family?" Jed shouted.

"You've already said it," she said, trying to stay calm. "They know you're sorry."

"You don't get it," he said.

"If I knew what 'it' was, I might," she said.

"This was an attempted political assassination. Gale got in the way. The politician survived."

"That's the way things turned out," Libby said. "You didn't plan it."

"Just doing the will of the people, I was," he said, and then his anger exploded like a meth lab. "Dammit," he said, pounding the table. "An attack on the prosecutor for doing his job is an attack on the people."

His mood swung again, and he coughed, leaving expectorant in his napkin. He whined. "What the hell am I supposed to say to Lee Ann?"

"Well, maybe Thresher meant to kill both of you," Libby said.

Jed gasped. "And that would make it any easier for *her*?"

"Of course not, but – "

"Whatever – I'm not interested. I'm going to my room," he said, getting up. He coughed as he went down the hall.

Shaking and nauseous, she propped elbows on the table. The dog padded into the dining room and gazed up at her. "I guess I blew it just now," she said to the terrier.

Agonizing, she cleared the table and washed dishes. She looked at the floor tile, dull as usual. She would wax it. Perhaps he would emerge from his room later. In the cabinet under the sink, she found a box of floor cleaner and a still-sealed bottle of wax, but no bucket. "Bucket in the garage?" she asked the terrier, who strutted to his door flap and waited.

In the garage, she found a bucket and a mop in the corner. Grim-faced, she went about the task. The dog apparently knew to stay off the fresh coat of wax. "Good dog," she said, picking him up and going to the living room.

It was quiet. Despite the air conditioning, the atmosphere was heavy, stressing the dehumidifier. The walls needed painting, and she could see

264

lighter patches once covered by pictures that went to Florida with Jed's mother. Libby sat in a wing chair upholstered in floral chintz. The well-constructed throne was comfortable. She put the dog at her feet and leaned back, closing her eyes.

Jed was grieving, struggling with guilt. She thought of him alone with his aching body and soul. She wished she hadn't chastised him for ignoring her calls.

She dozed, startled from sleep by a commanding bark. The dog's ears tensed, and she listened, too. Outside, a persistent buzz swelled, faded, and re-inflated. She could have investigated from the front stoop, but she didn't know how to reset the burglar alarm. The kitchen windows would offer a wide view, and she went to look.

The sky was green. Trashcans flew across neighbors' yards and slammed into the sides of houses. The buzz was a storm siren, rotating and fluctuating in volume. Her arms were goose flesh. The storm was here.

"*Los*!" Libby bellowed, at a run. Her diction was perfect. The little dog ran like he'd been fired from a U-Boat. They sprinted to the end of the hallway to the sleeping quarters. Only one door was shut, and she guessed it was Jed's room. She pounded on the door.

"Jed. It's a bad storm. Get up!"

He opened the door and smiled for the first time that day. "Really?" he said.

He led Libby and the dog to the basement door. "After you," he said, flipping the light switch at the top of the stairs. She started down, and then the power went off.

"Shit," she said. Jed chuckled.

"She's human," he said. "Don't move. I'll get a flashlight."

Moments later, he trained a beam on the steps and she continued down, followed by Jed and the dog. They huddled in the dark.

Listening to the roar of the wind, they heard a tapping sound.

"Hail," Jed said.

"Mary," Libby said, after a beat.

"Lutherans always come home when the going gets tough," he said.

The old Jed was emerging, to Libby's relief.

After the wind died down, they went upstairs.

"One nice thing about a brick house," Jed said. "No siding to be ripped off. I guess I'll have to call somebody to inspect the roof for hail damage. But not today."

He coughed, dropping into a chair at the kitchen table. He held his head in his hands.

Libby knew what she had to do.

"Let's get you packed. I'm taking you home with me. And the dog – and the dog potty. Especially that," she said.

"What about the visiting nurse?"

"We'll call and give directions to my house," Libby said. "You'll be well cared for."

"You don't like my house?" Jed said.

"It's a good house, for someone who's not here most of the time. But all the color left with your mother. Come on," she held out her hand, and he stood.

CHAPTER 61
The Present Day – Vulnerability

Libby worried that Jed wouldn't make progress without medication. He'd start physical therapy soon, but he wasn't talking about his experience, his grief, or his guilt. For the first few days after he came to stay, she let him mope. But on the fourth evening, she told him he couldn't hang around all day in his bathrobe, and that he had to get dressed, even if he didn't have an appointment.

"Or what?" Jed said in a monotone.

"Or . . . you can get a new girlfriend," she said. "I mean it. I didn't bring you over here so you could go to Hell."

"Yes, ma'am," he said. Tears fell from his eyes. "I'm sorry."

Libby embraced him in a bear hug. "Sweetie, I'd like to help you find a psychiatrist. You might need an anti-depressant to kick-start the chemicals in your brain.

"There's no shame in it. Just a low dose, nothing to make you gain weight and start making paper airplanes," she said. "Would you let me help you get things set up?"

He nodded his assent. The next morning, she made a three-way call with Jed to his physician to get a referral.

Libby chose Dr. Jukka Bostrum, a medical school professor who maintained a private practice. An appointment slot opened after a cancellation, and Jed had his first meeting with Bostrum within a week.

As Libby predicted, Jed was put on medication expected to yield noticeable results in about thirty days.

CHAPTER 62
History – August 1921

Mary told her mother she was going for a long walk and probably wouldn't return until lunchtime.

She walked, but it was to Doc Welburn's office. She'd been there last month to find out more about the circumstances of her birth. To coax him, she made it sound like her mother had spoken of the adoption. She had, in fact, but only because Mary was eavesdropping.

Mary greeted his nurse, Mrs. Emilyne Cort, a matronly woman of fifty years who'd nursed soldiers in England during the Great War. Short and stout, she was the most reassuring person anyone ever knew.

"Good morning, Mary! What can we do for you?"

"I'd like to see the doctor, please."

"Doctor is on house calls, but he'll be back. I'm surprised your mother didn't call him over."

"I'm not so sick I couldn't come by."

"Is there anything I can do for you?" Mrs. Cort said.

"No. Well, maybe. I just -- I have this problem. It's under my bloomers." She turned red. "I have these blisters."

"Oh, well, dear – nothing we can't handle. Why don't we go into the exam room so I can take a look?" the nurse said.

"If you want," Mary said.

Briefly examining Mary, the nurse was expressionless. She blinked once. Wrapping Mary in a sheet, she said, "Thank you, dear. I believe the doctor would have more to say than I would. He should be here soon."

The nurse excused herself and disappeared down the hall. Mary heard someone come in the back door. Welburn entered the exam room and was about to greet Mary when the nurse hustled into their midst.

"Doctor, before you get started, may I see you for a minute?" Mrs. Cort said. "In your private office."

"Of course." When they returned, he was tired and sad. "Hello, my lamb." he said to Mary.

"Can you do without me for a few minutes while I call in our pharmacy order? I want to make the deadline for the courier," Mrs. Cort said.

"That's fine," Welburn said.

The nurse was about to finish her phone call when she heard a heart-rending wail from Mary.

"No, I don't want to! I can't," she heard Mary say.

Welburn called out, "Em – for God's sake, now!" Mrs. Cort apologized and hung up on the pharmacist. She ran down the hall.

Mary's sobs echoed as the nurse shut the door.

After Mary went home, Mrs. Cort fixed the doctor a cup of tea, and he added a shot of whiskey from a flask stored in his desk.

"They ought to horsewhip that son-of-a-bitch on Monument Circle," the doctor said. The nurse poured some whiskey for herself without the tea.

"I doubt if she'll tell her parents before you stop by," Mrs. Cort said.

"She's probably afraid to face Laurinda." the doctor said.

He sipped his tea. "For Christ's sake, I'd like to horsewhip the bastard myself."

Back at the Hobson's, Mary wanted to skip lunch and take a nap.

"All right, but don't complain when your stomach starts rumbling," her mother said.

Mary was holed up in the bedroom until mid-afternoon. She walked in stocking feet to the bathroom and retrieved a bottle from the shelf of cleaning supplies under the sink. Staring down the hall at the open door to her parents' bedroom, she listened to the voice in the kitchen. The polished wooden floor was shinier than usual, reflecting the beaded curtain hiding the alcove for the bath towels. The wall sconce with a single electric candle was her silent partner.

She waited until her mother was occupied with important phone calls that conveyed gossip about Catholics, Jews, and anyone who was a little off.

The steep stairs to the attic were hidden behind a closet door in her parents' room. Heading there, tip-toeing shoeless, she heard her mother's voice.

"This particular dry cleaner keeps a crucifix on the wall behind the counter, and he gives the clothes back with the buttons missing. And then – he overcharges and gives the money to the Church. It's totally indecent.

"But guess what? He carries on with the seamstress who does the alterations at his shop. And his wife is having another baby."

Reaching the bedroom, the girl saw herself in the mirror over the dresser. A child of seventeen with sad eyes and the energy of a disappearing plume of smoke. At the closet, she gave the door a stealthy tug to release the seal of humidity. She slipped inside and left the door a smidge open. Garments hung on rods perpendicular to the door, and she stood in the space between them. Directly ahead – the attic door.

She waited, distracted by the pink striped hatbox on the shelf above the dresses, and by the patterns in her father's neckties dangling from pegs.

Sighing, she opened the attic door. The first step was about eighteen inches from the floor. She hefted herself up and grabbed the banister. Though she'd climbed this trip many times, she was spent, straining to keep from falling backwards.

The afternoon light of late summer streamed at sharp angles from windows at both ends of the attic. She crept to a hiding place for her belongings behind a slat at the end of the house that overlooked the roof of the front porch. Her diary and a fountain pen were concealed there. She put the bottle she carried in the hiding place. Pulling out the book and examining each page, she lingered over a cartoon of Clay Zell, the grasshopper.

"I love you, Clay Zell," she whispered. She kissed the drawing. Her mother threw out the bug collection, but she'd never find these sketches.

Mary dated a blank page and drew a new cartoon, a weeping butterfly sitting on a rock alone in the forest. Perfecting the details, she spent about twenty minutes on the cartoon.

But she knew she only had so much time, so she willed herself to be satisfied with the drawing. Hiding the book and the pen, again, she took out the bottle. She removed the stopper and hid it, also.

Lest she spill her chance, she held the bottle with both hands and went to the center of the attic.

Her mother finished the poisonous conversations a half-hour later. She

270

poured some lemonade. Maybe her daughter would like a glass, but no one answered when the woman called.

***

In the attic, the girl was stunned. She was floating. Nothing made sense now. She was looking down at herself sprawled on the floor. Laying over her crosswise – the limp body of her mother.

A faint voice echoed, calling names, and a man came up the stairs. He knelt over the bodies and appeared to cry out, yet the girl couldn't understand what he was saying. His voice grew even fainter. The three below her disappeared, and the attic shrank away. Enveloped in darkness, she forgot what happened.

CHAPTER 63
Eternal Time

In the darkness, the girl saw a tiny circle of light that grew larger until she was within the light, and she found herself standing in a room with gray walls, a conference table with chairs, and one window. The light outside the window was whiter than anything she'd ever seen.

Two men, one tall and skinny, and the other, short and plump, sat side by side at the table. They were smiling. The tall one nodded his head toward the window as if to say, "Look outside."

She gaped. A beautiful crystal path wound through a rolling meadow of light, and people were strolling, not rushing along the path. She strained to see where they were going, but the white light ahead was so pure, they disappeared into glory. She wanted to go, too, and she turned to query the hosts, who knew her thoughts.

The short one spoke. "You have to pay for your journey," he said, making a cordial gesture offering the seat across from them.

"Do you remember how you got here?" the tall man said.

She sat down. "No."

"Do you remember anything about your actions?" the short one with baby fat said.

"I do not."

"The act of recollection is only a portion of the fee," the tall man said. "You must help someone with a struggle, and he must help you, in return.

"When these requirements are met, you can go," he said. The tall one had a white goatee and wore a farmer's hat.

"What's your name?" she said.

"I'm Hill," the tall one said. "And he's Billy."

The two men wore deadpan expressions.

The girl smiled.

"Actually, his name is Luther," Billy said. "What's your name?"

In contrast to his friend, he was youthful with peach fuzz.

With a whisper, she conceded. "I don't know."

"But you understand you must remember who you were, and what you did?" Billy said. "It's hard, sometimes. But essential."

"Who I was . . . but not, 'am'?" she said.

Luther stood. "That's right," he said. "Your soul is active, but you no longer have a use for your physical body.

"For example, we don't need this furniture, but when people arrive, they haven't figured out they don't need to sit down."

"Where am I?" she said.

"A meeting room, nothing more," Luther said. "You can't stay here."

"Where will I go?"

The men were silent, letting her figure it out.

"I have to go back?" she said.

"Yes," Billy said. "You need to return, but you won't have the freedom to go anywhere else."

"Until you've met the requirements," Luther said.

"You'll be confined to that space," Billy said.

"Like prison" she said.

"Only if you choose to make it your prison," Luther said.

"Do you tell everyone that?" she said.

"We don't tell anyone anything. We're assigned to you and only you." Billy said. "You'll never be alone. But you do the work by yourself."

"What if I can't remember?" she said.

"You'll remember," Luther said. "The information is embedded in your soul. But we're allowed to give you a hint to get you started."

"What's my hint?"

"Pen –" Luther said.

"And ink," Billy said. "You'll never be alone. Just do the work."

The meeting room grew dim, and her new friends faded. She was in the attic.

CHAPTER 64
Eternal Time

Mary's soul showed a steady growth in self-awareness at a rate that couldn't be measured by the living world's concept of time. But while she fathomed more about herself, the temporal world required two decades for the excesses of the Jazz Age and the penny-pinching of the Great Depression. In Irvington, the national Ku Klux Klan leader D.C. Stephenson was convicted of murder, and soon after, the Klan fist that pounded the electorate collapsed into a limp handshake.

At the bungalow, Mary's father died of a stroke from uncontrolled high blood pressure when he was only fifty-seven years old. Although financially comfortable, her mother took a job working as a hospital receptionist, a post she held until age sixty, when she married a retired Army chaplain who volunteered at the hospital.

Undisturbed by the mania of mortals, Mary sat in a tiny circle of warmth with Luther and Billy in the attic.

"I wanted to ask if I could walk around the house." she said.

"That depends on what you've remembered," Billy said. "You know the rules."

"My name is Mary," she said. "I remember being in the kitchen with my mother. There was a phone in the kitchen. She was always on the phone. And I remember I didn't like the things she said.

"And the clue you gave me, about the pen and ink. I liked to draw – a lot. I wanted to be an artist," she said. "I needed to learn more, but I trusted a teacher who didn't care."

"Didn't care?" Luther said. "Is that what it was?"

Billy said nothing.

Mary faltered. "It was – It was . . . I don't know. I can't say."

"When you can, we'll take you on a tour of the house," Billy said. "You're making progress."

Her friends faded.

***

Mary's soul was screaming. "Monster! Monster! Monster! I didn't want it! I didn't want it. I said so. Monster!"

Luther and Billy appeared in a circle of light, now bigger and warmer.

"You must say it, child. You must name it," Luther said.

"I can't say it. I can't," Mary said.

"Name it," Luther said. "Until you do, you can't move forward."

"You were a good soul, then, and a good one, now," Billy said.

"He raped me," she said. "He stole from me. I never got to know what true love was."

Luther stroked his beard. "Your soul journey isn't over, Mary. You could find love."

Billy took her by the hand. "Let's walk," he said.

At once they were in the living room. She studied the painting of the auction.

"We went to an estate sale like that one," she said. "I just remembered my mother bought a cast iron skillet."

They went to the kitchen. "She made fried potatoes in the skillet," Mary said. "I can smell them."

"Who liked the fried potatoes?" Billy said.

"I did. I loved fried potatoes. She made them because I asked her to," Mary said. "She loved me."

Luther and Billy nodded but said nothing.

"She loved me. I'm so sorry," Mary said.

"Why are you sorry?" Luther said.

"I don't really know," Mary said.

"Do you remember how you left things with her?" Luther said.

"No," she said.

275

They were back in the attic.
"Keep pushing forward," Billy said.

CHAPTER 65
Eternal Time

In her attic cell, Mary saw herself thrashing on the floor.
"Help! Someone help me!" the girl croaked. "Help me!"
But no one came, and she saw herself convulse one last time.
"Just as it was," Mary said. "Just as it was."

***

The world Mary left behind went to war. European Jews were thrown into furnaces, and then, the Nazi stooges who let it happen disappeared into the wallpaper of the German post-war bureaucracy. But courageous prosecutors fought to hold trials that forced the German public to accept the truth about Hitler's crimes. On the winning side, Americans settled into the Cold War and the Golden Age of Television. The war was a story line for numerous films and TV shows, and politicians learned to use TV to scare people.

***

Reviewing her demise, Mary kept repeating, "Lord, Lord, my God, please help me. I'm sorry. I'm so sorry."
Luther and Billy found her staring out a window at the trees, older and taller than in her lifetime. She was now able to perceive the physical world outside the house.
"The trees last longer than we do," she said.

"If given a chance," Luther said.

"We know you reviewed your last day," Billy said. "It's time for your next commitment."

She was apprehensive. "You said I need to help someone – and he needs to help me – so I can go Home. But I don't have anything to give, and I can't leave this space. I don't know where to start."

"But you do have something," Billy said.

"Right under your nose," Luther said.

"Something of extraordinary value to the finder," Billy said.

"There's nothing to find up here," she said.

"But you know that's not true," Luther said. "Think about your last memory of this room."

Mary was stumped. "There were some books, and a chest with Christmas decorations. But they're gone."

Billy took another approach. "Whose books?"

"My father's," she said.

"Did you have anything tucked away up here?" Billy said.

"No."

"When you walked up the stairs for the last time, what did you do?" Luther said.

She looked at the stairwell. "I went to get my diary from its hiding place."

"That's right," Luther said. "And what did you do with the diary?"

"I leafed through it . . . and I drew . . . and I put it back?" She went to the hiding place behind a wooden slat.

"It's still here!" she said. "I can't believe it . . . but I can't move it."

"You can, but you'll have to marshal your energy to will it to move." Luther said.

"So even if I get it to move, what do I do with it?" she said.

"First things, first," Billy said. And she was alone again in the attic.

CHAPTER 66
Eternal Time

Mary was alone with one book stuck in its hiding place, while the world of mortals venerated its literary celebrities, including the self-help gurus, tell-all biographers, and gourmet cooks. Among the living, decades slid by like loose casino chips. Books featured beatniks, conscientious objectors, conscience-free yuppies, fitness joggers and investment floggers, angels and atheists, and characters in award-winning fiction with four-dollar words. Paperbacks enticed from pristine stacks at bookstores, later challenged by digital platforms for publishing. Yet while the access to books was wider, the estimation of their worth was narrowing. Holders of extreme viewpoints condemned certain books as well as the librarians and teachers who collected them.

But Mary had just one book to wrestle with, and it was a book about her. She concluded the book was to be read by someone who could help her. She was trying to identify the lucky reader.

"Who lives here?" Billy said.

"A woman."

"And someone new, yes?" he said.

"Yes, a man. I hear his voice," she said.

"And who needs more help – the man, or the woman?" Luther said.

Mary thought about it. "I guess the man. I don't know why, but I think it's the man."

"That's a good guess," Billy said. "Now, what do you have to give?"

"Nothing but the diary," she said.

"The diary is everything," Luther said. "We'll see you later." And the visitors vanished.

***

Now that Mary was free to roam the house, she visited every room. Hoping to see her mother's back as she worked at the stove, she always wound up in the kitchen. But she only found the woman who lived with her gentleman friend. They weren't married, but they were close.

"This is how it should be," she said, watching them make love in the front bedroom. Like a guardian, she wanted to make sure nothing spoiled their happiness. What she knew of sex in her lifetime was violent and shameful, but they were solicitous and gentle. To her, as they landed on each other, they were like wild ducks skimming the surface of a lake. She felt no titillation. Each picture the lovers made as they changed positions was like a scene from nature. They were noisy, but it was like listening to birds saying goodnight at sundown in the woods.

However, seeing the man mope alone, Mary believed her assignment was to help him.

CHAPTER 67
Eternal Time

With the force of her electromagnetic energy, Mary managed to slide the diary from its hiding place behind the wooden slat. The book was now on the floor, but she couldn't make it levitate. She heard the man in the bedroom below. She needed to throw the book hard against the floor, so that he'd come upstairs to investigate. She was desperate to connect with him.

She strained with waning force.

"Perhaps I could assist?" a man said. A warm sun entered her soul. A new friend appeared in the attic.

"Did Luther and Billy send you?" she said.

"No, but I think you called for me," the big, gentle man said. "When people need help in an emergency, they usually call the police."

"The police? Attic police?" Mary said.

The man laughed, pointing at the book. "My energy is a little fresher than yours. I think I know what you want to accomplish."

He focused a stare at the book, and it rose, floating above them. "Now!" he said.

The book slammed to the floor, making a sound like a curve ball landing in a catcher's glove. "Again," he said. The book rose, and he seemed to bore a hole in it with his glare. The diary slammed to the floor.

"If that doesn't make the boy curious, I don't know what will," he said.

CHAPTER 68
The Present Day – Not Alone

In the afternoon while Libby was at work, Jed lay on the bed. He'd driven himself to physical therapy in the morning and then to a session with Dr. Jukka Bostrum. Lunch was a fast-food taco, and he fixed a banana shake when he came home to Libby's.

Staring at the ceiling, he thought over his conversation with Bostrum.

"Be honest with yourself, even if you don't like what you see," the doctor had said. "Do you think you'd rather change places with Gale?"

Jed had frozen. He felt like he was on the witness stand.

Bostrum was relentless. "You're still young, good-looking, in love with a fantastic woman. But you'd rather be dead, isn't that so? You tell yourself you should have died, so you look better in your own eyes – Isn't that the truth? Makes you feel noble, doesn't it?

"You'd rather be dead, so you can leave work undone, leave a love unfulfilled. You don't really want to be with Libby, do you? You'd like to have an excuse to walk away, and you could if you were dead – "

"That's not true! I love Libby," Jed said. "I would not rather be dead." He was yelling.

***

"I love Libby," Jed said to the bedroom ceiling.

He heard a distinct thud from above. The ceiling had answered. He heard a second thud.

282

Now he was concerned. Were vermin crawling? Was there a bat? Surely not a human intruder.

Clad in a T-shirt and boxer shorts, he grabbed a large flashlight Libby kept on the bottom shelf of the nightstand. He knew the attic door was in the closet. Entering, he unlocked the inner door, stuck from lack of use. He yanked, and it made a cracking sound as it opened. A steep staircase was before him. He was in stocking feet, and he turned back to put on gym shoes.

He climbed the stairs. The higher he went, the colder he got. It occurred to him that it should be stifling in the attic.

"This is creepy," he said.

He reached the top. Sunlight was visible from windows at both ends of the house, but most of the enclosure was dark. Shining the flashlight in a slow path up and down the walls, he rotated a full circle. The attic was empty.

At the spot above Libby's bedroom, he swept light over the floor. His skin prickled, and he sensed excitement in each hair follicle on his legs. He spied a bound book.

Picking it up, Jed sniffed, recalling the thrill of smelling volumes of old law journals that hadn't been read for years. He took care not to tear the pages. The inside cover held a clue, "M.H., 1921."

"Holy crap," he said. He was freezing now and hurried downstairs. He slammed the attic door.

"Get food, get food . . . read book, read book," he muttered on his way to the kitchen. He made a peanut butter and jelly sandwich and a cup of instant coffee.

At the table, he browsed through the diary page by page. He found a cartoon of grasshoppers with Klan hoods. The crowd stood in a menacing circle around a cringing little grasshopper.

"Klan-hoppers." he said.

He discovered a handwritten copy of a poem he recognized, "To a Waterfowl," by William Cullen Bryant. Someone had decorated the page with an ink border of flowers and birds, and at the bottom of the entry, a pond.

Jed zipped through mundane entries about birthday parties and train trips, and then he settled on a disturbing passage written as a letter. Filled with a profound resignation, he felt as if he were gripping the hand of someone dangling from the edge of a cliff.

Dear Deck,

How can I say these things to someone? I cannot, and so I will say them here.

When I was with you, I always felt like I should ask if you were finished with dinner, and whether you wished to have your clothes pressed. I felt like an imposter, a little nobody in the presence of an aristocrat. And though you never said so, I always suspected you felt the same way. Do you know you make me feel inferior?

But I am a rebel, and I am starting to suspect that your kind, that is, the rich kind, are the real nobodies. What do you do for other people?

I know what you did to me. The memory of it is too much sometimes. I just think about it, and I am overcome. At night I try to escape in the darkness of my bedroom. I remember what you did, and how it was. And I can't go to sleep. You did that to me.

But what have you done for me? And what have I done for you? Each time we said goodbye, I felt like you went back to your real friends, and that I was never a part of your circle. And I was ashamed, as if you came to my front door for real and I let you in to meet my parents. And that you would see how ordinary we were.

But lately, I don't feel ordinary. I found out I was adopted. And I found out that I was taken from a woman who was called a mental defective because she fell and had fits. But I don't think she was defective.

I found this out by going to my doctor and telling him I knew everything. I only overheard that I was adopted. But I made him think I knew more.

She had me out of wedlock and I was taken away. Then, she got sent by the state to a special farm and they sterilized her. The doctor said it was legal, because of the eugenics law. He said I was lucky to be adopted, but that he always felt bad about the way it happened.

He said he knew my story because he had to check me out before my parents could bring me home. I decided the only thing wrong with my real mother was that she was poor.

And what have the rich kind done to help anyone in this town? I am not sure. But I remember what you did to me. And I remember and remember and remember.

"God," Jed said. He tore off a piece of the sandwich and chewed. He was starved. The state eugenics law. "God," he said with his mouth full. He sipped the coffee. What happened to this kid? He flipped to the last entry, a cartoon of a weeping lady butterfly, alone on a rock in a dark forest. It was one of the saddest depictions he'd ever seen, dated August 16, 1921.

He was on fire. How did this book wind up in the attic? Who lived here before? The property abstract! It was mid-afternoon, and he couldn't expect Libby to cancel her appointments to dredge up her ownership papers. But the library might have clues.

On a mission for the first time in weeks, he dressed and went to the basement door to shout to the dog, "Be back soon." The dog barked an OK.

CHAPTER 69
Present Day – From the Archives

The downtown library was moderately busy, and patrons idled, chatting beneath the soaring Neo-Gothic ceilings of the building's recent addition. Jed took the escalator to the second-floor reference desk. The librarian sent him to a room with microfiche readers, where he set up a reel of newspapers from 1921. Ever the history buff, Jed was soon intrigued by accounts of train robberies, Congressional follies, and fluctuations in the price of coal. He forgot about his sore shoulder.

After twenty minutes, he spotted a photo of a small group posing at a corporate celebration. The headline said, "C. Deck Whittenger feted at annual bank picnic." The paragraph beneath the photo explained that Whittenger was celebrating his twenty-fifth year as chairman of the board.

"Deck?" Jed murmured, judging this Deck to be too old, too flaccid for the mysterious M.H. But maybe there was a son, a nephew, or a grandson? At least he had a last name. He was about to get up to search through old city directories, when he heard a voice in his right ear. It was as if he'd been listening to a conch shell and someone inside the shell had spoken.

"Don't stop now," the voice said, gentle and firm.

"Gale?" Jed rasped. He looked around, embarrassed to be seen talking to himself. "What are you doing here?"

"I have to go now. I love you – Bye."

"I love you, too." Jed said, almost like a ventriloquist.

Gale said don't stop, and Jed assumed he should keep reading.

A peace fell over Jed. With his elbows propped on the desk, he rested his head against his clasped hands for several minutes. Gale had come to see him. During all Jed's training as a Roman Catholic, no one said things like this would happen. But Gale had been there. He whispered a "Hail Mary" and asked for intervention on Gale's behalf.

He resumed his survey of stories about the installation of water lines throughout the city, and of accidents involving the Interurban line. He scanned florid passages describing suicides, which, in the custom of the day, were covered in detail.

For example, Benny Reynolds ended his life "in a most violent manner" by stepping in front of a truck, the driver of which was on a run to deliver "gastronomical delights" to a women's club gathering. And Miss Shirley Bing, who lived alone in an apartment above a tavern, jumped from a bridge over the White River at her "loneliest hour." She was known around her neighborhood as "Shirley Butter," because she worked at a dairy. Acquaintances said she spoke of losing her beloved in the Great War.

"She got tired of working for her 'Bing and Butter,' " Jed whispered.

He held his breath. The next headline: "Irvington Student Takes Own Life."

Friends and family of Miss Mary Hobson are puzzled and distraught after her suicide yesterday at home in Irvington, where she lived with her parents, Laurinda and Barker Hobson. Miss Hobson was called to supper, and when she failed to respond, her parents searched the house. Their daughter was found deceased in the attic. Police said she swallowed carbolic acid from a bottle.

The grieving mother required medical attention after she fainted upon discovering the body, authorities said, adding the young woman did not leave a note to explain her actions.

A senior in high school, Miss Hobson was active in the Art and Home Economics clubs. She also belonged to a salon, Creedmore Hall, and she attended her mother's church, Homestead Community, in Greenfield.

A neighbor, Mrs. John Willingham, said Miss Hobson was a friend to all and took care of neighbors' pets while the owners were out of town.

The newspaper listed the name of the street the Hobsons lived on. It matched Libby's, and the story was published the day after the last entry in the diary.

Jed bowed his head. The poor girl killed herself in the attic of Libby's home. He wasn't sure he wanted Libby to know, but he would get into trouble if he didn't tell all.

The police said M.H. hadn't left a note. Yes, she did, Jed countered. The diary. The letter to Deck. And the weeping butterfly. But what did the butterfly know? The letter cast her in the light of someone who was self-aware. But something finally overwhelmed her. What was it?

His thoughts returned to Libby. The attic was empty, except for the journal, and it had to have fallen from some perch. Libby herself said she didn't like the attic and didn't go up there. She wouldn't be able to explain the journal. He sat for a minute staring into space. And then he settled on what he thought should have been obvious.

Gale. Somehow, Gale was getting Jed to focus on the diary and its author. But why? What did he want Jed to do about it? The girl had been dead for a century. If it happened today, what would Gale want? Justice? Justice for the girl. Forgiveness and understanding. Help for the survivors.

The survivors were long gone. But what kind of justice was she owed? Acknowledgment of her sorrow? Other factors – Was she persecuted? And then Jed had chills.

"How dumb of me!" Jed muttered to himself. "She's still in the house."

He checked his watch. Libby would be coming home soon. He'd better get moving. His wounded shoulder protested when he hopped up from his chair.

***

Libby was waiting at home. She searched his face when he walked in.

"You don't look bad," she said. "Did you get to your appointments?"

"Yes," Jed said. "And I went to the library."

She brightened. "That's good. Are you hungry?"

"Yes, yes, I am."

"That's great! Let's try homemade vegetable soup and a baguette."

"Do you have any popcorn," he said.

"Yes, I have popcorn, Junior. Do you want a hot dog to go with it?"

"Popcorn for later, I mean . . . I think I should go back to work half-days," Jed said.

"Whoa! Where did that come from? You're not even done with physical therapy."

"I have the ability to focus on problems, so I should be lending a hand to my assistants."

"At least wait for the doctor to clear you to go back . . . So, what really happened today?"

She's incredible, Jed thought.

"I don't know how to explain this." His stance wavered with fatigue.

"I think you should start by sitting down," she said, pulling out a chair and motioning for him to fill it. She went to the refrigerator and pulled out a jug. "Mint tea." She filled a glass with ice and poured. She handed it over, and he sipped, grateful.

"Compose your narrative while I get the beef stock going in the soup pot, and then we'll hash things out after I dump in the goodies," she said.

He watched her backside as she worked at the stove. I want to do this every night, he thought. She brandished a knife, slicing into the baguette. She arranged the pieces on a platter and presented it along with a bowl of spinach dip. She got herself a glass of tea and sat down across from him.

My wife, he thought.

She waited.

"I know I was just drooping around in my underwear," Jed said.

She shrugged.

"And I was – on the bed. And then, there was a loud thump in the attic. I sat up," he said.

She frowned. "Mice?"

"Nooooooo." Bracing, he looked at her. "Ghost."

"What kind of ghost?"

"The ghostly kind," he said, faltering. She rolled her eyes.

"But she left evidence behind," he added.

"She?"

"Yes. M.H." He pulled the diary out of his inside jacket pocket. Leaning over, he pointed to the initials on the inside cover.

"Jed, my attic was empty. Who could have put this up there?"

"I think it was there all along. But – something . . . caused it to fall from a hiding place, maybe? I found it on the floor, right over the bedroom."

He flipped pages to the sad letter to Deck. "Read this and tell me what you think."

Libby read, shaking her head in disbelief. "What in the world?" She browsed through the cartoons. "Pretty good!" She turned to the last entry and studied the weeping butterfly.

"So?" Jed said.

"A messed-up teenager, probably compromised by this Deck guy."

"My conclusion as well. But there's a noble conscience in these drawings. She was no airhead."

Libby was cool, but under wraps, elated at the improvement in Jed's disposition. He was engrossed in a problem and his appetite for life was coming back.

Indeed, Jed was the prosecutor of Marion County. "The decedent killed herself in the attic by swallowing carbolic acid," he said.

Libby sucked in her breath. "Oh my God!"

"The police could not determine a motive."

"It's all in here," she said, pointing at the diary.

"Except for the final provocation."

"Why couldn't it have been a gradual build-up until she was overcome by hopelessness?" she said.

"It could have been so. This is entirely subjective, but the person who comes through in the cartoons is tough-minded. These grasshoppers wearing Klan hoods – considering the preeminence of the Klan in those days – indicate she held unpopular views," he said.

"And she was isolated," Libby said. "But how did you find out she committed suicide?"

"The library newspaper archives. I matched an account of a local death with the initials M.H. She was Mary Hobson. The Hobsons lived here."

Libby shivered. "What about Deck?"

Jed smiled. "Only a hunch."

Libby got up to check the soup. "What about an autopsy?" she said.

"That, too. I might ask Army Hauser to dig it up. I don't want gossip about the wounded prosecutor spending time investigating a century-old death. But Army can say he's doing historical research. No one will care."

Jed's old political calculation was returning, too, Libby thought, but it didn't rankle as it once might have.

"And the eugenics law – the one she mentions in the letter to the jerk – What was this law, anyway?" she said.

"It was intended to rid our pristine state of paupers, deviates, and the feeble-minded. The original was struck down in state court as a violation of due process. But revisions were made, so we sterilized over two thousand citizens until we finally got rid of these laws in the seventies.

"If this boils it down for you, Hitler liked our eugenics program so well he mentioned it in *The Final Solution*."

"Jesus, Mary, and Joseph," Libby said.

CHAPTER 70
Present Day – Grasshopper News

During dinner Jed said, "Does it bother you that she killed herself here? I debated not telling you, but I don't want to hide anything from you."

"It depends on whether you believe in the existence of haunted houses," Libby said. "I've never liked the attic, but I don't care much for the basement, either. Just something about the desolation.

"But *Los!* seems to be handling the basement well," she said.

"He handles anything that involves dog treats," Jed said. "But he really needs to run around. I need to chain a long leash to a stake. That is, if you want a stake in your backyard."

"Wouldn't bother me," she said.

"What if I chained myself to your bed?"

"Wouldn't bother me."

"You didn't say how you really feel about living with the story of Mary Hobson," he said.

"I chose Irvington after I went on the haunted house tour. I knew what I was getting into. Mary isn't a malevolent ghost. I'm not even sure she's here. Maybe some other entity lured you up to the attic," she said.

"Who would it be?" He was going to keep Gale out of it for the moment.

"Don't know. Maybe an angel. This didn't happen until after you came to stay. Mary could have haunted me a long time ago." She paused. "But now that I think about it– my funny dreams and all the cold drafts – maybe she was here all along." She suspected it was Teddy, but she didn't want to make Jed feel insecure when he was on a comeback.

"An excellent point . . . Have I disrupted your life?" he said.

"Yes, but in a good way. We're having fun right now."

They ate in silence for a few minutes, and then Jed said, "My mother thinks I should put my house on the market."

"When did you talk to her?"

"Yesterday. She thinks I've gotten into a rut, won't try new things . . . new ways of living." He gave Libby a direct stare.

Libby dipped a crust into the spinach dip and took a bite.

"The slow crunch is a plea bargain," Jed said. The corners of her mouth curved a little into a smile.

"You've been with me through the worst in life. And we're still able to sit and talk over dinner. We can handle anything," he said.

Libby swallowed and washed down the bread with a swig of tea. She patted her mouth with a napkin.

"I think you're healing and showing me your true character – and it's a damn good thing Gale dropped that book on my attic floor," she said.

Jed's eyes widened and he laughed. "Dr. Booth, I present you with the haunted diploma of honor."

***

"Jed, it's good to hear your voice. The young dentist bringing you around one of these days?" Armistead Hauser answered his cell phone on the ninth hole of his golf game.

"I'm driving myself now," Jed said. "But I'm not ready to go back to work. I'm contemplating half-days, but I haven't run it by the doctor." My psychiatrist, that is, Jed thought.

"You are top drawer," Hauser said. "I was right about you from the start. But tell me this – You're not mad at me for seducing you into the promised land of elective office? I've worried that you have regrets about running – and becoming a target."

"Army, you have a hold harmless waiver, as far as I'm concerned."

After a pause, Hauser said, "It's a different world without Gale. Not as much fun. So, what's going on today?"

"Actually, I have a favor to ask. Maybe, if it's one you can fulfill, you'll get a new hobby," Jed said.

"Yes?"

"Could you find an autopsy report for me from nineteen-twenty-one? Date of death August sixteenth. Decedent's name is Mary Hobson. Died in Marion County at her residence after ingesting carbolic acid. I need to know what else was wrong with her."

"Nineteen-twenty-one? How about that! I know better than to ask. Yep, spell that last name for me?" Hauser wrote it on the back of his score card.

About a week later, Hauser called, polite and direct, holding back any sign of emotion, including curiosity. "I have your report. Mary Hobson was three months pregnant, and she was in the early stages of syphilis."

"Jeez."

"Does this fulfill your request, or is there a codicil?"

"It does, Army, it does. It explains a lot. I don't want to try to fill you in right now. It's something I'd rather do over several drinks."

"My liquor cabinet is unusually well-stocked, and my wife is asking about you. Don't tarry," Hauser said.

***

Jed sat on the steps of the front porch at Libby's house. A light breeze flirted with his forehead. The sun was directly overhead. Holding the journal of M.H., he studied the last entry, the depiction of the weeping butterfly, drawn in black ink. The disconsolate figure was utterly alone against the backdrop of the dark forest. He squinted, looking closer at the sketch of the woods, when he realized a pair of menacing eyes peered out from the darkness.

"Gosh, that kid was scared," he said. She must have known she had syphilis. He'd been surfing the Internet to brush up on the history of the treatment of venereal disease. In those days, she would have faced treatments of arsenic mixed with mercury or bismuth. And he felt sick just thinking of the damage to the fetus.

This girl had been through a lot in her short life. Perhaps she believed she couldn't measure up to others' expectations. Jed counted all the judgments piling up: The so-called boyfriend – if that's what he'd been to her – looked down his nose at her; she learned her birth mother came from a humble and troubled background; she herself had a pregnancy and a sexually transmitted disease.

And juxtaposed against the personal history, all the cartoons about the KKK. Why was the Klan of particular interest to this sweet child, a member of the Art and Home Economics clubs?

He studied the cartoons featuring her hero, Clay Zell, the bespectacled grasshopper who edited the *Grasshopper Gazette*. A crusading journalist, Zell stood up to the Knights of the Green Grasshopper. Hah! Just like the Knights of the White Camelia. Jed appreciated M.H. even more. He snorted at the cartoon of Clay Zell standing outside his newspaper office while a mob of hooded grasshoppers threw books onto a bonfire.

Zell's comment was, "You notice they never burn their dime novels?"

The crusader also went to a lemonade sale run by church ladies. At a booth with a sign announcing, "Proceeds Benefit KGG," the lady grasshoppers sold treats to fellow parishioners in the churchyard. Looking over the scene, Clay Zell quoted the Book of Isaiah, "It is He who sits above the circle of the earth, And its inhabitants are like grasshoppers "

Peeking from behind a gravestone in the churchyard, a grasshopper wearing a Klan hood queried, "Have you washed your sins in the blood of the Grand Grasshopper?"

Jed laughed, but then he noticed the name of the church above the door. "Homestead Community." Wait a minute – the same name as the mother's church. He remembered it from the newspaper story. But what did it mean? The mother's church supported the Klan, and the mother did, too? A lemonade stand for the Klan? "Klemon-ade?" he said.

Yet another qualifier in the girl's life. Narrow minds, mobs, adoption secrets, lousy rich guy, pregnancy, disease . . . and suicide.

It certainly made sense. He was getting angry. She was gifted, perceptive, and caring, but suffering from low self-esteem and a sense of doom. Who would have recognized a teen at risk in 1921?

Then, he had a horrible thought. Who would recognize the same teen, today? And what choices would she have, now? Not many, he knew Libby would say.

He was so engrossed he didn't notice the woman coming down the sidewalk with her dog. She stopped near the end of the front walk.

CHAPTER 71
Present Day – Shortbread

The dog walker recognized him as the county prosecutor who'd been under a black cloud. And now he was here at the special house, which meant that matters had come to a head. This was her moment.

"Good afternoon!" she said.

Jed looked up, startled, and then he smiled. "Hi!" he said.

"I'm glad I took the day off, or I wouldn't have met you. I'm Darla Dixon, Mr. Harkness. I recognize you from the news.

"I'm sorry about what happened to you and the policeman. I'm glad you're better. You look like you're on the mend."

"Thank you, Ms. Dixon," he said.

"Please, call me Darla."

She noticed he held an olive-green book close to his heart. She sensed the book had something to do with the spirit trapped in the house. This was a good sign.

"You appeared lost in your book. Is it a mystery?" she said.

"In a way, yes." He didn't want to say too much.

"I like a good read. That's an unusual looking cover. Is it an old book?" she said.

"Yes, I found it in the attic."

"The attic. You know, this is an old house, and some unusual things have happened here," she said.

"Like what," he said.

"A girl, a teenager, died here a long time ago," she said.

"During the flu pandemic?"

The dog walker decided to be direct. "No. I suspect this young woman killed herself."

"That's awful," Jed said. "Does anyone know why?"

She looked at him, appreciating his guile, and sympathizing with his desire to appear nonchalant.

"Perhaps she had very low self-esteem and thought no one was on her side," the woman said.

"How do you know? Did she leave a note?" he said.

The woman smiled. "I think she left more than that."

Jed clutched the book tighter. "How do you know?"

"I've known her spirit is trapped here. I think you know it, too, and you want to help." She smiled again.

Jed found her to be truthful and sincere. But how did she know all this?

"Are you a mind-reader?" he said.

She raised her eyebrows. "No, not exactly. But I do have paranormal abilities, and so do most people, by the way. It's just they don't like to talk about psychic stuff for fear of being ridiculed, and they block the messages they're getting."

"But you know she's in there," Jed said.

"Of course. And she's ready to go Home."

"Then why doesn't she just leave?" Jed said.

"Sometimes spirits need help crossing over. Or maybe they have a job to complete before they go," she said.

"So how do we mortals help them?" he said, still playing dumb.

"Well, a lot depends on your faith system. Sometimes just practicing the rituals of your own faith are a way to communicate with the spirit world.

"I mean, if the rituals don't reach their intended audience, what good are they?"

"I don't know," Jed said.

"Like, if you say, 'Saint So-and-So, pray for us,' you're assuming Saint So-and-So can hear you. And if you really believe it, why would you be surprised if other spirits heard you, too?" she said.

"Point taken," Jed said.

"The story of the Resurrection is the greatest ghost story ever told," she said.

"True," he said, with a sheepish smile.

The dog walker thought the seed was planted, and that it was time to move on. "I'll leave you to your book. I need to get home because I'm taking Trevor to the vet. It was nice talking with you. Good luck with everything!"

"Thank you, Darla. Have a good visit, Trevor!"

They turned and left Jed on the steps.

He slapped his knees and stood up, stiff. He went inside and sat on the sofa. He considered he was like a teenager at risk, as he struggled with survivor's guilt and railed against the unfairness of it all.

But I'm lucky, he thought. Libby and his doctors were helping him. He couldn't bring Gale back, though. And he couldn't bring back M.H. His chin dropped as fatigue came over him and he stretched out on the sofa. What could he do for them? He napped about forty-five minutes.

It was so easy, so obvious, now. He got up, shaved, changed into a casual summer suit, and went to his parish church.

***

Father Jack Cordele answered the rectory door about a minute after Jed knocked. The priest's hair was tousled, and his chin, stubbly with gray shadow.

"Jed!" Cordele threw the door open wide and extended his hands. "It's early in the afternoon for bourbon, but the occasion warrants."

Jed embraced the priest and the two went back to Cordele's study.

"Sit down, sit down! Put your feet up, if you like. Are you all right, Jed?" Cordele stared at him for a few seconds. "I was a chaplain in Desert Storm and saw men blown up right in front of me, but I don't think I've ever been as upset as I was the day you were shot.

"You've been in my prayers every day," the priest said.

Jed sat in a wing chair in front of Cordele's desk. "Thank you very much. I'm OK, but in all sorts of therapy. The doctors don't see any vascular or nerve damage so far, but I'm not taking anything for granted."

"Very wise. Let's get a snack going," Cordele said, picking up his office phone. He rang the housekeeper. "Marty, Jed Harkness is here! Would you be so kind as to bring a tray of shortbread and some beer nuts? Thank you."

Cordele went to an oaken cupboard and pulled out a bottle of bourbon and two shot glasses. "You're not on any painkillers are you," the priest said.

"No, but I should hold myself to one serving, because I'm driving. Gale used to drive me everywhere. And I'm still taking an anti-depressant."

Cordele filled the shot glasses. "You know I attended his funeral as you requested?"

"Yes, and I really appreciated it. He's the reason I'm here. And for one other person."

Cordele handed a glass to Jed and sat down, pushing his drink to the side for a minute. "How can I help?"

"I came to buy an indulgence," Jed said, smiling.

The priest rolled his eyes. "This has been a bad week for corruption in the Church. Another diocesan scandal with the molesters, and now this shady real estate deal on the Ohio River.

"If you want to buy an indulgence or two, I'm not going to stop you," Cordele said. "But I will put the money to good use for my greens fees." They both laughed. The Church had ended the sale of indulgences long ago.

A brief knock at the door meant the snack had arrived, and Marty the housekeeper came through, putting a tray of food in front of Cordele. Going to Jed, she wrapped an arm around his shoulders as she expressed thanks for his survival.

Jed said, "I'm all for shortbread, but not a short life." She chucked him under the chin and left.

Cordele raised his shot glass. "To 'short' bread and a long life."

"Cheers," Jed said, and they drank. Cordele pushed the tray toward Jed, and he took a slice of shortbread.

"I'm gonna get crumbs everywhere," Jed said.

"And they will multiply, so you can feed the masses," Cordele said, getting a small plate from the oaken cupboard. "Here, fancy-schmancy." Jed put his treat on the plate.

"Now what's this all about, my son," Cordele put on an Irish accent.

"Bless me, Father, for I have sinned."

"You're in good company. Now what did you do?"

"I have not forgiven the person who killed Gale," Jed said.

"Understandable. You probably play the scene over and over in your head."

"I do." Jed said. "I've been going to a psychiatrist, and I'm on the medicine. It appears to be working, or I'd probably be at home in my underwear. But I know I must forgive. I just can't wrap my head around it."

"Hardest problem for any human," the priest said. "Christ forgave his tormenters even as he was on the Cross. But he was the Son of God. We can't be Jesus, but we can follow his example. How well we follow him varies with the person and with time.

"If you think it's hard to forgive now, just think how hard it would be if you were a teenager. Remember how it was to recognize the flaws in your own parents and accept them for who they were? Or any other childhood idol?" Cordele said.

Jed was quiet, thinking about M.H. She must have found it hard to accept her mother's support of the Klan.

Tipping his glass, Cordele finished his bourbon. "I'll have another, thanks," the priest said, pouring himself a second. He looked at his watch. "It's almost four. Don't worry. I'll not overdo this evening."

Jed took a bite of the shortbread. Munching, he nodded his head. At last, he said, "I would like to arrange Mass intentions for Gale and one other person. I know it's not required, but I'd like to donate a hundred dollars for each if that's OK with you."

"Perfectly fine," Cordele said. "As we celebrate Mass with Gale in mind, we'll also pray for those impacted by his passing, including his killer. But tell me about the other person."

"She was a teen suicide in nineteen-twenty-one. I don't think her soul is at peace." He related the story of the diary and his subsequent findings to Cordele, who lowered his head at times during Jed's narrative. But at the end, he was exuberant.

"The best haunting this week!" Cordele said, slapping the desktop. "We'll have Mass intentions for sure, but I must also visit the attic. We're on a crusade now.

"Do you think your girlfriend would mind if you had me over to say a little prayer or two in the attic?" the priest said.

"No, but I will tell her first," Jed said. "When do you want to come by?"

"Soon. Before I say the Mass. Can I come tomorrow?"

"Yes. Let me buy lunch. After we're done upstairs, we can walk down to Washington Street to a restaurant – that is, if you have the time," Jed said.

"Where angels go, gravy follows," Cordele said, taking out beads. "May God grant you pardon and peace, and I absolve you from your sins, in the name of the Father, and of the Son, and of the Holy Spirit.

"And now, for help with forgiveness, we're going to pray the Rosary together."

CHAPTER 72
Present Day – Forgiveness

"A priest wants to pray in my attic," Libby said at dinner. "Did you explain it's a Lutheran attic with occasional forays into Buddhism?"

"You're a lapsed Lutheran," Jed said.

"She's a non-denominational ghost, if she's up there," Libby said.

"Point taken. But she's up there."

She left him watching an exhibition football game after dinner while she went for a walk. The sunset had been sent straight from Mesopotamia in orange and purple, majestic colors that only the heavens could mix. Now, a deep darkness descended because of the new moon.

She felt a stab of desire. Now that Jed was up and around, tackling problems, making decisions, he was the vital man she'd come to love.

He moved in of necessity, and it felt like a simple change of clothes. But after all, it was her house, and she needed to state her expectations. He'd want to know if he should wind up his visit, and whether *Los!* would be welcome much longer.

The dog could have a chain in the backyard. Why would that be such a big deal? And Libby never spent time in the backyard, except to mow.

Still, Jed needed a man cave. Her pace quickened as she realized what to do.

Libby stopped at a corner to observe the night sky. "Thank you, God, for giving us a second chance," she said.

***

Father Cordele grunted as he climbed the attic stairs, but he made it to the top. He and Jed stood in the center of the attic in silence as Cordele looked around at the eaves. Finally, the priest spoke, crossing himself.

"In the name of the Father, and of the Son, and of the Holy Spirit."

"Amen," Jed said, also making the sign of the Cross.

"Let us pray in the words that Jesus taught us," and Jed's eyes filled with tears as they lifted their hands and recited the Lord's Prayer. Saying this brought him home. He remembered his father always hugged and kissed him after the prayer at each Mass.

"Now Mary Hobson, we commend your spirit to Heaven," Cordele said. "You know you made a mistake, but you have the gift of grace as a child of God. He desires you to be with Him, enveloped in His love, in concert with the angels. Leave this space behind and fly, sweet child. May God grant you mercy and salvation.

"We understand your pain. You thought you could not handle the trials of life. But the greater trial is separation from God. We pray for your soul, and ours, and ask Lord Jesus Christ, who lives and reigns with the Father, to lift you into His celestial presence, and to comfort all those like you who despair and want to give up.

"Lord, please accept the soul of Miss Mary Hobson, a talented artist and concerned citizen, whose earthly energy was stifled too soon, but whose love needs to be in communion with You and the angels and saints in Heaven."

Jed wiped his eyes. The priest said another short prayer, and they stood in silence with heads bowed for a minute. When Jed looked up. Cordele was watching him.

"Ready?" Jed said.

The priest nodded. "Thanks for letting me do this. I realize that because of the scandals, our status is tarnished as the vessel connecting the faithful to Spirit.

"A lot of people in my own parish keep me at arm's length, don't confide, don't confess, just – don't. Even the number of dinner invitations I get has dropped.

"I do serve a ceremonial function, which is important. But I appreciate that you took me into your confidence."

"I can always come to you. Let's go eat," Jed said.

***

Jed surprised his staff on a Monday morning by appearing with doughnuts. Cheers and applause greeted the boss, and even the steely Fabiola de Torre did a little jig. Jed said he'd be in the office half-days for a week, and then back full-time.

He and his leadership team went into a meeting, and when they got around to discussing the case of Gale's murder, Jed said an attorney in private practice, Steve Jelks, would be the special prosecutor. Jelks was a chief deputy prosecutor in a neighboring county before joining a large firm.

The others nodded.

"It'll be up to Steve to decide whether to file for the death penalty," Jed said.

"The cops want it," Fabiola said.

Jed paused, framing his thoughts. "When he was a child, Malik Thresher's birth father dangled him by his heels outside a second-story window – more than once.

"He was whipped with electrical cords, burned with cigarettes, and even made to eat his own excrement.

"He never had a chance." The friends at "Sink or Swim" had done an elaborate investigation for their favorite customer.

Jed was far away, and then he said, "If there's an execution in Michigan City, I don't want to attend as a witness."

All were silent. Finally, Jim cleared his throat. He nodded in deference to Ray Stonehill, the lead trial deputy, but sending a look that he thought Stonehill should speak.

"The accused has been making unusual jailhouse statements," Stonehill said. The others stiffened as if fearing something else would injure the boss, a bird with a broken wing. Jed waited.

Stonehill sighed. "According to the guards, the defendant keeps saying he wants the death penalty."

Jed slumped.

CHAPTER 73
Eternal Time

Gale waved as Mary walked out of the conference room into the perfect light. She followed Billy, who explained he was her uncle – her birth mother's younger brother. He drowned in a fishing accident before Mary was born.

Gale turned to Luther. "Grandpa, it's good to see you. Any good whiskey up here?"

Luther snorted. "Where we're going, you'll be able to summon a bartender any time with the power of your imagination. But you won't have the craving."

"That's what I figured. I guess we're supposed to be free from things that don't matter," Gale said.

"That's right. You'll be busy pondering the things that do. Let's go, boy," Luther said, leading him through the door.

They disappeared into the white horizon.

CHAPTER 74
The Present Day – September

Libby gathered the staff in her private office for coffee cake before the practice opened on a Friday morning. "What do you think about a November bride?" she said. They all laughed when Marquita gasped and covered her eyes with her hands.

"You don't know the half of it," Libby said. "Jed doesn't even know we're getting married." They laughed again, and then Marquita said, "Seriously?"

"Yes. But he will find out this week." They all looked at each other. "It's a long story," Libby said. "But he will be happy, I promise." They all looked at each other, again.

"I thought if the wedding was on the Saturday before Thanksgiving, we could just close the office for the whole week. We only need to reschedule a handful of people if we do it right away. No worries, you'll be paid for those days.

"Of course, your families are invited to the wedding," Libby said.

"Where will it be," Marquita said.

"Oh, I don't know," Libby said. Trying not to laugh, they all looked at each other. "But the food will be fantastic. I promise," Libby said. She looked at her watch. "It's five 'til. We'd better wrap this up. I'll mail out invitations. Thanks, everybody!"

They dispersed. As Marquita went down the hall, she was singing, "Here comes the *local*/All dressed in mocha."

After work, Libby called Denise. "I need you to come with me to Jed's house."

"Why?"

"We're going to steal his TV," Libby said.

"No, really, why are we going to Jed's house?" Denise said.

"To get his TV."

Denise sighed. "I know there's a logical explanation. I'm only searching for simplicity.

"I just finished a therapy session with an obsessive-compulsive who kept bringing up the time his stove was struck by lightning while he was standing right next to the stove.

"Not on the other side of the kitchen, but right next to the stove. And he was getting ready to make hot chocolate, and he was right next to the stove, not a few feet away.

"And he was right next to the stove," Denise said, drained.

"Was he next to the stove?" Libby said

"Oh, ALL RIGHT! We're stealing Jed's TV," Denise said, laughing.

Libby obtained Jed's house key after suggesting she pick up more clothing for him now that he was back to work. "It's close enough to my office that I can go right after I'm done, so you don't have to drive all the way out there from downtown," she said.

"OK, but you'll need the alarm code. You put it in within two minutes of entry, or the cavalry shows up. And remember to lock yourself in." He wrote the code on the back of a business card and gave it to her. "You have to put it in again before you leave, and press 'Arm' and then go out locking the door within two minutes."

Denise met her at the office and followed her to Jed's. They conquered the alarm and went to Jed's den.

"This is why I needed help," Libby said, pointing at the sixty-five-inch TV. "I didn't want to break it all by myself.

"It's a surprise. I'm redoing a room into a den for Jed, and I need to put in the TV," Libby said.

Denise put her hands on her hips. "Libby, if I didn't know better, I'd say you were taking a big risk with this guy. You should at least make it look like it was his idea. Men are funny about their stuff."

Libby smiled and held out her hand to Denise, who clasped it. "He tried to ask me to marry him before he was shot. I said I wasn't ready to talk about it. This is my way of telling him I'm ready. I know he doesn't want to come home to this dusty house. This was his parents' home. There's nothing here for him now."

"Except this gorgeous leather recliner that looks brand new," Denise said. "And the wet bar."

"We'll get someone to haul the chair," Libby said. "I'd have to plumb in the bar, and he would probably object if I spent a lot of money on it. So we'll see.

"But I'm telling him 'Yes' as soon as I get the room set up. We might have to find another house, eventually, but for now, it'll be OK." Denise pulled her close and hugged her.

The pair unhooked the cable and wrapped the screen in a bedsheet Libby found in the linen closet.

"When do you want to have the ceremony?" Denise said.

"November feels right. It's a lucky month for Jed. He won his election last November," she said. "And it's good for me, too, because I can piggyback things with Thanksgiving and give my staff extra time off."

"So, is this a big church wedding, and in whose faith, if I'm not being too presumptuous?" Denise said.

"Not a big wedding, but we'll have to include a priest. I wouldn't dream of asking Jed to forgo that, after a lifetime in his faith. I haven't decided what I what for myself."

"And the shindig after?" Denise said.

"If I keep it small enough, will you cater?" Libby said. "I'd consider it a wedding gift. Your food is fantastic, and the way you present things – just an eyeful.

"Naturally, I'd cover all the expenses," she added.

"I will absolutely do it!" Denise said, skipping a small circle into the carpet. "I can't wait to start sketching how I want the buffet laid out, and the color scheme. Not to rush you, but you'll have to pick your colors soon," she said, turning to skip in the other direction.

"Thank you. I won't make you do anything at the last minute." Libby posted a mental note that she would get a magnetic plaque for the side of Denise's car to herald "Shrink Catering."

They carried the TV and its rectangular table into Libby's house and placed them along a wall in the new den. Libby still had to schedule the cable installation. All else was ready. On a Saturday when Jed was away, Libby had painted the walls terra cotta, and the wainscoting, an ocean blue. Instead of curtains, she'd put in wooden shutters with cherry stain and a valence in purple and blue paisley at the top. She opened the window to let out the odor of paint, and simply closed the door, because she knew Jed wouldn't bother to look inside. Later, she added a small microwave and a minifridge. The shelf under the microwave was stocked with popcorn, and Jed's favorite brand of beer was in the fridge.

Denise looked around. "Very nice. What if he wants those guy things like pictures of green ducks and lithographs of golf clubs?"

"He can repaint the room if he wants. I just cleaned it up. It was a dirty off-white with a plastic window shade."

"Are you leaving the wood floors bare?" Denise said.

Libby shrugged. "I'll let him choose. If it were my choice, I'd go with an area rug.

"But I think he likes subdued lighting, so we'll probably wind up getting a dimmer."

"More cave-like," Denise said, nodding.

Suddenly, they heard Jed shouting *"Los!"* as he came in the back door. The women gulped. Eager barks came up from the basement, and the friends heard Jed going down the stairs. They tiptoed out of the den and shut the door.

"Saved by the dog," Denise whispered. "I'd better go. Good thing I parked in front." She sprinted to the door and blew Libby a kiss. "Call me," she mouthed.

After feeding his dog and offering many expressions of affection, Jed came upstairs. It was almost seven-thirty.

Maybe now, Libby thought.

"Hungry?" she said.

"Always," Jed said, coming to kiss her on the neck.

His touch was inspirational. "I have just the thing. Let's get a pizza. I'll go get it." She grabbed her purse and keys. "It'll probably take about a half-hour if they're busy." And she ran out the back door before he could say anything.

At the restaurant, she put in a special order. "Here's what I want on top as an extra, and please use banana peppers and olives." She wrote her instructions on the back of a carryout menu and handed it to the young hostess.

"Oh! OK, yeah, yes!" the girl said. Her reaction is worth a big tip, Libby thought.

Back at the house, she put the closed box on the kitchen table. "Maybe you'd like to open a couple of beers?" she said.

"I think we're out," he said, looking into the refrigerator.

"You might try the refrigerator in your room," Libby said.

"What are you talking about?" Jed said.

"In your room. The door next to the bathroom door."

"What?"

"Go ahead, look," she said, keeping a straight face.

He went to the hall, turned the knob on the designated door. The door stuck a little from the paint job, and he pushed his way in. The light was already on.

He stood there. "My TV," he said, finally. He opened the minifridge. Beer! He took out two bottles and went back to the kitchen. He put the bottles on the table and pulled Libby into a bear hug.

"You didn't need to pick up my clothes. You kidnapped my TV, you wench." He squeezed her tighter.

"Open your pizza box," she said, muffled in his chest.

With one arm around her, he opened the box. He sucked in his breath. Laced together in banana peppers and black olives was a question, "Marry?" He balled up a fist and covered his mouth. Then, from somewhere in his throat, he heard a raspy, "I will."

"I can't hear-rrr you," Libby sang.

"I will," he said, firm and loud, as he pulled her toward their bedroom.

CHAPTER 75
Present Day – September

The next day, Libby called Tony and Kerry to find out if their daughter would serve as flower girl at the wedding.

"We'd love it. I'm honored you thought of us," Tony said.

"We'll be delighted to have you. I'm thinking one of you will need to hold her hand and walk her down the aisle."

"I can bring her down, but I don't know how long she'll stay in one place. She needs to sit with us during the ceremony, and then she can go back down the aisle behind the bridesmaids, if that's a detail you want."

"Jed's dog is one of his attendants, so I think I'm in a position to be flexible," she said, and Tony laughed.

"We just got a new pet, and Evvie walks him on a leash – with our supervision, of course."

"Tell me all about him," Libby said.

**

Later that night, Denise called about cake frosting.

"I don't think the frosting has to match the wedding colors," Libby said. She'd chosen orange gold with grape accents. "Just pretty frosting that you like, that's the important thing."

"OK. But what about the tablecloths and napkins – you want those to coordinate, right?"

"Yes, but if it's an ordeal, don't worry about it. The dresses, flowers,

311

ribbons – those are in the wedding colors. But it won't be the end of the world if everything is white at the reception," Libby said.

"Oh no, I couldn't look at white for several hours," Denise said. "Makes me see spots, and then after a while, it looks like paper products at the grocery, you know, toilet paper and towels."

"Tell you what – we'll use real cloth – white for the table covers and purple for the napkins, nice and stiff. Doll it up with tall purple candles in gold candleholders, two on each table. We should be able to get LED candles that fit the bill for safety," Libby said.

"Chair covers?" Denise said.

"No. Too fussy. Just something uniformly presented, no seating assignments except at the head table."

"Head table decorated the same way?"

"Yes and no. Let's elevate the head table, and since it's long and rectangular, we'll put a candelabra front and center and then several small bouquets spaced evenly along the table."

"Free at the bar?"

"Lots of lawyers will be there, so, yes."

***

That same night, Jed came into the kitchen from work around nine-thirty. He looked tired. Libby opened her arms, and he walked into them.

"Got any leftovers?" Jed whispered into her ear.

"Better. Freshly made squash casserole with cheese sauce, and a salmon patty."

"You're a genius." He held her tight, then loosened his grip and looked into her eyes. He needed to come clean.

"I should share some information with you about the case," he said.

"What?" she said.

"It hasn't been decided whether the state will file for the death penalty against Malik Thresher. There's some sentiment for it in Gale's family, and the defendant himself has made provocative statements about wanting it."

"No! No!" Libby cried. Pulling away from him, she paced the kitchen. Jed watched her, curious at first, then alarmed. He had never seen his cool clinician so distraught. She'd been his rock, but now, she needed him to man up.

"If we have to live with this, then so does he!" she said. Her face was contorted in anger, and Jed had never seen her so bitter.

"We'd be starting marriage with his execution hanging over us. It's like marrying him, too – May as well engrave his name on the license," she said. "How can this be possible?" she shrieked.

Jed took a deep breath. "A defendant can volunteer for execution by entering a plea of guilty to a crime for which the prosecution is seeking the death penalty.

"Doesn't mean the judge will go along. Or, if a capital case goes to trial and he's found guilty, the defendant can waive his right to present mitigating evidence during sentencing.

"So, to begin with, the special prosecutor would have to file for the death penalty as a sentencing option," he said, making a stop gesture with his hand. "That hasn't happened yet. And Thresher's attorney hasn't said anything, even though the jailers are hearing directly from Thresher."

"Then he can hang himself in his cell," she said, putting her hands on her hips.

Jed snorted. "Normally, I would be appalled by such a remark, but from you, it's – refreshing."

Libby was about to erupt, but Jed held up both hands. "Wait, sweetheart. Remember – Gale left a widow," he said. "And some very opinionated family members. They have a strong voice in recommending whether to make this a capital case.

"I went to see Lee Ann and the family tonight."

"And?" Libby said, frozen for the moment.

"I think she wants it to be over as much as you do. Even more so. But some – including a son-in-law who revered Gale – have other ideas.

"Bottom line – they're still torn up, and they want revenge," Jed said.

"They said that?"

"In so many words," he said. "No one who favors the death penalty ever uses the word 'revenge' in front of me, because it sounds base and petty.

"So they try to elevate the case by talking in Biblical terms, eye for an eye – or resort to the discredited argument that the death penalty deters crime. It does not.

"The one argument that Lee Ann said she could hold with is that crimes against the state, like the murder of a police officer, should carry the most severe punishment," he said.

"So she wants the state to ask for death?" Libby said, pressing her hands to her chest.

"She hasn't decided. I get the sense she's trying to work through this so the kids will cool down. But the cops made them aware that Thresher has been telling anyone who will listen that he wants to die.

"So it's harder to convince them the family would be stuck with enduring years of appeals, when the defendant is doing everything he can to speed to the death chamber," Jed said.

"You're not going to cave into him, are you?" Libby said.

"It's not my call," he said. "I was shot, saw my treasured friend die – but that's why we have a special prosecutor."

"It never stops," Libby shouted as she stamped her foot and began to sob. "Our wedding, our wedding!" She cried, broken-hearted.

Jed stood open-mouthed. Recovering himself, he took her right hand in his own and dropped to one knee. "Libby, Libby . . . Look at me."

He was a begging blur on the floor. She wiped her eyes with her free hand.

"I love you. You're going to marry me," he said. "We will stand by each other, for better or for worse. And we will have a wedding for the ages – because Army Hauser said he's picking up the tab for the booze."

Libby burst out laughing and fell to her knees. They rolled to the floor in a tight hug.

***

In a courthouse conference room, Special Prosecutor Steve Jelks sat across from Malik Thresher's attorney, Mark Phalen, a capable scholar just a year out of law school.

"Mr. Phalen, a plea of not guilty was entered at the initial hearing. But the outdoor surveillance cameras clearly show your client firing the murder weapon.

"On top of this, he discussed his motives during the interrogation after his arrest. I have the videotape of the interrogation, and I'd like us to watch it now, if you don't mind," Jelks said.

314

"I've seen it," Phalen said, "But we may as well watch it."

On the tape, the interrogating officer began, "Mr. Thresher, you were advised of your right to an attorney, and that anything you say can be held against you. Are you speaking with me now of your free will?"

"Yeah," Thresher said, barely audible.

"Why were you mad at Jed Harkness?" the officer said.

"Brother I run with, he get hard time," Thresher said, mumbling into his chest.

"Why were you out on Market Street that day?"

"Don't remember," Thresher said.

The officer sighed. "That's not good enough."

Thresher's hands trembled. "He mine . . . he mine . . . he always mine . . . Now he everybody bitch . . . I got nobody," Thresher said, crying with his hands over his face.

Jelks stopped the tape. "Thresher had a close friend with whom he was intimate. That guy was sent to prison after a trial supervised by Jed Harkness. Thresher had a motive."

He turned up the pressure on Phalen. "Counsel, we're keeping it simple. No deals will be offered – but we're filing for life without parole. The victim's widow has requested it."

"Crime of passion, sudden heat. A jury might go for voluntary manslaughter," Phalen said.

"It was premeditated. He was stalking Harkness, articulating intention," Jelks said.

"To whom? A bunch of crackheads, not credible witnesses," Phalen said.

"Do you really intend to mount a defense?" Jelks said. "Thresher has all but asked the jailers for a lynching party."

"I think a jury can weigh his case," Phalen said.

"I'll tell you what they're going to weigh," Jelks said. "A police officer died in the middle of the street because a lonely guy was missing his boyfriend."

"The canons require a vigorous defense, and I intend to provide one," Phalen said.

After a few moments, Jelks said, "I checked you out. You graduated in the top ten percent of your class, and your zeal is admirable – but I'll gut your client if you put him out there.

"There was no sudden heat – no basis for the crime of passion," Jelks said. "Harkness and the victim were going to lunch. Thresher never had a conversation with them. Nothing precipitated the shooting at the time. Your client planned it.

"It'll be a big waste of effort – and he'll still get life without parole," Jelks said.

After the meeting, Jelks dropped in at Jed's office. With a hopeful expression, Jed nodded to Jelks in the doorway.

Jelks shrugged. "We might have a trial, but I think I talked Phalen down off the ledge."

Jed threw up his hands in frustration.

"Don't lose heart. He's a smart boy. He's just still in the phase where he's toying with the role of defense attorney. When he thinks about it, he'll see that it's better for his client not to have a public spectacle," Jelks said.

CHAPTER 76
Present Day – All Hallows Eve

The November wedding drew near. In the last week of October, Historic Irvington celebrated its annual Halloween Festival, which culminated in a street fair that drew thousands of visitors. The weather held on the sunny side, and vendors couldn't move fast enough to serve customers. Around lunchtime, Libby and Jed strolled up and down Washington Street. They stopped to chat with roving volunteers passing out political pamphlets.

While Jed lingered with the campaigners, Libby wandered to a stall with embroidered goods on display. A purple headband caught her eye. She could wear it under her bridal veil. "Something old, something new," she whispered.

"Do you have a question?" a pleasant woman asked.

"Did you make this?" Libby said.

"I did. If it's a gift, I can put it in a box," the vendor said, holding up a tiny orange box decorated with black cats.

"That'd be fine," Libby said. "It's a present for me to wear on my wedding day."

"Oh!" the seamstress said. "That's so special. I'm very honored that you'd wear something I made to your wedding. When is your big day?"

"The weekend before Thanksgiving," Libby said, handing over cash. "The box and the headband will be a nice keepsake to store with my wedding sachet."

"That's wonderful. I can coast on this for the rest of my day," the vendor said, handing her the boxed trinket. "Congratulations! I wish you all the happiness in the world." she said.

"Thank you. Hope you sell out today – good luck!" Libby said, turning to look for Jed, who spotted her as he shook hands in parting with an acquaintance.

"Get something?" Jed said as he caught up to her.

"Just a little doodad for me, for my trousseau. Of course, you can't see it."

"Trousseau – Didn't he come up with the social contract theory?"

"That was Rousseau, and you knew that," Libby said. They were approaching a homemade candy stand. She leaned over and whispered. "Let's buy some fudge and take it back to the house right away."

"Why do we have to take it home right away?" Jed whispered back.

"We might smudge it on our clothing. But if we go home, we can take off our clothes."

"And we're out of stain remover," he said, pulling out his wallet. "Wait right here."

***

Darla Dixon talked it over with Trevor, and she decided to take a chance on being discovered by her university colleagues. For the first time, she had her own booth at the Halloween festival, a very public outing. Hoping to clear some Christmas money after expenses, she would give ten-minute psychic readings for a fee.

Trevor sat with her at the festival, and when it was time for the costume parade, she'd walk him in his outfit. He was going as an angel.

She borrowed a portable picnic shelter to cover her street space on a corner spot. Using tie-dyed bedsheets, she made three walls under the awning. A velveteen privacy curtain was strung to conceal her customers, so that only she could be seen by passersby while she gave readings.

At the street fair, throngs went by as she waved. She passed out hundreds of business cards. During the first hour, she snared a high school football player and his girlfriend, who insisted on a joint reading. The day's venture was worthwhile.

Needing a bathroom break, she was about to leave Trevor with a friend, when the woman who lived in the special bungalow stopped at the craft booth next door.

Yes, our queen is happy, but challenges are right on top of her, Darla thought, seeing calamity and question marks. Big question marks. That lady was being chased by punctuation.

A man caught up with the bungalow queen. It was the prosecutor, and Darla didn't want him to be uncomfortable running into her. She slid behind the velveteen curtain and watched their backs as they walked away, whispering and laughing.

They were sexy, the observer saw, turning away from the couple as her bladder sent a message of torment. With an anxious face, she motioned for her friend to hurry over from the line at the taco truck. "I'll buy you lunch when I come back," she said, passing the dog leash to her buddy.

***

On Sunday morning, Libby slid a chuck roast into the oven and poured herself another cup of coffee. Finishing toast, Jed was sitting at the kitchen table as he watched a network news show. He would duck out soon to attend Mass. It occurred to Libby that Jed himself might appear on a network show if he pursued his option to run for attorney general. In all the planning for the wedding, the couple hadn't discussed his electoral ambitions. But maybe we should, she realized.

She sat down gazing at her future husband, and then his cell phone rang. His phone is our reality, she conceded, sipping the coffee.

"What?" Jed said as he rushed to the living room with his phone. She could hear him yelling.

"GODDAMMIT! Goddamn it!" he said. "How in the hell did THAT happen? What did he DO IT with?"

Libby felt queasy.

"Well, who in the hell gave him THAT?"

Libby feared what was coming.

"GODDAMMIT! They were supposed to keep watch. You'd better find out who fucked up, and so help me, if they did it on purpose, I'm gonna INDICT somebody's worthless ass! And YOU get to announce it to the media. It's not MY jail, goddammit. I'm going now!"

Libby heard nothing for a moment, and then she leapt out of her seat when she heard Jed wailing, "God damn . . . Goddammit."

She rushed to him. "What? What?" she said.

"That was the sheriff. Thresher hanged himself. He got a belt somehow." Clutching his phone, Jed sank to the living room floor and held his head.

Libby pressed her fingers to her temples. "Oh my God, I said it. I said he could hang himself. I didn't mean for him to do it." Still pressing her temples, she squatted next to Jed. "I never should have put words to it."

With his head drooping, Jed sat, defeated. Moving behind him, Libby put her arms and legs around him and rested her head against his back.

"I wish I hadn't said it," she said. "I so wish I hadn't said it. It was a horrible thing to say. I didn't mean to put that energy out into the world." She hugged him.

"It's not your fault," he said, finally.

"It's not yours either," she said.

"I know. I'm not upset because he's dead," Jed said. "I'm upset because I'm relieved. I'm sad and ashamed."

"I wish I hadn't said it," she said. Jed looped his right leg over Libby's and kissed her left hand, now adorned with the engagement ring he'd bought last week.

"Are you going to call Lee Ann?" she said.

"She probably already knows. The cop grapevine is better than the Internet. But I guess I'd better." He punched a speed dial and waited. "Hi," he said gruffly. "Yes, I just heard." Libby crawled around to face him.

"This is one time I'm glad the sheriff is a Republican," Jed said after the phone call. "I'll ask the state police to make an investigation, because the deputies will be suspected of 'assisting' in the suicide."

"The deputies didn't murder him, I hope?" Libby said.

"I don't think so. They all knew Gale, but they understand that when a cop killer dies in custody, everyone is scrutinized." He heaved a couple of deep breaths, like someone who'd just run to catch a bus. Libby pulled him to her, and exhausted, they sprawled on the rug.

They listened to the grandfather clock ticking. "Why do we wind up on the floor?" Libby said.

"It's our meeting place," Jed said.

After a minute or so, Libby said, "Are you going to run for attorney general?"

Jed closed his eyes. "I don't know, sweetheart. But I also know not to make up my mind during a whirlwind. Let's just get married," he said.

A whirlwind. Libby stared up at the ceiling. One of the dreams about Teddy came back to her. He was outside in the wind, and garbage cans were blowing down the street. And he was laughing.

She and Jed were still, and then they fell asleep.

CHAPTER 77
Present Day – Union

The day had arrived. *Los!* had been taken to the dog groomer, and now he was wearing a dog tuxedo. Even Jed's mother, who was never fond of dogs, was gushing, calling him "Los-ie."

"You're going to give him a complex," Jed said. "You gave me a complex when you called me 'Jed-die.' "

"Oh, hush," his mother said. "I wish Dad were here."

"Dad is here, Mom," Jed said in a low voice. "You just can't see him."

Father Cordele overheard the exchange, and he said, "That's right, Corinne. He wouldn't miss it for the world."

The groom's immediate relatives, including his sister, Melanie, and her family, were assembled in a suite at the Morton Plaza, where the wedding was to be held. Jim was standing up for Jed as best man, and three old friends were the groomsmen. An honorary groomsman, *Los!* would stand up for Jed as well.

The wedding was at four o'clock, to be followed by a reception with cocktails, a dinner buffet, and dancing. Libby opted for recorded music and no announcer, just a technician who could keep the music going. But the hall had a special dance space with multi-colored disco lights.

The Harkness family gathered for a prayer with Cordele, who agreed to co-officiate with a Lutheran minister, Bill Wardell, from Libby's hometown in Iowa. At the rehearsal dinner the previous night, Jed went overboard with jokes about a Lutheran and a Catholic playing golf, walking into a bar, and being on an airplane about to crash.

Finally, Cordele looked sideways at Wardell and said, "This is why I only do one Lutheran wedding every 37 years."

Wardell smiled and said, "Try doing thirty-seven in one year." Cordele groaned and ordered another bourbon.

"I hope this is strong enough to wash away the stain of Jed's jokes," the priest said.

"Here's hoping he remembers what to say during the ceremony," Wardell said, lifting his glass of cola.

"Cheers," Cordele said. The two then huddled and talked about sports.

Now in the hour before the wedding, the Harkness clan made a protective shell around Jed and the priest. Cordele thanked them for loving and raising Jed, and the priest asked for the family's continued support for Jed and Libby in their new life.

Afterward, the family went down to the event hall, but Cordele and Jed lingered with *Los!*

"I need to walk him outside for a minute so he can empty himself. I forgot to bring the dog potty," Jed said.

"I'll walk out with you," Cordele said.

They went outside to a stiff breeze. In the late afternoon, the sky was showing purple streaks.

"I don't see any hydrants or trees," Jed said.

"There's an alley over here. We can duck in for a second, and he'll be all right," Cordele said.

The men entered the alley just as a car full of testy teenagers went by. A boy yelled out the car window, "Pervert priest getting a blow job!"

Jed looked at Cordele. "Do you see any priests here?" Jed said.

"No. The winos must have moved over to the next block." Cordele said.

They waited while *Los!* sniffed and found a suitable spot. They went back inside with wind-tousled hair and cold noses.

About twenty minutes later, it was time to assemble with the best man and the groomsmen. Jed handed each a sealed envelope with a personal note of thanks and tickets to a game between the Chicago Bears and the Green Bay Packers. "Open these later," he said. "I love you guys."

Jim looked at *Los!* "Libby is so cool to let your dog be in the wedding."

"She has been most liberal," Jed said.

"Need to share something," Jim said. "I'm going to start dating an auburn-

323

haired beauty who is one of the brains in your office."

Jed's mouth fell open for a moment and then he said, "Jim, *prima facie* sexual harassment. You're in a leadership role."

"Yes, but the lady in question is turning in her resignation," Jim said. "She's leaving the twenty-seventh of December."

"Then I'll have one less brain. Wait a minute – Are you talking about Army's niece, Sheri?" Jed said.

"The very same."

"Does she know you're interested in her?" Jed said.

"She's leaving because she's interested in *me*," Jim said. "Can you believe it?"

"She said that?" Jed said.

"Oh yeah. See, we wound up sitting next to each other at Gale's funeral. She forgot to bring a hankie, so I loaned her mine. But then I needed it. By the time it was over, every acre of that hankie was soaked and snotty.

"I had to throw it away," Jim said.

Jed laughed.

"So then after the service," Jim continued, "Sheri said, 'I'm all dressed up on a Saturday with no place to go.' And I said, 'Let's go to lunch, my treat.' So we went and it felt good. Just what we needed.

"So a couple times a week since then, we've taken turns buying lunch. Very harmless. But then Sheri knocked me off my feet. She wanted to go on a dinner date, but said we'd get into trouble."

"Yep," Jed said.

"I said, 'We could hold hands as we stand in the unemployment line.'

"And then she said, 'What if I found another job?'

"And I said, *'Señorita,* my history is yours to write.' And she laughed and said she'd ask her uncle for advice."

"Plot thickens," Jed said.

"Big time. Army gave his blessing, which also blew me away. He made a few calls and set up an interview in Johnson County. So she'll start with the prosecutor there after New Year's," Jim said.

"And you'll have a guilt-free date on New Year's Eve," Jed said, smiling.

"That is the plan," Jim said. He looked at his watch. "My brother, it's almost time."

Hugging him, Jed said, "I love you, man. I'm happy for you. We'll have you guys over for dinner very soon."

Cordele approached them. "Well, men, are we ready?"

"Are we ever!" Jed said.

Cordele's eyes misted. "This is the happiest I've been for some time. Let's get to it!"

With *Los!* trailing Jed, the groom's party walked to the meeting hall. The men entered and walked down a side aisle to the front, where they lined up.

A decorative white arch with orange and gold flowers and purple ribbons framed the space behind the altar, a rectangular table draped in purple with two tall candles burning on either side of a gold Cross. Lecterns had been placed at both sides of the altar.

The plan was for the concelebrants to take turns giving Scripture readings. The Catholic would give a short homily, and the Lutheran would lead the wedding vows. Jed would be given Communion by his priest, and Libby, by her minister.

Jim whispered to Jed, "Sheri's got an olive Chanel suit on. She bought it just for this occasion."

"To match the olives in your martini," Jed whispered back.

***

Libby's mother finished dressing the bride and went to check on Libby's father, waiting near the entrance to the event hall. Denise came up to the dressing room before going to her seat, from which she would flee after the ceremony to supervise the catering team. After Jed had presented his guest list, Libby and Denise looked at each other in despair. The small wedding was now an affair for three-hundred guests. Denise wouldn't be able to handle the food by herself as planned, so they hired a caterer to execute her plans to the letter.

"You're beautiful," Denise said. "After my divorce, I forgot how good it feels to be sentimental. Thank you."

"I can't thank you enough for putting all this together," Libby said, hugging her.

Denise pulled a hankie from her purse. "I'd better go down now. I don't want to drip snot on your wedding gown." They clasped hands for a minute, and then Libby was alone. Sitting at the desk, she pulled out a piece of hotel stationery and a pen and began to write.

Wedding Day

Morbid year, be on the run.
Leaden sky, and fleeting sun.
Days short, and lovers tall,
Looking down on cruel and small.
Monsters dumb, fresh out of stun,
The invincible We, in union free,
One, at last, the sojourn done.

She folded the paper and tucked it into her cosmetics bag. She was ready to marry Jed.

***

The wedding processional began. A harpsichordist played J.S. Bach as the four bridesmaids walked in single file. Libby's sister was matron of honor. Murmurs of appreciation came from guests as they viewed the orange-gold satin gowns, each with a purple cinch at the waistline.

Then, people gasped, laughing when the dog barked at the flower girl entering the hall. All smiles, she was tiny in a purple lace minidress. She held a leash on her pet skunk, who wore a frilly purple collar, like an Elizabethan skunk.

The clerics looked at each other. "I didn't know anything about it, Jack," Wardell said.

Los! barked and growled at the offending intruder. Jed just stared.

"Remember, you said Libby has been most liberal," Jim whispered.

"This is more like critical skunk theory," Jed muttered, bewildered.

The guests laughed as *Los!* continued growling. The skunk stopped midway down the aisle and raised its tail.

"He's gonna spray," a man yelled, bolting from his seat. Men along the aisle jumped up, and women cringed, holding up handbags in front of their faces.

"No worries," Tony said as he accompanied his daughter. He addressed the crowd. "He's had his smeller taken out."

Helpless, Jed looked at Armistead Hauser and his wife, who were in a fit of hysterical laughter as they clung to each other.

Jed sighed. "*Los!* Quiet!" he said in a low voice. The dog obeyed.

The skunk and the flower girl continued, taking their places in the line-up before the altar.

The harpsichordist played a fanfare, and the guests rose. A string quartet joined the keyboardist as Libby and her father came down the aisle.

With the wedding party fully assembled, Cordele began. "We're grateful to have you here today. You know, on the way over, I heard a story – A Lutheran, a Catholic, and a skunk walked into a bar."

The guests laughed, and Jed and Libby were married.

At the reception, Lee Ann Mooneyham took them aside. Lee Ann was crying, and they surrounded her in a hug.

"I'm sorry, I can't help it. Gale wanted this so much for you. I think he was here today."

"Yes," Jed and Libby said in unison.

"During the ceremony, I felt this cold draft hitting my face, and I got cold all over. And I thought, why are they running the air conditioning?" Lee Ann said. "But no one else around me seemed to notice."

"Hmm," Jed said. "Sounds like someone was trying to make a point with you."

"I just know he was here," Lee Ann said. "And that skunk! Gale would have talked about it for the rest of his days."

"By way of explanation," Jed said. "*Los!* got sprayed by a skunk once, so that's why he reacted the way he did." He nodded in the direction of the little group around Kerry and Tony. "But judging from that scene over there, he and the skunk have established rapport." The two animals on the floor were eating dog treats from the same plate.

Lee Ann wiped her eyes, and they released from their huddle. The recorded music blared the opening chords of Elvis' "Jailhouse Rock."

"I believe Gale would like the pleasure of this dance," Jed said, taking Lee Ann by the hand to the dance floor. "Don't stray too far, wife," he said over his shoulder to Libby.

Denise hurried over to Libby. "The free booze is a hit," Denise said. "Do these people have designated drivers?"

"Army thought of that, too. He's got a limo service coming by at eight for anyone too smashed to drive," Libby said. "But as an incentive, the guests don't know it. Here's hoping they consume responsibly."

"They're eating well. The hot ham and avocado dip is going fast with the baguettes. And the chicken salad in the fruit wreaths will be demolished," Denise said.

"It was a beautiful spread," Libby said. She sighed.

"What's wrong," Denise said.

"Nothing. I just realized how tired I am."

Denise smiled. "Tonight, you'll feel much better, when you're finally alone, and you've taken off everything except your wedding ring."

Libby nodded. "Yes."

"Are you telling anyone where you're going on your honeymoon?" Denise said.

"I can tell *you*. First, we're going to spend tonight in a cabin in Brown County. Then we're driving to Tennessee to visit some historic sites, and then from Nashville, we'll fly to London and stay for four days."

"Fantastic," Denise said. "I won't tell a soul where you are. Call me when you get home, if you feel like it. I won't ask about all the smutty parts."

Libby laughed. "Who knows? I might want to talk about all the smutty parts."

"I'm going back to the caterer," Denise said, kissing Libby on the cheek and whirling away.

***

Libby and Jed emerged in jeans and heavy sweaters and made their way to Jed's car in the hotel parking garage.

As Jed started the car, he said, "Boy, I could use a hamburger."

"After all that food?" Libby said.

"I didn't eat much," he said. "Too many sidebar conferences."

"I didn't eat much," Libby said.

"I guess our first official act as a married couple will be to go to a drive-up window," he said. "I thought that my ravishing you would be our first official act, but a hamburger it is."

"It can have special sauce," Libby said.

"You're naughty. I think I'll keep you," he said.

During the trip south, they agreed a highlight was Army Hauser having his picture taken with the flower girl and the skunk. And with a bit of guilt, they laughed about the long good-byes from each of their mothers.

"In their defense, they only get to see us a few times a year," Libby said. "You know, you're not exactly the type a girl takes home to mother, unless mother is out of state," Libby said.

"Preferably, out of the country," Jed said.

"Do you want my fries?" she said.

"I want all your fries," he said. She dipped one in ketchup and fed it to him. He licked her fingers.

"This is the longest forty-five miles I've ever driven," Jed said.

The cabin was cold. Jed turned on the heat. "Ravish-ee," he said. "When I booked the cabin, I didn't think to inquire if they had room service."

"At a cabin in the woods?" Libby said, incredulous.

"That's good because we won't be interrupted," he said, rubbing his hands together. "Now what did I do with my cell phone?" He pulled it out of his jeans pocket. "Gotta turn the ringer 'off' so I can turn the lady 'on.'"

This was the first time he turned off the ringer, so that crime and politics could not intrude. But knowing him, she also saw they needed to make the most of their privacy while it lasted.

Silent, she stripped off everything, except the ring. Feet planted, she straightened to her full height and threw her shoulders back. She stood still in the cold cabin. Jed rushed to her.

CHAPTER 78
Present Day – Back to Earth

Libby's office staff was subdued when they returned after Thanksgiving. She wondered what was up, and so she asked them.

"Job security," Marquita said. "Like when your babies start coming."

"Marquita!" Keisha said.

"She did ask. I'm being honest," Marquita said.

"And that's OK," Libby said. "Reality has settled in for me, too. I don't know what the future holds because I married someone in politics. I roll with it. But trust me to provide for your futures as well as for my own. We're still in this together," Libby said.

And with that, they went to work.

***

After Jed won re-election to a second term, he turned his ambitions to a new post. Standing with Libby on the steps of the Statehouse, he announced his campaign for state attorney general. Jim and Sheri, now married, flanked them along with Armistead Hauser, looking rested after treatments for leukemia. Hauser was as sharp as ever, and he was certain Jed could win.

A few months after the wedding, Hauser had made his case to Jed and Libby over dinner at Hauser's. At the time, he'd just been diagnosed with leukemia. Libby thought their friend was sicker than he admitted, because his wife, Jean, kept close like someone watching a candy thermometer.

"Now is the time, Jed. Everything I'm hearing is the Republicans will have a weak ticket, thanks be," Hauser said.

"The problem is getting the voters interested. They don't know how appeals are handled by the attorney general," Jed said. "The voters have no clue what the AG does all day."

"True. But the AG is an advocate in countless other ways," Hauser said. "Just think of the multi-state effort for lawsuits against big tobacco. And securities scams. What about polluters? This is a dirty state. Dirty air, dirty water."

"So you envision a populist campaign by a caped crusader?" Jed said.

"The cape is optional, but the passion is a requirement. Don't do it if you don't want to." Hauser said. "But a good reason is for the judicial appointments it could lead to. No question it would enhance your credentials."

"And my other options?" Jed said.

"Run for a local judgeship, or as a longshot, run for the US Senate."

"But don't keep running for prosecutor?" Jed said. "I could envision getting to a third term."

"You can, but the longer you stay in one place, the more things stick to you. Better to keep moving," Hauser said.

"I don't think I have baggage, at least nothing I'm aware of," Jed said. "I'll be elected to a second term without too much grief. But if I run for AG and lose, then I really would need a job."

"Why?" Jean said. "The prosecutor runs in the off-year elections. Your first term will end two years before the presidential year when the AG is on the ballot.

"So if you're re-elected prosecutor, you don't have to resign from office to run the AG campaign. Even if you did lose, you'd still be prosecutor for another two years."

"Well, I know, but – I'd want to fulfil my duties as prosecutor, and not campaign when I'm supposed to be in the office. If I were in the middle of a second term, perhaps it would be better to resign if I won the nomination at the state convention," Jed said.

"Hogwash," Hauser said. "The campaign heats up after Labor Day, and we're only talking two months. You can save vacation time to use for weekday appearances.

"But you know as well as I do that raising money for TV ads will be the bigger challenge."

Jed sighed.

Hauser continued. "Just keep in mind that the federal judges in the Southern District aren't making noise about retiring, so an appointment to the bench would be down the road. At least with the AG election, you'd increase your political base."

Jed looked at Libby. She looked back, somber.

"We'll think it over," Jed said.

"In the meantime, there is something you can do for me," Hauser said.

"Anything," Jed said, meaning it.

"I want you to bring a case against a madam who runs an escort service."

"Why?" Jed said.

"She's a blackmailer," Hauser said. "We need to pile up charges so we have leverage to get information about prostitution on the dark Web."

Jed looked sideways at Libby, and then at Army.

"It's OK. She can hear it because she won't tell anybody. It's good for her. She needs to know you do things," Hauser said. "God, I would love a cigar right now."

"Out of the question," his wife said.

"Satan," Hauser said, casting his wife a look of loving appreciation.

"This pillar of the community – she here in town?" Jed said.

"She's everywhere," Hauser said. "I'll have my first assistant contact you with the particulars tomorrow."

"Have you heard Jim and Sheri's big news?" Jean Hauser said.

"Maybe you should let Jim break it when he wants to," Hauser said.

Libby spoke up. "If you're talking about their engagement, Sheri called me yesterday."

Jed looked at Libby. "You didn't tell me."

"Not on purpose," Libby said. "She called during lunch, and then I had a challenging afternoon. I just forgot."

"It's six months until the wedding, so you'll have plenty of time to talk about it," Jean said.

Jed looked forlorn for a moment, and Hauser studied him.

Then Hauser said, "If you run, you can win. But if for some reason you don't, you'll still get a job."

Libby saw what Jed's reservations were. They'd decided not to attempt a pregnancy until he finished at least half of his first term as prosecutor. After that, Libby couldn't postpone any longer. She said even if he were re-elected, he would need to scale back his political activities to be a dedicated father, just as she would need to balance her career with motherhood.

"You won't be able to hang out with people just to hang out, like you do now," she said.

"I guess I could be more selective about the meetings I go to," Jed said. "So much of politics is inseparable from the activities of everyday life."

"Like poker games," she said.

"And trips to Wrigley Field," he said.

But tonight, they were talking about ramping up his political life. It would never end. She felt queasy. In fact, she thought she was going to throw up.

"Would you mind excusing me for just a minute?" she said, pushing her chair back. The others nodded and she hurried to the bathroom, out of earshot and just in time as her dinner came up.

When she returned to the table, the others were talking about a Colts football game that ended in a loss. Jean shook her head. "I honestly think they tried to decapitate the quarterback," she said.

Miserable, Libby turned down dessert, which the others savored.

They sat in the living room for coffee, and Army reminisced about his days as an FBI agent. Libby got lost in his storytelling, and by the end of the evening, she was renewed.

After a week's worth of pillow talk, Libby and Jed decided that he'd run for re-election as local prosecutor and then pursue the nomination for attorney general, and that she'd stop taking birth control pills right away.

She couldn't put off motherhood, but she wouldn't deny him his grand tour of county fairs, banquet rooms, and union halls.

CHAPTER 79
Present Day – Flashbulbs

As Jed predicted, he won re-election to a second term as prosecutor. Back in office, he traveled under the radar to the far corners of the state on weekends as he mined for support for the AG bid. Whenever possible, Libby accompanied him, and they managed to find the privacy for ardent evenings, often spent at state park inns.

The hard days of work, the nights alone, and the weekend scrambles took a toll on Libby. Having stuck to Jed's schedule, they were surrounded by district party officials at a small dinner in Grant County. Libby felt dizzy. Now is not the time to flake out, she reminded herself. But then a wave of nausea came over her.

After stopping the birth control, her body adjusted to new hormone levels, and her cycles were irregular for several months. But the doctor said Libby was ovulating and should be able to support a pregnancy. Still, it was taking longer than Libby anticipated to start a baby. They'd been trying for over a year. After nearly passing out in Grant County, she took a pregnancy test when they got home.

Indeed, it was positive, but she wouldn't tell Jed until she knew for sure. That night, she awoke at three a.m. with cramps. Sensing moisture between her thighs, she slid from under the covers, and blood dripped on her knee as she stood.

She looked at the sleeping Jed. This is one time he didn't need to know, she decided. Bleeding heavily the next day, she canceled her appointments for the first time since taking over the practice. Her doctor saw her late in the afternoon.

"You can try again," the doctor said. "Don't stress over it. Let it be."

But before dinner, Jed wanted to know why she canceled her appointments. "Cramps and bleeding," she said.

He looked at her hard. Coming to her, he cupped her face in his hands. He kissed her forehead. "Tell the truth."

She melted under his gaze. "I miscarried. It's very common. I'm OK."

He hugged her tight. "Don't ever keep a secret like that from me again," he said.

"I feel like crap," she said.

Months passed, and still no pregnancy – but the summer nominating convention was at hand. Jed's opponent hung on, but with support from only a fourth of the delegates. Jed was the official nominee.

He and Libby mounted the stage to applause and cheers. With one arm around Libby, Jed was smiling and waving to the occasional face in the crowd for special recognition. Recorded music blared an up-tempo "Back Home Again in Indiana." Libby felt like a blow-up doll.

Dang it! We need to be in it to win it, she thought, broadening her smile as she raised her right arm and waved a victory sign. Camera flashes went off.

Sitting in the front row, Armistead Hauser caught Jed's eye and nodded his appreciation.

***

Jed's campaign commercials began running in late August. The first ad was a biographical introduction with photos, video clips, and voiceovers from Jed discussing the ideals he strove to uphold.

Two weeks later, the second ad appeared, and Jed was saying the attorney general's office should hold corporations accountable for reckless behavior. He cited examples of retaliation against workers who reported violations of safety laws. He promised help for whistle-blowers exposing fraud at pharmaceutical and health-care companies.

In late September, the polls Jed commissioned gave him a slight edge in the race. His consultants explained the Republican opponent, Brent Kraznik, was closing the gap by outspending Jed on advertising. The Kraznik ads, which featured a catchy bluegrass jingle, were scoring "high positives."

In private, Jed muttered to an exasperated Army Hauser that the so-called weak Republican was proving to be potent.

"I have to admit," Hauser said. "I didn't see this guy coming. When you throw him against the wall, he sticks. I caught my wife tapping her toe to his jingle."

Jed's advisors simply fell back on, "Spend more." Needing an infusion of cash, he attended fundraisers every night for 10 days and netted "only" $250,000, he told Libby.

"Have you thought about taking up dentistry?" Libby said. "It's a nice vocation, not nearly the pressure.

"And your hands will be in people's mouths, instead of their pockets," she said.

"Hah!" Jed said. "Between us, I'm the one who actually takes the direct route to someone's pocket." He swatted her behind.

Just when she feared she'd never be a mother, her last pregnancy test was positive. She craved the right moment to tell Jed, but the campaign never seemed to provide one.

On a Saturday, she accompanied him to a county political dinner on the west side of the state. On the way home, they snoozed, propped against each other in the back of the campaign van driven by his assistant.

They passed through a small town and waited at a stop light. Jed stirred, checking to see where they were. Libby watched a sign blink in the window of a local bar. On green, the van moved forward, and the couple settled cheek to check.

Bam! The van hit a large pothole. Libby cradled her abdomen with both hands, and Jed observed the protective gesture. His leaned forward, speaking to his driver.

"Could you pull into that gas mart and get me a cup of coffee, Larry?" Jed said.

"Sure." Larry parked the van at the edge of the station's lot and went inside.

"OK, he's gone for the minute," Jed said, pulling Libby close until her mouth met his. "What are you hiding, missy?"

Libby smiled. "We're having a deputy AG."

He kissed her. "How far along?" he said.

"Three months," Libby said. "I went to the doctor on Tuesday.

"If it's a boy, I thought we'd name him 'Theo' after the guy you beat in your first campaign," she said.

Jed burst out laughing. "Poor Theo. He says his wife wants to spend January in Argentina, so she can go down to Tierra del Fuego.

"He's trying to get cases put on the docket in January, so he has an excuse not to go."

"Why? Sounds like a neat trip," she said.

"Not when you're paying for your son at Harvard," Jed said.

"Oh," Libby said.

"We'll have to start a college fund for our little deposition," he said.

They nuzzled for a while, and then Jed craned to look out. "Here comes Larry," he said. "He's a great assistant."

"Baby 'our secret' until after the election?" she said.

"Yep," Jed said. "I love you, by the way."

"I love you, too."

CHAPTER 80
Present Day – Thwarts and All

In the first week of October, a Republican ex-president came to campaign for his party's state ticket. Appearing with him – a pro football player who made country music recording hits, and a popular evangelist who wrote an inspirational bestseller. The three would speak at a mega-event in downtown Indianapolis. Several thousand were expected to attend, and for the preview reception, tickets ran from $1000 to $5000.

Since the Democratic president seeking re-election was not waging a battleground campaign in Indiana, the Republicans could devote this high-dollar event to state races. As a result, Jed's opponent was the beneficiary of an impressive sum from the party.

"You're being targeted more intensely now," Army Hauser told Jed over lunch. "The GOP finally woke up. They sent their overachievers.

"I got told by an ex-county GOP chairman they don't want you to have a platform to run for the Senate when the next seat comes up," Hauser said.

"But I'm not ambitious for the Senate," Jed said. "I'm an attorney. I'm focused on the law, not on farm subsidies."

Hauser shrugged. "I know. But in politics, the chessmen try to eliminate threats. At least it's a tribute to your appeal."

Jed's shoulders sagged. "This fund raising," he said. "And I thought a local race was bad."

"Don't give up now," Hauser said. "You're doing very well."

"I am, and I'm not," Jed said. "I just bought a focus group survey. They

338

tested only Republicans. What it boils down to is – all you do is give Indiana Republicans a likeable Republican. That's the maximum requirement.

"Kraznik has managed to do it with his stupid jingle," Jed said.

"That jingle is a musical hemorrhoid," Hauser said.

"And my opponent collects money like the IRS," Jed said.

"Nothing you can't overcome," Hauser said. Jed detected a plaintive tone in Army's voice.

"How are you?" Jed said.

"What do you mean?" Hauser said.

"You know what I mean, Army. The cancer. How are you?"

"I'm clean," Hauser said.

"But something's bugging you."

"I heard something I don't want to believe," Hauser said.

Jed leaned closer. "Such as?"

"Did you pressure Gale's wife not to go for the death penalty for Thresher?"

"No," Jed said.

"Did you ask the special prosecutor not to file for it?"

"No, I did not." Jed said. "He met with Lee Ann to discuss her wishes and proceeded accordingly."

Hauser pursed his lips and nodded his head.

"Army, what?"

"I think they're going to make a run at you over the way Gale's murder case was handled," Hauser said.

"That's insane. I recused myself and got a special prosecutor. What could they possibly have to complain about?"

"That has yet to be revealed," Hauser said. "I hope it's not true."

"Me, too," Jed said.

Jed wished he knew more. He didn't use "Sink or Swim" for opposition research. That was his rule. The security firm was there to guard against breaches, but not to eavesdrop on the enemy's campaign strategy. Yet, the rumor was troubling.

After lunch, Jed went for a walk. He found himself standing at the corner of Market and Alabama streets, and he stared at the place where he and Gale had fallen.

Gale died across from the former site of the old Market Square arena, where Elvis gave his last concert. Gale loved "The Jailhouse Rock." It would make a great music bed for a campaign commercial, but paying for the right to use it would be prohibitive, Jed speculated.

He was tapping his foot. *Oh wait*, the beat. The beat. He knew what he needed to do.

He pulled out his phone and called his campaign manager.

CHAPTER 81
Present Day – October Surprises

During the campaign, Jed met his daily responsibilities as the county prosecutor. He believed he owed it to the public, but he knew he was giving his opponent an advantage. The Republican Kraznik was in private practice and could dictate his hours. Jed got calls from tipsters who said they'd seen Kraznik at civic club luncheons around the state during the week, all invitations Jed couldn't accept.

But Jed was about to use vacation time in the last few weeks before the election to travel every day. Libby couldn't go along.

Libby had come home from a swim after work and fixed a chicken enchilada for supper. Jed went to a meeting in Columbus and wouldn't be home until around nine-thirty. She turned on the TV in the kitchen to catch the evening news.

During a break, she saw a campaign ad. The narrator said, "This message is paid for by Indiana Watch for Justice."

A melancholy harmonica vamp caught her attention – and then she was stunned to see Gale's picture with his name.

"A veteran police officer, fallen in the line of duty," the voiceover began.

"Oh, my God," Libby said.

"Killed – as he threw himself on top of his friend to save his life."

Gale's son-in-law Terry appeared on screen and began to speak.

"When a gunman tried to kill the county prosecutor, Jed Harkness, my wife's father, Gale Mooneyham, took the bullet, instead.

"We wanted the state to file for the death penalty. I was surprised when

341

we talked about it with Jed, because he said didn't believe in the death penalty. And he's a lawman.

"I thought he would stand up for police officers, no matter what."

A picture of Jed appeared next to a flashing red question mark. The voiceover concluded, "Jed Harkness – Tough enough to be Indiana attorney general?"

Libby crossed her hands over her heart. "Oh, dear God" she said. She felt a sudden message from her bladder. Pregnancy was catching up with her. "Oh God," she said, running to the bathroom.

As she unleashed against the toilet, she remembered Gale's daughter and son-in-law were the only members of his surviving family who didn't attend Libby and Jed's wedding. She brushed it off, because Lee Ann said her daughter paid far in advance for a cruise. But were they holding a grudge?

And what would be the point? The killer had done himself in, so didn't they get what they wanted?

Back in the kitchen, she filled another glass of water to replace the one she eliminated.

"Why did they have to do that?" she said to the birds outside the window over her sink.

The land line rang. It was Hauser calling.

"I just saw it," Libby said, right after Hauser said, "Hello."

"Try not to absorb it," he said.

"How can I not?" she said.

"It was a very clever manipulation," Hauser said. "Bottom line is that Jed has done nothing improper, sleazy, or scandalous."

"No, but they made him sound like a wuss," Libby said.

"Yes, they did. It was a shameful commercial, and I'm sorry for Gale's wife. She doesn't deserve this, especially from her own kids. I suspect the daughter is just following her husband's lead," he said.

"My guess is that Jed hasn't seen it, but he'll hear about it before he comes home," Libby said.

"All the more reason you should be there with love and support," Hauser said.

"OK, Army. Do you want me to give him a message?"

"No, that's OK. I have his cell number. I really wanted to speak with you. You take care, all right?" he said.

"Thanks very much, I will. Have a good evening."

She peeked in the oven at the enchilada. Not bubbling yet.

"Oh, boy!" She sighed, going to the cookie jar. She removed a large fudge cookie with macadamia nuts. "Perfect nuts for a night like this," she muttered. She sank her teeth into the cookie.

The network news came on, and half-way through, the phone rang. It was Lee Ann Mooneyham.

"Did you see the ad," she said.

"Don't worry, Lee Ann. It's OK. It'll be all right," Libby said.

"I called to apologize for my daughter and her husband. I thought they were smarter than to be used like that," Lee Ann said.

"There's a clique of conservative cops who have a blog, and my son-in-law, Terry, reads the dumb thing. He posted a comment about Gale, and those guys swarmed around, treating Terry like a celebrity. But this is what comes of it.

"I think they set him up to be used," Lee Ann said.

"It's hard to know who's behind these things," Libby said. "What's done is done." They were both silent for moment. And then Libby thought to ask, "Did Jed really tell Terry he was against the death penalty?"

"Not in that way," Lee Ann said. "My memory of it – and it seems like just yesterday – is that Jed came over to be with the family for dinner, and later, we sat around the table and talked about everything. He told us the special prosecutor would be handling the case.

"At some point, he said he didn't like the death penalty, and that it bothered him that it's used more on blacks than on whites for the same type of crime, and that he was raised to be against it.

"But he also said his opinions didn't matter, that the special prosecutor would abide by my wishes," Lee Ann said.

"But technically, he said he was against it, in general, and Terry was there," Libby said.

"Well, yes," Lee Ann said. "But as far as I'm concerned, Terry stuck his nose into something he doesn't know very much about.

"He's a good husband to my daughter, loyal, always helpful to me, attentive even when my own sons forget," Lee Ann said. "But he really blew it with this one."

"I know you'll forgive him, and if you do, then I'm sure Jed will find a way," Libby said.

"Can you hold on a second? I'm getting a beep." Lee Ann left the line for a moment. "That was my daughter," she said. "She's falling apart and coming over. It's just as I thought."

"I'm so sorry, Lee Ann," Libby said. "It sounds like it's going to be a long night."

"Afraid so. This was the time of evening when Gale sat in his easy chair, and I'd bring him pie and coffee. Maybe that's what she needs, too," Lee Ann said.

After the call, Libby was exhausted. Nothing good was served by the commercial. Gale wasn't honored, and poor Terry – she didn't know what to think about him. And the public – they didn't know Jed any better, and now an issue had been raised the roving pack wouldn't let go of.

But the enchilada was ready to eat.

Friday arrived, and it was time for the weekly political talk show. Jed had begun his full-time road tour. The TV host was waiting for him at a breakfast meeting in Bloomington. Jed was going to speak before health-care executives about initiatives reviewed by the attorney general's office. He'd done his homework, and he was looking forward to the encounter.

Until he saw the camera man.

Microphone in hand, the reporter Bill Stedlow stepped from behind the camera man and walked up to Jed.

"Mr. Harkness, a question about the ads running by Indiana Watch for Justice. Is it correct to say that you do not support the use of the death penalty?"

Jed looked him in the eye. "I don't like the idea, but my personal beliefs don't count when it comes to serving the families of crime victims. In a case eligible for the death penalty, the wishes of the victim's survivors are paramount."

"So you would still support the use of it?" the reporter said.

"It's not appropriate in every case. But in making decisions about whether to file for the death penalty, I believe it's important to consult with the victim's family," Jed said.

"But what about when police officers are murdered? Should these cases all be treated the same way?" the reporter said.

"No. Law enforcement professionals want to see a very tough response to violence against police, and that's understandable, and even desirable. But again, the wishes of the families must be considered. If you study the convictions of cop killers, you'll find that sentences of life without parole have been imposed in some high-profile cases."

"And it was because the families wanted it that way?" the reporter said.

"I think that's a very large part of it, yes," Jed said. "I'm going to have to conclude our talk. I'm due at a meeting shortly."

"Just one more thing – How do you respond to Indiana Watch for Justice's question about whether you're tough enough to be attorney general?"

Jed smiled. "Justice is blind, but she is tough. I leave it to the laws of the land and the ethics of my profession to dictate how tough we should be – and not to someone with the cash to waste on frivolous TV commercials."

But negative ads kept running. After the carpet of stinkbugs from Gale's son-in-law, a blanket of venom spilled over Jed's campaign. Libby viewed the new TV commercial in her office during a lunch break.

"A child molester got a six-hour release from jail to attend his mother's funeral, and while he was out, he walked away from the funeral home and socialized with twelve-year-old boys. Was anyone standing in the way? Not prosecutor Jed Harkness – He never opposed the temporary release of this dangerous inmate.

"Now, Harkness wants to be Indiana attorney general – But is he tough enough?" The red question mark blinked next to Jed's photo.

Another beauty from Indiana Watch for Justice. Libby was concerned. She and Jed hadn't discussed the molesting case. She would reserve judgment until she heard every detail from him.

That night he called from a small town on the Ohio River to say he'd be home around midnight. She wasn't going to ask him about the commercial, but he brought it up.

"It wasn't that we didn't worry about letting the inmate out," Jed said. "His cousin was on the sheriff's department, and he said he would keep an eye on him at the funeral.

"We thought this was sufficient. But the deputy's own mother fell ill at the funeral. She was apparently overcome with grief.

"So, the deputy was preoccupied with taking care of his own mother, and he took his eye off the inmate. He wandered down the street from the funeral home to a convenience store.

"Said he wanted cigarettes. These middle-school boys rode up on bicycles just as he came out of the store. He asked them why they weren't locking up their bikes, and they said they didn't have any locks.

"And he tells them he'll watch the bikes while they're in the store," Jed said, continuing. "He grabs a smoke, and then these two kids come back out with snacks and offer him potato chips.

"They stand around eating chips and talking, and then the deputy finally comes down the street in his car. He's looking, and he's mad.

"The deputy sees the guy with these kids, and he pulls into the lot like Starsky and Hutch.

"He handcuffs his cousin. When they get back to jail, he's charged with attempting to escape."

"So, there was no molesting while he was out?" Libby said.

"None," Jed said. "He made the judge, the sheriff, and the prosecutor look silly. Unfortunately, I'm on the list."

"Then technically, the commercial is accurate."

"It's factual," Jed sighed. "We try to be compassionate when a jail inmate loses a member of his immediate family. Plus, he hadn't been convicted of anything at that point. But it looks and sounds bad."

"But the ad called him a child molester. Had he done it before?" Libby said.

"Not that we know of – but he was convicted, eventually," Jed said.

"It's such a waste of time and money to blow this up and take it out of context," Libby said.

"It's the reality of TV ads," Jed said. "We all hate it, but as long as it's legal, the practice will continue."

"Just a few more weeks," Libby said.

"And not nearly long enough, I'm finding," Jed said.

.

CHAPTER 82
Present Day – A Convoy

Jed's campaign advisors wanted attack ads against Kraznik to run as soon as possible. Jed demurred, much to his team's frustration.

"I don't want to do negative ads," he said. "Too many running, already. Look at the manure pile in the Congressional races." He recited a string of allegations: 'Not good for Indiana, not telling the truth, lying about his record, lying about my record.

"To stand out in this trash heap, we'd have to say 'Kraznik is not from Planet Earth,' " Jed said.

Jed's consultants looked at each other. "Well, he *is* a little pale," the campaign manager said. After a beat, he added, adopting a faux-tired demeanor, "We have to say *something* about why he's not as qualified as you."

"I'd rather speak directly to the press about the groups giving him campaign contributions. The gun lobby. I can't believe that even after all these mass shootings, he's dumb enough to take gun money. But he has. Let's talk about it," Jed said.

"That's fine," the polling consultant tossed in. "But you only get the 24-hour news cycle to beat that drum, when you really need advertising to beat it for weeks.

"And to be honest," the pollster concluded, "You're getting pelted with Kraznik's bluegrass jingle. I doubt any pledge from you about campaign contributions is going to cover the din. It's not exactly the battle of the bands."

"OK, then we'll run our own commercial. 'Unlike my opponent, I don't accept money from the gun lobby,' " Jed said.

The ad agency working for Jed came back with a story line, "Planet Earth." It opened with scenes of children entering a school building. The students appear to study botany in a classroom with potted plants and then appear before a science fair display on sustainability. The montage was interspersed with clips of a gunman poised to start firing into a classroom. Jed's narration addressed the gun lobby's role in the campaign. He concluded, "The youth of today want to save our planet. Let's not sacrifice our children to the gun lobby."

"It's still too soft," the campaign manager muttered.

In response, Kraznik turned up the volume on his bluegrass, which now accompanied the rapidly spinning tires of a semi driven by the candidate. The camera panned to the driver's cab, and Kraznik tooted the horn and waved. A wide shot revealed "Kraznik" painted across the length of the semi's trailer.

Wearing a plaid shirt, Kraznik said he'd make sure safety regulations were fair to Indiana truckers. "We can be safe on the road without making things too hard for truckers just trying to make a living."

As the commercial ended, Kraznik approached the rear doors of the trailer and said, "Here's my payload." As he opened the doors, the scene transformed, making it look as though he'd walked into a law library. Now in a business suit, Kraznik pulled a law book from a shelf and addressed the camera. "At home or on the road, I'm livin' the law."

"Oh, bullshit," Jed said, watching.

"A point of interest," his campaign manager said. "About one in fourteen Indiana jobs are related to the trucking industry, according to Kraznik's press release."

"Could I entice you into running a teeny-weeny attack ad?" the manager said. "Along the lines of, 'Kraznik supports reckless people doing reckless things – providing automatic assault weapons, reducing highway safety,' " he said.

"I hate attack ads," Jed said.

"That's OK," the campaign manager said. "But you can't be a caped crusader if you don't have a diabolical enemy. You actually need to win."

The assembled campaign staff waited for Jed's reaction. Finally, he shrugged. "The hell with it," he said. "Make a list of his vices, pick one. Have it ready to go by tomorrow night – I don't want much."

And he left the room.

Another of Jed's positive messages started the next day. Called "The Beat," his Elvis-inspired soundtrack had a rock-a-billy bass guitar controlling the pulse of the narrative. It highlighted the success of Jed's efforts as prosecutor – the percentage of convictions in serious felony cases, and his leadership in the fight against domestic abuse.

Libby's staff came back with favorable comments about the ad, and they weren't just playing up to her. Optimistic, she looked forward to the weekend trip to South Bend. The lone debate with Kraznik would take place on the campus of the University of Notre Dame.

Before then, Jed's campaign finally released an attack ad, which fueled a bitter response from a Kraznik spokesman, who called the charges "volatile and vindictive."

The ad said Kraznik helped a now-disgraced investment counselor, who enlisted Kraznik to offer advice at seminars for potential investors.

The securities salesman was later charged with bilking his clients, and while Kraznik wasn't reprimanded by the state, his association with the fraudster was an embarrassment.

But not so embarrassing that Kraznik couldn't resort to using more banjoes. His trucking ads expanded to a convoy. As the furious bluegrass tune whipped the trucks into high gear, Kraznik made campaign pledges appeasing not only the logistics industry, but agriculture. With each promise to challenge "silly" farming regulations, a new truck with "Kraznik" on the side joined the convoy.

The ad ended with Kraznik again saying, "At home or on the road, I'm livin' the law," he said.

"Shithead," Jed said to himself.

On Sunday night during the ride home from the debate, Jed voiced doubts about his standing. "I did well tonight, but it won't be a game-changer," he said, muffled as he and Libby huddled in the back seat.

"It might make a difference to the people who watch public television," Libby said. "After all, if they were bothering to watch, they were hoping to learn something."

"OK," Jed said, preoccupied. She kissed his cheek.

"Let's stop at the next town to pick up some pizza," he told their driver. "And some breadsticks." Libby was alarmed. She was surprised to hear Jed ask for his favorite comfort food that late into the evening.

***

Election Day arrived. On the previous weekend, the wire services distributed a local story from Indianapolis, "AG Race Tossed Salad."

The account summarized the back-and-forth of the Harkness-Kraznik contest.

Jed and Libby were in a hotel suite at the Morton and would go down to the Democratic election headquarters. Libby asked Jed if he'd written a victory speech.

He took her by the hand and led her to the bathroom away from his assistants. He closed the door.

"Sweetheart, I'm not going to win this election."

Libby looked down at the sink counter. She studied the pink sculpted soaps in a dish. "How do you know?" she said.

"The returns from typically Democratic regions are lackluster."

Jed continued. "The Republican presidential huckster has quite a following here. Michigan is not in, yet, and neither is Pennsylvania. He won't take them. But he'll carry Indiana with coattails.

"We'll wait it out. I'm hungry." he said.

"Eat an apple, and then we'll have a little more when it's over, OK?" Libby said. "I don't want you to throw up before this is finished."

He smiled. "Dr. Booth, I will follow both your advice and your attractive backside."

Later, they stood before a sympathetic crowd as he announced he'd made a concession call to his opponent. The race ended with Kraznik carrying 51.5 percent, and stray tabulations wouldn't be enough to overcome his lead.

Jed was graceful, even funny, in his short speech. He made it look easy. But as he held Libby's hand, his squeeze got tighter and tighter. She squeezed back with what remained of her hand. They waved goodbye to the crowd and returned to their suite.

They were alone. Jed pulled her close and they hugged for a long time.

Then, he buried his face in her shoulder, and she felt it grow damp. She squeezed him hard, and they stood, rocking from side to side like slow dancers. When he straightened, she saw tears in his eyes, but he was relaxed. She could see he would recover.

"Fixing myself a bourbon and Coke," he said. "Do you want a glass of sparkling water?"

"Sure."

They sat on the edge of the bed and clinked their drinks together. "To our deposition," he said. They sipped, idle and not talking.

"So, what do I do now?" Jed said after a bit.

"Paint my den to get the nursery ready," Libby said. "My darling, I'm very disappointed. But I'm not the one who went to Pencil-tucky and back.

"I know you'll be run down for a while. Wallow in it, and then move on. You've been through much, much worse. And you can always talk to Dr. Jukka Bostrom," she said. "I'll go with you, if you want."

"Jukka says there's no credit limit on lousy feelings, just on lousy decisions," Jed said, lifting his glass. "Here's to feelings." He wiped a solitary tear resting under his right eye.

"Pink or blue paint?" he said.

They just looked at each other. They chose not to know the baby's gender ahead of time.

At last, Libby said, "Pale pink. We can stencil blue animals on the wall. I'll make the stencils, and you can spray paint over them.

"But let's not do it right away. We have several months," she said.

"The holidays are coming. Maybe we should take a trip," he said.

"Our anniversary is in a couple of weeks," she said. "And there's Thanksgiving weekend. Maybe we should visit your mother in Florida for a couple of days?

"Maybe we're dumb enough to think we can still book seats to fly out on the Wednesday night before Thanksgiving?" Libby said.

"That's a good idea," he said. "We haven't told our parents about the baby, so now would be the time."

***

The next day Libby was having lunch in her private office, when Jed called with news about their vacation plans.

"Great news. Economy is booked, so we're flying first class," he said.

"Jed! Are you really spending the money?" Libby said.

"Why not? You'll lean back and receive the tender ministrations of the flight attendant."

"What about you?"

"They'll be serving me honey-roasted nuts."

"Along with your split of champagne?" she said.

"I detest champagne," he said.

"Seriously? Didn't you know your mother has been roasting turkey in a bag with champagne for years? Didn't you know that?"

"Are you making this up?" Jed said.

"I am not. We had a long discussion last year about Thanksgiving recipes. That's funny – You detest champagne. She'll get a kick out of that."

She smiled. "How are you today, honey?" she said.

"Better than I thought I'd be. Army called, and he's very down. He thinks he goaded me into running, and I reminded him that I'd been talking about running for several years. And then he practically begged me to let him buy lunch.

"I told him, 'I have a standing invitation to eat lunch whenever you're buying.'

"I'm leaving to meet him after we hang up," Jed said.

"What about the campaign staff? When is their last day?" she said.

"The core staff is having a twelve-martini lunch on me today at an undisclosed location, and they have designated drivers – don't worry. I thought it best to give them the time without me, so they can bitch all they want.

"The receptionist, Brandi, is done after today, and my campaign manager is contracted until the end of month. He'll coordinate with the campaign treasurer. The driver, Larry, is done today. He's a graduate student in political science, so he'll be going back to school next semester.

"Dooley, the advance guy, already has a job lined up with the state party." he said.

"How do you thank your volunteer leaders?" she said.

"Very carefully," Jed said. "I have a phone list to call for the special touch, and to follow up, warm letters of gratitude that *Los!* will help me draft."

"Speaking of which, he seems pretty listless these last few days," Libby said.

"Probably sensing the big letdown," Jed said. "I read the newspaper to him this morning, and he just put his head down and closed his eyes."

Keisha knocked on Libby's door and stuck her head in. "Can I bug you about an invoice for a second when you're free?" she said. The lunch hour was over.

CHAPTER 83
Present Day – Movie Night

The week after Thanksgiving, Jed called Libby at work.

"Something's wrong with my dog," Jed said. "He can't get up on his own."

Libby drew in her breath and exhaled an imaginary cigarette puff. "OK. Can you do me a favor? Open his mouth and look at his gums? Are they pink or gray?

"Hang on, putting the phone down," he said. She heard him say "Come on, buddy – open up. That's a good boy – let me see."

Back on the phone, Jed was starting to huff. "They're gray. I've never seen that. What does it mean?"

"Try not to panic. Just call the vet and see if they can take him now. If not, you should go to the animal hospital, but it'll be more expensive," she said.

"The hospital? Why?" he said.

"What would you do if I couldn't get up on my own?" she said.

"I get it," he said.

"Call me when you find out," she said.

He called again before her last appointment.

"I'm at the vet," he said. "It's bad. Diabetes. *Los!* is staying here for a few days and we'll have to give him shots from now on."

"I'm sorry. I thought it was. Did the vet say whether the dog is dehydrated?" Libby said.

"He is. They've got him hooked up to some stuff."

"Right. Well, OK. How long will you be there?"

"I need to speak with the vet, but I'll probably be home before six. I feel so guilty. I should have seen this."

"We've been gone a lot. We didn't see how often he was peeing, or that he was thirsty all the time. We'll just have to chart some notes when we notice something new," Libby said.

"Yeah," Jed said. "Here's the vet. I'll see you later."

Libby went swimming after hours and expected to find Jed at home. But the house was still, with only the kitchen lamp glowing over the sink. She tried reaching him, but the call went to voicemail.

She rummaged in the refrigerator for leftover chicken breasts and a half-full jar of tomato sauce. She covered the chicken with sauce in a frying pan on low heat and added water and garlic cloves. Leaving the dish to simmer under a lid, she washed a fresh head of lettuce.

Still no Jed.

She made a chopped salad and threw in blueberries and walnuts tossed with a raspberry vinagrette. She set the table. The house was still, like a library after dark with the doors locked. She lit a fat pillar candle and placed it in the center of the kitchen table.

No Jed.

She started angel hair pasta in a boiling pot. The garlic aroma from the sauce intensified.

Highlighting a snow flurry, car lights illuminated the backyard. She rushed to open the back door. Jed got out of his car and walked with his head down to the house.

She stepped back to let him in. He opened the basement door as if to call *Los!* He looked down the stairwell. Libby left him alone. Eventually, he closed the door and turned to her.

"*Los!* is not coming home. He had complications, and he died," Jed said.

"Oh, *Los!*" Libby said, trembling. She went to Jed and unzipped his bomber jacket. "Come," she said. "You need to get warm."

She led him to the lounger in his den and wrapped him in a fleece throw.

"I'm just about done fixing dinner," she said.

He reached out and pulled her into his lap. "Don't go," he said.

They held each other for almost five minutes. "I should turn off the heat under the food, maybe?" Libby said.

"No, we can eat now," he said. "But I feel like it's my last supper."

"Come on, honey," she said, getting up.

"I can take losing an election. That's not nearly as important as a basketball game. But my dog – I'm so stupid, I had no idea it would hurt this much," he said, voice cracking.

"Yes, he was yours when you had no one else, and he loved you more than you could ever know." Tears ran down Libby's face. "He loved you every single day."

A consideration occurred to her. "Does the vet have a burial service?"

"Yes," he said. "They'll make a model of his front paw prints and then he'll be cremated. I'll get the ashes."

"That's good," she said, wiping her face with her fingertips.

They went to supper. They didn't say much, but as they split an apple for dessert, Jed asked, "After the baby is born, can we get a puppy?"

"I don't see why not," Libby said. "But a puppy can wear you out, and you'll have late nights with the baby. You don't have to decide right away," she said.

"Good point," he said. And then, he burst out, "Don't ever leave me!"

Libby reached across the table and took his hands into hers.

"Jed, I have no intention of leaving. We're parents, yes? Life goes on," she said. "*Los!* was a senior citizen. He just didn't seem that way. But he took care of us, got us married.

"It's going to be all right," she said.

"I want a beer," Jed said.

"Now, I know you're OK," she said. "You know what?" She jumped a little in her seat.

"What?" Jed said, surprised.

"I've never seen that movie."

"Which one?" he said.

"The one you took the dog's name from – for the submarine command – *Los!*"

"You mean *The Enemy Below*. I thought we watched it," he said.

"Never," she said. "We can make popcorn."

"Popcorn, beer, Curt Jurgens and Robert Mitchum. You're my girl!" he said, going to set up the movie in the den.

Libby sat still for a minute. Her chest was warm, like love had crawled in

356

and snuggled.

"I know you're here, *Los!*" she whispered.

CHAPTER 84
Present Day – Summons

Working hard to close the books on his campaign, Jed was eager for the diversion of shopping, even more so than Libby. On a Saturday morning, they put on their coats to embark on a spree.

"I want to hang holiday lights on the front porch," he said. "Let's buy some stuff. And luminaria bags." Irvington observed an annual Sunday for luminaria.

"OK," she said.

"And I want a fresh green wreath for the dining room wall," Jed said.

"OK."

"And I think we should have miniature stuff on the mantle over the gas fireplace," he said.

"OK," she said.

"I'm speaking of a crèche, Three Wise Men –"

"Cattle lowing," she said.

"And cattle," he said. "When do you want to put up the Christmas tree? Should we get a fake one, for fire safety? Or do you want the real thing?"

"I'm fine with an artificial tree," she said. "Just nothing garish."

"We define garish as . . ." Jed said.

"You know, things that look like they belong in a saloon. Blue-and-white lights for the Colts."

"Those are all over Irvington," Jed said, laughing.

"Not in our living room," she said.

"Yes, *Fraulein*."

"Hey, Sheri and Jim are having an open house next Friday night," Libby said as they walked to Jed's car. "We should take them a Christmas gift – maybe a crystal tree ornament?"

"And something for the baby girl," Jed said. "Jim says that Melinda Mary, already nicknamed Mimi, is the apple of Great-Uncle Armistead Hauser's eye."

"How is Army?" she said. "I haven't spoken with him since right after the election."

"I don't know," Jed said, underscoring each word. "He's been very mysterious lately."

Jed found out soon enough.

"Glad you could meet on short notice," Army said the next morning at a diner on the southwest side of Indianapolis. The piped-in country music, and the conversation among hungry truckers gave him perfect cover as he leaned to speak in confidence. Whenever Army summoned him to this grill, Jed understood two things: They would dress down, and something was up.

"These portions are huge," Jed said, looking at plates on other tables. "As I near forty, I can't handle truck-sized meals. I think I'm in the small delivery-van stage."

"While I was getting chemo, I was in the tricycle stage. I didn't feel like eating," Army said. "Jean kept force-feeding me protein shakes."

"How is she," Jed said.

"That's why I'm here," Army said.

Jed sobered.

"She got bad news from the eye doctor. Macular degeneration," Army said.

"I'm so sorry," Jed said.

Army nodded his head in appreciation. "At first she was pretty upset."

"Was she not seeing well all of a sudden?"

"Sort of. Nothing dramatic, just felt like she was getting old. But she went to a specialist after her optometrist recommended it. The specialist said Jean is in the early stages, and he wants to stall it."

"I don't know much about the condition, but from what I've heard, not everyone who has it goes blind," Jed said.

"That's true," Army said. "It could be a while before the disease advances, if at all."

359

"That should make her feel better," Jed said.

"It already has – but it doesn't make me feel better," Army said.

Jed waited.

"I've never taken my wife to Europe in all the years we've been married," Army said.

"Wait a minute, I distinctly remember you went to London and took the train to Scotland," Jed said.

"But that's not Europe," Army said. "I mean France, Germany, Italy, Spain, the Low Countries, Scandinavia.

"I was stationed in Germany in the military right after college – before I went to the FBI. But Jean wasn't with me. I met her when I came back to the States."

"I thought you took your whole family on vacation when the children were at home?" Jed said.

"I did. We went to the Grand Canyon, Grand Tetons, Great Smokey Mountains – all the great and grand. But she's never seen the splendor of the European capitals."

"Sounds like a vacation in the offing," Jed said.

"More than that," Army said. "I'm quitting."

Jed was confused. "Do what now?"

"You heard right. I'm quitting."

"Why do you have to quit? Why can't you just take a vacation?" Jed said.

"I will be on vacation. I'm retiring."

Jed opened his mouth and then closed it.

"No, go on – What were you going to say?" Army said.

"It's – none of my business, except that you're sharing because you obviously need to. I can't presume to tell you when to retire," Jed said.

"But you think I shouldn't?"

"I don't have a vote. I'm confused about why you feel the urgency, because you already said it might be a while before her vision gets worse, if it's going to," Jed said.

"I can't be sure that it won't, but that's not what's bugging me," Army said. "She was so vulnerable when she told me, and I realized what a bastard I've been – not all the time, but some of the time.

"It was when she said, 'I was looking forward to when I'd finally have you all to myself, and now I might not be able to see well enough to enjoy it.' And she talked about how lonely she's been.

"She sacrificed for me, nursed me. If she has good vision now, we need to live in the now – and not count on hypotheticals.

"Besides, as you well know, I can always have a recurrence of leukemia.

"I owe it to her – to walk away from politics and the son-of-a-bitching president," Army said.

The waitress came with glasses of water. "Ready to order?"

"Yes," Jed said. "We'll take two orders of humble pie."

Armistead Hauser laughed. "A la mode," he said.

The waitress rolled her eyes. "We're fresh out of humbles. But the Holiday Humdinger is back on the seasonal breakfast menu. You guys look like you might be able to split one between you."

"Is that allowed?" Jed said.

"Honey, I can do anything I want," she said. "I can bring one Humdinger and two plates, if that's what you'd like."

"We'll take it," Army said. "And a pot of coffee, black."

After she left, Jed said, "About the president."

"Right," Army said. "He knows. I called the Justice Department earlier this week and had quite a conversation with the attorney general. The president doesn't want the hassle of pushing judicial appointees through the Senate as soon as his second term begins.

"I gather his legacy-building involves infrastructure projects that will need bipartisan support. Maybe he's going to name a national park after himself. I don't know," Army said.

"But the AG was not enthused about having to find a replacement," Jed said.

"No, he was not. If I just up and leave, the first assistant takes over according to certain rules. But all presidents want to use political capital to their benefit, and they'd rather appoint people who make others happy," Army said.

"And the president is a second termer looking at his legacy full time. Maybe he can get his face carved in granite on Mount Decrepit," he said.

Jed smiled. "I don't know much about your first assistant, except that he's quite a drudge. But if he did take over, the public would benefit from a prosecutor who's serious about reading law books."

"As opposed to 'livin' the law'?" Army said. "I still can't believe Kraznik

Marianne Coil

won. He'll do something to screw up."

"No, Army, I screwed up. For one thing, I waited too late in the game to play the card about Kraznik's association with the crook. I don't know why I was so reluctant. And even then, it wasn't a carotid blow, because Kraznik skated in the fraud investigation.

"I think I was trying too hard to impress my angelic wife by acting like a choir boy. And it wasn't her fault. She never made any noise about our strategy.

"It was all about me. And the lesson I got? It's not all about me," Jed said, shrugging. "It's supposed to be about people like our very decent waitress, who doesn't seem to know who either one of us is.

"And this place is full of truckers. But Kraznik was the one who went to them," Jed said. "He made a straight-forward appeal to anyone who does manual labor."

"Try not to overthink it, my friend," Army said. "You ran a hell of a good campaign, but the other guy got more votes."

"Yep," Jed said. "He did, but not by as much as he should have, considering all the jack he spent."

"Now you're talking. You're still marketable, Jed. This wasn't an embarrassing defeat," Army said. "Not by any means. You polled better than anyone else on the state ticket, including the gubernatorial candidate."

"But you should take advantage of this right away," he added, just as the waitress returned with the pile of breakfast food.

They ate in silence. In their long friendship, they were comfortable not saying much.

They drained the coffee pitcher, and the waitress came back with a replacement.

Army took a sip. "So now – the Democrats have provisional control of the Senate," he said.

"You're talking about the recount lawsuit that could tip things one way or the other?" Jed said.

"Yes. Assuming the Democrat hangs on, the president will have a consensus group for about five minutes," Army said.

"Five minutes is an eternity in politics," Jed said.

"A lot happens. Look – here's my point. I want you to replace me," Army said.

362

Jed had not seen it coming. Cold all over, he hugged himself, massaging his arms.

"I'd have to be confirmed by the Senate," he said.

"Not right away. You can be interim US attorney, and this would give the president time to prepare for the confirmation vote," Army said.

"What if he wants someone else?" Jed said.

"Such as?"

"Maybe there's an old political hand who covets the job," Jed said.

"Could be," Army said. "But if I present you – all tied up with a ribbon, so they don't have to spend time considering my replacement – they'll be eager to move on. Politically, you're more bankable than any other potential nominee. And I can always let them know you won't take the interim unless they intend to recommend you for confirmation."

Jed flinched a little. "Sounds like an ultimatum."

"Not at all," Army said. "They understand why someone waiting on a new baby wouldn't want a temporary job."

Falling to earth, Jed landed on his rear end. "I can't do this without consulting Libby," he said. "She may have some big reservations."

"Discuss it with her. Just do it in the next three days. I need to call the attorney general as soon as possible," Army said.

"So you haven't turned in your letter of resignation?" Jed said.

"Not yet. I need to make sure you're all set," Army said. "This is nothing against my first assistant, by the way. He's a brilliant guy, organized, energetic."

"Then why aren't you pushing for him?" Jed said.

"Number one, he's a Republican. Number two, he's all cattle and no hat."

"What does that mean?" Jed said, laughing.

"He's got no hat to wear in public. Not a person for the media. He cringes whenever we schedule a press conference. But he's one hell of a lawyer. I'm probably doing him a favor," Army said.

"Would he resent me?" Jed said.

"For about five seconds. But you can take heat, and he'll back you. It'll all work out. Besides, he thinks you're a drudge, too, in case you didn't know."

Libby did have reservations. Informed of Army's proposal, she got up from the kitchen table and made a cup of hot cinnamon tea. A bright red spot outside the kitchen window caught her eye, and she went to stare out the back door. A male cardinal perched on the lonely peg for the dog chain that once danced around the yard as *Los!* cavorted.

"I thought this would be a Christmas without politics," she said, after inhaling steam from the teacup.

Jed fixed a glass of ice water, as if to steel himself for the conversation. Watching him, she returned to the table when he sat down.

"It is Christmas without a campaign, my love," Jed said. "This is a classic backroom maneuver, of which Army is the undisputed world 'cham-peen.' I don't have to do anything but be well-groomed and beam with gratitude.

"At least the president doesn't want to interview me. More important, you don't have to do anything, except cook Christmas dinner – if I'm still invited."

"Don't be silly," she said. "You weren't invited to begin with."

"Ouch," he said, toasting her with his glass.

Each tried to read the other's mind. They sat in silence, until Jed spoke.

"I have to work somewhere," he said. "Let's say I don't take the US job. And let's say I stay in the prosecutor's office for two more years, and then go with a big law firm that wants a rainmaker to dredge up business.

"And that'll work for a day or two, until I meet some poor grandmother who's raising her druggie daughter's children and needs help.

"And you know I'll help her for free. And then the daughter's boyfriend will be charged with stealing cars, and I'll wind up defending him – because he never learned to read –"

"And you'll appear unproductive," Libby said. "Unless you're handling some other case that brings in money."

"Every lawyer has an obligation to provide *pro bono* services," he said. But you bring in the money to be a partner."

"So you're more likely to be called, 'of counsel,' than to make partner?" she said.

He looked at her. "You've done a little homework. But yes, to make partner, you generate a deep-pocket buzz. And you need to look right, smell right, whatever that means.

"That doesn't mean I wouldn't make good money. There are plenty 'of counsel' who rake in over three-hundred thousand a year."

"You don't want to defend pharmaceutical companies and medical device makers. That's it, isn't it?" Libby said. "And the gambling industry. And alcoholic beverage and financial services – and you're a do-gooding pain in the ass.

"You don't look right or smell right," she said.

"I think you paid me a compliment, but my demerits are obvious," he said.

"Couldn't you start your own firm?" she said.

"I'd still have to be the rainmaker."

He sighed. "And there's this – maybe the most important thing – I'm in criminal justice, not wills and trusts. It's what I do." He smiled. "I am not ready to walk away from law enforcement."

"So, you'll be working a lot of nights, no matter what," she said, feeling like the cardinal perched on the peg.

"Lawyers work late. Dentists have office hours. I'm glad you're the one who's having the baby," he said.

"But we're both having the baby. I want you here for the first words, the first steps, the first high fever –"

"And I'm going to do my best to be here for all of it," he said. "If I thought I wouldn't go crazy, I'd be a stay-at-home dad."

"The last time you stayed home, you found a ghost in the attic," she said.

"Yeah," he trailed off in the mist of memory. He hadn't thought about Mary Hobson in a long time.

They were quiet, again, listening as the grandfather clock heralded the half-hour.

"But it's not like running a campaign," Jed said. "I think the last year was so abnormal, maybe anything associated with my career looks dismal.

"Whichever way I go, the travel should be minimal compared with the campaign."

Libby yawned. "I guess I should start the potato soup," she said.

"With little chunks of ham?" Jed said.

"Or bacon, whichever you want."

"Ham," he said. "Do I need to go to the store for anything, like dinner rolls?"

"No, Worship," she said. "But you'd better call Army, if we're going to do this."

"Yes, Dr. Booth."

CHAPTER 85
Present Day -- Nativity

Christmas Eve arrived.

"I'll go with you to Midnight Mass if you want," Libby said.

"Then I won't be able to take the attractive lady who lives down the street," Jed said. "But if you insist."

They turned off the TV after the evening news and listened to a classical music station. Nuzzling on the sofa, they sat in the dark, enjoying the lights on the Christmas tree. Through a window, they could see snowflakes teasing the streetlights.

Around ten o'clock, Libby fixed cocoa and surprised Jed with a plate of shortbread.

"They're from Father Cordele's housekeeper, Marty," she said.

"Isn't that wonderful!" Jed said, taking a bite. "She really is the salt of the earth."

He swallowed and said, "The snow doesn't look too bad," Jed said. "But the seats at my old church fill up fast. We probably ought to leave as soon as we finish our cocoa. But let's enjoy it. I have to dip the shortbread."

En route to church, Libby said, "I've hired an associate. He's going to take all my cases for twelve weeks while I'm on leave, and then I'll go back to work part time.

"After that, he'll stay on. I think I can afford a full-time associate, but he's very ambitious to teach. So, he'll be working with undergrads at the dental school when he's not in my office."

"What's his name?" Jed said.

"Joey. Joe Bob Fulweiler. He's from Texas. Hence Joe Bob. But he goes by Joey."

"How'd ya find him?" Jed said, talking like a cowboy.

"I put up a notice on the job board at school, and he called me the next day. My old professors were all for him," she said. "He finished his master's in orthodontics this year, and he's been filling in for a dentist who had a coronary bypass."

"When you go back, who has the baby during the day?"

"I do," she said.

They came to a stoplight, and Jed looked at her.

"Really? How's that going to work?" he said.

"I'll be home every morning," she said. "Then the baby comes to work with me in the afternoon. For the first year, he or she will nap a lot, but we'll have a very active playtime in the morning."

The light changed and Jed resumed their trip. "What about Saturdays? Baby still going with you?"

"That's something you and I need to work out. I'm going to need help. It's either you or a babysitter."

"I don't like babysitters," Jed said. "I've read too many case reports. No way on a babysitter, at least not for an infant," he said. "But I'll be able to watch a lot of football with a bouncing baby."

"Thank you. I didn't want a babysitter either," Libby said. "Once in a great while, we might have to resort to it. But Denise said she can pitch in every so often."

"I could see it working for the first year – but for a 'Terrible Two' opening the refrigerator and climbing on furniture – I don't see how the half-day confinement in your office is going to work," Jed said.

"It probably won't," Libby said. "At least not without a creative work-around."

"What does that mean?"

"I could always hire a child-care assistant to come to the office," she said. "Play games, have snacks, read stories, watch a little TV."

"In your private office?" Jed said.

"No. There's an empty room gathering dust. Just big enough to be a playroom," she said. "A half-day would be OK. At age three, I think pre-school might work. I went to pre-school when I was three."

"But not for the whole day," Jed said.

"I don't remember when I came home every day," Libby said. "But it was a positive experience."

"I salute you for not wanting to palm off your newborn on total strangers," he said.

"But I'm leaving the baby with you on Saturdays," she said.

"That's different," Jed said. "I'm just totally strange."

After New Year's, Armistead Hauser announced his retirement. Speculation about his replacement was cut short the next day, when the US Dept. of Justice released a statement naming Jed the interim US Attorney for the Southern District of Indiana, effective the first of February. In turn, Jed announced his resignation as county prosecutor. A party caucus would choose his successor.

"I still got invited to the inaugural ball," Army said, when Jed came to look over his new suite in the office building down the street from the federal courthouse.

"Are you going?" Jed said.

"Oh, hell no," Army said. "But for Valentine's, Jean and I are going to Rome."

Jed was wistful. "You'll be gone a lot, now. You always turned up wherever I was. I'll miss that."

"I made a point of it. I saw something in you I never saw in anyone else. I had to water my plant," Army said.

"I'll try not to wilt," Jed said.

"Let's take a walk. Let's drop in on the hidden closets full of government lawyers.

"Peek in the closet, often, but don't bug them for very long – just a touch to let them know you're paying attention.

"Then we need to meet with the FBI special agent in charge. He's coming over at two to give us a briefing. Now, something to know about this agent, Delph Broderick – he likes bottled sparkling water. It makes me belch, but he drinks it whenever we meet. So have a case on hand," Army said.

"Fancy water for the Bureau. Duly noted," Jed said.

"And he really likes Italian food. Really, really, likes it," Army said.

"Better not tell him you're going to Rome. He might want to come along,"

Jed said.

"Oh, God," Army said. "The things I do for love."

CHAPTER 86
Present Day – A Parade

Libby started maternity leave in the second week of March. The baby was due on the twentieth. The annual Saint Patrick's Day parade was starting, and Libby wanted to attend and meet Jed for lunch.

Although the day arrived with blustery winds, sunny skies coaxed a large turnout. Libby parked in a garage and walked to the corner of Ohio and Pennsylvania streets. A fife-and-drum corps advanced down Penn. The crisp sound of the snares made her blood rush, and she would always remember how happy she was that morning.

When he was county prosecutor, Jed marched in the parade. He had a framed picture of himself wearing a bright green overcoat. The photo caught him flashing a joyous smile and waving. It made her change her mind about the holiday, which she once ignored.

"Wherever did you find a coat that color?" she said.

"Ay, milady, some secrets are not for the knowin'," was his reply.

Today he was watching out a window of the federal courthouse if he had the time. The wind picked up, and she pulled her collar a little closer.

One of the best parade units walked by. In the manner of a rifle corps, a brigade of men carrying lawn chairs folded and unfolded the chairs, tapped them rhythmically on the street, and then hoisted the chairs over their left shoulders in unison.

Libby laughed. The people standing around her were frantic, capturing the spectacle on phone video. She laughed even harder. And then she felt a sogginess in her dress pants.

She couldn't have wet her pants. She hadn't even felt the urge.

Today was the seventeenth. Had her water broken? She looked down at her feet and saw that a dribble ran from under her right pants leg down the side of her shoe.

She was glad she wore a full-length black coat and a pair of black dress pants with lining. At least she had some cover. But now she needed to tell Jed. She dialed her cell, but the call went to voicemail. He wasn't expecting her until around one o'clock. She decided to go into the courthouse.

The security guard at the east entrance on Ohio Street asked if she had court business.

"No, it's personal. I'm Libby Doherty Harkness. My husband is Jed Harkness, and I need to see him urgently."

"Everything all right, ma'am?" the guard said.

"It will be. But time is of the essence," she said. "I just went into labor."

"Yes, ma'am," he said, like a waiter getting her the best table. "Time is of the essence. I'll have our security director locate him."

"OK, but first, let me try again on my phone. If it goes to voicemail, then I'll need help." She dialed, and as she half-expected, he didn't answer. She left a message. "Jed, I'm downstairs at the east entrance with the guard. My water broke. Please call or text as soon as you get this.

"In the meantime, the posse is looking for you."

The security guard laughed. "The posse," he said. He radioed the director, who said he was on the move.

"I feel like a bomb threat," Libby said.

Another guard brought coffee to his comrade, who explained Libby's presence. "Wouldn't you like to sit down?" the newcomer said, pointing to a chair in the corner.

"No thanks – I'm probably better off standing," she said.

"Can I get you something to drink?" he said.

"Oh, no, but thank you."

She checked her phone. No messages.

The first guard saw someone exit from an office down the corridor, and he shouted to her, "Angie, have you seen Mr. Harkness?"

"Yes," she turned to walk toward them. "About an hour ago. He stopped in the clerk's office to book time in the Steckler courtroom for today."

"Is there a special event?" the guard said.

371

"No," Angie said. "He just likes to sit in there all by himself." She stopped, shrugging. "I guess it's a good place to think."

"Thanks," the guard said, and she nodded and went the other way. He radioed the director, again, advising to check the historic courtroom.

Libby felt a stiffness in her lower back. "Come on, Jed," she said to herself. The guards looked concerned, so she decided to make talk.

"You're so lucky to work in a magnificent place like this," she said. "My husband took me on a brief tour after he was appointed, but we didn't have time to appreciate the murals.

"Someday – when I'm not in labor –" and she smiled at her own joke, "I'd like to spend an afternoon just wandering around."

"It's a lot to take in," the first guard said. "But that makes what we do even more important."

The director cut in, reporting via radio that he'd found Jed. "They should be down in a couple of minutes," the second guard said.

Soon approaching, Jed saw Libby and started jogging ahead of the director.

Greeting her with a kiss on the cheek, Jed put a protective arm around her. He thanked the guards for helping.

"Do you need a lift to the hospital?" the security director said.

"I've got my car, thank you," Jed said. "But we're trapped by the parade. It's snaking around the building. We planned to have lunch, later, but the baby had other ideas.

"Today of all days, I decided to get some exercise, and I walked over here and left the car in the garage under the executive office. We need to cross Meridian to get there. But the parade is turning north right here onto Meridian.

"So we're kind of stuck," Jed said.

The security director furrowed his brow. "This show is probably about half over," he said. "Maybe if you wait at the corner for the last unit to pass, you can hurry across." He addressed Libby. "Do you think you're up to that?"

"No, not really," she said. The soggy pants were making her feel tired and heavy.

"By the way, how did you get here?" the director said.

"I'm parked at the fieldhouse garage on the roof," she said.

"Oh, well, you can't get there, either. And it's a longer walk, anyway," the director said. "Tell you what – I think you should stay put right here, where it's warm, until the parade clears Ohio Street.

"I'm going to arrange to have a police unit pick you up at the curb to take you to get Mr. Harkness' car. And that way, if you're not up to switching cars, the cop can just take you to the hospital.

"I think this is the safest thing to do," the director said.

"I agree," Jed said.

And so they waited, until the last leprechaun pranced by the federal courthouse, and then the couple bid the guards a happy St. Patrick's Day.

"I'll be around with cigars," Jed said. The guards smiled and nodded in appreciation. Jed steered Libby to the curb where they met the patrol car.

"Your suitcase is in my trunk, just as we planned," Jed said, after they settled in the back seat.

"But what about my car?" she said.

"Problematic, but not a crisis. We'll just wind up paying to leave it for a few days," he said.

"So you're calling your Mom, right?" Libby said.

"Correct. Then I will call your mother. Between the two of them, you know, the word will get out."

"We haven't put together the diaper-changing table we bought last week," she said.

"I'll just have to do it," he said.

"I'm hungry," she said.

"I don't know how to respond to that," Jed said.

"Is Army back home from Europe," she said.

"Yes, he is, as a matter of fact," Jed said.

"Then you should call him," she said. "And Jim. They're like family."

"You are so smart, all the time," he said, dialing. "Getting his voicemail. 'Army – Jed. Just wanted to let you know we're going to the hospital. Our future federal judge is on the way.' "

"Doctor," Libby said.

The police officer studied the couple in his rearview mirror.

***

Labor lasted eight hours. Libby asked for the journal tucked into her suitcase. It was a book of poems written during her pregnancy, and she passed the time entering new ones. She meditated on liquid nourishment:

Icy Chip, Warm Broth

The sting of ice against my tongue, the life I led when I was young.
The warming brew from chicken gone, a stifled cheep.
But new life stirs, a brand new quirk,
a brand new broth,
First cold, then hot.
Catch every driblet fast,
For waste and wait, a loss,
Tarnished spoons from a lonely past.

CHAPTER 87
Present Day – Dessert

The family was at home. Libby's den was converted into the baby's bedroom. Jed was spending hours next to the crib so he could watch his sleeping daughter. Libby was amused at how he'd taken to whispering.

At the hospital, they considered many names for the baby. She arrived on St. Paddy's night, and Jed thought her name should be Patricia. But Libby didn't like the diminutives Patty and Trish, so Jed said maybe Patricia could be her middle name.

Libby agreed, so they debated a first name.

"Wait a minute. Why is this so hard?" Libby said. "It's right in front of us."

"We can't name the baby '*Los!*'" Jed said. "As much as I'd like to."

"No," Libby said. "Gale. Only we'd spell it G-a-i-l. As in Abigail."

"Abigail Patricia Harkness," Jed said.

"Precisely," Libby said.

"Judge Abigail P. Harkness," Jed said, stretching it out.

"Now wait a minute," Libby said.

"We haven't even picked a school," Jed said.

***

Libby had dinner on the table. Jed sauntered into the kitchen.

"Still asleep?" she said.

"Judge Harkness is resting in chambers," Jed said.

375

Libby laughed.

"Got a note of congratulations today from Army," Jed said. "He wants us to come over with the baby and watch his travel slides."

"The baby needs to mature a little bit before we start taking her around," Libby said. "But we should make it a short visit, because of all the feeding and diapering. His slides will keep, and I'm sure Jean will see it that way."

They sat down to eat. The mention of Army made her recall he suggested Jed could run for the Senate someday. And Jed had responded that he wasn't interested in farm subsidies.

As they finished their beef stew, she said, "You still not interested in farm subsidies?"

"Apropos of what?" Jed said, scratching his head.

"Running for the Senate."

He stopped his fork in mid-air. "There's a seat open next year. Kevin Fadely already announced he's going to retire. Dr. Booth, do you actually want me to run?" he said.

"If you built a career in Washington, I could send my kid to medical school behind your back." She had no intention of trying to program her child to pick a certain ambition, but she liked teasing Jed.

"In that case, forget it," he said. "What's for dessert?"

"Pecan pie."

"May I please have some ice cream with it?" he said.

"Yes, Worship."

She extended her right hand, and Jed brought it to his lips.

"You are all my campaigns," he said.

From the baby monitor on the kitchen counter, they heard a cry.

"I'll go," they said in unison.

They looked at each other and smiled.

His phone rang. Libby held up a hand signaling he should stay, and she went to change the baby's diaper. When she returned to the kitchen, he was finishing the call.

"Yes, I agree," Jed said. "Let's hold off on making a statement. Tell the FBI we want a nine o'clock meeting. Get the coffee going early in the conference room, OK? Hey – Thanks for calling. See you tomorrow."

"Everything all right?" she said.

"Swastikas," he said.

"What?"

"A whole bunch – painted in black all over a synagogue, where the windows were broken as well – and across town, all over an African Methodist Episcopal church," he said. "And it looked like the vandals planned to set the church on fire – but they ran off when a deacon drove up. They threw gas all over the wooden doors."

"At least they're equal-opportunity haters," she said.

"Yes," he said. "Where were we?"

"Oh," she said. "I think you wanted ice cream."

"I still want the ice cream," he said.

"Coming right up." She gave him a slice of pie with vanilla ice cream on the side.

"Hold it," she said. She got a bottle of chocolate syrup from the refrigerator and squirted a swastika onto the ice cream.

Eyes gleaming, Jed looked at her. "Your point being?" he said.

"How do you know the difference between a prank and a crime?"

Jed laughed. "Tonight, I don't. All I know is, I got a phone call that saved me from changing a diaper. And the irony is, I wanted to change the diaper." He dug into his dessert. Libby filled their coffee cups. She sat back, taking in Jed as he enjoyed his treat. At last he spoke.

"You just taught me something," he said.

"I did?" she said.

"It's about empathy," he said. "You caught me off guard with a joke, but that's all it was – for *me*. I didn't lose my ancestors in the death camps, and I'm not a black guy.

"But a swastika is more than a cultural artifact to the targets of racism. The swastika revives the insult, and the pain – and hints at the promise of more," Jed said.

"So when does a prank by someone who lacks empathy turn into a crime?" she said.

"When the statutes and the courts say so," he said.

"We're going to get fat on your desserts," she said.

"You didn't eat any," he said.

"Not yet. But I'm going to."

"I love you, Libby," he said.

She walked over to sit on his lap.

377

"I love you, Jed." She kissed him.

"When I'm recovered from this feat of childbearing, would you like to come up and see my empathetic pranks?" she said.

"Dr. Booth! I'm a married man with a new baby!"

A wail pealed from the baby monitor.

"See?" he said, and they laughed, getting up.

The End

ABOUT THE AUTHOR

Marianne Coil lived in Irvington, the locale for this novel, on the east side of Indianapolis for 25 years. She and her black cat, Binx Carlotta, now live on the city's northwest side, and they are working on a new project.

Made in the USA
Monee, IL
28 October 2024

68776881R00225